the
memory

# BOOKS BY LUCY DAWSON

LUCY DAWSON

# the
# memory

bookouture

Published by Bookouture in 2018

An imprint of StoryFire Ltd.

Carmelite House
50 Victoria Embankment
London EC4Y 0DZ

www.bookouture.com

ISBN: 978-1-78681-748-8
eBook ISBN: 978-1-78681-747-1

*For Jenny Thompson.*
*Loved and missed.*

# CHAPTER ONE

## Eve

He asked me out again as the class was about to start, while the kids were taking their shoes and socks off. The other mothers were watching us and I saw them whispering to each other as they made their way to the door of the sports hall, on their way to get hot chocolate from the vending machine by the changing rooms.

'Just a Christmas drink.' Paul deliberately placed his hands on his hips so that his judo jacket widened to reveal his smooth and over-muscled chest. I imagined him shaving it and felt sick.

'Thank you, but I'm going to be busy.'

'I haven't even said when yet.' He looked affronted.

'I mean that Christmas is a really busy time for everyone, especially when there's only one of you doing everything.' I didn't want to play the widow card, but I thought perhaps I could be excused on this occasion, given the circumstances.

He frowned and scratched his head. 'Yeah, it's just I've asked you more than once now and you said no then too. A lot of women round here would be hellish pleased to go on a date with Paul Jones; you probably don't know that yet.'

I couldn't help staring at him in disbelief. He'd really just referred to himself in the third person? 'I didn't know that – you're right.'

'No problem.' He rolled up his sleeves and crossed his arms to show off his biceps. 'Anywise,' he continued, 'I thought we could go down the pub on Christmas, Eve.' He smiled widely, delighted at his own joke.

'Very good, I see what you did there. My name is Eve and *Christmas* Eve.' I forced a polite smile, and he chuckled, looking down at the floor modestly.

'Well I've always been known for being funny-like too, Eve, you see? That and being international and three times national mixed martial arts champion, obviously.' His smile vanished. 'Which is *no* joke.'

'Obviously. Well, it's very kind of you to ask, but I'm still going to decline, thanks anyway.'

He frowned. 'Ah c'mon, Eve. I'm getting sick of asking, and you've got to get out there again while you're still young enough.'

'I'm only twenty-eight.'

'But you've got to have your own life. He's not coming back, is he?'

My own smile vanished completely.

'I know that might sound harsh,' he continued, 'saying it like it is about your dead fella, but I'm straight up and down. That's good though, see?' He pointed right at me. 'I won't mess you around, like. You'll know where you are, and that's a promise. Sometimes you need someone to tell it as it is.'

I cleared my throat. 'Can I be "straight up" with you, too, then? It was only the six-month anniversary of my husband's death yesterday, but even if it had been six years, or sixteen years,' my voice started to strengthen as I spoke and carried across the sports hall, 'I still wouldn't want to go out with you. I don't fancy you. Sorry.'

One of the mothers who had hung around to earwig stared at me in disbelief, as the other – with wide delighted eyes – gleefully grabbed her friend and burst out of the door to gossip.

Jones watched them leave, looked down at the floor again, and snorted. 'All right. There's no need to be like that. *It's just a drink, dahhhhling.*' He mimicked my English accent. 'A word of advice, Eve. People round here don't like airs and graces. You're no better than anyone else, you know?'

'I never said I was.'

'You're acting like it. You're behaving like someone who thinks she's much smarter than the person she's talking to, and that's not nice, Eve. There's folks round here that don't like English people looking down on them, moving in and taking their homes. It could get dangerous for a girl like you on your own. Did you ever think of that?'

My heart thumped. 'You can't possibly be comparing the local people – who have been nothing but kind to me since we moved here – with the Meibion Glyndwr protesters who burn down English holiday homes? Plus, you do realise that technically this town is English?'

'We're right on the border, love. I consider myself Welsh and I'm proud of it.'

'You should be – Wales is lovely. But I'm confused – who are you saying is threatening me then, because it seems to just be… you?'

'You're obviously taking it that way, which is weird. I'm saying I could look out for you, if you wanted. People respect me.' He shrugged.

I glanced across at my seven-year-old daughter who was watching us, waiting with the other kids to start, apparently listening to every word we were saying. 'Again, thank you for the invitation, but I just don't want to go out with you, Mr Jones, even if that does make me an unusual woman, or will mean that I won't have your protection.' I spoke clearly and confidently for Isobel's benefit. 'People should never be forced into something they don't want to do.'

He took a disgusted step back. 'Man alive, what are you on about now?' He gave me a confused look then an amused leer spread across his face. 'Oh I get it – you're one of *them* as well, aren't you? Keep your knickers on, you daft cow. Look, just forget it. You're not all that, anyway, just so you know. I was only trying to be nice cos you're on your own, like, but I'm not that bothered.

'Come on you lot!' He spun around on the spot and clapped his hands at his students. 'Line up to start, please! Dyke.' He casually threw the last insult at me over his shoulder as he walked away.

My mouth was still open as Isobel stood there uncertainly. I should have just taken her home then and there, but the ridiculous truth is, I didn't want to make a scene. I didn't want to make my little girl feel uncomfortable. The whole point of bringing her to the classes in the first place was to improve her self-confidence, help her make friends outside of school and give our Saturday mornings a focus that wasn't the gaping, lonely and unbearable absence of Michael.

'Go on, sweet,' I mouthed and smiled encouragingly for her to join the others, to show her I was fine. She turned and did as she was told. I went and sat down on the wooden bench by the door, smiling brightly like I wasn't 'bothered' either, even though, ridiculously, I wanted to cry. It shouldn't have mattered what some idiot meathead said to me, but I suddenly missed Michael with such acute longing it made me gasp and I had to cover my mouth with my hands – making it look like I was coughing – to cover the sound.

I cleared my throat, determined to stay strong and not let Isobel see I was upset – or give Jones the satisfaction of realising he'd got to me. This would be Isobel's last class. I'd tell him at the end we wouldn't be coming back in the New Year. I'd just thought he fancied himself and expected everyone else to. I'd had no idea quite how unpleasant he really was. I wasn't having a man like him teach Isobel.

As the lesson progressed, however, it became apparent that for all his insistence otherwise, Jones was pretty bothered by what had happened as well. He was much shorter than usual with the children, barking instructions at them, crossly insisting they weren't doing the exercises and drills properly. There were only four of them in any case – perhaps that was why he was annoyed, too.

Towards the middle of the session, one of his teenage helpers from the adult class arrived to assist with some pad work. I had retrieved a book from my bag that I was pretending to read, but was glancing up regularly, anxiously waiting for Isobel's turn to work one-on-one with Jones. I caught my breath as he got to her and she began kicking the pad he was holding, I could see him urging her to go harder. He wasn't going to take out what had happened on her, was he? I watched as he leant forward and said something I was too far away to hear. Isobel stopped completely and stared up at him, bewildered. Shit – he was. I tensed and put my book in my lap. What was going on?

'I don't want to,' Isobel said clearly, and I stood up.

She didn't want to what?

But Jones just laughed, reached out and ruffled her hair. I was about to walk over when he beckoned the next child forward. Whatever had just happened during their exchange, it seemed the moment had already passed. I sank back down again slowly.

'Dewi!' Jones called over his shoulder, to his young assistant. 'Come here a moment.' I watched the boy run across obediently and Jones whispered something in his ear. Dewi nodded, hurried back to Jones's pile of belongings, picked something up and sprinted to the emergency exit that led to the car park.

Satisfied that everything seemed to have settled down, I returned back to my book. I was actually pretty thirsty but didn't fancy running the gauntlet of the two other mothers in the foyer. I couldn't face the nosy questions but also didn't want to make things worse. Least said soonest mended, as my grandmother used to say. Instead I tried to concentrate on reading.

So I didn't actually see Dewi Roberts come back into the hall carrying the gun.

He'd left the emergency exit slightly ajar enabling him to just slip back in again. The children were doing shuttle runs by this point, up and down the hall. Jones had been shouting at them to go faster, but he suddenly yelled 'COME ON!' ferociously, and, alarmed, I looked up properly, to see he was *holding a machine gun*.

I'm almost certain that's when I stood up again, in shock. The four children had stopped running and were staring at him, too.

'Isobel says she "doesn't want to" do pad work,' he put on a mock whingey voice, 'and none of *you* lot is even trying. This time – let's see you RUN!' He shoved the gun at his shoulder. One of the boys, Izzie's little friend Adam Owen, laughed nervously thinking he was joking.

'I said RUN!' He looked down the sight and took aim right at them. Their expressions changed; they turned on their heels and fled – as he pulled the trigger.

The 'pffft' of the big, black gun firing, sounded exactly like a machine gun in a movie, only echoing eerily around the sports hall we'd spent the last six consecutive Saturday mornings in. As the first burst stopped, I could hear the children's panicked bare feet on the badminton court floor, like fluttering birds, as they approached the barrier, turned and desperately ran *back towards us*, obediently continuing their shuttles as they'd been told. I looked wildly right at my daughter – and I remember this bit very clearly – she was already sobbing with terror.

'Pffffffftttt!' The gun began again and someone screamed. It might have been me. I couldn't be certain though. I started to run towards her, but my shoe caught on the strap of my bag lying at my feet. I stumbled, crashed to the floor and looked up to see one of the three small boys scrabbling through a break in the plywood barrier sectioning off our area from the other badminton courts behind. There was enough of a gap, running underneath, to reveal his bottom. He'd sat down and was cowering to take shelter. Jones laughed – *laughed* – and pointed the gun right at him. I heard another cry but twisted back to Isobel. She was about to pass in front of us, less than twenty feet away. The gun stopped again and so did she. Adam, still running, accidentally thudded into her, knocking her off balance. I heard the squeak of the skin on her toes against the shiny wooden floor and the slap of her other foot go down as she tried to steady herself, but instead fell to her knees.

'Get up!' Jones shouted. And he took aim right at her.

I was almost standing again but I couldn't get there fast enough. Nothing went in slow motion. It was horrifyingly quick. Adam had frozen and was staring down at Isobel in fright.

'Pfffffttt' went the gun again, as the last remaining boy deliberately dived in front of my daughter to shield her. They huddled together on the floor, alongside each other, hands about their heads, the boy's small arm protectively around my little girl's back. I heard them yelping as the shots made contact with their bodies.

Then silence. Everything stopped. The whole episode had lasted less than ten seconds.

My breath was rasping and my body started to judder as I rushed over to them, trying to make sense of what I was looking at, what I'd just seen. He'd shot them? Actually shot them? Isobel wasn't moving. *My daughter was not moving.*

Jones turned to me and pointed behind me, at the floor. 'You've dropped your book.' I stared at him, horrified, still unable to process what he'd just done.

He scowled with annoyance. 'Calm down. It's not real. They're just pellets, not bullets. Even the kids know that.' He turned abruptly, walked back over to the pile of pads next to his bag, and carefully propped up the gun. I looked back at the children who were slowly, miraculously, unfolding like flowers. They were white, shaking, and all three of them, without exception, were crying. It had felt just as real to me, too.

'Get out from behind that fence,' Jones shouted at the boy still sat out of sight, who re-emerged, weeping.

'On your feet for bows – all of you.'

The children scrambled into a line. It was as if they'd been caught in a hailstorm – hundreds of tiny white balls rolled around at their feet.

The children bowed at Jones. '*Sensei.*' They managed, just about audibly and Jones nodded, apparently satisfied.

'See? You *can* do it properly. Do it first go next time, all right? I'll see you all after Christmas. Remind your mams and dads to bring the money to the first class back, please.'

Dismissed, Isobel ran and flattened herself onto me, wrapping her arms round my legs so tightly I almost wobbled over as she buried her face in my jeans, just as the sports hall door opened and the two oblivious mothers walked back in laughing and chatting, holding their purses, and chocolate bars for their children.

I bent down to whisper to Isobel: 'Where's your coat?' – even looking around for it before I realised *it didn't matter*. We needed to get out. Paul Jones had gone mad. He had a gun. He said it wasn't real, but what if that was a lie and he had real bullets in a bag back there? Should I shout? Should I tell the other parents who hadn't seen what had just happened to *get the children out now*! The father of the boy who had jumped in front of Isobel arrived; Adam's mother and the other woman were frowning down at their sons, beginning to notice they'd been crying – all of the children were accounted for. I looked at the gun again and I began to shake. We had to leave. I had to get Isobel out immediately.

I reached into my pocket for my keys as one of the little boys ran up to Jones, holding a Christmas gift that his dad had unwittingly given him to hand over to the teacher who had just shot him. I watched Jones take the wine as the boy turned and dashed away, before Jones looked up and right across at me, clutching the bottle tightly round the neck. I pulled Isobel from my legs and almost dragged her in my haste towards the emergency exit doors at the back of the gym. My ankle throbbed as I pushed down on the cold, metal bar to release us. Isobel shivered involuntarily in her judo kit and stopped on the threshold.

'I've got no shoes, Mummy.'

We'd left them behind.

'Should I just walk anyway?' She looked up at me, red eyes still wide with fear.

'Quick! Jump up into my arms.' I reached out and braced for her whole weight as she put her arms around my neck, leapt up and buried her face in my shoulder, clinging on like a baby monkey. I panted as I staggered towards the car, determined that my ankle would not give way. *Forget my bag, her shoes – everything.*

'Here,' I sat her on the bonnet as I fumbled with the keys, repeatedly glancing behind me in fear, half expecting Jones to come bursting out of the doors behind us waving the gun again. 'Get in quickly.' I bundled her into the back seat and roared out of the car park as fast as I could.

We swung onto the main road and Izzie blurted: 'I'm sorry, Mummy. I didn't mean to make him angry! I'm sorry. I was trying to kick as hard as I could.'

*He'd shot her.* 'It wasn't your fault, baby. What did he say to you when you were doing the pad work? You told him you didn't want to do something?' *That had actually happened? He'd just shot her?*

'He wanted us to kick harder. He'd been mean to you,' Isobel cut across me, 'and I didn't like it. I didn't want to do it any more.'

'What did he say to you though, darling?' *He held a gun to his shoulder and he aimed it at her.*

'He said: "none of your dirty English ways".' Isobel's voice was soft and small.

Everything froze – crystallised for a second – then I actually felt the explosion of rage within me. Blood thundered against my eardrums and my ribcage. I swerved left and stopped suddenly in front of the Red Lion pub. The bastard, the mad, racist dangerous bastard. She was seven! SEVEN.

Running round to the back seat, I flung the door open. 'Quick, darling! Jump in my arms again.' She did as she was told and, this time, I barely noticed her weight as I wove my way unsteadily up to the front door, shoving it violently with my hip, praying that it would be open. It wasn't – but it rattled enough in the frame for a shadow to quickly appear behind the glass as keys threw back in the lock.

The fifty-something landlord appeared clutching a tea towel, staring down at me holding Isobel in my arms.

'Can I use your phone?' I must have looked wild, deranged almost. 'There's a man at the leisure centre with a gun. He's just shot at the children. I need to call the police.'

He'd obviously seen enough drama in his time not to ask stupid questions, instead just rushed me through the back, to a cold red-tiled hall adjoining the bar and the lounge where the payphone was attached to the wall between the ladies toilets and the closed pub kitchen door.

I set Isobel down who flinched at the chill on her bare feet, but didn't complain. As I dialled 999, the landlord disappeared into the ladies loos, and came back with a hand towel, which he laid down at Isobel's feet.

'Stand on that, bab.'

He and Isobel listened as I told the call handler I needed the police. My daughter's instructor had fired a gun in the sports hall. No, my daughter wasn't injured, I didn't think, but I wasn't sure if he had any other weapons. Yes, he'd deliberately fired at the children in the enclosed sports hall. He'd said they weren't working hard enough, his assistant had gone out to his car via the emergency exit and come back with a big, black machine gun and Jones had shot them. He was still there now with other parents and children.

'It was Paul Jones who did it?' The landlord was frowning as I hung up, white with fury and shock.

I nodded.

'Well, there we go then,' the landlord sighed, without passing any further comment. 'You both need a drink.'

He took us back through into the empty bar urging us not to trip on the hoover lead snaking invisibly across the brightly patterned carpet, sat us at one of the tables in the window and gave Isobel a small bottle of orange juice with a straw and me a brandy. The winter sun was shining in through the glass so brightly it illuminated slowly swirling flecks of dust – hitting the highly polished mahogany table top with such a powerful glare it made me squint as I turned to Isobel to inspect her, gently turning her small head this way and that looking for marks or any obvious wounds.

'My arm and my toe hurt,' she confessed, lifting up her right foot.

I gasped as the landlord reappeared over my shoulder, and we both looked at Isobel's big toenail – which was already turning black around a small circular blast hole right in the centre of the nail bed. An unmistakable shot wound.

'Let me see your arm?' I slipped her jacket back from her right shoulder to reveal her white vest and three small, angry and perfectly circular welts on her skin. One was bleeding where the skin had broken.

'Ah – that's pellet marks, they are,' the landlord said.

'In an enclosed area! Can you believe it?' I exclaimed quickly. 'He could have blinded them!'

'I tried to run faster, Mummy,' Isobel apologised again. 'I'm sorry.'

'You didn't do anything wrong,' I repeated. I pulled her to me and stroked her poor little head.

We heard sirens approaching and a flashing blue light went whizzing past the window. *Good*, I thought savagely, picking up my brandy and downing it in one. The back of my throat burned, and the landlord straightened up. 'That's it then. Chris Davies is on his way to sort it out. When you came in here a moment ago saying someone had shot people I thought it was Hungerford all over again.'

'Thank you for these drinks,' I interrupted hastily. I didn't want Isobel to hear the horror of what had happened only three years earlier in a small, close community just like this one.

'You must have thought so, too,' he added kindly. 'Thank God it wasn't, eh?'

'I didn't know what to think, to be honest. It all happened very fast.'

I was already replaying the events in my mind – Jones holding the gun... and me just standing there. *Why hadn't I moved more quickly?* I started to feel sick. It wasn't the unaccustomed brandy on an empty stomach at that time of the morning, but horror that I hadn't been fast enough to leap in front of the children. I watched someone shoot at my daughter and I didn't protect her. A boy instinctively did it instead – the Vaughan child threw himself in the line of fire rather than me.

I had failed Isobel.

Nearly thirty years on, that self-disgust at my own inadequacy has not gone. Friends have been kind each and every time I have returned to that morning of 22 December 1990, asking myself how I could have let it happen to her.

I tripped – they tell me – it wasn't my fault. The police assured me it's a very natural reaction not to move at *all*, but rather to freeze completely. None of us know how we will react in moments of extreme trauma apparently, until it actually happens. Other people said that was complete rubbish. *Of course* a parent would move to protect their child: 'I don't care what anyone says, if there's a gun pointing at my little girl or boy, I'm getting in between it and them, no questions asked.'

I tried to apologise to Izzie the night it happened – tried to explain how I'd fallen but that I would always be there to protect her: 'Most of all, darling, I don't want you to feel worried that it will happen again. It was really scary, but it wasn't a real gun, Iz. It was a toy one.'

'Then why did the police shoot him?' She was sat up in her bed, pale, with wide eyes.

I swallowed. 'Because they *thought* it was a real gun. Mr Jones was waving it around in the car park after we left, the police told him to put it down and he didn't. They were worried he might hurt people.'

'Do the police shoot everyone who doesn't do as they're told?' Her voice went a little higher with fear.

'No, no darling. The police are good. They look after us.'

'But Mr Jones died when they shot him because they used real guns?'

I nodded, with difficulty.

'Because we phoned the police and told them he had a gun?'

'Yes, Izzie.' I forced a smile. 'But you're safe now, darling, try to snuggle down and go to sleep.'

This being nearly thirty years ago, we weren't offered counselling or anything like that. The best I had to offer Isobel was that she could come and get into my bed if she woke up feeling scared.

'Will Mr Jones go to Heaven?'

I could see where she was going with this – what she was afraid of – and it broke my heart all over again.

'No, my angel, he won't. Daddy will be safe, don't worry.'

She visibly relaxed. 'And I don't have to go to class any more on Saturdays? Because Mr Jones is dead?' She was only trying to piece it all together, to make sense of it, but her childish factuality unnerved me, even though I have always encouraged her to be honest and open.

'Yes, because he's dead.'

*

After I called the police they went screaming round to the sports hall. An angrily defensive Jones – loading his kit into the boot of his car – refused to hand over his weapons, then pointed the gun at them and forced the police back. A sixty-minute siege followed, culminating in him being shot dead in the leisure centre car park. The month-long inquest afterwards determined that the two police marksmen who killed him acted lawfully, believing the gun he was waving around as he walked towards them was the real deal. The police repeatedly reminded everyone at the inquest that although all of the guns found at his flat afterwards were discovered to be replicas – in addition to the pellets found scattered in the sports hall – the marksmen involved believed the weapon was genuine, that they were in danger and so asked Mr Jones to put down the gun – which he did not. Jones's parents were on the scene by that point, begging the police to let them talk to their son, insisting it was a replica weapon. They weren't allowed to approach him – in Hungerford, one of the many people Michael Ryan had shot was his own mother.

I saw Mrs Jones in the street, six months after that fateful day, just before they moved away from the area. By then the whole town had read every detail of the inquest in the papers. They all knew Jones had asked me out for a drink just before the lesson had started. I'd said no… he was angry, Isobel had cheeked him – not my words – and he eventually lost his temper. Mrs Jones knew it was me that had called the police. Everyone did. She stopped on the opposite side of the street and stared as I hurried past her. She could have shouted something, abused me. But she didn't and somehow her silence was worse. Without saying a word she made it crystal clear she thought I was responsible for what had happened to her son.

And if truth be told, I do sometimes feel a sense of disquiet about the phone call I made from the pub that morning. I don't doubt in principle it was the right thing to do – when someone shoots a gun and people are injured, you call the police.

What I've never discussed with anyone, however, is that I saw the pellets on the ground – I *knew* it was a replica gun and I didn't say that to the 999 call handler. I said Jones had shot the children – which was true – he did. But did I deliberately omit the fact that the gun wasn't real because I was angry with Jones and wanted him punished? I just don't know. I couldn't say for certain.

No one else behaved as if I was to blame for Jones's death. In spite of his warning to me that Izzie and I were regarded as unwelcome, the town couldn't have been kinder to us. They wrapped us in their arms. We were looked after. Meals were made and brought round, reporters were shooed out of our front garden by cross, protective neighbours – we were supported. Timothy Vaughan rightly became a local hero for jumping in front of Izzie; it was a tragedy that kept the town busy for months. The press cast Jones as a psycho in waiting and regardless of his personal political stance – such as it was – everyone agreed that it was madness to take a gun into a class full of children, replica or not. Eventually the chatter quietened down… but it didn't stop completely. Significant local events are never forgotten, they become woven into the fabric of the community – sometimes becoming luxuriantly embellished as time passes, or as has happened in our case, the stiches can appear simplistic and old-fashioned when viewed through modern eyes. Especially eyes that are desensitised by the violence everyone carries around in their back pocket these days, on those wretched tiny screens no one looks up from any more.

Mary Morgan was in the wool shop only this afternoon, talking about it all when I arrived to choose some buttons for Izzie. Busily shaking her head that next week would mark the *twenty-seventh anniversary* of the shooting. I could tell she was settling in for a gossip, not having heard or seen me come in, as she stood by the till with her back to the door.

'Thing is – Paul Jones was always on the edge – even when we were at school, wasn't he?' She was addressing Ann, the shop owner. 'He gave me a Chinese burn once and it really hurt. He wouldn't let go – he just kept saying he could squeeze and squeeze and break my wrist if he wanted to and I think he would have, but my God – those eyes! He was a *very* good-looking man. He shouldn't have taken that gun in where there were kiddies, I'm not saying that – but maybe he was just showing off again, a bit overexcited, like. Children use those BB guns all the time now – my own grandson shoots rats out the back barn when he comes to us. He loves it! It'd sting you, like, if one of the pellets caught you – but not *hurt*. Paintballing's worse, you know? Gareth did that for Rich's stag do and was covered in bruises for days after. I said you're too old for that sort of lark, you daft sod! Anyway, when you think Paul Jones *died* because of all that.'

She had the grace to blush furiously when I coughed and she turned to see me standing there. 'Eve! You all right? Oh lovey – never mind me. I'm not having a pop at you, but you know that, don't you? It's the police I'm talking about, what *they* did.'

I didn't say anything, just held up the packet of buttons I'd chosen. 'I'll just take these, please Ann. Izzie's keeping busy making a jumper,' I looked pointedly at Mary, 'as this time of year is always particularly tough for her.'

The two women pulled sympathetic faces and tutted.

'Of course it is,' said Mary. 'I see you haven't had any luck with selling the house yet then? I expect that's unsettling too, isn't it? Not knowing where you'll be?' She waited hopefully.

'We'll stay local,' I confirmed. 'Just not at Fox Cottage.'

'That's it, then!' Mary agreed. 'It's such a big old place for you. I've always thought that – and there's some nice new houses being built. Some just across the fields from where you are now, aren't they? You wouldn't have to do a thing – all ready to move into! Although you won't be able to do those artist whatsits when you move, will you? What do you call them?'

'Retreats.' I was starting to feel tired and wished that I'd not come in at all. 'I've decided to stop the workshops and residential courses anyway. Izzie struggles a bit with lots of strangers in the house.'

'Well, I don't think I'd want someone I didn't really know wandering around my kitchen either, to be honest. I think you're brave to have done it at all, Eve. Does Adam Owen still use your barn to do his paintings?'

'Yes, he does, but he's hardly a stranger.'

'Oh I know! That's not what I meant. He's a lovely boy. Is he with you most days then?'

I nodded.

'Ah – that's nice. Talk about committed. Ever since he was a little lad he's been her shadow, hasn't he? Bless.' She smiled innocently at me. 'So you think you'll be hat shopping any time soon, Eve?'

I looked back at her steadily. 'He is indeed a lovely boy. I'm very fond of him.'

'Well, you've been good to him, too, since he moved out sharp-ish when his mam remarried that Craig Evans – and I don't blame him!' She shuddered. 'Does he still see his dad much, though? Last I heard *he* was in Thailand of all places! Got himself one of those Thai brides, did he?'

'Adam is busy concentrating on becoming an exceptional artist,' I replied sharply. 'He's finally starting to get quite a lot of attention from some very good galleries.' The latter was sadly not true, although it deserved to be.

'Oh! Lovely!' Mary nodded politely. 'Does he paint people? Or fruit?'

God, she was a cretin. 'Landscapes are his thing.' Dark, bleak hills and stormy threatening seas – the poor boy. I didn't tell Mary Morgan *that*, obviously.

'Clouds and fields. Very nice!' she beamed. 'He'll be sad when you sell Fox Cottage too, then?'

I gritted my teeth. 'It's going to be a big change, yes. But the right one, I think.'

'Definitely!' she agreed. 'It's funny really, Eve, but you know, Fox Cottage has always been tricky. The people you and Michael bought it off – I don't suppose you remember them, the Begleys, they were called – when they tried to run it as a pub again it didn't work at all. The stress is what made Dave Begley have to sell up. He couldn't take it any more. Sian, his wife, ended up *hating* the place. That's why you got it so cheap, you see, when you and Michael bought it. They wanted rid and it had been on the market for years, hadn't it, Ann?'

'Oh yes,' agreed Ann. 'They had a bad time with it.'

'Anyway,' continued Mary, 'my sister's daughter-in-law used to clean there and it gave her the creeps a bit, to be honest. She IS sensitive to that sort of thing – she goes to those mediums, or psychics – whatever you're meant to call them – and someone *always* tries to contact her. Anyway, when she worked at your place for Sian, a plug popped out of the wall when she was boiling the kettle! Do you ever find funny things happen?'

'No, never. I simply don't believe in rubbish like that,' I said rudely, starting to lose my temper.

'I don't either, actually,' she agreed, not remotely bothered. 'I expect it was just wiring that wants doing. You'll probably laugh about this too, but you know that big old hook in the beam what's in your sitting room now? Well, that used to be the pub lounge bar, see – and when we were kids, someone started a story that the landlord hung his wife off it – when it was a really old pub, like – because she disappeared. Only the Begleys actually did find things buried in the walls when they did it up. A bloodstained woman's shoe, bits of old letters. Love letters, I'd wager. The husband found out she was up to no good and did her in.' Mary Morgan nodded at me knowingly.

I held her gaze. 'Placing shoes inside a wall was a common phenomenon back in the day. People did it to ward off witches. It was probably bloodstained because it was ill-fitting. Although I appreciate that doesn't support your story so nicely. Sorry.'

'I have actually heard that too,' said Ann. 'You're supposed to leave the shoes where you find them, aren't you? It's bad luck otherwise.'

'Well, my sister's daughter-in-law, she never liked going in that room on her own after that, I can tell you.' Mary was not to be derailed. 'I don't know if she sensed the spirit of him or his wife though. I'll ask her when I see her next, but what—'

I exhaled slowly. She had barely drawn breath. How the bloody hell had Richard Morgan put up with such verbal incontinence their whole married life?

'—that house needs now is someone from out of town to come in with more money than sense: spend a fortune, make it into a family house and have done with it. You don't want to do that, Eve. You're very sensible to let someone else do all the hard work now and foot the bills. Mark my words – that's who will buy it, not someone from round here. Then you can finally have a new start! You just need to hang on in there, love! They'll turn up eventually.'

'Actually, there's someone coming to view it the day after tomorrow,' I snapped crossly.

Mary wrinkled her nose. 'On a Saturday? This close to Christmas? Well, they'll either be desperate or time-wasters. They're probably just staying with family and fancy a nose to see how much space you can get up here for your money. I'd cancel it if I were you, Eve. All that cleaning for nothing. You'll regret it, trust me.'

I wanted to scream when I finally escaped back out onto the street. Sometimes I wish I'd done the same as Paul Jones's mother and moved away from the town straight away too – started again somewhere else with Izzie, but I know back then I felt I needed to stay. Michael was buried in the local churchyard. I couldn't leave him. On the whole it's been better, I think, because horrifically invasive though it is that people round here know *everything* about our history, they do at least make allowances for my daughter. And while I also *hate* that they all know I NEED to sell Fox Cottage, facts are facts. I just can't do it any more; the cost of preventing it from crumbling away is crippling me. The retreats aren't worth the increasing agitation they cause Izzie but neither is my art teacher's salary enough on its own.

I actually hoped Bloody Mary was right for once, and the viewers would turn out to be desperate and buy it – because the time had come. There was no more money. We were going to be forced to have our 'new start' one way or the other.

I started my trudge home, towards the outskirts of town, past the quiet churchyard.

*It'd sting you, like, if one of the pellets caught you – but not hurt. When you think Paul Jones died for that…*

Mary Morgan isn't malicious, just pig ignorant and insensitive. She has no idea about 'hurt'. What she and people like her really forget is that these were *children*. Mary Morgan – with her blissfully straightforward farmer's wife life, grown-up sons and grandchildren – has no imagination, no understanding of what it might be like to be seven, to really, truly believe that your teacher is shooting you for not running fast enough.

Lucky her. It looked and sounded like a real semi-automatic M4 – the second most manufactured gun in the world after the AK-47. It stuns me that people can have no empathy for what those ten seconds must have felt like to them: ten seconds of deep trauma that has forced those children to become adults they were never meant to be.

True – Jones didn't tear their muscles or break their bones, but he violently shattered their small souls. Paul Jones stole so many futures that day – and when I think about *that,* I have not the slightest regret that I didn't tell the police the gun wasn't real. I'm glad they shot the bastard dead.

In fact, I would kill him with my bare hands for the damage he did, all over again, if he was stood in front of me now. I'd choke the life out of him slowly and deliberately. I would watch him suffer and I would enjoy it.

I wonder what Mary Morgan would say to that?

# CHAPTER TWO

## Claire

'Oooh. Junction 10A…' I remark happily, seeing the sign. 'Nearly on the M54! I always feel we're mostly there when we get to this bit.' I turn around and glance at Rosie who is fast asleep in the back, head hanging forward over her seat belt, forced to sit bolt upright on her booster. 'Poor kid. I meant to get her one of those inflatable plane pillows, but I forgot. Still, we should be there by ten, didn't you say?'

'Yes, definitely.' Tim glances at the illuminated clock on the dashboard.

'Will your mum be back by then?'

'I'm not sure. She's been in court today.'

'She must be knackered. I don't know how she does it.'

'She's only part human, that's how.' He looks in his mirror and pulls into the outside lane to overtake. 'Rampaging through the legal jungle like *Predator*, collecting her scalps while wheeling her suitcase of court documents behind her.'

'Tim!' I rebuke him. 'That's not very nice.'

'She's hard-core, is all I mean.'

I frown at him. 'Whatever – it's not exactly a flattering comparison. In any case, yes, you're right, she's very capable, but everyone has their limits.'

Tim says nothing, just yawns.

'I'll drive if you're getting tired,' I offer immediately, and he glances across before putting a reassuring hand on my leg.

'Thanks, but I'm fine. I promise.'

'OK, but say if you change your mind.' I reach for another sweet. 'I can't stop eating these now.' My thoughts return to his parents. 'How exactly *are* they going to have the time to oversee a major house renovation on top of everything else?'

'Sorry, what?' Tim says absently. He's not really listening.

'This project house they're going to buy,' I repeat, 'your mum is flat out at work and your dad is busier than ever.'

'Well he won't do any of the hands-on stuff.' Tim pulls back into the slow lane carefully. 'He's past that now, but he'll definitely be involved.' He clears his throat.

'I still don't see why they need *my* opinion on this place? They don't usually have a problem with doing what they want. I mean that in a nice way,' I add quickly. 'They're decisive. That's what I should have said.'

'I know what you mean, it's OK.' Tim reaches for a Haribo. 'Hang on – you've nearly eaten the whole bag!'

'Sorry.' I make an apologetic face. 'I've got a mini hot cross bun if you want? Or a banana?'

'I'm trying not to eat bread during the week though, aren't I?' Tim sighs.

'Then have the banana.' I reach down and produce it from the snack bag.

He shakes his head. 'I don't fancy it. I'll just have a hot cross bun and start again tomorrow. Mum and Dad want you to look at the house because you're good with property. Thanks.' He takes the bun I hold out and eats it in one go. 'Can I have another one, please?'

I roll my eyes, but say nothing and reach into the packet again. 'I don't think I'm "good with property" at all. I've not found *us* anywhere else to buy yet, have I?'

'Not for the want of looking,' Tim says kindly.

'Thanks, babe.' I sigh, then brighten. 'At least when the right place comes along we'll be able to grab it, now that we've got nothing to sell. Anyway, yes – I'll happily look at these houses for them. It still blows my mind that you can get a whole massive house up here for the same price as a two-bed flat where we are. Why don't they just do that, out of interest, if they want an investment? It would be a lot less hassle.'

'I don't know.' Tim shifts uncomfortably in his seat. I know how he feels; my bum has gone numb too. Three and a half hours is too long to be in a car.

'They've made you appointments for tomorrow morning at the three places they've shortlisted. I'm going to stay and look after Rosie.'

'You're not coming with me?' I reach for one of the last remaining sweets.

'No. Just you.'

I glance up in surprise. '*No one* is coming with me? Not even your Mum?'

He clears his throat again. 'Mum has a favourite, so does Dad. They want you to decide without being swayed by them.'

'Oh no, so *that's* it – I'm the arbiter? Great.' I immediately go right off the idea. 'Why are you doing your nervous cough thing?'

'Am I? Sorry. I'm fine.' He swallows instead. 'I forgot to mention, you can't let on that Mum and Dad are the potential purchasers. If the agents ask, you'll need to pretend you're the one who is buying.'

'Why can't I just be honest?' I'm confused.

'Because everyone knows Mum and Dad. If they went to look at a house locally then didn't buy it and maybe bought something else instead, that might cause some resentment.'

I eat the last of the sweets and put the empty packet back in my bag. 'But surely they've *already* viewed these houses? They're not just going to blow £350k on something they've not even *looked* at? That's mental!'

He shrugs. 'I've no idea.'

I hesitate and realise perhaps he's upset because Tony and Susannah have asked for my opinion and not his.

'I suppose they know the places well enough,' I say carefully. 'They've lived locally for nearly thirty years, after all.'

He glances sideways at me. 'Which is also why I can't come with you. Everyone knows me too, don't they?'

'Oh yeah,' I admit. 'I hadn't thought of that.'

'It's no big deal, Claire. They just want to know which one you'd choose. That's all.' He exhales, sounding stressed and I look at him again more carefully.

'I'm really sorry you didn't hear about the audition, Tim. I know you wanted to be able to tell your dad you'd got the part.'

'It would have been nice, yes,' he agrees, 'but what will be, will be.'

I look away. I know this is all front. He wants this role really badly, but I also know he should have heard from his agent by now if he'd got it. I reach out and squeeze his hand supportively.

'Why don't you close your eyes for five minutes?' he says.

Fair enough. He doesn't want to discuss it. 'Hint taken,' I say, and swing the spotlight off his apparent latest rejection, by adding kindly: 'no more house talk, I promise.'

He smiles gratefully and I do as I'm told. The rumble of the motorway beneath us, and the dark of the car, is seductive. It's been a long week at work and I am tired.

It doesn't occur to me to suspect a thing.

What a fool.

# CHAPTER THREE

## Eve

There is a knock on the door at precisely quarter to eleven. Hurrying through the sitting room – my hands outstretched as if I am about to perform a papal blessing – I bitterly curse Ms Claire Waters for being fifteen minutes *early* and possessing neither the breeding or gumption to drive around the area for a bit, until our allotted viewing time. I try to twist the stiff door knob to the inner hall with my wrists so I don't get oil all over it, but of course, that doesn't work, so I give up and crossly yank it open, earning my first look at Ms Waters, who has actually pressed her little snub nose right up against the small square of glass in our front door, to get a better look in.

My eyes narrow, and darting forward I wrench it with all my might, but of course, the bloody thing sticks on the floor tiles with a clonk – as it has every day for the last two decades – so the effect is ruined and she doesn't fall in through it at all, just jumps and stares at me.

'Sorry about that,' I say briskly. 'We've got so used to it over the years we don't notice it any more, but I'm sure it could be fixed with a simple re-hanging. I'm Eve Parkes. You must be Claire Waters?'

'Yes, I am,' she says cheerfully. I glance at her car on the forecourt, a thoroughly unflashy family Volvo, which tells me absolutely nothing about her financial status, but as said family are not getting out of it, pretty much everything about her intent. A serious potential buyer would have at least brought *someone* with her – if not her children, which she obviously has, as I can spy a booster seat in the back. Blast Mary Morgan, she's absolutely right. This woman is a time-waster. As my shoulders tense, I step to one side. 'Would you like to come in?'

She gratefully leaps out of the bitter wind roaring up the valley like Jack Frost himself, ready with his hoary fingers to snatch away anyone who isn't safely inside. Obviously not a local either – Bloody Mary has called that correctly too – as her coat is some sort of camel-coloured, oversized, curiously mannish affair, the like of which one might see in a glossy women's magazine. Almost a hairy dressing gown. Even if she was tall enough to pull the style off – which she isn't – it would still be perfectly repellent and needs a hood at the very least to give it any practical purpose whatsoever. If she is this into appearances it's going to be a *very* short viewing. I look down to see she's teamed the coat with some rather extraordinary – and slightly tacky – red leather ankle boots. Out of nowhere, I'm suddenly reminded of a Paddington Bear toy Michael bought for Isobel not long after she was born. I soften slightly and realise she's extended her hand to me in greeting.

'I would,' I say, 'but I've just been grappling with the Rayburn and I'm covered in oil. Come in, I'll wash my hands and we'll start again, shall we?'

I turn abruptly on the spot and march off through the sitting room. She has the sense to follow me as we proceed on to the dining room and then into the kitchen.

'I've already lost my bearings, even though I studied the floor plan last night!' she says rather breathlessly, hovering in the doorway while I bend over the sink and scrub at my hands under the tap. 'It's big, isn't it?'

I glance at her. 'Yes it is. I'm sorry about the godawful smell.'

'Oh please don't worry. I can't smell a thing,' she says.

I snort and peer over my half-moon spectacles. 'Really – you don't have to be polite, it's dreadful.' I can't see the point in us not acknowledging it, she isn't going to buy the place anyway. 'That thing,' I nod at the Rayburn and dry my hands on a tea towel, 'is a menace. It blows out constantly and did it again this morning – hence the overpowering fumes.'

She looks a little embarrassed. 'No, I mean I actually have no sense of smell at all, so you could have got away with not mentioning it in my case.'

I stare at her, then laugh, taking off my glasses. 'Really? Bugger. What are the chances? Oh well, there we go. Take it from me then, it absolutely reeks.'

She shrugs and gives me an apologetic smile, but I've heard the stair creak and my attention is already elsewhere. Isobel. I take a step forward, in time to see the door behind Ms Waters slowly pulling to. Ms Waters turns and looks over her shoulder into the apparently empty room. But *I* can see my daughter's sylph outline behind the obscured glass door panel, as she waits for a moment, listening to us.

'Are you coming in?' I call pointedly, so she knows I've spotted her, only for the door to slam crossly, before the thumping of feet running upstairs reverberates throughout the house.

I sigh. 'Sorry, that's my daughter, Isobel.' I rub my face with a hand, before putting my glasses back on. 'She's just off to see a friend, I think.' If only that were true. 'Can I offer you a tea or coffee?' I say, albeit in a tone that doesn't invite acceptance.

'No, thank you,' Ms Waters replies dutifully, better brought up than I thought after all; but then suddenly I go blank and completely forget where we were, too busy worrying about Izzie and hoping she isn't gearing up for a scene.

'Sorry – Ms Waters, what was I saying, before we were interrupted?'

'Please, call me Claire,' she invites. 'You were telling me about the Aga going out all the time?'

'Rayburn,' I correct. 'You cook on it like an Aga but a Rayburn will do the hot water, too – when it's working, obviously. There's an immersion switch you can flick when it goes out, although that gets the water dangerously hot if you forget about it. I mean it would literally blanch the skin from your bones if you stepped into a full bath inadvertently or put a child in, unawares. I noticed you had a booster seat in the back of your car, which is why I mention it – and there's the cost, of course. Dreadfully expensive to heat like that.'

Ms Waters – Claire – raises two shocked eyebrows and I realise I am *almost* starting to enjoy myself. 'Yes, you're right,' I agree. 'This is exactly why people aren't allowed to conduct their own viewings, isn't it? The agents usually do them for me, but on a Saturday they won't, they say it's too far to drive over here from their offices in Shrewsbury when they've only got a skeleton staff. I didn't want to use a local firm. I probably should have, but there we are. So tell me, Claire – the agents knew almost nothing about you at all when I asked – where do you hail from?'

'Surrey.'

Of course she does.

'And what brings you to Shropshire?'

'I'm visiting my partner's family.'

I nod. So far, so predictable. 'Have you been looking to buy around here for a while?'

'Not exactly.'

Well, at least she's honest about that. I turn into the kitchen, walk across the room and throw open the back door. 'OK, out here is what used to be pub urinals in a former life.' I watch her nose wrinkle. 'It's now where I have the washing machine, big fridge, coats and boots – that sort of thing. There's a door to the garden *there* and an arctic downstairs loo at the far end, if you want to take a look?'

'I better had,' she says, squeezing past me. 'So that goes out to the garden,' she points left – 'and where does this lead?' She gestures to her right.

'Oh this house is a little bit like Alice in Wonderland, Claire,' I say airily. 'Doors everywhere. If you go *that* way,' I nod in the direction she's pointing, 'you wind up in the library. Not as grand as it sounds, it's just where I keep my boxes of books and the computer – that sort of thing. It was originally going to be a big communal dining room. My husband and I were going to run Fox Cottage as a B&B – or a boutique hotel as I think they're now called – but shortly after we did all of the work, he died.'

'Oh – I'm so sorry,' she says immediately.

'Thank you,' I reply. 'It was a long time ago now. He was twenty-nine. It wasn't here in the house or anything.' I wave a dismissive hand. 'I know some people worry about these things. He lost control while we were driving home after a night out and smacked into a telegraph pole. He wasn't even going that fast, but his injuries…' I tap my own head lightly to illustrate and see ghostly trees flashing past the car window seconds before the impact.

I was in bad temper. Michael had gently removed my glass while I'd been chatting perfectly innocently to a chap in the pub and I'd been incensed in the car afterwards.

'You tell me I've got to give this place a chance, and then when I *do* interact with someone, you treat me like a lush!'

'It was hot tonight; I know that's the only reason you drank more than you would normally.' He spoke soothingly. 'It's easy to create the wrong impression, that's all. People were starting to stare.' Gripping the wheel, he held on sensibly at two and ten. 'You're too smart and funny to need propping up with Dutch courage, anyway.'

Patronised, I'd crossed my arms and slumped into a glowering, sullen silence; although he was right, of course, red wine always makes me belligerent, I have no idea why. 'Dutch courage?' I snapped a moment later, spoiling for a fight. 'Hardly. I was simply talking. Actually, that's not true – I was flirting,' I lied. 'There, I've said it. It was nice to be spoken to like a human being, not just "Mummy" who also happens to do all of the cooking, ironing, washing… I wasn't ready to leave, Michael. I was having fun – for once. I don't want to go back to that *hole* of a house.' I flicked the hair from my eyes crossly and looked in the wing mirror. There was a car some distance behind, the headlights tracking us. I stared at them, getting closer, as we drove past the iron-gated entrance to a lonely farm; the otherwise deserted road on one side lined with tall, foreboding pine trees, and the other giving way to a steep drop off down into the valley. This could be the start of a film. Someone following us, an unknown threatening presence in the car… but they suddenly turned off and disappeared. Bored again, I sighed heavily, and Michael glanced across.

'I don't think of you as just Mummy. I think you're beautiful.' He hesitated. 'Do you honestly still hate the house?'

'Yes!' I exclaimed. 'It's a draughty money pit. We were mad to buy it.'

'I really, really want you to try and give it a chance. It's so important to me. Please?' he begged. I ignored him.

He sighed and, moments later, valiantly tried again. 'It's so eerie the way all of the moths are drawn out of the darkness, isn't it? No control over their destiny at all. The poor things…' He shivered. 'I keep seeing little eyes in the hedges, too, do you? Wow! Look!' he exclaimed excitedly, swerving slightly. 'A badger! Did you see? Just disappearing into that field! We must remember to tell Izzie in the morning!'

Still, I said nothing, just yawned. I wasn't making a point, I was genuinely sleepy.

'Oh, don't be like this, Evie,' he pleaded. 'I'm sorry I took your drink away. You're right, I shouldn't have. Eve? Please look at me!'

He put his hand on my arm, and I petulantly yanked myself free, refusing to be placated. I felt the car start to speed up – but oddly it felt as if there was no grip on the road at all – we were almost gliding… before it swerved and smashed into something head-on. When I opened my eyes again, Michael was staring right at the pole buried in the crumpled bonnet, only his forehead was oozing blood, his eyes were unblinking and his arms hung lifelessly at his side – his seat belt was taking the weight of his chest.

I ran back to the farm we'd passed, for help. The only sound in the otherwise dark, still summer night was my feet pounding on the tarmac road and my breath coming in terrified gasps.

*

Was he distracted and lost control, accidentally selecting too high a gear? Did he swerve on purpose to force a reaction, and it all went horribly wrong? But Michael was such a sensitive and sensible soul. I can't believe he would have done that. I would so dearly love to know what happened, even after all these years.

'We had one of those rows you can't even remember the point of afterwards.' I stare into the middle distance for a moment. 'So silly.'

'I'm very sorry,' Claire repeats and I hear a tremble in her voice. 'I really do understand. My parents died in a car accident.'

I spin back to her in astonishment. 'Oh my dear girl!'

Her eyes are shining brightly with unshed tears that I watch her blink back. 'I was eighteen. They were on the way home from taking me to university. A seventy-nine-year-old lady drifted across onto the carriageway and ploughed straight into them.' She shrugs and gives me a desperately sad smile.

I walk back over, and to both of our surprise, take her hand in mine and quietly hold it for a moment.

'Thank you.' She squeezes it a little more tightly before letting go. 'It will be twenty-three years this June. I think of them every day.'

'Being forced to go forward into a new life you didn't choose and would never have wanted is very hard. Are you sure I can't make you a tea?' I say, sincerely this time.

'No, really, I'm fine, but thank you.' She takes a deep breath to steady herself. She looks so young, suddenly, and I feel ashamed of my uncharitable first assessment of her nose. For all of her attempts at high-end fashion, you really *couldn't* describe her as pretty, but attractive, or sexy, perhaps. Certainly not a boat rocker or someone who colours outside the lines though – so why on earth isn't she viewing some smart, safe glass box in Esher, rather than my crap hole of a property in Shropshire? Something isn't sitting quite right.

'Look, Claire – do you really *want* to look at the rest of the house?' Our moment of shared understanding encourages me to lay it all out on the table. I'm not exasperated, just confused.

She flushes bright red. 'Yes, of course I do! Sorry – have I done something wrong?'

'No, not at all, but—'

'I suppose usually people viewing a family home would bring their family with them?' she says slowly. 'I wouldn't bring my daughter to look at anything until I thought it was a serious prospect. It would be too unsettling for her otherwise. But I *am* interested in your house and,' she lowers her voice to a confidential whisper, 'it's a cash purchase.'

Well. That's me told. 'Shall we move on to the small sitting room then?'

I walk past her, gesturing the way, and trying to squash down the excited extra thump of my heart. Not really, not *finally* after all these years? I try to imagine packing up boxes and turning the key in the front door for the last time. I have to push the image away. It's too much – I feel almost light-headed.

'So this room does what it says on the tin really. It's nice to have another space to escape to if you've got a houseful, where people can read or have some peace, if the TV's blaring in the other room. It's actually the oldest part of the house and has fifteenth-century origins.' I point at a one foot by one foot hole in the thick stone wall of the fireplace. 'That opening is the old bread oven from when this bit was probably a bakery—'

'I thought you said it was a pub?' She looks confused.

'It's been lots of things: pub, shop, bakery, possibly even the local abattoir at one point. There are hooks in the beams all over the place and there used to be a stream that ran outside the house many moons ago – you would have wanted running water nearby to sluice the blood away,' I explain, only for her blank expression to give way to one of horror. 'Not any more, obviously,' I say gently, and obviously feeling a bit foolish, she laughs at her own reaction. 'Sorry.'

I smile and turn back to the bread oven. 'Because the chimney leads off from here up to the roof, you can't have a traditional fire in this room, just a decorative one. Although maybe you could fit one of those wood burners that are all the rage now and feed the flue up there – I'm not sure. You said you were visiting your partner's family? Do they live nearby?'

'Yes, they do.'

I open my mouth to ask if I know them, but before I have the chance, she says: 'My daughter Rosamund – Rosie – is eight. She'd love a big garden to run around in and we can't afford that where we are now. I liked the pictures of your garden very much.'

I suddenly remember Izzie's delight on the very first day we moved into Fox Cottage, exploring the vast garden and orchard, announcing she was going to get guinea pigs, wobbling on her bike around the rather uneven path that tracked the perimeter of the garden. It was such a hot summer that year and she practically lived outside for those first blissful months. My heart seizes at the memory.

'It's the perfect garden for children,' I admit. 'Let's just finish the downstairs tour and I'll take you out there to see for yourself.' I move to the back of the room. 'Another door,' I remark drily as I turn the large iron key in the lock. 'This one leads to the section of the house that – once upon a time – was used for grain storage.'

I lead her through the small, narrow corridor past the second downstairs loo in which sits the old-fashioned pull-chain lavatory. The paint on the walls is flaking away with the damp, and the carpet is blackened with mould in sections. If she's still interested after this bit, I'll start getting properly excited.

'You'll notice it needs a bit of work.' I give a rather nervous laugh. 'We obviously don't really use this section to live in; it's still a storage area right now, in fact! Not grain though, obviously.'

We walk into the large room absolutely stuffed to the rafters with Adam's belongings and, again, I see it through her eyes, and feel cross that I didn't ask Adam to at least stack things more neatly.

'My daughter's boyfriend is between flats right now,' I try to explain. 'He asked if he could keep everything here for a while. I hadn't anticipated any more viewings before Christmas, so I thought it would be all right to say yes. I apologise that it looks so… cluttered.'

I watch her look in astonishment at the two free-standing pine wardrobes, stacked sofas, a bed with a bare mattress – duvet and pillow tossed onto it – a mountain bike, suitcases, a box of vinyl, a couple of amplifiers, two guitars and at least two dozen cardboard boxes. 'I don't think he's sleeping here too, but it's sometimes quite hard to tell,' I remark, frowning at the bed. It looks like a dosshouse – why didn't I notice this earlier? I decide I need to move her on, quickly. 'Now through *here* is the barn, which you'll have seen on the particulars has planning consent for conversion into a separate four-bedroom house.' I pause, as she's still looking open-mouthed at Adam's sad collection of worldly goods. 'Claire?'

'Yes, I'm coming. Sorry.'

'Adam – the same boy – also rents *this* space as an art studio.' I throw over my shoulder, waiting for her to catch me up.

'Oh my God,' she says in disbelief, stepping into the cavernous room and starting to walk around it in wonder, rubbing her arms against the cold. 'It's enormous! This place goes on forever!'

'Yes, it does a bit.' I look around me and try to remember how I felt the first time I viewed the house, as she is now. I'd been enchanted by the barn. It had been going to be *my* studio – even, and this makes me want to laugh now, gallery – but as soon as I started teaching full-time up at the school, I stopped wanting to paint for pleasure.

I watch Claire glance at the large, French windows set into the heavy stone walls – rotten as anything; I hope to God she isn't going to touch them. Luckily, a distracting shaft of sunlight breaks through the cloud and illuminates Adam's easel, with his work in progress set upon it, right in the centre of the room.

It's another of his disturbing seascapes, which is unfortunate, not helped by the mad scatter of half-squeezed tubes of oils he's left littered on the floor. Only the upturned box next to the paint-ing – covered in an old, stained towel – lays claim to some sort of ordered mind at work. His neat selection of brushes and palette knifes are clean and ready to start again.

Stepping to the rear of the room, however, I jump to see an enormous oil canvas of a sheep's skull I haven't previously noticed, propped up at an angle against the saggy, faded old sofa on the back wall. Two gnarly horns curl up around the edge of the picture like they belong to Lucifer himself. I roll my eyes and sigh. *Throw me a bone, here, Adam. You're really not helping.*

'My goodness.' Claire catches sight of it too. 'That's – arresting.' But then she walks around to the other side of the sofa, frowns, bends down and peers closely at a much smaller canvas, at the front of several more stacked prints. '*That's* lovely though.'

I walk across to join her, removing my glasses to clean them on my apron for a better look.

It's a portrait of Izzie, copied from the photograph that has been carelessly tossed on the floor next to the painting. She is sat on this very sofa – only when it was new and the once-vibrant purple cushions plump – looking out of the windows. One leg is drawn up to her chest, long, red hair spilling loosely over her shoulders and the other hand propping up her head, tiredly; capturing her forever apparently on the verge of the release of sleep. Claire is right, it's exquisite.

'He should call that *Day-dreaming*,' Claire remarks, obviously pleased with her pedestrian title suggestion. 'How does he paint in here, it's *freezing*.'

'He has a small plug-in heater. He manages.' I pick the photograph up, silently put it in my apron pocket and turn away, waiting by the door until Claire has finished looking. The painting has completely unsettled me and I have an overwhelming desire to get the rest of the viewing over and done with, so she'll leave.

'Where do those stairs lead to?' She points at the open flight right along the left-hand wall, and the tiny hatch at the top.

'Nowhere,' I say tiredly. 'Behind the door is a small mezzanine. You could just about squeeze into it, but that's all. I wouldn't though, I'm not sure the floor is sound – it's the shed space below, where I keep the lawnmower and garden things. I wouldn't want you to fall through.'

She is looking at me, concerned. 'Are you all right? You look a little pale.' She reaches out and puts a steadying hand on my arm.

'I'm fine, thank you. I think, after all, perhaps we'll do the upstairs before the garden.' I keep my own hand in my apron pocket, holding the picture of Izzie, my voice brusque with the guilt of having established any sort of rapport with this girl when my daughter is the one I ought to be thinking of. 'Brace yourself.'

*

'So every bedroom has got separate sinks and fitted wardrobes built into them?' Claire says in astonishment, as we re-emerge back out onto the landing in the middle section of the house. 'All *seven* of them?'

'Back then it was the vogue,' I explain. 'Washing facilities in every room. I know it's very old-fashioned now and the fixtures are all horribly dated, but at the time they were cutting edge, I can assure you. The only room that has an en suite is the master bedroom, which now belongs to my daughter.' I force my tone to sound matter-of-fact. 'It's over here.' I walk across the hall and pause outside the closed door. 'Would you mind if I just check that she *has* gone out? I think she has, I just… don't want to surprise her if not?'

'Of course.'

Claire waits politely as I knock softly. 'Isobel? Can I come in?' There's no answer. 'I think we're safe,' I push the door slowly open. As the room is revealed, Claire gasps and steps past me.

'This is so beautiful!' She turns around on the spot in the elongated triangular eaves room. Clouds are rolling across the large, slightly open skylight that I had installed, at great expense, ten years ago now. I can hear our resident robin singing in the back garden, and the five-foot cherry blossom tree that I painted across the sloping walls looks like it is dancing in the breeze, shedding pale pink petals in clouds of confetti, as birds of paradise take flight from the branches. 'It's like an enchanted tree house!' Claire exclaims.

I half smile. 'Thank you. That's the effect I was going for. It used to be a shut off, unused loft space over the kitchen and I had it converted. There's a bathroom through there.' I gesture at the closed door to our left. 'Sometimes when it's particularly windy outside, you can almost feel the room rocking you. But in a good way,' I add hurriedly. 'It's just a very old house. The walls breathe in a way new properties don't; the roof lifts slightly when there are gusts in the right direction. It's all very normal and it's stood for hundreds of years.'

'You did this though? It's stunning! Rosie would *love it*!' Claire looks at the tree in wonder, then at the white sleigh bed, frilly pink duvet tucked in, cushions carefully arranged on top. I watch her eyes alight on the old-fashioned doll's house, front neatly closed. On top of the full bookcase are the assorted cuddly toys, mermaids and unicorns, and when finally she notices the white built-in wardrobe in the right-hand corner on the back wall, she laughs, pointing at it. 'There you go. No escape.'

I shrug tiredly. 'What can I tell you? As I said, it could use a little updating.'

'Oh not at all! It's the perfect dream bedroom for a little girl.'

She smiles at me, and then I see the confusion flit across her face as it suddenly dawns on her that I am far too old to have a daughter the same age as her Rosie. I see her remember Adam's adult belongings downstairs, the person I described as my daughter's boyfriend. She hesitates and looks around her again.

'I'm just going to close this now.' I gesture at the skylight. 'It's getting a bit cold in here.' I walk past her, reach under the bed and pull out the pole, pushing the skylight tightly shut with one practised movement, cutting off the birdsong, before I replace it back out of sight and straighten up. Claire is watching me carefully. I can see she has questions about Izzie, but isn't quite brave enough to ask.

As she stands there in her too-big coat, I suddenly see myself, all those years ago. Perhaps it's what she's shared with me – our commonality – but out of nowhere, the best part of thirty years roll back in an instant as I wonder what would have happened, had I not let Michael persuade me to take on such a ludicrous project at such a young age on barely more than a whim. How different life might have been, had my little family not moved here?

'Don't buy this place,' I beseech my younger self desperately, out loud.

Her eyes widen further still. Everything has gone very quiet. I can feel the house holding its breath too.

'It really is a lot of hard work, and I'm not sure I think it would make you terribly happy.'

I blink and see Claire standing in front of me once again. Unlike earlier, I feel embarrassed and immediately wish I hadn't spoken. I need to sell. This woman is paying cash and is nothing to me – a total stranger. What do I care if she is about to make a huge mistake?

And yet, I find, I do. I think about another innocent little girl sleeping under the branches of the bewitching cherry tree – Rosamund is such a pretty name – and feel slightly sick with anxiety. Neither of us moves… and suddenly a door slams somewhere downstairs. We both jump out of our skins.

'For God's sake, Izzie!' I shout suddenly, and Claire takes a step back from me. 'I'm so sorry.' I rub my forehead lightly, trying to regain a sense of equilibrium. 'My daughter sometimes finds visitors a little unsettling. She's lived in this house for so long that anything new or different is *very* different.' I exhale deeply – my heart is racing. 'Look, I shouldn't have said anything just then, about what you should or shouldn't do. I don't know your circumstances; your situation is none of my business and I spoke out of turn. I shan't do another house viewing again! Now, you wanted to see the garden, I think? Do you still?' I look at her desperately.

She nods silently. She seems to have lost the power of speech. I can't blame her really. We take the main staircase as it's closer, rather than the back one. 'Not many houses can claim to have three separate flights of stairs!' I joke, trying hard to lighten the atmosphere, but we are well past that point. We make our way to the garden in silence.

Once we are outside, however, I feel instantly better, as I always do. The cold wind cools my anger as we arrive on the main lawn. I turn my face to the hills and fields for a moment, looking towards the just-visible roofs of the new development Mary so 'helpfully' mentioned in the shop – and take a gulp of air, before looking back at the house. The skeleton of the bare, overgrown honeysuckle is clinging to the stones, although more accurately, probably propping the house up. I'm scanning the bedroom windows when Claire eventually speaks again.

'This is a stunning garden. Do you do all of this yourself?'

I nod as I glance at the ordered beds, the rockery, the pergola, the apple tree with the swing, right down through to the orchard and vegetable patch. 'It *is* nice in summer,' I admit. 'I mow little paths through the orchard. Rosie would probably like that. And in the spring, the farmer puts lambs in the fields behind the house.' I point at the back hedge. 'The garden is what I will miss most.'

'My late grandmother was a good gardener. Very instinctive and she knew all of the Latin names for everything. Now, I'd love to learn from her, but I didn't appreciate her knowledge when I was younger.'

'It's not so complicated,' I confess. 'You'd very quickly get the hang of it if you spent a little time working alongside someone in your garden and being introduced to some of the plants. People are afraid of making mistakes, but gardens are very forgiving.'

'That's a good idea. I should try and arrange something. An in-garden tutorial. Thank you.' She smiles.

'You're very welcome.'

We stand in silence for a moment alongside each other, until the robin begins to sing again and breaks the spell. I gather myself and remember my manners.

'Well, thank you for coming, Claire. I'll show you out.'

'It was very nice to meet you, Eve.' She holds out her hand on the doorstep. 'Happy Christmas.'

'And to you,' I say.

We shake and she smiles at me before turning to make her way back to her car.

I close the door and stand well back in the gloom of the hall, watching her through the glass as she climbs into the Volvo and starts it up. I feel oddly sad to see her go. Although, actually, there is nothing odd about it at all. She's a cash buyer and I just told her not to buy this place. Urgh. What is *wrong* with me? I am NEVER going to sell this damn house.

I sigh, then shriek, leaping about ten feet in the air as someone right behind me blows on the back of my neck. 'Jesus Christ, Isobel!'

I hear her giggle – having finally succeeded in pushing me over the edge – and sense the change in the air as she darts back out, slamming the sitting room door so quickly behind her that by the time I've spun round, clutching at my heart, she is already gone.

I furiously throw it open again. 'I'm glad you think this is funny!' I shout into the house. 'Isobel?'

I wait, but hear not so much as a whisper in response.

# CHAPTER FOUR

## Claire

I can just about make out Eve's face as she stands motionless inside the small hall, watching me through the glass panel in the front door. I start the car and take one last look at Fox Cottage. Such a pretty name... but made for chocolate-box prettiness and gardens of wild flowers – not this sprawling pebble-dash monstrosity with its murky, mustard lintels. Either side of the front door stand two shiny-leafed bay trees in modern, square planters – an obvious attempt to smarten it up for sale – but all it does is make it appear as if Eve is somehow standing sentry within, like a life-sized doll ready to come to life again when someone next knocks on the door.

I pull off the forecourt and begin the drive back. When the estate agent told me the owner of Fox Cottage – an art teacher up at the local high school – would be showing me around, I immediately pictured a Germaine Greer-type in a hessian smock top, self-made silver jewellery, loose trousers and flat, round-toed leather shoes. Eve has completely wrong-footed me. I didn't expect someone so attractive – very few women her age keep their hair long. She's let it go past her shoulders, and it's exactly the sort of burnt bracken colour I've always wanted but never been brave enough to try. In any case, I don't think you can fake that particular Celtic tone, although she has to be in her fifties... it can't still be natural, surely?

And when she took my hand – just like that – after I told her about Mum and Dad. To my huge surprise, tears spring to my eyes at the memory of her warm kindness. Most people just stare at the floor or do the sympathetic head on one side bit, but she obviously understands exactly how it feels when you violently lose someone you love.

I hear the echo of her voice in my head warning me not to buy Fox Cottage because it won't make me happy, and sigh. The poor woman was so obviously talking about her own experiences – the devastation of *her* grief. I imagine her arriving as a young wife, the excited effort of doing up Fox Cottage with her husband... *Please God, she didn't lose the little girl as well?* I don't think I could bear it if that's what happened, because apart from the beautiful cherry blossom bedroom full of unplayed-with toys... I didn't actually *see* the daughter she insisted was in the house. And how could she possibly be Rosie's age now in any case? She'd be grown-up, surely?

It's all wrong and Eve is too vibrant to be trapped in that tumbledown house, alone. I bite my lip, thinking about those brown eyes looking back at me, her amused smile lifting apple cheeks. The vividly floral dress over a black polo neck had a Biba vibe, hugging her petite but ample figure and all topped off with that frilly apron. She ought to be the head of some large farmhouse family: an adoring husband, strapping sons, their wives and grandchildren everywhere as she competently bakes bread, hangs out clean washing on blustery days, paints and sells her work in local galleries... motherly and voluptuous all at once. I've never met a woman so obviously living the wrong life. Just tragic.

I try, instead, to clear my head and focus on the job in hand. I ought to be getting ready to deliver my report on the houses themselves – Tony, in particular, will want my opinion the second I get back...

But when I arrive at The Rectory, Susannah's car is missing from the drive and nobody appears when I call. Only Tony's fat, black Labrador, Badger, comes waddling out into the hall, lazily waving his tail. Assuming they are all out, I dump my bag on the floor, hang up my coat above the boot rack and wander through into the enormous kitchen to put the kettle on, reaching for my phone in my back pocket as I sling the large cast iron kettle on the Aga plate.

'Aha! You're back!' says a sudden voice behind me. I turn to see Tony standing in the doorway smiling, slippers and reading glasses on, holding *The Telegraph* and a mug. 'What did you think? Did you get to see all three houses? Oh sorry – you're about to make a call?'

'It can wait.' I put my phone away. 'Yes, I did see them. Would you like a cup of tea?' I point at the kettle.

He shakes his head determinedly. 'I won't, thanks, darling.' He raises the mug he's holding and puts it down on the side. 'I've just had a coffee. Come on then – put me out of my misery. Which would you buy?' He raises a quizzical eyebrow.

I hesitate. 'Well, it needs the most work, but I think you'd make the most profit from Fox Cottage because you could easily split it into four properties. Although I don't know what the tax implications would be; you'll be more up to speed with that than me.'

'Ha HA!' he says delightedly and thwacks the kitchen table with his paper. 'That's my girl!' He points *The Telegraph* at me. 'I knew I could rely on you!'

I groan. 'So it's your choice? I'm not going to be popular with Susannah.'

'Ah – she'll come round.' He waves dismissively. 'Well, that's marvellous. Thank you for that. Have you seen Timothy since you've been back?'

'No – not yet.'

He nods. 'Right-o – well, when you do – I'm in my study. Excellent!' He begins to whistle a happy tune under his breath and makes to leave the room.

'Tony,' I say suddenly, imagining Eve walking out of the house into bright sunshine, shutting the door behind her for the final time. 'The woman who lives there – Eve Parkes. She mentioned she had a daughter?'

Tony pauses in the doorway. 'Isobel.'

'That's right. Is she?—'

He holds up a hand to silence me and listens carefully. 'Hold that thought – I can hear my wretched phone ringing. *Uno momento!*' He spins on the spot and strides off down the corridor as suddenly as he arrived.

I return to the kettle. Since his retirement, if anything, Tony has become busier. He's constantly on the phone offering advice, involved in this and that project/charity/ initiative, taking various meetings in London, improving his already impressive golf handicap and managing the small estate in which The Rectory sits. As well as maintaining both the house and outbuildings, he looks after the gardens and surrounding fields. All family requests for him to slow down have fallen on deaf ears.

'What, and drop down dead at the ninth hole like poor old Hugh Portman?' he said indignantly the last time he and Susannah had a row about it over supper, while Tim and I tried to steer the conversation onto less controversial ground. 'Stopping is the *last* thing you want to do. That's when your body just gives up. The secret is maintaining a manageable but constant level of stress. You shan't be getting your hands on *my* insurance policy anytime soon, I'm afraid.' He finished his mouthful of food and took a large gulp of wine. 'I fully intend to hang around like the proverbial bad smell for many years to come.'

In fairness to him, I'm not sure how someone mentally taxed day in and day out by complex legal issues could be expected to just give that up for a life of *Bargain Hunt* and a spot of light gardening. I've seen Tony presiding in court and was both very impressed and secretly a bit proud. He was every inch the charismatic, kind, considered but authoritative judge. You can't operate as an important part of the Establishment one day and simply walk away from a lifetime's work the next. I retrieve my mobile from my pocket to return to the call *I* was about to make.

'Hello!'

I turn, to find Tim stood in the doorway this time, smiling, where his father was moments earlier. They really do look so alike, except for Tim's brown hair, where his father's is silver. It's a bit odd sometimes, knowing exactly what Tim is going to look like when he's older – although I can't see him adopting his father's 'gentleman of a certain age' uniform of a well-cut shirt and cords without a fight.

Tim pulls the jumper I bought him for his birthday over his head and comes to sling it on the rack above the Aga, padding across the cold tiled floor in thick socks which he's tucked his jeans into. He's obviously been working outside.

'I thought you were out!' I say, pleased. 'Cup of tea?'

'No, thanks.' He reaches for a tissue from the box on the side and blows his nose, his cheeks ruddy. 'I was outside doing a bonfire but it's just started to rain, which is annoying. I thought I heard the car.'

I put my phone back in my pocket, put my arms round his waist and kiss him. His skin is refreshingly icy. 'I love you.'

'I love you, too,' he says, surprised. 'You all right?'

I release him, still thinking about Eve Parkes. 'Yes, just lucky to have you, that's all. You're freezing. Are you sure you don't want a tea? Is Rosie wearing her coat, hat and gloves if she's outside, by the way? And she's not on her own near the pool, is she?'

'She's gone out into town with Mum actually, but for the last time, the pool cover is on, the safety fence is up, and yes, of course she's wearing them.'

I don't say anything, but it's far from guaranteed that any of them would have put sensible clothing on Rosie. Tony and

Susannah are fully paid up members of the 'fresh air' club: family swims at windswept beaches in all temperatures, shoving on an extra jumper rather than turning the heating up, building fires, chopping wood, riding horses and walking the dogs. While Rosie loves the lifestyle and becomes practically feral every time we visit, I feel like I spend most of my time running around after her checking her lips haven't gone blue.

'Anyway, were you about to make a phone call?' Tim has also inherited his father's eye for detail.

'Only my sister, but it's no problem. She'll probably be out on the town – it's 11 p.m. their time. I'll try her tomorrow morning instead.' I huddle next to the Aga. 'Do you know, I would very much like to be in Sydney right now myself.' I shiver. 'Perhaps we should think again and move there after all?' I grin teasingly at Tim.

He smiles briefly. 'Perhaps.'

I pretend to pick my jaw off the ground. 'Who are you?' I joke as I take the now-boiling kettle off, 'and what have you done with the man I love, who hates spiders?'

'It's more the snakes, to be honest. Don't forget the snakes.' He scratches his stubble as he sits down at the kitchen table and looks up at me. 'Can I talk to you about something, Claire?'

'Of course. What's up?' I reach for a cup and teabag.

'I didn't say anything, but I had some bad news yesterday.'

My heart sinks and I turn to face him. 'Oh – you didn't get the part? I'm so sorry. You did say the audition didn't go very well.' I *knew* that was why he was quiet in the car on the way up.

'No, it's not that. I still haven't heard anything about that.' He clears his throat. 'Charles Blake, a bloke I was at school with, committed suicide on Thursday night. He jumped out of the window at work.'

'Oh, Tim!' I put the cup down, make my way over to the table to sit down and take his hand. 'I'm so sorry. How sad, and what a horrible shock.'

He nods and doesn't say anything.

'Was it work-related then?' I say carefully.

'Yeah, kind of.' Tim looks down at our clasped hands. 'He was under a lot of pressure. His wife called Harry yesterday, to let him know and then Harry called me. It's going to be all over the news.'

'Has he got children?' I whisper, thinking first of Rosie and then my mum and dad.

'No.' He shakes his head. 'Which is something, I guess.' He gives my hand a squeeze.

'But his poor wife though.' I reach an arm out, put it around his shoulder and he leans his head briefly on mine.

'They'd only been married a year, I think,' he says. 'That's just no time, is it? No time at all.' He straightens up again. He has tears in his eyes. 'Sorry.' He wipes them away quickly. 'I didn't even know him that well any more, to be honest. I mean, we were close at school, but not so much recently. Harry saw him far more regularly than me. They… did a lot of deals together. Charlie made a huge property investment on Harry's recommendation last week actually.'

'Oh shit…' I say, seeing where this is going.

'No, it came good. Harry knows his stuff.'

'Well, that was lucky.'

'It's not luck, Claire. Harry's very skilled at what he does.'

'What went wrong then?' I say diplomatically. 'If they'd just made a load of cash?'

Tim takes a deep breath. 'Harry had the nod about a bit of land that was coming up for sale. The plan was to buy it, sit on it for a few weeks, then sell it on once the council approved some new development plan – Charlie stood to get double his original investment back. He paid the cash into Harry's company; the company bought the land: everything was great. Only then, you know Harry also makes those random air conditioning units?'

I nod.

'One of them caught fire last week and it nearly burnt down some shopping centre in the States. There's been a massive safety recall, all of the orders dried up overnight, the bank pulled Harry's finance, a legal action has been launched against him – he's gone bust, basically – and not only is the land they bought now going to be sold to help pay off hundreds of creditors all over the place, Harry told Charlie he couldn't withdraw Charlie's original investment from the company accounts because everything has been frozen.'

'In other words, Harry hasn't got it to give back.'

'Yeah. Basically, Charlie lost everything.'

'And he killed himself because of that?'

Tim takes his hand back. 'Yes. I can't make sense of it. It feels so unreal.' He puts his elbows on the table, his hands over his mouth and exhales slowly through his fingers, then looks me straight in the eye. 'Claire, I gave Harry all of our money, too.'

I freeze and jerk back away from him. I hear my chair scrape on the tiled floor. 'What?'

'I gave Harry the money we had in the bank. He said this land sale was a life-changing opportunity – and it would have come good.'

I just stare at him. 'But that money was from selling my parents' house. It's so we can buy our own house.' I am speaking like a child. 'How much did you give him?'

Tim swallows and looks at me with frightened eyes. 'All of it.'

I half cry out and jump to my feet. 'You gave him two hundred and forty-eight thousand pounds?' I cover my mouth with my hands. 'Please tell me this is some sort of really bad joke?'

He shakes his head. 'I gave him two hundred and fifty. I borrowed £2k from Mum to round it up. We doubled our money – I want you to know that; it's really important to me that you understand I didn't risk it on something that wasn't going to work. The plot has already doubled in value.'

'What are you talking about?' I exclaim. 'It *didn't* work! You've lost it! All of our money is in Harry's bust company! How could you even do this without talking to me first?' I feel sick. Like I am actually going to vomit in my hands.

Tim hangs his head. 'I knew you'd say no! You always shut down everything like this. When I wanted to buy a bitcoin all that time ago, you said it would never—'

'But we're not talking about a *bitcoin*!' I explode, taking a couple of steps away from him, then returning to the fight. 'We're talking about a quarter of a million pounds for our *house*!'

Tim holds out his hands. 'Please, try and calm down.'

'Calm down?' I put *my* hands either side of my head. I can't believe this. 'You've given every penny we have to the friend of yours we both know I hate – have always hated – he's effectively done a runner with it, and you want me to CALM DOWN?'

'You don't need to shout at me.' Tim tries to reach out and I jump back, yanking my arm out of his grasp. 'I know I've made a terrible, terrible mistake. I understand that you're angry. Please try and see that I wanted us to have proper financial security. You've been amazing about me having this job break for six months, but I'm dreading going back.'

'I KNOW, Tim! You tell me constantly how desperate you are to make acting work this time and that you've hated every single job you've had since I met you that *isn't* acting and how scared you are that you're going to run out of time; but adults with children to support sometimes have to do jobs they hate because *that's life*.' I stop for a moment, breathless with sudden anger. 'Jesus – what have you DONE?' I stare up at the ceiling. *This can't be happening. We've lost everything?*

'But the investment worked. That's the point. We would have been able to buy a house outright, in cash – it came good! This was not my fault! It wasn't Harry's fault either.'

'How many times? No – it *didn't* work, because the money is ALL GONE! The whole thing *is* your fault. What are we going to do now? We've got no house, no money, all of our stuff is in storage and we're living in a tiny rental flat! *What were you thinking?* I shout the last bit so loudly Tim flinches and closes his eyes. I hear Badger bark somewhere from deep within the house and realise why Susannah has taken Rosie out. They already know. He's told his parents before me. My mouth falls open in disbelief.

Tim hasn't noticed. 'I'm so sorry. I am so, *so* sorry. I deserve everything you've said. You're right – there are no excuses; however it happened, the money is gone. I've let you and Rosie down so badly. And when I think about Charlie…' He shakes his head and the tears return. 'He was only thirty-six. I'm not saying that to make you feel glad to still have me, by the way. I know what I've done is unforgiveable. I'm so ashamed of myself. But I'm going to sort this out. I'm going to make sure we are all right.'

'We were already all right.' I feel numb. I am unable to comfort him, despite his obvious distress.

'What I mean is, I'll do anything it takes to make this better again! I know I've not always been the strong, reliable partner you deserve, and *you've* had to sort everything out in the past when I've buckled. But I will be now – I swear. I'm going to make you and Rosie proud of me.'

I close my eyes and clench my jaw. I've heard this before. I even know what's coming next.

'Dad has said he will help us—'

There we go. I let my head drop. 'Oh God…'

'I know!' he says. 'I know how that sounds and how it makes you feel, believe me.'

'You don't, actually. When did you tell him about the money?'

'On Wednesday. Why?' He appears genuinely confused at my question, and I don't have it in me to explain why that's wrong, too. All of a sudden I feel exhausted and like *I* want to cry. How can he have done this?

'I had to get a plan in place,' Tim continues. 'I didn't want to tell you what's happened and not have any answers, which would make you feel like you had to sort it all out. Dad's got some ideas. I know you're beyond angry with me, and you're right to be, but would you come and hear him out? He's waiting in his study.'

*

The fire is lit and Antony is sitting behind his desk as we walk in, staring thoughtfully at the flames. He looks up at us and smiles sympathetically.

I stay standing as Tim quietly sits down on one of the leather armchairs. 'Do you think there is any chance of recovering the money?' I come straight to the point.

Tony leans back in his chair. 'I'm sorry to say I think it's virtually non-existent. There's no paper trail, no contract – just a payment from your account into Harry's company. It's a limited company, so he has no personal liability at all, unless he's been a very silly boy, which I doubt. He might choose to repay you from any personal funds separate to the business, as a matter of honour given you are friends, but legally, he doesn't *have* to.' He glances at Tim. 'In the meantime – because this will not reach a conclusion anytime soon, if at all – we need a more immediate plan of action.' He sits forward in his chair again and leans his elbows on the desk. 'You've how long left on the lease of the flat you're renting?'

'It goes onto a rolling contract as of 14th January, with one month's notice. The whole point was to make everything as flexible as possible so that when we found something we wanted to buy, we could just go for it.'

'Of course,' Tony says. 'It was a very sensible idea.' He takes off his glasses and sighs sadly. 'And all of your furniture is still in storage?'

'Yes. We're sharing the monthly cost with my sister while she's working in Australia. She needed somewhere to store all of her belongings too, until she's back in the summer.'

He nods understandingly. 'Forgive me, Claire, I'm not prying, just clarifying; the quarter of a million pounds Timothy took without your knowledge from your joint savings account and gave to Harry Asquith – that was from the sale of your late parents' house? Just your share – not your sister's too?'

'That's correct.' Shock is making me functional. 'We split £525k equally. I banked my half, Jen did the same. She still has hers. She intends to buy a flat on her return. You probably know we'd considered buying my sister out of my parents' house when Jen said she wanted to buy her own place, but we came to the conclusion it would be better for us to have a fresh start too. It was a very tough decision to sell it though and one that I now obviously very much regret.' My voice shakes as I look at Tim.

'I am so sorry,' he repeats.

Tony taps the desk thoughtfully with a pen he's picked up. 'I think we're all agreed that Timothy's betrayal is unforgivable, but *my* primary concern at the moment is setting things right. Claire, I feel very strongly that I have a responsibility to provide my granddaughter with somewhere to live.' He contemplates this for a moment and points the pen at me. 'I'd like to buy you a house.'

'I'm sorry?'

'In your name only.'

Tim jerks his head up in shock. 'What? This isn't what we discussed!'

'Now, now old chap!' Tony rebukes him. 'The defendant may not address anyone directly unless it's through a court clerk. You know the rules!'

'This isn't a joke, Pa.' Tim stares at him.

'No, it most certainly isn't,' agrees Tony and the smile fades from his face. 'Perhaps it would be better if you stayed quiet though, hmm?'

'But Pa—' Tim is now sitting up, pale and ramrod straight. 'You didn't say a word of this when we spoke on the phone. You just said you'd help us find a house!'

'And I am!' Tony gestures widely. 'There's nothing sinister about this. I'm sure Claire will let you live in it, too. I just want to demonstrate you won't be able to dispose of it without her say so. I think it's only fair under the circumstances to give Claire as much reassurance as possible, although I'm encouraged you fully accept your failings.'

'Of course Claire's going to let me live with them.' I can hear the panic in Tim's voice. 'You don't need to make a point of that. Yes I've made a mistake; yes it was a lot of money. She's right to be very, very angry with me but we love each other. We have a daughter together!' He gets to his feet uncertainly. 'I asked you to help me!'

Tony looks astonished. 'But, darling boy, I am!'

'No you're point scoring and you know it. *I* need to accept *my* own "failings"… really, Dad?' Tim stares at his father. 'When you have children it's supposed to make you forgive your own parents their flaws. Just so you know, I've never felt that way about you. In fact, you come off even worse.'

My eyes widen with shock and embarrassment, but Tony merely gives a deep sigh.

'You know, of course, that when I was a child, Grandpa used to cane me across the bare buttocks? It made me determined never to lay a finger on a child of mine. I wonder if perhaps it would have been kinder if I had?' He stares at Tim for a moment then returns to me. 'The house you viewed this morning, the one you said *you* would buy. I'm going to purchase it for you. You will all live in the house for a year while it's renovated – Timothy has agreed to work unpaid as a labourer. You will not have to pay any rent. At the end of the year we will divide the house into two properties. You will own one, I will own the other. You may do with yours as you will: sell it and move back to Surrey, stay and live in it, split it into two again and give one to Rosie... the choice is yours. In the unlikely event of your property being worth less than £250k, I shall refund the shortfall to you. There, you see?' He gestures widely with his hands and looks up at Tim. 'Exactly as promised. The moral of the story is, wait for the whole picture before you pass judgement.'

I mentally rerun my tour of Fox Cottage. We can't live there, with its dark, depressing rooms, damp everywhere, stained carpets and toilet like something out of *Trainspotting*. Apart from everything else, it's at the wrong end of the country. I don't mind visiting now and again, but I don't want us to *live* here. We have a life in Surrey. A very nice life. We are happy there. It rains all the bloody time here and the quality of light is different. I mentioned it to Susannah once and she looked at me as if I was mad, but I'm not. It's genuinely gloomier, even on a dry day. All I do when I'm here is want to huddle by the fire, watch TV and eat stodge. I'll be the size of a water buffalo by the end of a year.

'That's why you asked me to view the houses on my own? You wanted me to choose the one I was going to have to live in?' I manage to speak eventually.

'I know moving to Shropshire would require some considerable adjustments to your lifestyle, although perhaps not ones that are insurmountable.' He shrugs gently. 'It would mean a new school for Rosie, but equally, grandparents on hand to help. She likes coming here and young children adapt well to big changes—'

'Children adapt because they don't have any choice,' Tim interjects. 'It's not—'

'And because you work largely from home already, Claire, your job will be unaffected.' Tony speaks over his son, ignoring him completely. It's as if Tim hasn't said a word. 'On the days that you need to travel into London… one or two a week I believe… Susie – when she's around – and I, will help out with childcare for Rosie. She's such a super little girl, and of course, Timothy will always be on site. A year is no time at all, really. Think of it as an adventure, perhaps, if that helps? I can't pretend we wouldn't very much enjoy having you living here. We'd adore it.' He stands up, and Badger obediently gets to his feet too, wagging his tail at his master.

'Timothy, can you please confirm for Claire that you've agreed to those terms, should she decide to accept them?' It's like he's giving dictation instructions to a secretary. 'You'll work on the house to help repay your debt and give up on this notion of acting for a living, once and for all?' He looks down at the carpet, listening carefully.

'Yes,' Tim says eventually. 'I give you both my word.'

Tony smiles broadly. 'Well, there we are. Good chap.' He walks past Tim and briefly pats his son's back. 'In any event, you don't need to decide tonight, Claire. Sleep on it and let me know if you want to proceed with the purchase of Fox Cottage in the morning.' He makes for the door.

'Hang on a minute, Fox Cottage?' Tim looks at his father in shock. 'Mrs Parkes and Isobel? You're joking, right?'

'I had nothing to do with the selection,' Tony insists. 'Claire made the decision, unprompted, just as we agreed.'

'Bullshit,' says Tim slowly. 'It wasn't "unprompted" at all. You only gave her three places to choose from and you certainly didn't tell me *that* one was on the list. I'm not living there! Are you out of your mind? It's madness!'

'I don't understand?' I look between them. 'What's the significance of Fox Cottage?'

Tim is now visibly shaking. 'Even after all of this time? Well… fuck you.'

I flinch as he spits the last words at Tony – who closes his eyes – as Tim roughly pushes past his father and barges from the room.

We both jump as seconds later a door slams from deeper within the house.

'Oh dear,' remarks Tony. 'I'm so sorry about that, Claire. Obviously we know how dramatic Timothy can be, but I hope, perhaps, when he calms down he'll see I'm only trying to help…' He pauses and sits in the armchair Tim occupied moments ago, wincing as he stiffly stretches his legs out. 'I really cannot apologise enough for what my son has done. Yanking someone's security from under their feet like that is an appalling act of unkindness and selfishness. I apologise unreservedly on his behalf and I will stand by my obligation to you and Rosie. You don't have to accept my offer, of course. I won't be offended if you decide to return to Surrey and rent. We'll be sad, of course, but we'd understand. The choice is yours.'

# CHAPTER FIVE

## Claire

I can see Tim at the bottom of the garden by the remains of the bonfire. It's started to drizzle and beneath The Rectory, a low-lying mist is rolling in across the valley floor, engulfing neighbouring farms. As they submerge and slip from view, the mountains in the distance appear to rise eerily from an enormous body of water. I walk past the swimming pool – just as Tim said, safely fenced off. Dead leaves are collecting in the centre of the floating cover and on redundant wooden loungers stripped of their comfy summer cushions. Wrapping my arms around me at the bite of the chill wind, I make my way across the main lawn to Tim, the acrid tang of smoke catching in my throat. Crouched down, he's angrily prodding at the dying embers with a large stick, trying to force life back into them.

He glances up as I arrive alongside him.

'I apologise for losing my temper like that. I never learn. He knows exactly how to push my buttons and I fall for it every time, *every single time*! I keep putting my head above the parapet. I'm thirty-five – you think I'd have learnt by now! I'm a fucking idiot.'

I don't respond, just look out over the spindly bare branches of the apple trees in the orchard to my right.

'Sorry – you're right. I should calm down. You probably guessed he didn't warn me this was going to be just your house.'

'I don't think that's what he meant,' I say truthfully. 'He wanted to reassure me.'

Tim snorts. 'He was making the point he has no intention of bailing *me* out. He could perfectly well just give me the money, and he knows it. They're emotionally blackmailing us, using what I've done to force a move that *they'd* like to see happen, and it stinks.'

I move out of the way of the smoke, only for the wind to gust contrarily again and blow it right in my eyes, making them smart and water. I blink and squint at Tim. 'But why *should* he bail us out and give us the money? It's your mistake, not his.'

Tim pauses, surprised, then carries on raking at the embers. 'Because I'm his son and I've asked him for help? You'd do that for Rosie, wouldn't you?'

I don't answer.

'Exactly. I'm very aware this is my mistake. I asked Dad to help me – that's all – not see an opportunity and grab it with both hands.' He glances up at me and stops. 'You're crying?'

'No, it's the fire.' I point at it, then stop and pick a small piece of ash from my mouth, trying to sidestep the smoke again.

He returns to his furious jabbing. His hands are clenched tightly around the stick and I can *see* the rage just bubbling away under the surface. 'I've allowed him right where he likes to be, back in control of everything.'

'But this isn't really about you and your dad, though, is it?' I try to keep my voice even. 'You just took quarter of a million pounds out of our joint savings account without telling me and effectively set fire to it. The money that came from selling my parents' house, which was one of the hardest things I've ever had to do.'

He throws the stick on the ashes, straightens to a stand and turns to face me. 'I know and it doesn't sound enough to say sorry.

It *isn't* enough. If I could go back, and undo it – I would. I've made a terrible mistake.'

'The thing is…' My earlier energetic anger is already being replaced with a slowly hardening, icy calm. 'I pay all of the bills, I manage everything. You must have dug out the blue box file, got the savings folder, found the sheet of paper with our customer ID number – and the other one I've written the password on – then transferred it all into our joint account. Given that the bank stopped a transaction when I tried to buy Rosie a *coat* online last week, but they didn't contact me to say a quarter of a million quid had just landed in our account, you must have moved it out again bloody quickly, so it didn't even really register on the system. Not long enough for alarm bells to ring anyway. That's pretty premeditated, wouldn't you say? Not exactly something you accidentally do in the heat of the moment?'

Tim clears his throat. 'No, you're right. It wasn't an accident. I meant to do it.'

'But you *know* how I feel about Harry. That I would have said absolutely no way to this "deal", yet you went ahead anyway and gave him that money deliberately and purposefully.'

He rubs the back of his neck as if it's tight and aching. 'I know you don't mean to, but you're starting to sound a bit patronising. I was worried that the way you feel about Harry would prevent you from seeing the opportunity we had. That's why I didn't say anything.'

'Oh come *on*! You're not seriously trying to make out you were *protecting* me in some way, by not telling me? That's scraping the barrel a bit, isn't it? And patronising? Really? You want to have a go at me right now?'

'Of course not!' Tim looks down at the ground. 'I know you're angry but the land HAS doubled in value – Harry was right. He didn't know his company was going to go bust because of this fire.'

'That's what he's told you.'

Tim jerks his head up. 'No, that's not fair. He's my friend. If he had the money he'd give it to me – he doesn't, so he can't.'

'*He's your friend?*' I turn to face him. 'You actually just said that? What are you – five? I don't care about Harry and his excuses as to why the money has gone. Just tell me why *you* took all of our money – my money, really, if we're being honest – in the first place? Was it really just so that you didn't have to go back to your old job, but could carry on trying to make acting work after this six months trial is up?'

He looks at me, astonished. 'You *know* I'm not that selfish.' He kicks the stick back on the smouldering pile as it rolls off. 'It's like you said, you manage everything: it's *your* job that pays the bills, *your* job that the new mortgage was going to be based on—'

'So all of this is my fault for earning more than you?'

'No!' He looks genuinely surprised at that too. 'I wanted to contribute something. That's all. We would have been able to buy a house outright for cash. But I also can't lie – it felt exhilarating when Harry called and told me we doubled our money. I felt brave.'

Before I can stop myself, I exclaim in frustration, and Tim looks at me sadly.

'Yeah, you're right – it sounds pathetic, doesn't it? But it's true. I can't explain it, sometimes my life just feels so small – so constrictive. I wanted some bigger experiences.'

Of everything, this is what cuts me to the quick.

*Life feels so small?*

It is so painful to hear, I don't know how to respond. Instead I just stand there gaping because my mind can't work fast enough to process what he's actually just said. And still he doesn't see it, reaching out a hand.

'Talk to me,' he says desperately.

I put my hands in my back pockets.

'Are you going to take Dad's offer?'

I can't answer.

'You don't want to leave me, do you? Is that what this is about?' He sounds frightened.

My voice is thick with tears when eventually I do manage to speak. 'Your life is not small. You *have* done something with your life. You have me and you have Rosie. You're lucky to have a life full stop.'

'That's not what I meant at all!' He glances up at the overcast sky in disbelief as if he can't believe how everything has gone so wrong. 'Please, Claire. I messed up. I've messed up hugely, but of course I love you and Rosie and I know you love me. We're a family!' He waits and when I still don't say anything, he continues. 'What's happened to Charlie is horrendous. Surely *you* can understand, in comparison to that, the money I've lost is meaningless?'

I gasp and step back away from him. *Now* the words are there. 'So because I know what it feels like to have someone I love die, but I still have you, I should forgive you anything?'

'No!' he says urgently. 'Why are you being like this? I don't understand! I'm not being manipulative or playing a card here – I'm trying to be honest. I shouldn't have done this and it's going to have huge ramifications, but we've still got *us*. We've not lost the most important thing. That's what I mean! Tell me we've still got us?' He pleads, reaching out and *pulling* my cold hands free to hold them in his.

'You know how difficult it was for me to sell my parents' house in the first place, how much I didn't want to.' I am properly crying now. I can see it in my mind; every familiar corner, the layout of the sitting room, the kitchen, Rosie's room. If I close my eyes it's as if the whole house is still out there right now, just as it always has been, waiting for us to walk back into it… not all dismantled, packed up and gone forever.

'Your sister was ready to move on and get her own place. We couldn't all stay living there together. She wants to start the next bit of her life; meet someone she can settle down with. Maybe have her own children. And that's how it should be.'

'We could have bought her out.'

He shakes his head. 'We talked about this for ages. *You* decided it was the right thing to do, to get somewhere fresh for us to start a new part of our life; you, me and Rosie. You were worried you wouldn't cope with Jen not being in the house any more. That it would feel too hard. I deliberately didn't offer an opinion one way or the other because it had to be your decision. You said it was starting to feel full of ghosts. It had stopped being a comfort. Remember?'

I nod eventually. 'But you MUST see how it feels to discover that money is now gone? It was all I had from them.'

'Of course I can. I've never regretted doing something so much in my whole life.' He shrugs helplessly. 'What more can I say?'

I pause and shake free so that I can stem the flow of tears with the heels of my hands. 'So how do I trust you not to do something like this again for kicks, because you want to make your life "bigger"?'

'You just do. I can only say I'm sorry and make amends the best way I can.'

I feel like I'm in a scene of a programme on TV. It's a very weird sensation – almost like an out-of-body experience. What would I be saying if I was watching this?

*Walk away! They're just words! He's an actor for crying out loud!*

'I'll give up on acting.' He reads my mind. 'I'll move here and do whatever Dad wants – work for free, labouring, I don't care as long as we stay together.'

'Unless I choose Fox Cottage, apparently. What was all of the shit back in your dad's office about *that*?'

He sighs and turns away, looking out over his parents' garden. 'Did you meet her? When you went to look at it?'

'Who – Eve Parkes?' I watch him carefully. 'Yes, I did. She was very kind to me. She lost her husband in a car accident.'

'I know. Did you tell her who you were? As in your connection to me and Mum and Dad?'

'No, because you told me not to!' I can hear the exasperation in my voice.

He doesn't say anything for a moment. 'You remember what happened to me that Christmas?'

'The shooting, you mean?' I pull an irritating piece of hair off my face that the wind has whipped up.

'Yes. It was Eve's daughter Isobel that I shielded.' He looks at me and waits. 'You know? When everyone went crazy and told me I was a hero for jumping in front of her and Dad responded by packing me back off to the other end of the country? That's why I don't want to go and live in their house. It's too close for comfort. I wasn't even supposed to be there. Dad made me do a taster class with Paul Jones that Saturday because he couldn't think of anything else to do with me.'

I hesitate and see Tim as a little boy as he's been described to me before: huddled on the floor positioned in front of a small girl, his arm bravely round her as they are shot at, and as always, the image both tears at my heart and rips out my stomach with fear at the thought of that happening to *my* child.

'I'm not saying it wasn't a truly horrible experience, Tim… but you haven't kept in touch, have you?'

'No, I haven't seen Eve or Isobel for years.'

'Then I'm not really sure I get the problem in buying a house from them? She's still alive, the daughter?'

He gives me a strange look. 'Yes. Why do you ask?'

'I didn't see her, that's all, Eve was making out like she was there in the house and she wasn't. It was a bit weird… but anyway.' I hold up my hands, determined not to become distracted. 'If I can be expected to sell Mum and Dad's house, shouldn't you also be able to move into the house of someone you used to know? After all, they're just buildings, according to you?'

'Fair point,' he admits. 'But honestly? No, I don't want to come back and live here.' He gestures back at the imposing house behind us. 'Of course I don't! I can't think of anything I want to do *less* than come and live this near to my parents and all that entails, where everyone knows everything about me, in the back end of beyond and where I've got no chance whatsoever of getting to auditions, but I'll do it, because I accept I've completely ballsed up. The *only thing* I really care about is keeping the three of us together. You know you and Rosie are everything to me, so if you think buying Fox Cottage is how we make the best of this situation, then fine. I'll do it. But yes, I'd much rather we – you – chose one of the other houses.'

'Eve's house has the most potential,' I say truthfully.

He gestures his hands widely. 'OK then, whatever you think.' Like you said, it's just a house. But you should probably know I also had a thing with Isobel Parkes.'

'Well, I understand your reluctance a little more now,' I respond, 'but that was a long time ago too, wasn't it?'

'Yes.' He looks suddenly exhausted. 'I was involved with her the summer before I went off to university. It was nothing major, but I'm telling you in the interests of total honesty… and you're right, I'll live anywhere you want me to, if it means we all stay together.'

We both look back in the direction of the house at the sound of a car pulling up on the gravel and Badger barking. Rosie appears seconds later, running around the corner and across the lawns towards us, a huge smile plastered over her face, her bunches bobbing up and down, as she clutches a large, plush unicorn.

'Mummy! Daddy!' she calls, delighted to find us together. 'Look what Granny bought me!'

'Wow! Lucky girl! Let's see?' I hold my arms out and smile brightly although I want to cry again. She doesn't deserve any of this. She is a happy little girl, with friends and a life she loves.

How could I possibly tell her that all has to change?

\*

'I'm so sorry – I know how late it is with you now, but I just needed to talk to someone.' I huddle on the windowsill, shivering in Tony and Susannah's guest bedroom overlooking the garden where Rosie is throwing a ball for Badger, who is gamefully trotting to collect it for her. 'Hello? Jen? Can you still hear me?'

'I'm still here.'

'I'm sorry, the reception is shocking. It's all the hills.'

'Stop apologising. It's fine and I'm GLAD you called me. I'd have been really pissed off if you hadn't. I'm sorry I'm a couple of drinks up though, I'll try and concentrate. I'm back at home now and on water, by the way. So,' she clears her throat, 'that Tim did that in the first place and then they got you to view those houses without telling you the real reason why? It's all beyond messed up.'

'It was to ensure I *genuinely* chose the one I liked best, apparently.' I feel wired with the adrenaline of acute stress in a way I've not felt for many, many years. It's unpleasantly familiar.

'Yeah, because it's important to be *happy* in the house they've preselected for you to make up for Tim flushing quarter of a million quid down the bog. I know this sounds an odd thing to say,' Jen says slowly, slurring very slightly, 'but the whole thing about Tim handing the cash over to Harry – that's real, right? This isn't just some mental plan they've all come up with, to get you to move to the other end of the country and they're actually using YOUR money to buy this house?'

I half laugh. 'Moving back here is the last thing Tim wants. He'd never do it voluntarily. He's only ever been able to cope with his parents in small bursts. I'm certain the money is gone. I could ask him to show me his bank statement – and I will at some point – but right now I think it might push me over the edge to see it in black and white: all of my money going into that disgusting man's account. I hate Harry so much.'

'I just cannot believe Tim would do this.' I can hear the disbelief in my little sister's voice. 'It's all my fault. If I hadn't said I wanted to buy my own place—'

'No, no, no,' I correct her fiercely. 'It's not your fault at all. It was his choice to give our money away. I can't wrap my head around it, Jen. I love my friends, you know I do. I wouldn't give a single one of them a quarter of a million quid.'

'Yeah – but that's the weird boarding school thing though, I suppose,' Jen says slowly and yawns. 'They're not just friends, are they? It's like a fucked-up version of family. I'm with you on Harry – he's a terrible excuse for a person – but Tim's lived with him all his life. You'd give it to me, wouldn't you, if I said I knew I could double the money for you?'

'Not without talking to Tim first.'

'That's a fair point,' Jen agrees. 'He one hundred per cent should not have taken it without asking you. I've got to be honest though and say I can see where he's coming from a bit. Why can't Judge Tony just give you the £250k no strings attached, instead of forcing you to move to Shropshire just because it's what *they* want, so that Tim has to give up on cracking acting? Although let's be honest, that might not be a bad thing. It's never going to happen, is it?' The booze has completely loosened her tongue.

'He's about to turn thirty-six. He's the same age as Eddie Redmayne, seven years younger than Benedict Cumberbatch and *eleven* years younger than Damian Lewis,' I repeat Tim's obsessive holy trinity automatically. 'The thing is, Jen, I can't tell him this sort of shit doesn't happen in real life because it *does* happen to all of them. So many of his friends – and lots of other "terribly nice boys" he was at school with – are doing exactly what he wants to be doing and they've made it look normal. He sees them and thinks "Why not me too? I've only got one life…" And never mind the school lot – it's not just Sam winning bloody Oscars – it's all of his university friends from that stupid Footlights society too. I can't so much as switch on the TV without one of them popping up in something.'

'The bastards,' she says vehemently. 'I get it – it must screw with his head, being surrounded by people who make it look easy, but to be fair to Sam, he grafted for thirteen years before he got his big break. What's Tim got on his CV apart from a couple of plays, one of which he walked out on, mid-performance?'

'He couldn't help that,' I say quickly. 'He had an all-out panic attack *on* stage. Proper post-traumatic stress. He was doing the talking to the ghost bit in *Hamlet* and he felt like the man who shot him – and then was shot dead himself – was on stage with him, just staring at him.'

Jen giggles. 'Sorry – I shouldn't laugh. It's not funny. OK, Hamlet probably wasn't the *ideal* part for him, but shit happens and fifteen years later is a bit too much of a gap to decide he can make it work as a career after all, don't you think? Come on! Let's have a dose of real life here! You wanted to be a ballerina when we were kids. I don't see you dusting off your tutu and quitting your bloody job, because you're a GROWN-UP.'

I fall silent and wonder for a moment if Tim would have been better off with someone taking this approach with him from the start, rather than always listening and encouraging him, as I have. Jen's got a point. Who says you can achieve anything if you want it badly enough, and that you should never give up on your dreams? That's just the stuff of shitty memes on Facebook. I never sat dreaming of selling data for a living when I was a little girl. I do it because someone pays me to and I have a daughter to support.

'Let's count some blessings here, shall we?' Jen is on a roll now. 'He's got you, he's got Rosie, he's got his health. He's a lucky man. And while his dad might be a control freak, he's still going to *give* him – or you, whatever – a house! I mean… come on! Champagne problems doesn't even come close! *My diamond shoes are too high to walk in…* so get a cab!'

When she puts it like that, it *does* sound ridiculous.

'Not that you have to do it, you know that, right?' Her voice becomes firm. 'You don't *have* to stay with him. You and Rosie can come and live with me. I'll buy us somewhere with my half of the money? *We* could get a mortgage together.'

'That would defeat the whole object of you moving out in the first place.' I smile sadly at her generosity.

'I'd do it for you in a flash and you know it. Family, innit?'

I feel tears start to well up again. 'Thank you,' I whisper.

'Oh don't cry,' begs Jen. 'I wish I was there to hug you. Don't get me wrong – I might be trying to make out this isn't as bad as it seems, but I'm still *furious* with Tim.'

'Me too.' I look down at Rosie on the lawn, throwing the ball as high in the air as she can and trying to catch it, before closing my eyes. 'Me too.'

Jen pauses. 'But on the other hand again, he's never done anything like this before. He can be pathetically precious when he wants to be, but you and Rosie mean everything to him. It's been that way right from the start for him. You weren't even that interested!'

'No, I liked him straight away; he made me laugh. But I didn't trust him. Who wants to date an actor?' I say truthfully. 'All that excitement and passion until they get bored and move on to the next girl, or co-star… and who also honestly ends up with a guest they snog when they're waitressing a wedding?' I open my eyes again. 'I should have listened to myself. Stuff only goes wrong when you don't listen to that inner voice.'

'Yeah, but you've got Rosie now – you can't apply the same rules as back then. They don't exist any more. Bottom line – Tim loves you. That's not in doubt here, he's not that good an actor, believe me. He's fucked up hugely – but do you really want to chuck everything out of the window because of one mistake? He hasn't had an affair or anything. In some ways, he's sort of right – it's just money, although shitloads of it.' She sighs. 'He's such a dick.'

'Yes, he is.'

There's a long pause and then delivering that sugar-free dose of medicine that only a close family member can administer, she says suddenly: 'Let's face it, Claire, Tim is very funny, one of the most charming and charismatic people I've ever met; kind, generous, a great dad, but he's also angry a lot of the time, damaged, frustrated, fragile and difficult. I know you love him but he's a complicated sum of pieces and you don't have to be the glue that holds him together any more if you don't want to. He knew what he was doing when he gave Harry that money. It's a huge deal to expect someone to say "never mind, darling! Yes, let's pack up our lives and move two hundred miles away from our friends, school and work and do up some dump of a house!" All because what he's done isn't as bad as him cheating on you.'

'Did I also mention said dump of a house is also owned by his ex-girlfriend, who he shielded at that shooting incident when he was eight?' I add. 'I told you that bit, right?'

There's an appalled silence. 'Well now he's just taking the piss,' Jen says. 'I suppose he's not just finally having the nervous breakdown he's been teetering on the edge of as long as we've known him?'

I sigh and look down into the garden to see that Tim has come out to join Rosie and the two of them are playing Frisbee. He looks completely relaxed.

'It's just for a year though, right?' Jen says. 'Then you can do whatever you want with this place?'

'Apparently. Would you do it?' I feel suddenly exhausted.

'Honestly?' She pauses. 'Yeah – I think I would. So it was some girlfriend's house… it's not like you have to live there *with* her. Do it up, make the money back, sell it on, come home. Think of it as the gap year you never got to have because you dropped out to look after me. A shit gap year, I'll grant you, but a gap year nonetheless. You can still do your job from Shropshire, can't you?'

'Probably,' I rub my forehead wearily, 'with some effort on the commuting front.'

'Then do it. He's Rosie's dad. Ultimately, we both know you're going to stay with him for her sake anyway, because you don't want her not to have the two of you together. So give him the chance to make this up to you.'

I sit in the bedroom a little longer after I've let her go and crawl into bed on the other side of the world, watching Rosie rush over to Tim so she can leap on his back. I can just about hear her laughter through the glass as he gallops her around the garden.

I glance down at my wrist and the tattoo I got the day after Mum and Dad's funeral – two small stars, inspired by Peter Pan taking the second star to the right and going straight on until morning…

Life is too short to make mistakes and waste precious time.

I get up suddenly and go downstairs to find Tony. He's sat in his study, leant back in his chair with his eyes closed, listening to Radio 4. I hover in the doorway, uncertain if he's actually asleep and jump when he says suddenly, and without opening his eyes: 'Reached a verdict then?'

'Yes,' I say clearly. 'I've made my decision.'

# CHAPTER SIX

## Eve

My hand is shaking as I hang up on my solicitor, his kind congratulations ringing in my ears. I've barely been back from work for five minutes and we have just exchanged contracts. It is now definite. We will be completing and moving out of Fox Cottage forever, in just under two weeks, on Valentine's Day.

I look around the kitchen. I thought I would feel relief, but now the moment has finally come… I tremble and place my hand on the side to steady myself amid the small space where I've cooked thousands of meals and worn a path to the cupboards putting away endless rounds of washing-up.

Bewildered, I make my way through the dining room to the sitting room, taking in the inglenook fireplace, the desk in the corner, photos on the wall where they have hung for almost exactly twenty-eight years. We moved in on the 1st of March 1990. Sinking down onto one of the shabby sofas, I cover my mouth with my hand. I close my eyes too, wanting so very badly to feel Michael's presence at this pivotal moment – everything we wanted and hoped for in this house and were never able to share comes rushing towards me so suddenly I feel as if I'm being swept off my feet by an unexpectedly large wave. I reach out my hands, but of course, he is not there; I grasp at nothing and let out a sob. I can feel the house watching me curiously; the mad old woman sat waving her hands around, crying. I can't let Izzie come back to see me like this. It won't do at all – so, clumsily, I get to my feet, hurry through the passage into the utility room, fumble with the key in the back door and burst out into the freezing courtyard.

The wooden door set in the deep stone wall – I used to refer to it as the 'secret garden' door – bangs open as I rush outside. Reaching the lawn, I stop, shiver and close my eyes again, feeling the cold wind blowing about me, stroking my hair and soothing my brow as I breathe deeply. I can hear crows cawing in the field as the sun sets out of sight behind thick cloud – but nothing else… and the stillness is calming. I give an odd moan of release and straighten up a little taller, opening my eyes and looking at the house from the outside. It's done. My gaze alights on the crumbling pointing, the gutter hanging off. They are no longer my problem. I turn my back and look at the garden instead: tiny green tips of bulbs poking through the earth, buds beginning to form on the branches. I won't be here to see them bloom. How odd. I shall miss this garden so very much. It has been my refuge.

I wander over to the bench and sit down heavily in the twilight, before glancing at the empty swing on the branch of the apple tree as it moves slightly in the breeze. How strange that another little girl – almost exactly the same age as Izzie was when we first came here – will be sitting on that swing soon.

I was shocked and unsettled when the estate agent told me that Claire Waters had made an asking price offer after the viewing. She's not the first to have wanted to buy Fox Cottage – there were others, although every single deal fell through and the buyers pulled out. But I meant every word I said to Claire. I couldn't bear the thought of another young couple and their daughter moving into this place – it felt too much like history repeating itself: three innocents being thrown at the mercy of this hungry house; but now I can see perhaps this time round will reset the balance.

Claire Waters is not me, her daughter is not Izzie, her father not Michael. Their story will be different – and I will not have the monthly stress of wondering how on earth I am going to pay yet another sheaf of maintenance bills. I cannot pretend this purchase hasn't been the answer to my prayers. I will have some money in the bank. I will also, it must be said, have a considerably smaller garden… I think about the handkerchief-sized square at the new house; the borders stuffed full of ghastly indoor marigolds by the developers in a bid to make the properties appear 'aspirational'. They were probably all removed and returned to the garden centre the second I left.

But I refuse to tread the path of 'what might have been' a second longer. I am determined to move on, in every sense, now. I squint over at the swing again as a sudden last shaft of weak sunlight breaks through. I will explain to Izzie that another little girl is moving here, which might help – because now the sale is official, I *must* tell Izzie we are moving. This will be the hard bit.

I don't get any further with my worries than that, however, as I hear one of the two back gates – they sit at either end of the garden – clank shut and straighten up with a frown. Someone has come in. I remember just in time that Adam told me he was coming to get another load of his belongings and smile at the footsteps approaching on the gravel path, but my welcoming expression falls from my face as quickly as the sun disappears, when I realise the man who has walked into the garden is not Adam at all, but Antony Vaughan.

'What on earth are you doing here?' is the best I can manage, both astonished and furious to be caught like this, sitting in the cold garden in slippers – as if I'm some sort of care-home resident who has been shoved outside for their daily fresh air but forgotten – and even more livid to find I give a hoot what he thinks.

'May I come in?' He smiles winningly, hovering on the edge of the lawn.

'You already have,' I retort, and his grin broadens, before he begins to gingerly pick his way across the garden in his smart leather boat shoes.

'Do you want to hitch the hem of those up too?' Irritated, I nod at his ridiculous salmon pink cords.

'This grass is a disgrace.' He gestures around him. 'It needs cutting.'

'Fuck off,' I reply shortly, and he laughs.

'That you are responsible for the shaping of young minds will never cease to terrify me.' He sits down next to me, and I move right to the end of the bench. He notices and rolls his eyes. 'It's nice to see you, too.'

'I loathe droppers-in. You've put on weight,' I say rudely, nodding at the small, soft belly that's rounding out the front of his biscuit-coloured cashmere jumper. 'Retirement treating you well, then?'

'I'm certainly keeping busy. No rest for the wicked, Eve. You know that.'

I choose to ignore him and respond only with a starchy: 'I do actually have a lot to get through myself this evening. What do you want?'

'Yes, you look positively rushed off your feet.' He glances down at my slippers. 'Why *are* you sitting out here? It's practically dark. And freezing.'

'Well, you're still not coming in.' I hesitate for a moment, but then the excited urge to share my news with another grown-up becomes too much. 'I was having a moment, if you must know. I've sold the house. My solicitor just called to let me know we've exchanged.'

'Well, congratulations!' he says. 'That's been some time coming, hey?'

'Almost four years,' I admit. 'It's not exactly a buoyant market.'

'No,' he agrees. 'Not for a doer-upper of this magnitude.'

'I had other offers,' I sound defensive, 'they just didn't come to anything. This one has, that's all.'

'Are you staying local?'

'Yes, I shall be living—' I swing round and point across the now dark fields, 'over there.'

He looks surprised. 'One of the new builds? But they're soulless little boxes.'

'You're a dreadful snob, Antony Vaughan.'

'I'm not,' he says, stung. 'I just know you like period properties, that's what I mean.'

'You're right, I do,' I concede eventually, 'but it's affordable and docsn't need a thing doing to it. In any case, I'm starting to think character isn't all it's cracked up to be.'

'Well, there's that,' he agrees, 'perhaps a blank canvas is just the ticket this time.' He smiles at me.

It's so nice just to chat with someone, I almost forget myself and ask if he wants to come in for a cup of tea after all. That's how easily I could slip back down the slope.

'I didn't mean to sound mealy-mouthed,' I say suddenly. 'The truth is, I was hanging on by my fingernails. This has come in the nick of time. It's a blessed relief, frankly.' I hesitate. He's right, it's almost completely dark now. 'I shouldn't have been rude to you, Antony. I'm sorry. What can I do for you?'

He sits forward and twists the gold signet ring on his little finger, and I jolt slightly at the familiar nervous tic that I haven't seen him perform for years.

'It was me,' he says. 'I've bought Fox Cottage.'

I make a 'ha ha' face at him, even though I don't see how that is supposed to be funny. 'The buyer is a Claire Waters,' I correct him. 'She's moving here from Surrey with her daughter and partner.'

'That's right. Rosamund – Rosie. She's my granddaughter, and Timothy's daughter.'

I jump off the bench and away from him like I've been scalded.

He looks up at me smiling ruefully before holding wide his hands. 'Surprise.'

I sway on the spot as I stare at him in horror. 'You're lying.'

'No, I'm not. Claire Waters is my daughter-in-law – well, by proxy. She's not actually married to Timothy, but as good as.'

I whirl around on the spot and rush back to the house, hearing him call after me. Slamming back through the gate, I bang into the kitchen, breathing heavily as I watch him walk through the courtyard before appearing on the threshold of the kitchen.

I'm shivering with anger. 'You stupid, meddling old bastard.'

His eyebrows shoot up and he laughs, rubbing his chin. 'Not quite the thanks I envisaged.'

'"Thanks"?' I repeat, incredulously. 'Have you any idea what you've done? Timothy is going to come and live *here*? Are you out of your mind?'

'Darling, he's as good as married now.' He steps towards me. 'It's water under the bridge.'

'DO NOT call me that,' I shout, 'and no, no it isn't. Oh my God, Antony, you fool. What were you thinking? I told you – I TOLD you not to interfere.'

'I've bought this house because Timothy and his family need somewhere to live, for one reason or another, and as you've said it's hung around on the market forever, so it was a good deal. This isn't charity. I didn't do this to help you.'

'Rubbish – you just said this isn't the thanks you envisaged. You couldn't wait to come here and tell me what you'd done, show me how powerful you are!'

'Don't be ridiculous! I came to tell you that Timothy will be moving in here with Claire and Rosie, because I thought it would be better coming from me than as a shock on moving day.'

'It was you all along. *You* were the cash buyer?' I shake my head. 'I cannot believe this. But I dealt with Claire.' I look at him challengingly. 'She signed off on everything. She lied to me,' I realise, furiously.

'I gave her the money to buy it, but it's in her name.'

I sink onto a chair. 'You have no idea what this is going to do to Izzie.'

It's his turn to look irritated. 'You said yourself you were hanging on by your fingertips. This is a good thing, surely?'

'I told you, specifically, NOT to interfere, not to try and buy this place. That's why you sent Claire.' I'm working it through, catching up. 'I would never have sold it to you – so you made sure I didn't suspect a thing, and *she* went along with it. She came here, ingratiated herself and I fell for it. You're all in this together. How disgusting.' I manage to stand up. 'Get out.'

He looks bewildered and his shoulders sag. 'I wanted to do the right thing, for everyone. It seemed the perfect answer. What good is money sitting in the bank, when I can use it to help the ones I love?'

I stiffen and step back, away from him. 'Stop it. Now. You honestly thought you could walk back in here after all this time, start saying things like *that* and everything would be all right? Well you've made everything a hundred times worse!' I'm starting to feel wild with panic. 'I'll cancel the sale – I won't proceed to completion!'

He softens. 'Evie, you can't do that.'

'I don't want your money!'

'I mean, in the short-term, you'd still have to pay the estate agents, your solicitors, my solicitors, Claire and Timothy's temporary accommodation costs when they become homeless on the 14th of February; you'd lose the deposit you've paid to the developers for your new house… you'll also be in breach of contract and the courts will force you to complete in any case if Claire decides to sue you. You have to go ahead. You have no choice.'

I do not want to cry in front of him, but I'm unable to help the tears of frustration and rage that leap to my eyes as I stand there, with him carefully watching me. 'Get out,' I repeat and, finally, he turns without another word, leaving the way he came and disappears off into the dark.

I sink onto a kitchen chair and burst into noisy tears, the like of which I've not cried for a very long time. *Everything* I've done has been because I have no choice. I am Izzie's mother. It is my job to protect her from harm and I have failed again.

What Antony has done is going to break what's left of her heart.

*

'You're just going to have to tell her.' Adam has his hands curled round his mug of tea as we sit in the kitchen. 'My gut instinct is that it would be better to let her have some time to get used to the idea. Take the heat out of it.'

'Although it might also do the reverse and give her longer to build it up in her mind and turn it into something it isn't. The prodigal son and all that. Christ, this is a disaster.' I put my head in my hands. 'It's going to completely spin her out and she's not in good space as it is. What if once she knows he's coming back she refuses to leave the house? What do I do then? No.' I decide then and there. 'I'm going to keep it from her until the day we complete. I'll tell her we're moving, obviously – but I won't say who is really buying this house. Will you do the same, please?'

Adam sighs and nods.

'I'm sorry,' I say quietly. 'This must have come as a shock to you, too.'

He shifts position on the chair and pushes an unkempt curl out of his eyes. 'I can't deny I'd been hoping that once you two were finally out of this place,' he motions around the kitchen, 'that things might turn a corner for Iz – and us. You know I'll be gutted to lose the barn from a selfish point of view, but I don't think this house does her any good. It saps her energy. It does the same to me, if I'm honest.'

'Really?' I'm surprised to hear that.

'This middle bit is so dark with all of the overgrown ivy hanging down over the windows. It feels like a secret hideaway, except that's kind of the problem.' He sips his tea and puts the mug back down, before pulling the sleeves of his baggy jumper over his hands. 'Izzie retreats back into that bedroom and for her it's like time stands still, only it isn't – she's getting older and older. It makes me sad. I don't know what you think, but I feel like her moods have been worse recently, too.'

'I'd agree with that. She was watching TV last week and suddenly there was all of this shouting. I ran through and she was holding her head saying something had whispered hello to her, even though she was in the room alone. Some*thing*,' I say pointedly. 'She was adamant she'd heard it. She lost her house keys again, too; I got cross and she was in floods of tears saying it wasn't her fault, they "get hidden". "Who hides them, Izzie?" I said and she actually replied: "this bloody house".'

Adam exhales, shifts position again and shakes his head. 'I don't know what to say.'

'I found them yesterday down the back of the radiator. I mean why on earth would she put them there? She insisted she hadn't when I asked her and I heard her saying angrily in her room "it's not funny". I have no idea who she was talking to.'

'Maybe on a subconscious level she's starting to detach already. It's a huge thing for her, moving out of this place.' He looks up at me and shrugs. 'It's the only home she's ever really known and a lot has happened here.'

'True,' I admit. 'By the way, on that note, thank you for coming to get everything so late tonight so she wouldn't see. It's just upsetting her, the thought of everything changing; you moving your stuff out.'

Suddenly the baby monitor next to me crackles and we both freeze. 'She's waking up.' I look up at the kitchen clock showing 11 p.m. 'That's early – she only went up at ten.'

The green lights on the monitor react as they sense noise in Izzie's bedroom, and we both listen as I turn it right up so we can hear what's going on. It's an old second-hand monitor I bought from a charity shop and not very sensitive, so we have to crane hard.

'Is that her *crying*?' Adam says worriedly.

'I think so. Poor thing. I ought to go up.'

'Do you want me to come with you after what happened the day before yesterday?' Adam nods at my bruised wrists.

'Would you mind?' I look at him gratefully, and he shakes his head, getting to his feet.

At the top of the stairs, I push her bedroom door open quietly and as the light from the hall creeps into the dark bedroom, we see the outline of her body lying in the small bed beneath the cherry tree, fast asleep. She doesn't appear to be crying any more, but breath held, we watch and wait – before both jumping as her arm suddenly thrashes sideways and she emits some really horrible, low moan as her head turns restlessly to the other side on the pillow. It reminds me of the low warning growl a cornered animal might make before it attacks – and the hairs on the back of my neck stand up. Where is my poor child? What is she dreaming is happening to her?

We sit down on the carpet outside her room and then she starts to *giggle*. It wasn't her crying we heard – but laughing. I look at Adam and throw my hands up silently. He shrugs in despair before starting to fiddle with a loose thread on his jumper. Isobel carries on chuckling away to herself at nothing; well, nothing we are aware of anyway. Listening to laughing in the dark when you're not in on the joke is not funny at all and I'm suddenly very glad Adam is there. I even think on balance I prefer the growling sound, which is saying something. It's another moment or two until finally she falls quiet.

Is that it? Perhaps it won't be such a bad one after all. I shift, uncomfortably, from my low vantage point on the floor as I stare around the jumble in her room, dark shapes and piles of stuff in the gloom. I couldn't sleep in a room like this – no wonder her mind is so busy.

Unable to sit still any longer, both from a physical and mental point of view, I get up and begin to move about the room silently, picking things up, folding discarded clothes, sliding books into the shelves.

'Eve…' whispers Adam. 'Let's go back downstairs.'

I put my finger to my lips. I know he thinks that moving around disturbs Izzie even more, but she has no idea I'm here – I'm certain of that – she is deeply, deeply asleep. Two minutes and I'll be done.

I tiptoe over to the side of her bed and pick up a couple of tissues she's dropped on the floor. She seems to have calmed completely. I look down at her – always my little girl, and so beautiful. My heart softens.

I turn to motion to Adam that I think we can leave now, when Isobel suddenly springs bolt upright in bed like a jack-in-the-box, eyes wide open and a terrified expression on her face. Even her hands are reaching out, fingers splayed and grasping. I shrink back away from her and lift my hand to my thumping heart, but unfortunately, my elbow brushes her fingertips. The second she senses my touch she twists to the side and grabs me, squeezing my wrist so hard I whimper, her fingers digging into the bruises of the other night. It hurts so much I can't help but instinctively try and break free.

The movement makes her eyelids flutter, she blinks and her head jerks, before she gasps and lets go of me – shooting back into the headboard with a thud, like a scalded cat.

'Sweetest? You've just had a bad dream,' I say, still not entirely sure if she's awake or not. 'It's me – Mummy.'

She just stares at me for a moment, but then her eyes roll back and she falls backwards onto the pillow.

'Isobel?' I say frightened and pat her cheek several times. 'Can you hear me? She's passed out! Isobel?'

Adam scrambles to his feet as Isobel begins to stir again, pushing herself back up to seated, breathing heavily and wiping the sweat from her face. She lets her head drop and groans.

Adam hurries over to her. 'You're safe, Isobel,' he says. 'Do you know where you are?'

Izzie nods dumbly, blinking.

'Why don't you lie down and go back to sleep?' he suggests gently.

She silently does as she's told, sinking down onto the pillow, staring at us, eyes still wide, before turning suddenly away, her long hair trailing out behind her as if she's submerged underwater.

I listen as her breathing begins to regulate again, and Adam hears it too, because he gently takes my arm and leads me from the room.

'Do you want me to stay?' he asks quietly, once we've crept back downstairs and are stood in the small sitting room.

'She should be all right now, thank you.' I rub my sore wrists. 'You know the pattern. It's not often more than once in the night. I'll be unlucky if it is.'

'Even so,' he says.

'I'll be careful, but thank you, Adam,' I say sincerely. 'And I'll think about what you said: telling her it's Timothy that's moving in here, I mean.'

He nods. 'I wish it wasn't true just as much as you do.' He leans forward and kisses me on the cheek. 'Good night, Eve.'

'Good night, love. Drive carefully.'

He gives me a brief, grateful smile before leaving the room. I hear him carefully lift the front door over the sticking section so that it doesn't disturb Isobel. I make my way out to lock it and watch through the door panel, as he checks the doors of his van are secured.

I sigh heavily, seeing the small boy stood behind Isobel in the sports hall, watching in terror as Paul Jones lifts the gun and points it at her, unable to move with fear – only for Timothy Vaughan to leap into life and throw himself in front of Izzie.

Adam climbs into the van and switches on the lights and the engine, carefully looks to make sure both ways are clear – and pulls off the forecourt. He has loved Isobel for so long. It is impossibly unfair that Timothy is about to jump back into the frame and eclipse him all over again.

# CHAPTER SEVEN

## Claire

'Unaccustomed as I am to public speaking...' Sam pauses and inclines his head modestly as everyone cheers. We've all seen his recent gracious and self-deprecating acceptance speech on YouTube, watched him mouth a shocked 'Oh My God' as he walked up to collect his statuette from Helen Mirren. I feel Tim tighten his grip on my hand and force my smile to widen. 'No, no – please!' Sam holds up a hand. 'It's a total honour to raise this toast to one of my oldest pals, Tim, and his lovely Claire. Are your glasses charged?' He grins and looks around the crowded room as he waits for his audience to quieten down. 'I am full of admiration for people who walk the walk, and actually *do* something to dramatically change their lives. It's so easy to believe we always have tomorrow and yet time will eventually make fools of us all—'

I watch everyone gaze at him, hungrily gobbling up his every word. This is mad. Maybe it's because it's Sam giving this speech. He's everywhere right now, all over every magazine and Sunday supplement, yet here he is in real life too. *My* life. This big, pretend show that we are putting on today.

'Claire, Tim and Rosie are under no such illusions and have decided to seize the moment. In exactly one week's time they move to the gorgeous market town of Oswestry in Shropshire, snuggled on the edge of the Welsh border – I know, I had no idea about this privately held dream of theirs either – to begin new adventures in the valleys and hills while undertaking their own personal version of *Grand Designs*. Guys,' he lifts his glass and pauses for a moment, pretending to collect his thoughts, 'we wish you contractors who turn up when they say they will, fair weather, inspiration, fun and laughter – but most of all, may you enjoy building fabulous memories together. You will be dearly missed – but *bon voyage* and don't forget us! To Claire, Tim and Rosie!'

'Claire, Tim and Rosie!' echo our friends.

I take a sip of my Prosecco as a sea of friendly faces looks at me and I smile back at everyone. Now would be a really bad time to break down in tears.

'Speech!' cries someone, and I shake my head desperately, holding up a hand, but Tim takes over, letting go of me as he clears his throat. The excited and slightly drunken hum of chatter dies down.

'Thank you, Sam,' Tim lifts his glass a little higher, 'for those very kind words. That's why he gets the big bucks, ladies and gentleman. It's all in the delivery.' Everyone laughs good-naturedly. 'Thank you all, for coming today to wave us off as we embark on this new – slightly impulsive – stage of our family adventure.'

*Slightly impulsive?* I fix my face into a rictus grin and instinctively reach for Rosie's small, warm hand to anchor me back to reality, and remind me what I'm doing here.

'I've mentally run poor Claire through the mill a few times now, but this has got to take the biscuit. Shropshire doesn't have quite the same ring to it as Hollywood but I'm absolutely certain we're going to smash it. I can't wait to get my hands properly dirty and I'm so excited that she's given the green light to this particular project. I've always wanted to take on a build like this – Sam's right, it's been a privately cherished dream of mine for a long time now – and I'm so thankful to Claire for agreeing to let me make my way home, and have a go.' He turns to me and addresses me directly. 'You are an amazing woman – thank you for this chance. I won't let you down.' He looks me right in the eye as he says this and leans forward to kiss me. I listen to the cheers and whoops around us as I automatically close my eyes and his lips touch mine. He has fooled them all.

'I'm also so proud of Rosie for being the incredible daughter she is and not letting this faze her,' Tim continues, seconds later. 'She's very excited about moving to the country. The new pony has absolutely nothing to do with it, by the way.'

Everyone laughs as poor Rosie looks up at me in confusion, and I shake my head and smile down at her while mouthing 'Daddy's just joking'. So now she's wondering if she's getting a horse. He just doesn't think.

'Don't be strangers though,' Tim urges everyone. 'Come up and see us. Come and stay in one of the – how many is it, Claire,' he acts like he's not entirely sure, 'seven bedrooms? You're all welcome anytime. *Mi casa es su casa*—'

Well, strictly speaking, Tim, no – it's not. It's mine.

'Stay in touch and please don't hate us if we decide to do one of those really annoying property blogs.'

The fresh wave of laughter sounds tinny to me, like a bad sitcom studio audience. In a flash of realisation, I am suddenly crystal clear that I don't want this. I don't want to be saying goodbye to everyone. Rosie is happy here, I am happy here. Panic prickles up and over the skin of my back like marching ants. I take such a large gulp of my drink that I cough.

Tim laughs. 'See? Even Claire's appalled at that thought! So until we meet again… stay, drink, eat the cake. PLEASE eat the cake, I can't carry it back home, it weighs a tonne. We love you all. To friendship.' He lifts his glass and everyone echoes his toast back to him, amid 'hear hears'.

A slightly awkward moment of silence follows while everyone waits to see what's going to happen next – although not as much as I am, that's for sure – before someone has the sense to turn the music back up in the private room we've hired and they all start to happily chat again. Rosie wriggles out of my grasp and runs off to join her best friend as Tim ducks down and whispers: 'Thank you'. I say nothing and force another wide smile as *my* best friend approaches, trying equally as hard as me to look happy.

'Nice speech,' she says to Tim as he shakes hands with her husband and she mouths a quick 'you OK?' at me. I nod and she swiftly turns back to Tim. 'Are you available for bar mitzvahs and weddings?'

'Not any more,' he says and downs the remainder of his drink in one. 'Next stop – master builder.'

'I *beg* your pardon? Master what?' says Sam, appearing in front of us. 'You can take the boy out of boarding school…' He twinkles at us naughtily and, in spite of herself, Mel gives a starstruck giggle. Her husband looks down at her and she blushes furiously. Sam doesn't appear to notice, but rather offers his hand to Tim. 'I've got to shoot – literally I'm afraid.' He rolls his eyes. 'We start filming at some ungodly hour tomorrow morning, so I must make a movie! Take care my lovelies and give beautiful Shropshire my best.'

'Thanks for coming, pal!' Tim grins at him.

'Not at all, mate! Glad I was able to.'

They back slap and I can't bear it. I cannot bear the smugness of it all, the stupid quips, the front we are all presenting and the lies we are telling to our *friends*. I ought to be tapping my glass and telling them all the truth.

*Sorry, can I have your attention? We're actually doing this because Tim spunked a quarter of a million quid up the wall, so his dad has bought us some house in Oswestry, which he's forcing Tim to work on, because we can't afford to buy anywhere ourselves now! Tim's never so much as put up a shelf before, never mind overhauled a whole property! [cue studio laughter]. He doesn't want me to tell you*

*this though, because he's very embarrassed. I've promised him I won't
breathe a word to anyone. I haven't even told Mel the truth. My own
best friend! I know! Cheers everyone!*

Sam leans in and kisses me. 'You are a saint to put up with him,
darling Claire. You're a good deed in a naughty world. Ah there's
Squiffers – just in time!' He's already looking over my shoulder
and waves as I spin round to see Harry Asquith lounging elegantly
in the doorway, as ever, holding a glass. I almost drop my own in
horror. Tim did *not* invite him to our leaving party? Surely! After
all he's done?

I watch incredulously as Sam strides across the room and
shakes hands with Harry, leaning in and whispering something
that makes Harry's face split into a wide grin, before he whispers
something back and Sam roars with laughter and gives him a fist
bump. Harry does not look like a man traumatised by the collapse
of his company. He looks like he always does, faintly amused by
everyone beneath him. Tim says something to me, but I don't hear
what it is, I simply down the remainder of my drink and shove
the empty glass at him before marching across to confront Harry.

I arrive in front of him as Sam leaves. Harry eyes me warily,
but I smile, throw my arms open and to his surprise force him
into a hug, placing my lips at his ear.

'You've got a fucking nerve,' I whisper. 'I want you to leave,
now. You're not welcome here.' I draw back and twist to look over
my shoulder at Tim who is watching us anxiously, before giving
him a smile and wave that all is well.

Harry doesn't budge. 'No can do, I'm afraid. I've come to wish
my oldest friend *bon voyage.*'

'"Friend"?' I take a step closer to him again. I can almost *taste*
the musky, expensive cologne I've no doubt he's splashed all over
his smooth skin to mask last night's booze and garlic. 'Friends
don't stand by and watch lives fall apart because of something
they've done.'

'If I still had the money, I'd give it to him, Claire.'

'You're a liar. You know what I think? You needed a big cash injection. You knew Charlie and Tim had funds and you tapped them up even though you understood the risks. That was the money I made from selling my dead parents' house. My little girl is homeless because of you. You can really live with that? Honestly?'

He looks me in the eye. 'Homeless? Really? Seven bedrooms, I think I just heard Tim say? It must be terrible to be you.'

'Not as bad as it is to be Charlie, that's true,' I fire back but Harry doesn't react, because he is completely heartless. There's just a big black hole where it ought to be. 'Did Tim invite you here today?'

'Yes, he did.' I can see he enjoys telling me that, positively *revels* in the discomfort this additional disloyalty makes me feel.

'Right, well unless you've got my £250k tucked in your back pocket, I meant what I said. You can fuck off.'

He snorts. 'You've never liked me, have you, Claire?'

'No, I haven't.' I look at him unflinching. It feels good to be telling the truth.

'Well, you may not believe this, but Tim is pretty much the most important person in the world to me. I would never want to hurt him. I didn't know this was going to happen.'

'Important enough that you'd assault the girl he'd just met? Take all of his money? Force him to move back home? God knows how you must treat your enemies.'

'"Assault"?' Harry curls a lip in disgust. 'Not that, *still*? It was a test! I wanted to see how serious you were about Tim, if I could trust you… if *he* could trust you – or if you were the sort of aggressive social climber who might just be chasing the biggest… inheritance,' he adds nastily, 'and might break his poor little fragile heart. The fact that you're still going on about it all these years later says far more about you than me, I'm afraid.' He takes a mouthful of Prosecco. 'You're not ever going to be my type though, dear, whatever mood I find myself in. I'm so sorry to disappoint.'

'I wouldn't touch you if my life depended on it.'

He looks bored and straightens up. 'Look, I don't know if it's because you're that bit older or because of that chip on your shoulder – your inverse snobbery – but we can't help that we're better connected than you, that we're more *interesting* than you. We are what we are and I'm sorry that you're not part of the gang, but there it is.' He sighs. 'I can't spend a lifetime apologising for you being a little bit – cheap.' He pulls a sympathetic face. 'Now, let's talk of happier things! I'm so glad to hear Tim's "long cherished dream" is coming true.'

I pale. 'Don't, Harry. Don't play that game. He doesn't want anyone to know. You'll make him look pathetic. Just have your drink and go. Let him have today, at least.'

He looks suddenly angry. 'I've told you, I would never intentionally hurt him. And while we're being honest,' he lowers his voice so nobody can tell we're having a row, 'let's not pretend it doesn't suit you perfectly to go along with this, so you can keep his balls in that jar on your bedside table. He'd have been every bit as successful as Sam, you know, if it wasn't for you and your child holding him back.'

'*Our* child,' I correct, now trembling with anger. '*His* daughter. Who he loves, more than he'll ever love *you*. If what you say is true, and you were any kind of friend to him, you'd do whatever it takes to get that money back to him. It's because of *you* he's being forced to give up on this dream of his. No one else.'

'Don't be ridiculous! As if you thought he was going to make it anyway!' snaps Harry. 'He's too old now, even you can see that, surely? You've had the best years of his life! What a waste!'

'Claire,' says a voice behind us and we look up to see Tim, standing right behind us. He's obviously heard every word. 'Mel wants you… and it's becoming increasingly evident to everyone that you're both having words. Please don't. Not today.' He goes to turn away.

'Tim!' Harry says, quickly. 'Wait! You're right – we'll put a lid on it and behave. Let me buy you a leaving drink, at least. A proper one.' He sets his flute down.

'With Claire's money?' Tim asks.

Harry flushes. 'Touché. Crass of me, but I *will* get you the money back. I've promised you, haven't I?'

Tim nods silently.

'Listen, what you heard us saying just then…' Harry begins awkwardly.

'You'll have to excuse me now,' Tim cuts in, 'I need to go and say goodbye to a few people. Enjoy your drink.' He takes me by the hand and leads me away.

Once we're back in the throng, he turns to me in explanation. 'I invited him because it would have looked weird if I hadn't, like there was some sort of problem.'

'No, it wouldn't. People would have just assumed he was busy, that's all – but I'm not going to argue with him any more, so please try and relax.'

He doesn't seem to hear me. 'Do you think Harry meant what he said?'

'I would like to think so,' I confess, 'but I very much doubt we'll see the money again. I wouldn't hold your breath.'

'No, I mean about me being too old now.'

I stare at him and I want to scream. I want to open my mouth and let the sound explode out of me. I picture it shattering the glasses, the windows, flaying the skin from his face leaving him featureless. *Do you understand what Rosie and I are doing for you, Tim?*

'I still think I could have been a good professional shapeshifter.' He smiles at me desperately, not having noticed at all. 'Being paid to be someone else. Never mind.'

I swallow and manage to say calmly: 'Let's talk some more when we get back to the flat. It's not the right time now.'

'No, you're right. In fact I don't want to talk about it any more. I want you to understand that I'm totally committed to making this work. I'm not going to lie, I'm struggling with the prospect of moving back home and working for Dad. It's all messing with my mind. I don't feel… quite myself. I'm pretty depressed, I think.'

'Yeah, well you and me both,' I can't help saying. 'I'm feeling downright shit about moving.'

'You're right. I'm sorry. I have no right to bang on about anything. Hey listen, ignore me. I'm fine.' He looks determined, takes my hand and kisses it. 'It's going to be fine. I love you.'


I'm too tired to cook when we get home, so Tim goes to get the last takeaway from our favourite Indian because this time next week we shall be at his parents' house in Shropshire. He's just left when I pick up a text message from Mel.

*What's going on? You looked sad this afternoon. If anything was wrong, you would tell me? This is all so sudden and random. Maybe it's just me seeing something that isn't there because I DON'T WANT YOU TO GO.*

I throw the phone back on the sofa and pad through the flat into Rosie's bedroom, where she has brushed her teeth, is in her pyjamas and waiting for her story. I read her two chapters of one of *The Worst Witch* books while she plaits my hair in several eye-wincingly tight and tiny braids. 'Ooh, thank you!' I reach around and feel my head once we've both finished. 'They're amazing!'

'Look in the mirror!' she insists, so I do – and see a tired, middle-aged woman staring back at me, who has mad sticking-out plaits, but not the strength for this. For quite a while, I've felt smug about not ageing as fast as some of my friends. Good genes, I've told myself, assuming that, were Mum and Dad still here, they'd look suitably Peter Pan-ish. People even occasionally mistake me for being younger than Tim, despite my being five years older (as a friend once said to me brightly 'a toy boy, but not enough of an age gap to be creepy'). Instead, it all seems to have happened overnight. I don't recognise myself. The skin on my forehead is no longer smooth, but papery and faintly lined, my eyelids are drooping… only my roots are freshly done – I held off on my appointment until the very last minute because I don't know how soon I'll be able to come back again once we've moved.

Once we've moved…

I turn back to Rosie. 'Hop into bed, sweetheart.' She snuggles down and looks up at me, clutching Dog. I sit down on the duvet and start to stroke her hair as she yawns. 'It was a long day today, hey? Fun though, to see everyone!'

She nods. 'In the new house, if I don't like the bedroom you think I will – the one with the tree on the wall,' she sounds uncertain, as if she's tried to imagine it and not succeeded, 'can I choose another one?'

'Of course you can! There are loads of others, or you can just sleep in with me until you're used to the house and you've decided which one you would like.'

She looks relieved, but then troubled again. 'Won't Daddy mind?'

'No, he'll be fine. He won't mind sleeping in another room,' I say firmly.

She smiles happily.

'There isn't anything else you're worried about?' I stroke her head again.

'No. I'm excited to go to Granny and Grandpa's house, although it will be strange *living* there and not wishing we didn't have to come home, because we *will* be home!' She laughs. 'Although I will miss my friends,' her face clouds, 'but I'll make lots of new ones, too, I expect.' She brightens again.

'Of course you will.' Then I hesitate and my heart thumps. 'Sweetheart, I think Daddy's actually going to go and live in a different house to us.' I'm horrified to hear the words come out of my mouth before I know I'm going to say them.

'What?' she sits up in alarm. 'Where?'

I don't stop – I actually carry on. 'We might have to stay here and live with Aunty Jen so that Mummy can go to work and you can go to school here, and Daddy will go and live with Granny and Grandpa and build their house.'

'No!' she says and her eyes fill instantly with tears. 'I don't want him to! Please don't, Mummy. No!' She grabs my sleeve in wild panic. I have never seen her look so frightened. It's obvious she hasn't entirely processed the finality of what I mean, only that she knows whatever this is, it's bad and she doesn't want it to happen.

'OK, OK,' I say quickly. 'It's OK, Rosie, we won't do that.' *What's wrong with me?* I've already made this decision, what am I doing, hurting her unnecessarily like this? I pull her safely into my arms. 'We'll all go together, OK? You're right, that'd be a much better idea.' I kiss the top of her head and hold her tightly. 'I promise. It's OK. We'll all go together.'

I'm supposed to be the one who makes her feel safe! I'm overwhelmed with nauseous guilt and appalled by the damage I've probably already done by making such stupid remarks. Enough now! I have no idea why I just did that. It's a done deal.

I will make this work. I've come through far worse than this.

It's not as if I don't love him – I do – and we *will* be a happy family again, because I will do anything for my daughter. Whatever it takes.

# CHAPTER EIGHT

## Eve

'Isobel, please. You have to come out now,' I call outside the closed and locked bedroom door. 'The men are going to be here any minute to put our furniture and things in the van. They need to take it to the new house.' I wait and listen, but she doesn't answer and for a wild moment I picture the fire brigade going in via the skylight and dragging her out, kicking and screaming, but that of course will not need to happen, I must calm down. 'Please Izzie,' I beg, almost crying. 'I know this is hard, darling, and you don't want to go, but we have to. Do you remember I told you about the new little girl who is coming to live here?' My heart hardens as I picture Claire Waters and Timothy Vaughan standing in front of the apple tree watching their child swing backwards and forward, laughing happily as she goes higher and higher... In my mind she has golden hair. They have golden hair in all of the best fairy stories. Perfect little girls, perfect parents, perfect lives.

'Rosie needs to be able to move *her* things into this room now, angel. You don't need it any more, you know you don't. You've got a lovely bedroom at the new house. Come out now, please?'

I hear a creak on the stairs and turn to see Adam walking slowly up, to join me.

'Still nothing?' he whispers, and I shake my head wearily, before looking at my watch and trying to contain my panic.

We are set to complete at half past twelve today, at which point the agent will be arriving to collect the keys from me, to hand to *them*. I do NOT want Izzie to be here when Claire and Timothy arrive. I want the chance to explain to her that it is Timothy that will be living here once we have finally left and she is unable to get back in again.

'Izzie?' I repeat.

Adam sits down on the top stair and first rubs his eyes tiredly, then wipes his face – he always has a light sheen of oiliness across the bridge of his nose – before hugging his knees as we wait for a response, but the only sound is the rain lashing down on the skylight directly above my head. It is, of course, a filthy, cold day. Perfect for moving.

'Isobel!' I say eventually, my tone changing. 'Come along. Enough is enough now.'

Nothing.

'Isobel Parkes!' I shout suddenly, feeling my cheeks flush hotly. 'You are to come out now!'

And damn it, I think I hear her bloody well *laugh*.

'You think this is funny?' I lose my temper completely. 'Fine, if you won't come out – I'll come in and get you. Only *babies* behave this way, Isobel, not big, grown-up girls.' I shove my shoulder violently against the door and the hinges rattle, but the heavy, old-fashioned lock does not budge. The door will splinter around it sooner than it will open.

'Do you really want this?' I shout in warning. 'You *really* want me to find another way in? Because I am taking you out of this room, come hell or high water!'

'Eve! Stop – please.' Adam comes up the last of the stairs and puts a calming hand on my arm, his fingernails are full of paint. 'Let me sort it.'

He squeezes his wiry frame past me with ease and knocks gently on the door. 'Izzie? It's me. You have to come out now. It's time to go. I've packed my things up too. Come out and I'll take you to breakfast.' He looks at me quizzically, and I nod gratefully. 'We could go into Shrewsbury and see a movie at The Old Market Hall if we leave now? It's a good day for movies, all rainy. We could get a hot chocolate and a cake afterwards in the café bar?'

I soften. That sounds like such a nice day to me. He is a good boy.

Adam sits down on the floor, crosses his legs in his faded jeans, rolls the sleeves up on his enormous baggy, stripey jumper – I am not a natural knitter; I did not get the tension right in my stiches, it's almost grown bigger every time I've seen him wear it – and gives me a thumbs up. 'You go downstairs,' he whispers to me. 'I promise I've got this.'

I nod and reach into my back pocket where I have three £10 notes. I was going to offer them as a tip to each of the moving men, but if he's taking Izzie to the cinema, he'll need money. I hold the notes out, but he shakes his head and smiles.

'I'll phone you,' he mouths, making a handset shape with his thumb and little finger.

There is nothing else for it, but to do as I'm told.


I return to the kitchen, wash up my cereal bowl, dry it and pack it in the crockery box and then do the same with the little fruit knife I use to chop her banana every morning. I jump slightly, neatly slicing the end of my thumb and making it bleed, as I hear the slam of the front door. Hastening into the sitting room, sucking my thumb to stem the flow, through the window I'm just in time to see the back end of Adam's elderly transit van pulling off the forecourt. He's not done it? Oh clever old chap!

I hasten upstairs. The door to Izzie's room is indeed unlocked and still swinging open. I tiptoe in, but she's gone. I can feel it. I sigh with relief, but then look around at the clothes she has taken from her drawers and wardrobe; piling them in mountains on the floor. Toys are strewn across every surface. There are colouring pencils and drawing pads on the rug. Her music stand has shed loose scattered sheets and the tiny objects of crap she collects, are everywhere. Boxes and boxes of hairbands, clips, nail varnishes, shells, leaves, feathers, tiny dolls, misty marbles, pictures of Michael, sewing threads, buttons. My heart sinks at having to pack up this *entire room* before the removals men arrive, but it was the right thing to do. It's better, surely, that she's walked out this morning leaving her room exactly as it is – preserved in her memory – than having the distress of seeing it all dismantled and packed away, then left empty… bar her birds and tree on the wall.

I glance at the door and, on autopilot, take the large iron key from the lock and return it, through habit, back to where it lives on the *outside* – but then I realise what that would instantly reveal to the Vaughans – and hastily put it inside the door again. When we first moved into Fox Cottage, this was Michael's and my room. I kept it for some time after he died, until it seemed unfair, when Izzie had so many more belongings than me. All of which I must now pack.

I go and grab several boxes and set to work, only stopping to put a plaster on my thumb, which won't stop bleeding. I studiously avoid opening her diary, which I find in her underwear drawer. I cry when I find a picture of Michael and her I don't even remember taking. She is kissing his cheek and he is laughing in delight. It's in a tacky china frame with a Forever Friends bear holding either end of a moulded banner, which says 'My Daddy'. I pack it carefully – and then I find the Timothy shoebox at the bottom of her chest of drawers. There are several clippings from faded newspapers, one is a round-up of 'bright young things' set to conquer the screen and stage; Timothy's handsome teenage face beams back at me in among a group of other youngsters, some of whom look quite familiar too. I don't read the letters he sent her, carefully preserved in their envelopes; I don't disturb the Polaroid of my daughter lying on a bed apparently shrieking with laughter, and Timothy Vaughan's face, smiling, half in, half out of the shot, obviously taking the picture. There are some leather, plaited bracelets, stiff and faded with age – and a small, tarnished ring in a carefully folded piece of loo roll – two hands holding a heart in the centre. The only thing I pick up are the tarot cards, held together with a hairband, as my heart sinks. She bought another pack then. I knew she would.

Further investigation reveals a candle magic colour chart I've not seen before, which she has handwritten and painted. It's at least twenty coloured squares and carefully written descriptions of which emotion corresponds with which candle colour. There is also a lighter, a half burnt *red* candle (passion, sex, lust, vitality, courage, according to the chart; God help me) upon which she has carved some sort of symbols. It has also been decorated elaborately with rose thorns and reeks of some heavy, sickly cheap perfume. When I lift my fingers to my nose, I realise I have a residue all over my hands. I sit back on my heels in shock at the thought of her sitting up here quietly burning candles with me none the wiser. This bit of the house is timber framed – it would go up in a heartbeat.

I throw the candle back in the box and firmly wipe my hands on my apron. I'll have to think of a way of tackling this with her, without her realising I've found it. It's so incredibly dangerous, the poor, foolish girl.

Getting stiffly to my feet, I go to the edge of the room by the window and peel away the carpet – exposing the bare boards – pinning it down with my knees so it doesn't flap back, then gingerly ease my fingernails round the edge of the largest board before lifting it away in one clean motion, yelping as it also pulls the plaster from my thumb.

Oh Lord – and there it is. A new Ouija board and planchette. I want to cry with frustration as I look at the board and the ornate lettering, evidence of the cemetery Izzie carries around in her heart. Every time I think she's getting better and improving I am reminded that what I want for my daughter remains so hopelessly out of her reach. And now Timothy bloody Vaughan is going to make it all a thousand times worse, swanning back into the picture with everything Izzie will never have, putting his daughter to bed in her room.

I am suddenly *so* angry that I shove the board back, release the carpet by standing up, and march over to the Timothy box. Pulling out the red candle, my hands are shaking as I light it and red wax begins to pool at the top of the stick. I watch, mesmerised by the flame while the rain continues to hammer on the skylight. The sound is relentless but strangely soothing in the way that being undercover in a storm often is. I start to feel almost dreamlike as the wax begins to overflow. I could drop this candle now. It could all be a horrible accident. The whole place could go up. God knows I've thought about doing it time and time again over the years – but we're going to complete any moment now. It would be the *Vaughans'* heap of smouldering timbers. Their problem – and they would not be able to live here. Curse you, Antony, for your meddling. Curse all of the insufferable Vaughans. I close my eyes and swallow, the candle wavering in my hands.

But of course – I don't drop it. I blow the flame out viciously and the hot wax splatters all over the tree and on one of the birds on the wall behind me, like little drops of blood. I smile grimly, but then I remember that Rosie has done nothing wrong and I am a grown woman.

I swallow, feeling ashamed of myself and put the candle on the bedpost so that I can step forward and start to scratch the already hardening wax from a bleeding wing with my fingernail. I've hardly started when I hear a knock at the door and jump in panic. The men are here and I'm not even half done. I forget about the candle and the Ouija board, and run down to let them in.

Somehow they manage to get everything – bar the last bits that I am taking myself – loaded into the van that is making one drop off at the new house. The remainder is to be delivered to the storage unit, because it's too good to chuck out, but there's no room for it. I take the phone call that confirms we have completed, the funds have transferred successfully and Fox Cottage is no longer mine.

It is done. So small a moment for such a big change. Anticlimactic really.

As I hang up in the echoey kitchen, only just remembering to unplug the phone from the wall, I am wrapping the cable tightly around the handset when I hear a voice *within* the house: 'Hello? Is anyone here?'

Susannah Vaughan. I stiffen. The removal men must have left the door open – but she's let herself in? Surely not? The bloody cheek!

I shove the phone down and walk quickly through to find her standing in the empty small sitting room, looking around her, handbag tucked under her arm. She's wearing a *black fedora*, for God's sake, a cropped to the waist and fitted tweed jacket – multicoloured, black and white threads with piped edges – a huge chunky necklace around her throat, narrow crepe black trousers encasing her long, too thin legs and scarlet heels. I immediately feel even more matronly and tattier than usual. There is a certain set of women who live in Shropshire and work in London, even internationally, as barristers, surgeons, creative consultants – what ever that is – and perfume designers… one owns a private members club, I think. Susannah flies with this flock of gilded birds. I do not. My only consolation is that I suspect she looks ghastly out of clothes. Like a collection of coat hangers twisted into limbs.

'Eve.' She gives me a cool nod of the head. 'How nice that our paths are crossing again.'

I don't bother to say hello. We're long past that. 'I'm as delighted as you are.'

She shrugs. 'It is what it is. We're due to meet the agent here to collect the keys, but perhaps you'd prefer to hand them over to me directly?'

'I think I'm only supposed to give them to the agent or the owner, which I believe is your daughter-in-law, Claire?'

'Oh, I think you know who I am,' she says softly. 'It's not like handing them over to someone off the street now, is it?'

'Nonetheless.'

She fixes me with those piercing blue, cold eyes of hers and says nothing for a moment before smiling suddenly. 'How *is* Isobel?' She asks as if we are sitting down to tea and not stood opposite each other in a draughty, dusty and empty room that was mine moments ago and to all intents and purposes is now hers. This room has always felt oppressive – it's the low ceiling – right now, the atmosphere is unbearable.

'She's fine, thank you,' I lie. 'At the cinema with a friend.'

'Adam Owen?' Susannah says instantly.

My muscles tense defensively and I don't answer. I don't want to. It's none of her business.

Susannah doesn't pursue it. 'Claire should be here any minute. She stopped at the shop to get some bin bags. We forgot them and she wants to have a *really* good clean!'

I don't rise. 'Are you sure you're dressed for it?'

She laughs dismissively. 'Oh I shan't be helping. I'm going to head home and help Tony look after Rosie while Claire and Timothy co-ordinate the removals. It's you I've come to see. Now Eve, Isobel *does* know that Timothy is moving in here today, I take it? Do we need to prepare for any unpleasant scenes?'

I flush hotly and lie easily. 'Of course she knows. It was a teenage romance, Susannah. That's all.'

'It was a *little* more than that, wasn't it?' Susannah looks at me idly from under the brim of her ridiculous hat.

'No, I don't think so.'

Susannah pretends to hesitate, as if she's not sure about something, and I'm immediately on alert. She's never made an uncalculated move in her life. 'Oh dear,' she says eventually. 'I did wonder as much. She never told you, did she?'

Everything is silent and I realise the rain has finally stopped. I refuse to give Susannah the satisfaction of asking her to tell me what she's talking about, when I can see she's going to do it anyway.

'Well now, there was the pregnancy,' she says. 'Isobel came to me after Timothy left for university. She didn't know what to do. I think perhaps she saw me as an ally. Oh don't look like that, Eve! Would you have ever told your mother such a thing? I certainly wouldn't! It's not a personal affront to you! Girls just don't!'

'You're lying.' I gasp. 'I know everything about *my* girl!'

'No, you don't – and she's a grown woman,' she says calmly.

'What did you do?' My world is falling away. 'What did you tell her to do?'

'I didn't tell her to do anything!' retorts Susannah. 'I organised what she asked me to organise and I went with her to make sure it was safe.'

I cannot catch my breath – everything is crashing down around me, the walls I have built around us, to protect Izzie. 'You took her for an abortion? Where was I? I would have noticed!'

Susannah inclines her head to one side. 'You'll remember that week of work experience I arranged for her at my chambers, that September? When I was still trying hard to be a good friend by supporting and helping you, and wasn't *entirely* sure you were sleeping with my husband? In fact I pushed away my doubts because

I didn't believe anyone could be that ungrateful or callous as to repay me so heinously?' She smiles brightly. 'Remember *that*, Eve?'

'Yes. I remember.' Of course I do. I loathed letting Izzie get into the car with Susannah every morning to be driven into Shrewsbury, but how could I stop my daughter from seeing if she could cope with an office job? How could I openly reject Susannah's suffocating kindness without arousing more suspicion?

I regret it all.

'Well, on the first of those days we went to Birmingham, where one of my friends offers obstetric care. She has a very nice private practice there. She confirmed Isobel was indeed ten weeks pregnant. On the Wednesday we went to a clinic in Chester. It was a simple procedure: a pill. We went back on the Friday for another one, and that was it.'

That was it.

My eyes fill with tears. Isobel must have been so frightened. How has she *never* told me? Did she think I would be angry with her? How has she carried this alone, all of this time?

'You should have told me, Susannah. From one mother to another – regardless of anything else you thought or knew was going on – you should have told me.' I can barely get the words out.

'I'm sorry, but I disagree,' she says smoothly. 'She asked for my help; she was seventeen and legally entitled to make her own decision. For whatever reason, she didn't want to tell you, so I helped her. It had nothing to do with what was "going on" with you and Antony.' She shrugs. 'Izzie is, in some ways, far more capable than you give her credit for. You really must allow her to grow up, Eve. All of the children experienced the same trauma that Christmas – and while I appreciate Isobel was grieving for her father at the time, the boys have coped more than adequately, it doesn't define them at all. They were shot *at*, they weren't shot, per se.'

My mouth falls open. *Shot per se.* She just actually said that out loud? 'Our children were shot. Just shot – no per se, no conditions. It was terrifying and I say that as an adult.'

'My God, woman!' she raises her voice in exasperation. 'You are the only person still banging on about what happened! Do you not understand that? You make it worse for Isobel when you do this!'

'You're a lawyer!' I shout back. 'How can *you* not empathise with the kids or at least acknowledge what happened was wrong?'

'Of course it was *wrong*! But yes, I've seen far, far worse things happen to people. How does one cope with trauma? You move on, you don't let what happened have any power over you any more!'

'What a noble sentiment.' I am now shaking. 'Except sometimes you don't actually have a choice. A man shouts or a child screams suddenly in a crowded shopping centre, you just panic – you don't stop and intellectualise what's happening to you. Where does your "no power" argument come into that? How can you have taken someone as vulnerable as Isobel to have an abortion, without telling me?'

'Look – *you* have made Isobel into the person she now is by keeping her wings clipped. Yes, in some ways she's a little girl trapped in an adult body… to say she's socially awkward doesn't begin to cover it – but if you let her, she'd grow up. *I* saw a young woman determinedly taking control over her own future. It's unkind of you to keep her in this box.' Susannah has calmed her voice back down, regained control. 'It's actually got a name, too: Munchausen's syndrome by proxy, or fabricated or induced illness. It's where a parent or carer – most often a biological mother – exaggerates or causes symptoms of illness in their child. You're aware you do that, surely?'

I hear the shriek of pure rage that issues from my mouth seconds before I step forward and slap her smartly about the face.

She takes it with barely a flinch and eyes me challengingly. 'I suspect when you've had time to think about what I've said, you'll accept that I'm right.'

'*You* had no right!' Bizarrely, actually striking her makes *me* stagger backwards as if I'm the one physically wounded by everything she has just said. 'She's my daughter! I would have helped her.' The tears are now escaping wildly down my cheeks. 'I would have helped her keep a baby, if that's what she'd wanted.'

There is a silence. 'Yes. I'm sure you would have,' Susannah says eventually.

Oh – and there we are. I gasp – seeing it all, instantly. 'That's why you "helped" her. You didn't want her bound to your son forever. She's not quite what you imagined for your boy? Is that it? Or was it because you were taking out your feelings for me on her? You didn't want to be linked to *me* forever? What did you tell her? What did you say to make her do it?' I step towards Susannah again; but desperately this time – I have to know *exactly* what happened to Izzie. 'Did you tell her I'd be angry if she was pregnant? That she'd disappoint me in some way?'

Susannah says nothing, just stares at me defiantly.

'I want you to swear on your son's life that you didn't try to manipulate my very pliable daughter into doing something she wouldn't have otherwise done,' I say, my voice by turns now soft with danger.

'That is a revolting thing to suggest,' Susannah replies eventually. 'And no, I shan't swear. I never swear on anyone's life – I think it's a dreadful thing to do. I didn't influence Izzie either way. It was her own choice; her own decision – her body. But if you're asking me do I believe Isobel was mentally equipped for motherhood? No, I do not.'

'Who is, Susannah? Have you or I made any better job of it than Izzie would have?'

'That's a deliberately inflammatory comment.'

'Not at all. You criticise my parenting skills when *you* sent your son back to school rather than help him deal with his problems. At least I was actually here for Izzie… and I suspect when you've had time to consider what I've said, you'll accept that I'm right.'

It's a cheap shot, but I see it hit home, and I'm glad.

'There is nothing wrong with my son at all,' she says angrily. 'In fact, he's very happy and that's the single reason I'm telling you this now, because it's entirely clear to me that you've grossly underestimated the effect of Timothy's return on Izzie, and I do not want all of this raked over again. It's done. Let's not give the locals more cause for gossip, shall we?' I can hear the acid in her voice. 'Think about it, Eve, wouldn't it have been more useful to tell you this information about the abortion *years* ago if I'd been keen to make capital from it? Wouldn't it have been the ideal way to ensure you stayed away from our family – and my husband – rather than my having to bear the humiliation of *asking* you to finish it with Antony – as I did? I respected Izzie's wishes that no one should know. I felt very sorry for her. I have always felt sorry for her.'

I hesitate, reluctantly seeing the logic in her words. I want to collapse to the floor. Will we *never* escape this family? 'For God's sake, Susannah! Why did you let him do it, then?' I shout suddenly. 'Surely you TOLD Antony not to buy them this house? Just for once take an interest in what your husband does, hey?'

She pales instantly and, too late, I realise my mistake. 'Antony's told you *he* bought this place for Timothy and Claire?'

'It didn't take a genius to work out, once I realised – too late – who Claire was,' I try to cover my tracks. 'I can't imagine Timothy was exactly keen to move in here. It was obvious Tony was involved.'

'You're lying. He's definitely told you.' She looks at me in disgust. 'How pathetic of him. Well, let's face it – no one else was going to buy this money pit, were they? I'll bet he couldn't wait to roar up and tell you how he's financially saved the day for *you*. Still desperate to be your knight in shining armour after all these years.'

I feel my cheeks flame with guilt as she nails it, instantly – and I know she sees.

'Of course I asked him not to buy this place,' she retorts, 'but really, Eve, these days, do I look like the kind of woman who is prepared to beg?'

'Does Timothy know Izzie was pregnant?' I ask suddenly. 'I don't understand why she didn't tell him rather than you? That doesn't make sense. She was in love with him. They were seeing each other.'

'Staying the night at your house on one occasion over that summer, to my knowledge, does not a couple make,' she says crisply. 'I told you, he'd left for university. He'd ended whatever "it" was with her. Isobel was very specific that she did *not* want him to know because it would disrupt his studies. She was worried he might drop out under some misguided sense of obligation to her.' She shrugs. 'I'll admit, I *was* slightly suspicious myself. I wondered if perhaps it was Adam Owen's child instead. In fact I had my friend perform a paternity test that Monday, while we were at her clinic, but the subsequent results took a little while to come back. I didn't want to unnecessarily delay any action while we were waiting, so it seemed sensible to go to the clinic in Chester anyway, once it was clear she actually was pregnant.'

'"Unnecessarily delay?"' I seize on that. 'You didn't want to risk Izzie changing her mind and keeping the baby, you mean.'

'In any case, there was a DNA match with a sample of Timothy's hair.' She smoothly ignores that. 'So Izzie was telling the truth. Do you think that was easy for me – something I've found *comfortable* to keep from my son? But I gave her my word.'

I give a strange, half laugh of disbelief. *Yes, Susannah. It would have been all too easy for you.* My poor, poor Isobel. She could not have chosen a more dangerous confidante, but neither was she aware why. Yet again, this is all my fault.

As if reading my mind, Susannah says: 'Men have affairs, Eve. It happens. Usually, men like Tony have them with very bright, aggressive young female barristers who they then set up in their London flat – and eventually marry. It's not often someone like you, who looks like the wife at home.'

I try very hard not to say anything. I won't give her the satisfaction.

'Although, you know, ending it with him was the smartest thing you ever did.' She considers. 'I shouldn't have interfered and asked you to step back – I should have let him tire of you on his own as you lost your looks, because he would have done. Instead, in his mind, it seems you've become the one that got away. Irritatingly.'

'I didn't do it for your sake,' I blurt, truthfully but unnecessarily, knowing it will hurt her. 'I ended it for Isobel, because I knew it would be too painful for her to have to be around Timothy all the time if Antony and I became a proper couple, so don't beat yourself up that your "request" had anything to do with it at all. It didn't. You were irrelevant. You were not my friend. I gave you no thought.'

That bit is actually not true. The evening she came to Fox Cottage and begged me to sever contact with her husband and end our affair, I cried after she left. I was so ashamed of what I'd done and the hurt Antony and I had caused. I remember it very clearly. I can see him now, lying in my bed on the nights he secretly crept to Fox Cottage under the cover of darkness when Susannah was away and Isobel was asleep. I'd wake in the morning to find him gone.

Can that ever really be love? I know I thought it was at the time.

'Well, delightful though this catch-up has been,' Susannah cuts through my thoughts, 'I really did just want the opportunity to say that I don't want anyone to misinterpret Timothy's return for anything it isn't. He has a very happy relationship with Claire; he's keen to undertake a large renovation project. That's all this is.'

'I don't want my child anywhere near yours either.'

'Well then,' she says smoothly. 'You see? We have that in common too.' She holds out a hand.

'I'm not going to shake on it!' I look at her in disbelief. 'I'm not making a plan with you, or agreeing to anything behind anyone's back. All I'm prepared to do is exactly what I've done all her life: protect my daughter from harm.'

'I mean I want the key,' she says softly. 'You don't live here any more. Get out.'

I just about manage to keep my head held up high. 'I have some last few bits in the kitchen to gather up. Then I'll leave.' I roll up my sleeves.

Susannah stares at the bruises on my wrists and her mouth falls open. They *are* fairly spectacular colours: deep purple with yellow patches bleeding into black. Stick that in your 'there's nothing wrong with Isobel and you imagine it all' pipe and smoke it. I let her look and then I roll them back down.

'I'll just get them now,' I say quietly, and she nods, finally, mercifully, lost for words.

# CHAPTER NINE

## Eve

Propelled by anger, guilt and grief for what Izzie has suffered, once I arrive at the new house and have put away some shopping – breakfast bits for the morning to see us through – I am a whirlwind, channelling my fury into organising Isobel's new bedroom as soon as the removal men have placed the big items in the room for me. I am determined to have everything looking as nice as possible for her. I don't just make the bed: the rug goes down, her curtains go up, I open the doll's house to restack the furniture that toppled in transit. The vast assortment of cuddly toys return to sitting on the shelves that I stack with her books; her chest of drawers goes over by the far wall so I can plug in her lamp. It's a bit squashed next to the built-in wardrobe, but it just about works. By the time I'm finished, it is almost a complete replica layout of her old room. It's what swung buying this house for me. I knew I'd never find something else which had a top floor like this: a self-contained space accessed by one flight of stairs with a door at the top that can be safely shut, but that leads into the light, comparatively large space in the eaves – complete with two skylights and an en-suite shower. I will do whatever it takes to make sure she is happy here.

*Munchausen's syndrome by proxy.* The bitch. I sit back on my heels and look around me at the finished room. How bloody dare

Susannah Vaughan! As if she has the slightest understanding of the complexities of Izzie's very real needs. To suggest that I want Izzie's vulnerability and dependence on me to continue – that I *cause* it?

I am devastated by what she has said, in fact. Every single day, I watch my daughter's last chances to have a normal life and a family of her own slip further away and it breaks my heart. She is now thirty-four and living no different a life than she was ten years ago. She can't cope with more than a part-time/menial job, she dresses like a child, she has no friends, she becomes anxious in crowded spaces, she's hopeless with the money that I provide her with, she likes colouring and collects snow globes. She needs me.

I am certain that Paul Jones triggered serious mental health issues that day before Christmas: post-traumatic stress, OCD, depression, bipolar, borderline personality disorder… just some of the suggestions made by various doctors, psychiatrists and counsellors over the years. Pretty much a different diagnosis each time we see someone new, in fact, but only my worst nightmare is constant: the thought of something happening to me and Izzie being left to cope, bewildered and alone.

And Susannah thinks I want this to continue? Yes, *sometimes* Izzie plays up her 'weaknesses'. She's faked blackouts in the past when she's been stressed and occasionally when she's had her night terrors. I don't see how she can possibly not remember them the following morning – they are so violent, it's as if she truly is wrestling the devil himself – but there are no physiological explanations for any of these symptoms.

I was worried recently after a particularly upsetting night that she might have a brain tumour; she was writhing around the bed, eyes wide open and shouting as if she was in physical pain. They *did* scan her brain for me – eventually – but they found nothing. The new, much kinder GP Izzie was transferred to after I made the complaint about the way the previous one spoke to us, suggested it might be that Isobel constructs these 'symptoms' because she simply doesn't feel worthy of attention otherwise. While, sadly, I think there is a grain of truth in that, it's very different from saying the problems are something Isobel can control, as Susannah suggests. Isobel needs tolerance and understanding – not being told to pull herself together. If only treating mental illness were *that* easy.

And in any case, the utter hypocrisy of Susannah saying all of that to me after what *she* put Izzie through – because she didn't think her 'mentally equipped' for motherhood? She encouraged Izzie to undergo an invasive procedure, just to confirm it was Timothy's baby, then have an abortion? What kind of woman does that? She is a monster. She has hurt my child.

I am shaking with anger as I fix a lock to the outside of Izzie's new bedroom door. All of my old feelings towards the Vaughans have come alive again and are writhing around within my stomach like snakes. While I find I hate Susannah all over again, this time it's with an entirely fresh ferocity.

I give the screws one last vicious twist, and realise it's almost six o'clock. Where *are* Adam and Izzie? I finish up and take the tools downstairs, temporarily shoving the box in the cupboard under the stairs until I can think of somewhere better for it. I need to try and focus on the job in hand, and not on what Susannah has told me. I look around, exhausted. There are boxes everywhere. Perhaps once Isobel is asleep later I can unpack the kitchen at least. Which reminds me, I have no idea where I have packed the baby monitor. Unlike Fox Cottage, where I didn't always switch it on, I won't be able to hear a thing without it if she calls me when she's at the top of this house. Luckily, I find it in one of the kitchen containers and plug it in on the side to charge up. I also unpack and wash three plates, glasses, cutlery and find the ketchup, ready for the fish and chips that Adam texted to say he would pick up on their way back through.

I'm just deciding that I probably have enough time to make my own bed, if I'm quick – and I must turn down the new heating, it's subtropical in here, I'm not used to somewhere so heat efficient – when I hear the loud ring of my mobile phone on the table in the hall. I walk out quickly and see that it's Adam calling. I don't even get the chance to say my determined bright and cheerful 'Hello!' before his frightened voice asks: 'Is she with you?'

It's like a violin bow scratchily sliding down the strings. 'What do you mean, is she with me? I thought she was with *you*.'

'She was! I stopped to get the fish and chips. It was busy in there and she was tired, so I left her in the van… but it was all right, I could see her from where I was. They asked me what I wanted – I gave them the order and paid – then I looked back and she was gone!'

I instantly close my eyes and put my hand to my head as I try to contain the thoughts and not go blank with panic.

'I'm so sorry,' he gabbles. 'I should have taken her in, but she was so relaxed, we'd had such a great day. I didn't think it would be a problem.'

'It's OK,' I say, trying to cut through the white noise of his apology. 'She wouldn't come here. She'll have gone to Fox Cottage. Damn it!' I cannot help exclaiming in frustration as I hear Susannah's horrible *we're not going to have any scenes* comment from earlier. 'When did this happen?'

'Literally just now. I'm so sorry, Eve.'

'It's OK,' I say, although it isn't. 'She'll be walking and she'll go through the churchyard.'

'Do you want me to go on foot after her?' He sounds confused.

'No, drive straight to the house. We must get there before she does.'

There is a reproachful silence on the end of the phone.

'Yes, all right, I know!' I explode. 'You were right – I should have told her about Timothy sooner, but you *know* I wanted to wait until we'd got her out of that house. I was going to do it tonight. Let's just go, shall we? I'll meet you there.'

I hang up before he has the chance to say anything more, shove the phone into my back pocket and run out into the hall. Where are the keys to the new house? I glance around wildly, lifting up boxes and my bag before finding them dumped in the corner of the hall by the small cardboard box of pointless moving-in 'essentials' left by the developer. And where are the car keys?

Perhaps I should just run round there rather than waste more time looking for them? I dither in panic, lifting up a pile of coats, yanking open the drawer in the sideboard, rummaging through my handbag, but they are nowhere to be seen. I make a snap decision to go on foot and throw open the front door, stepping out into the now-icy February air.

I brace myself as the cold hits me and slam the door shut, before hurrying down the small drive. It would be quicker to cut across the field – but I'm not risking tripping on uneven earth in the dark. I'm better off on the pavement, and begin the five-minute walk from our development; the road tracing round in a large loop, before cutting back onto the main street, on which Fox Cottage sits.

I am panting heavily by the time I arrive at the front door, too old and unfit for this. I'm about to knock, when common sense prevails and I pause to quickly glance around the front of the house first for any sign of her. The streetlight opposite has always been pathetic; all I can see are shadows and dark corners. The Volvo I remember from Claire's viewing is there, so they are in – but the garage door is also unlatched and slightly open, as if they had a go at parking within it earlier and gave up, because the entrance is so narrow. It wasn't made for modern-day vehicles. I stride over and throw the metal door wide, letting in as much orange light as possible. The vast, unoiled hinges give their usual yawning groan of resistance, but I couldn't care less about the noise.

'Izzie?' I stand in the doorway. 'Darling, are you there? Please can you come out if you are? I can't really see you.' I peer into the dark, scanning the space carefully, but there are just three bikes, a scooter, a child's easel, a large fridge and what seems to be a dresser stacked on the side. No Izzie, crouching down, knees hugged to her chest.

'Can I help you?' says a voice behind me, making me jump, and I swing round to see Timothy Vaughan standing about five paces away from me, looking frightened. Claire Waters stands on the doorstep, her arms folded over her chest.

'Mrs Parkes?' Timothy says in confusion, and we both blink as Claire flicks on the outside light, illuminating our faces properly. 'It *is* you! Hello.'

He instinctively offers me his hand. That's what private education buys. Manners regardless of circumstances. Bravo them. I stare at him. He hasn't changed a bit. Just an older version of the charming teenage boy my daughter spent one perfect, enchanted summer with. The last time – pretty much the only time – she was truly happy.

It's a curious thing when you can see exactly what your child finds attractive in another. History repeating itself. He has exactly Antony's height, dark colouring and that direct and confident stare. His brown, slightly unruly hair is swept back and he's deliberately left slight stubble on his jaw, I suspect, to prevent himself looking too boyish. Susannah's striking eyes look back at me, only a deeper, warmer blue. He's terribly pretty but I know it doesn't explain the hold he has over Isobel. That's down to an entire life being built on a ten-second moment where one child protected another and she bound her soul to his forever in return. The power of it astonishes me every single time.

'Mrs Parkes? Did you forget something?'

'Yes, my daughter, apparently.' I give a strained, odd laugh and notice, out of the corner of my eye, Claire frown and tighten her arms at the cold. 'What I mean to say is, Isobel has gone missing.'

'Oh,' he says, confused. 'I see.'

'I wonder if I might—' I begin but the noise of Adam's van suddenly pulling up on the forecourt alongside us drowns me out. Adam climbs out, and Timothy looks at him in astonishment.

'God! Hi there! How are you? Wow! It's been a while.'

'Welcome home,' Adam says flatly. 'Hello,' he gives a small wave to Claire, 'I'm Adam.'

'Adam and I knew each other years ago,' Timothy explains to her, over his shoulder. 'Before I—'

'Timothy,' I say pointedly, 'I'm sorry to interrupt, but I really do need to find Isobel. Do you think I might check in your garden, round the back?'

His eyebrows shoot up in surprise, but he's too polite to refuse. 'Yes, of course. Can I help at all? Do you need a torch? Claire, have we got a torch?'

'Um.' She appears just as thrown. I might have written her off as useless as him, but I shan't make that mistake again. 'In a box somewhere, but...'

'Please don't worry.' I hold up a hand. 'We can manage. She hasn't – knocked on the door?'

Timothy shakes his head. 'We haven't heard a thing, but then we had the radio on while we unpacked in the kitchen. Our daughter isn't here tonight, she's with my parents, so the music was louder than usual.' He looks at Claire. 'You didn't hear anything?'

'I'm sorry to say I haven't seen any sign of anyone.' She looks at me oddly as she says that but I turn away. I simply don't have time for her right now. After what she's done and her duplicitous part in all of this, I won't ever have time for her again.

'We'll just take a look around the back then if you don't mind?' I address Timothy, ignoring Claire completely. An old car passes by us, heading out of town and backfires suddenly as it reaches the corner. All three of us leap in the air at the bang and Adam instinctively steps closer to me, reaching a hand to my arm.

'Anyway, please, carry on…' Tim says faintly as the sound dies away, gesturing towards the white metal gate.

When I first moved to the country I was fascinated by how dark the nights were, but actually, the moon is so bright tonight that as Adam clanks the gate shut behind us, I can make out the outlines of the familiar trees and shrubs quite easily, until Adam switches the torch on his mobile and they all vanish again as my eyes readjust.

'You should use your torch too,' he says, waiting as I fumble around with it, only finding the right function through luck rather than any expertise.

We stride out, crunching over the long, already frosting grass and Adam immediately breaks off to the left, to check the courtyard and the oil shed. I follow the gravel path, making my way across the main lawn, behind the house. I shine my torch onto the French windows that lead into the dining room and pull the handle, but they are locked, just as I left them this morning. I go round to the back door that's in the middle part of the house, but that's locked too. That leaves the rotten windows in the barn – the whole frame lifts out if it's pushed hard enough. *Izzie wouldn't do that and climb in, surely?*

I hesitate when a voice says behind me: 'It's all secured at the three-storey end.' It's Adam. 'You've checked the garden shed and by the swing?'

'No, I haven't!' My heart lifts with hope and we both hurry across to the apple tree – but when Adam shines a beam across the lawn, the swing is empty – the ropes and seat hanging eerily still in our artificial light. 'She's not there,' I say quickly, pushing his phone down. I don't want to look at it.

'Eve! Come quickly!' I hear a voice calling from some distance behind us – it's Claire. Hastening back towards the house until we reach the gravel path, she is standing in the brightly lit back doorway looking rather pale. 'Isobel is in the small sitting room.'

Christ – she *is* inside the house. I glance at Adam who is clearly thinking the same thing. We follow as Claire wordlessly leads us through my old kitchen, which has a too-big table in it, through the dining room, full of nothing but boxes. The house feels confused and sad. I can hear Timothy saying something, but as I arrive in the small sitting room between them, he has fallen quiet and is just staring at Izzie, who is gazing back at him, open-mouthed with silent tears streaming down her face. She couldn't look more thunderstruck if she tried.

I am instantly furious with myself for making the wrong decision – particularly in view of Susannah's earlier revelation. 'I'm so sorry, darling.' I make a snap decision to reframe the significance of this moment to protect my daughter from further humiliation. 'I should have told you exactly who was moving in so you didn't find out like this. I'm so very sorry!' I'd rather make this moment appear far bigger than it is; let Claire believe she's witnessing stars collide as the two lovers explode back into each other's lives, than have Izzie cast yet again as the local crazy girl who just broke into her ex-boyfriend's house. I'm just not having that. It's *not* how this is going to be.

Anyway, it's not as if Isobel isn't playing her part perfectly – my poor love – I watch her reach a hand forward, slowly. I can see that she wants to touch Timothy and make sure he's real. Her beautiful mouth opens as she laughs.

'You came back!'

I wince as Claire audibly gasps in astonishment. I can't pretend it doesn't hurt afresh every time someone hears my daughter speak and reacts as if she's a freak. What's particularly excruciating *this* time, is the rapt wonder in Isobel's high-pitched, little girl voice. Adam looks away from everyone. I don't think he can believe this is happening at all. Poor, poor Adam. Unrequited love is the only kind that lasts forever.

I step forward, taking my daughter by the arm. 'Isobel? We have to leave. Adam, would you please?'

He comes to life again and moves to gently take her other arm, leading her quietly from the room as I let go. Isobel is so shocked that, mercifully, she doesn't resist.

Once she is out of earshot, I turn back to Timothy. 'In view of your and Isobel's "history",' I let the word linger in the air ambiguously, 'do you think I might ask you to give her a little space? She's been doing so well recently.' Understandably he looks a little surprised – and confused – by my implication that he might have had any plans whatsoever to meet up with her and says 'of course!' without really thinking. He always was eager to please. Like a dog.

I nod, as if satisfied and in some ways I am. I think I've rectified this situation; successfully twisting the painting so they are confused and uncertain they were viewing it the right way up after all. Isobel has walked out of here with her dignity intact.

But I have underestimated Claire.

'Just to be clear,' she has recovered herself as I reach the threshold, 'there are no keys that Isobel still has, to any of the other doors here? In case she becomes "confused" and tries to get in again?'

I hesitate. 'Confused?'

'She *does* understand nothing here belongs to her any more? I mean that in the nicest possible way, Eve.'

My God. The apple hasn't fallen far from the tree. Timothy has chosen himself a little mini-Susannah. My hand grips the door handle more tightly. I think about my unwittingly showing Claire around Isobel's room, letting her peek at everything that was private to Izzie, what I exposed to her… how she tricked me. I think about holding her hand when she told me her parents died in a car crash. I wonder if that sob story was Antony's idea or hers?

I turn slowly to look at her. 'You were not honest, Ms Waters. At best you were evasive – at worst you deliberately deceived me.

You took advantage of my kindness and I won't forget that. I would not have sold you this house, had I known who you really were.'

She has just enough grace to blush violently. 'Yes, I was evasive, but—'

I hold up a hand to cut her off. 'You should have listened to me. I tried to warn you – this house will not make you happy. Good night.'

I walk out leaving the door swinging open behind me.

# CHAPTER TEN

## Claire

I am stunned. Tim and I just stand there in silence for a moment, before Tim moves to close the front door and turns back to face me, clearing his throat. 'I'm so sorry. Obviously she has no idea that you weren't in the full picture either and didn't set out to "deceive" her at all.'

I nod but tears have already rushed to my eyes.

Tim steps over and tries to hug me. 'Just ignore her. She doesn't know you and her anger isn't directed at you anyway, trust me.'

'Sorry,' I breathe, wriggling free, so I can try to stop the tears from falling. 'I liked her when we met, that's all. I don't want her to think badly of me when, as you say, this isn't *my* fault. Tim, what's wrong with her daughter's voice? Is she putting that on?'

He shakes his head, embarrassed. 'It's always been like that.'

'But she sounds like a child!' I say in disbelief. 'This tall… amazing-looking woman opens her mouth and that tinkly-glass, wind chime voice comes out?' I stare at the centre of the disordered room where Isobel stood, moments ago. 'It's actually a bit creepy. Like she's possessed or something.'

'Please don't,' Timothy says quickly and shudders.

'Does she do it because she thinks it's cute, do you think? Oh God!' I suddenly remember the cuddly toys, the rose-patterned duvet on her single bed, the little trinkets everywhere, in her bedroom above us. 'Has she got the mental age of a child, or something? Is that it? Is she not quite right in the head?'

'No! She's just a bit... different. I told you, I haven't seen her for years.' Tim walks over and sits down heavily on our sofa, dumped at an odd angle at the back of the room. 'Not since we dated. Which, like I just said – was only for a few weeks. That's it.'

'The way she looked at you, I felt like I was watching Juliet being reunited with Romeo,' I say quietly.

He sighs. 'What can I possibly say to that without sounding like an arsehole? OK, yes, she fell quite hard. I did like her, too, but I was only eighteen. I broke it off when I went to university, and she wrote to me for a bit. She was pretty upset and the letters were a bit much. I wrote back a couple of times, but I got bored and stopped – and eventually so did she. It was just normal teenage stuff. Life moved on.' He shrugs. 'I'm telling you the truth – it was no big love affair on *my* part. It was all very innocent actually. I never even slept with her. It wouldn't have been right.' He shifts uncomfortably. 'She's a little offbeat perhaps, but she's a sweet girl. She means well.'

'"A sweet girl"?' I repeat. 'Tim – she is also astonishingly beautiful. You didn't think to mention that either?'

'Um,' he looks puzzled. 'Why would I? Wouldn't that have been a really odd thing to say to you?'

'In her case,' I correct him, 'it's almost stranger that you *didn't* say anything. She's exquisite. I mean, Eve is attractive but Isobel... was her father Irish or something, with all that red hair and those green eyes? That's some childhood sweetheart you've got there.'

Tim stares at me. '"Exquisite"? Are you feeling all right? And she's not my childhood sweetheart. I told you – we barely dated for a summer.'

I pull the sleeves of my jumper over my hands to dab my eyes. 'How did she get into the house?'

'That's my fault,' Tim confesses. 'I'm pretty sure I left the front door open, and she would have heard us calling her name. I take your point, about what you said to Mrs Parkes, but I don't think she used a key. It's nice to see she's with Adam now though – he's a good bloke.'

The name rings bells again with me, and as I rack my brains, I remember Eve telling me about her daughter's boyfriend, Adam, storing his stuff at the house. 'He's the artist,' I say out loud, sitting down on the sofa opposite Tim.

He makes a bemused face. 'Honestly, Claire – I haven't a clue. I've not seen Adam in about sixteen years either. We hung out because he and Izzie were best friends – but that's it. We didn't exactly keep in touch.'

'He paints pictures of skulls and swirly seas.' I suddenly remember the mesmeric picture of the red-headed woman in his studio at the back of the house. 'He used to work here in the barn. And you're right, he's Isobel's boyfriend.'

Tim gestures helplessly. 'Well I'm not surprised. He always had a thing for her, ever since school, I think. He was also one of the kids that was there the day Jones shot us.' Tim leans back on the sofa and stretches his legs out. I will never understand how he can speak about it so casually. I know it's a coping mechanism, but still… 'There was one other boy too, who tried to hide behind the barrier and Jones deliberately shot him in the arse. What was *his* name?' He blinks and stares up at the bright, bare lightbulb hanging in the centre of the room. 'Richard! That's it. He ended up a prison officer in Derby, I think…' He exhales. 'Adam probably only started the class because Isobel was doing it. He wasn't exactly martial arts material. Or maybe his parents made him do it to toughen him up – they got more than they bargained for if that was the case. Anyway, we wouldn't even be having this conversation if Iz hadn't rocked up here tonight. Try not to let it all seem more than it is.'

Iz? I don't miss that telling, comfortable familiarity and, although I know it shouldn't, it unnerves me. I also remember suddenly how opposed Tim was to moving into Fox Cottage. Why is he downplaying what's just happened when it seems this is exactly what he was afraid of?

'Tim – are you sure Isobel didn't let herself into the house?' I ask slowly.

He frowns, running his fingers through his hair, making it stand up on end. 'I really don't think it was anything suspicious, if that's what you mean? Mrs Parkes and Adam went off round the back, you disappeared upstairs and I went into the kitchen. I called and then I heard her say my name – I came back in and she was just standing over there. Like I said, I think I probably left the front door open?'

He points at the empty space in the middle of the room and neither of us say anything for a moment. The silence in the house reminds me of watching someone screaming on TV with the sound turned down.

'Right, well I think I'll get the locks changed tomorrow morning,' I say. 'It's good practise when you move into a new house in any case.' I shiver and rub my arms to try and warm myself up. 'Let's do another hour and head back to your parents'.'

'You don't want to stay tonight after all then?'

'No! But not because of Isobel,' I say quickly. 'It's just bloody freezing in here.'

'I know, that Rayburn thing is stone cold and I haven't cracked the thermostat heating yet either. I'll try and get it sorted before we go.' He rubs his eyes tiredly and holds out a hand to me. 'Come and sit with me just for a second.'

I hesitate, we've got so much to do – but I do as he asks, crossing the room and sitting down. He pulls me into a hug and kisses the top of my head as I lean rather awkwardly on his chest.

'I'm sorry this has been such a crap start to us moving in,' he says. 'It's arctic, we've had a lovely chat about traumatic childhood events, my ex turned up in our sitting room and then her mother arrived and issued you with a dire gypsy warning of unhappiness forever. Happy Valentine's Day!'

I half laugh – and out of nowhere – yelp as overwhelmed tears return again. I pull free and sit up to search for a tissue in my sleeve. 'What did Eve mean, she wouldn't have sold it if she'd known who I was?' I blurt. 'Like you said, she doesn't know me full stop!' I wipe my eyes.

Tim groans and looks at the ceiling. 'You're my partner; I'm Dad's son. She meant she wouldn't have sold it to Dad.'

'Why?'

Tim whistles under his breath, lifts his head and looks at me flatly. 'Because I think they had an affair.'

'What?' I draw back from him. 'You're joking!'

'I don't know for certain.' He leans his head back again and closes his eyes. 'All I know is one minute Mum and Mrs Parkes became good friends and Mum was trying to help her out a lot, sending Dad round to fix a gutter here, reattach a tile there. That's kind of why I even started dating Isobel in the first place. I was at home for the holidays bored out of my brain, and Mum asked me to take Isobel out because Mrs Parkes was worried about Isobel not really ever going anywhere. The next minute – bam. Nothing. All contact stops; Mum in tears, shouting in the study when they didn't know I was home and could hear them – that kind of thing.'

'Why didn't you tell me? I would have chosen another house!'

He opens his eyes and stares at the ceiling again. 'Because in a way, you were right. They're just buildings and I didn't want to sound like I was making excuses. I'd have done whatever it took to keep us together. Plus, I'm not one hundred per cent certain that's what happened. It's just what I think.'

'You've never just asked your mum?'

He laughs. 'What do you think? You know we don't have that kind of relationship. Best foot forward and all that. Anyway, they obviously worked it all out, they're still together.' He twists his head and looks at me. 'I'm sorry, Claire. This is all so shit. I promise I will make this up to you.'

I pause and imagine him trying not to listen to the shouting echoing down the halls of The Rectory, having recently come back from boarding school, about to ship out again to university. Why do some people even bother having children? I reach out and squeeze his hand.

'Ignore me, I'm just tired,' I say, partly truthfully and then I take a deep breath and sit up straighter. 'You don't have to keep saying you're sorry, Tim. I know you are.' I blow my nose. 'I'm still dealing with what you did, but this isn't going to work if I blame you for every tiny thing that goes wrong from here on in, because things *are* going to go wrong. I'm determined not to fall into that trap, and we're going to make the best of this. It's just for a year – that's all. Everyone wobbles a bit when they move into a new house, that's normal, because it's not what you're used to apart from anything else. This place isn't that bad really.'

I pause and we look around us at the threadbare carpet, the faded walls with marked squares where once Eve's pictures hung and the paint peeling from the window frames. It doesn't just feel neglected, more like it has been abandoned. Our jumbled boxes and furniture only seem to add to the confusion. I haven't done a good job of cleaning in here either – there are still cobwebs on the ceiling, drifting in the air and lifting on whispering draughts we can't feel… and everything is so still and quiet. I actually miss noise – police cars going past, commuter trains rattling away in the distance, even the neighbours above and below us clonking around – signs of *life*.

'It just needs some new curtains,' says Tim wryly.

I snort and he smiles at me, before reaching for my hand again and holding it. 'Thank you,' he says simply.

I nod and then we both jump out of our skin as there's a sudden bang from one of the rooms above us.

'What the hell was that?' Tim says nervously, looking up the dark stairwell to the floor above.

'I left the window open in our bedroom. It smelt all musty. I expect it's blown shut, that's all – my fault.' I stand up. 'I'll go and close it now before I forget. That's probably why it's so cold, too. I'm a moron.'

He stands up too. 'No, you're not. You're just absolutely exhausted, that's all. Mentally and physically.' He hugs me to him and rubs my back. 'And I'm sorry about Isobel. I can't help having a past, but I promise you're the only future I want.'

I properly laugh for the first time in a while. 'Tim! That's such a naff line.'

'And I really mean it.' He grins.

I think about Isobel again, standing so very still while staring at him with such unnerving radiance, and immediately tip my face up to his, kissing him lightly on the lips. 'I still want to get the locks sorted though. Not because of her, but if the builders are starting next Wednesday in the barn end and storing materials in the *other* end of the house, it makes sense to secure this sandwiched middle bit we're actually going to be living in. I don't want Rosie wandering through the connecting doors and finding a load of sharp, dangerous tools on one side and exposed wires and rubble on the other.'

'Agreed,' says Tim. 'Plus I don't want the builders ambling through from one bit to the other whenever they want either. They can go round the back when they need to get something. This middle bit needs to feel like a home. As much as possible.' He looks around him again doubtfully.

'I think we can make it a lot nicer than it is now.' I chew my lip, put my hands on my hips and look at the boxes again. 'In fact, I wonder if we shouldn't just slap some paint over the walls before we unpack? Do you think your mum and dad would mind if we stayed at theirs another couple of nights? Or at least if Rosie does? Just so we could work really hard on it for the next two days? I'm not talking a professional job, obviously – just a freshen up. It's only three bedrooms and the bathroom in this bit – and I wouldn't paint in Rosie's room anyway, she'd be gutted to lose that tree – then down here it's the dining room, two sitting rooms and kitchen. OK, so we can't do *all* of it,' I realise aloud. 'But we could certainly do our room and at least one of the sitting rooms. That'd be enough to start with?'

'And so it begins,' says Tim. 'You've hit organising mode. It was always going to happen.'

I smile tiredly. 'I think I'm just firing on adrenaline.' It's true, I feel slightly wired. I should have hit a wall by now yet I can't quite seem to stop. It's an odd, unsettled excitement. 'Come on! Let's go and decide on a colour.' I reach out, take his hand and lead him up the dark stairs to the bedroom.

# CHAPTER ELEVEN

## Eve

We all squash onto the front seat in Adam's van, Isobel wedged between me on the left and Adam – who is driving – but she doesn't say a word, until we pull up outside our new home.

'Why didn't you tell me Timothy was coming back, that he was moving into our house?' The aura around her is palpable; she's positively shimmering with happiness – lit up from within. She looks at me, and Adam sits back, crossing his arms, and waits too.

'Darling, it's not our house any more,' I remind her. 'I wanted the right moment to tell you about Timothy because I knew it was going to upset you – and I was obviously right.' Worriedly, I reach out to take her hand. 'You can't just walk into Fox Cottage any more, Izzie. How *did* you get in anyway?'

She draws it back. 'I wasn't naughty. The front door was open and I heard him calling my name.' She catches her breath. 'So I went in and… he was just standing there, waiting for me.'

Oh God. She's constructed *that* out of him trying to help us look for her? An enchanted Disney moment all of her very own. 'But Izzie, you shouldn't have been there at all.' I try to steer her off course. 'Adam was getting the food and you just disappeared from the car. We were very frightened, weren't we, Adam?'

He nods. 'I have to say I was, Iz.'

'We didn't know where you were.'

She looks confused and immediately becomes anxious, starting to pick at her poor stubby nails, bitten back right to the quick.

'Leave them, sweetest.' I gently pull her hands apart. 'You'll make them so sore.'

'I'm sorry. I just suddenly remembered I'd left some important things at home. That's all. I went back to see if the new people would let me get them?'

I remember the Ouija board under the floor. 'You don't need to worry about that now. We've talked about all of this before. None of that is real, Isobel. The only damage it can do is to your mind. Now, tell me! What did you see at the cinema? I bet I can guess—' She frowns but I carry on quickly. '*Paddington 2!*'

'Right first time!' Adam interjects cheerfully.

'Oh no! Not again!' I force a laugh and Adam chuckles too. 'Lucky it's so good, eh, Iz? Hugh Grant is a revelation.'

'I'm tired,' she says suddenly, as Adam turns off the engine.

'I'm sure you are. It's been a big day.' I climb out of the car and watch as Adam holds the door open for her, but when she emerges, she's smiling again. She's absolutely ablaze within, I can see it; I can *feel* the terrifying warmth of the happiness radiating from her. 'You must be hungry, too?'

She shakes her head. 'I don't want to eat anything. So this is where we live now?' She looks at the house, and just for a moment, I'm released from thinking about the Vaughan family and turn my attention to the next challenge.

'Yes, it is. Would you like to come in and have a look around? Tell me what you think? I'll be interested to know.'

I hold my breath as she drifts over the threshold in a daze, but at least she's in. I open my mouth to tell her to take her shoes off now that we've actually got nice flooring, but instantly think better of it. I don't want to make any mistakes or strike a single wrong note. Adam shoots me a look and I know he feels the tension too.

'Oh hey, Iz! Look at this!' he says conversationally as they walk into the sitting room. 'The TV is set up already! The chairs are all organised. And there's a little fire. You've worked hard, Eve,' he says as I come in.

'I wanted to get it looking nice.' I smile wearily, suddenly realising how tired *I* am. Izzie doesn't say anything; she doesn't appear to be noticing any of it at all, although that's not necessarily a bad thing.

'Can I go up to my room now, please?' she says absently.

'Of course!'

We troop right to the top of the house. I'm leading the way, Adam bringing up the rear – Izzie deliberately sandwiched between us to make her feel safer.

'You're up here.' I stand to one side and let her walk in, watch her scan the room as her gaze settles on the closed door that leads to her en suite. 'That's right! You've got your own bathroom just like normal!' I say quickly. 'This whole floor is all for you!'

'Wow, Izzie!' Adam appears behind me. 'Look at this! You've got so much space.' He nods at the two skylights. 'And you'll still be able to watch the clouds.' He mimes closing his open mouth, and I smile gratefully.

'There are no birds,' she says suddenly and points at the blank wall.

'Not yet,' I say quickly.

'Maybe *I* could paint some for you this time?' Adam offers and she gives the briefest of shrugs.

Adam laughs. 'Thanks very much! Maybe paint your own then!'

'I just might,' she says softly and then, to my huge surprise, she walks suddenly across the room and gives me a hug. 'Thank you for doing this,' she says. 'I'm sorry I frightened you.'

I am so overwhelmed I actually feel tears rush to my eyes. I cannot remember the last time she thanked me, unprompted, or offered me a hug. I allow myself the luxury of feeling her head lean against my shoulder for the briefest of moments, but it's already too much for her and she's pulling away from me, before I get the chance to mentally bank the simple joy of holding her in my arms.

'I think she likes it, Adam!' I remark, choked, to cover my emotion.

'Who wouldn't! It's an amazing room!' Adam says cheerfully.

Every time I've asked him what's happening with his own living situation, he's brushed me off and told me he's fine. I know he's going to run out of friends' sofas before too long. And then what? But I can't worry about that now too. Not tonight. My head might explode if I try to fit something else in. It's time for bed and some well-earned rest.

But I'm premature. Izzie is peering at her chest of drawers in confusion, which I realise, too late, I have not shut properly.

'Have you been in my things, Mum?' she asks. Her voice is light, but a trained ear can hear it – a delicate string pulling so tight it might snap.

'I haven't been through them at all, Izzie, no,' I say firmly, in an attempt to head her off at the pass. 'I had to take the drawers out so that the removal men could lift them onto the van, but no one has looked through them. Let's go downstairs and watch some TV while Adam gets those fish and chips!' Again. 'Do you mind going back, Adam?'

But she is not listening, she's already opening the middle drawer, and Adam groans. She digs around inside the T-shirts and jumpers, then pulls out the Timothy box. She lifts the lid and rummages around in the contents, before, seemingly satisfied, starting to close it again, but then she hesitates and her eyes widen. She reaches in and scrabbles around urgently.

'Where is the candle?'

'What candle?' I feign ignorance because I've just remembered I have no bloody idea where it is. I did pack it, didn't I? It was on the bedpost.

'Mum, please!' She explodes suddenly. 'You *know* what I'm talking about. Don't treat me like I'm imagining things! Where is it? You didn't light it again?' She looks at me anxiously.

'No, I didn't!' I try to sound annoyed. 'Isobel, come along! Downstairs please.'

'You did, didn't you?' She stares at me. 'What were you thinking about when you lit it? This is very important, Mum. I know you don't believe me, but it could be dangerous.'

'Isobel Mary Parkes!' I'm starting to lose it myself. 'Darling, please, must we do this? The only dangerous thing about lighting a candle, is you doing it on your own, in your old bedroom. I didn't want to have to talk to you about this now, but since it's come up – I don't want you using candles without my being there too. The whole house could burn down.'

I watch Adam look at the floor and wait. He's bracing for the train to hurtle through the barrier.

But she is unusually calm. 'I know *you* don't believe in magic – but I do. Show me your hands!' She reaches out and grabs my wrist tightly, her thumbs digging into one of my bruises. It hurts and I yelp; nonetheless she forces my palms over.

'There,' she says immediately, pointing at my cut and painfully throbbing thumb. I didn't get round to putting another plaster back on.

'It's nothing. Just a cut!'

'Did you keep it covered when you held the candle? Otherwise, you've basically just performed blood magic.'

Blood magic? I could *scream*.

'I didn't bleed on anything and witchcraft is not real,' I manage. 'We've been over this. No more boards, no more chanting, summoning or spell casting. Please… *please*.' My voice cracks but she looks at me defiantly.

'This is your fault, Mum – not mine. If you hadn't gone through my things it would still be in there. I need to go back and look for it now.'

'To Fox Cottage?' I exclaim. 'For a bit of candle? You're joking, right?'

'It's important. I won't be able to sleep until I know it's safe.'

'OK – yes, I found it and yes, I burnt it – I burnt it to the end and I burnt that ridiculous board too!' I lie, finally losing my rag. 'It's *crazy*, Isobel. You have got to stop this, do you understand? It's unhealthy, dangerous thinking.'

'You're sure you burnt it out completely?' she says, ignoring everything else I've just said.

'Yes,' I practically shriek. 'I promise.'

She nods with relief. 'OK then. I really don't want any food, thank you. I still feel sick after the popcorn and sweets earlier.'

'But that was this morning. What have you eaten since then?'

'We went back again after lunch and watched another movie,' Adam says. 'We've had loads to eat, honestly. It was a Valentine's Day treat,' he adds sadly. 'I'll say good night, Iz.'

He comes over to kiss her and she deliberately twists her face so he only catches the back of her cheek and her hair. I look away, embarrassed for him.

'I'll see you downstairs, Eve,' he says quietly.

I nod and wait until he's out of earshot before I turn back to her. 'That wasn't very kind.'

'"People should never be forced into something they don't want to do",' she repeats aloud the words I said to Paul Jones all those years ago, and I freeze, recognising them instantly.

'Are you OK, Iz? Today has been very overwhelming, I think?'

She goes and climbs onto her bed and hugs her knees to her chest. She looks about five years old. 'No – it's been good. I like it here!' She smiles at me nervously, and I try to smile back at her, even though I know she is thinking about Timothy Vaughan again.

'I can't believe it, Mum!' she whispers, confirming my fears. The ominous sense of wonder has crept back into her voice. 'It worked!'

I risk walking over to her bed, sitting down and reaching out to stroke her hair from her face, but she lets me. I'm afraid to ask – I know what the answer is going to be – but I must. 'What worked, my love?'

'I brought him back,' she confides shyly and stares at the rose pattern on her bedspread, tracing the petals with her fingertip. 'That's partly what the candle was about.'

I take a deep breath. I don't want to do this, it would be so much easier not to, but it wouldn't be kind. I wouldn't be a good mother.

'Isobel, that woman in the house with Timothy lives with him. She's called Claire. He hasn't come back for you, darling.'

She looks down at the duvet, refusing to meet my eye.

'Izzie, there's something else,' this is going to be the hardest bit, 'he has a daughter now. She's eight and she's called Rosie.'

'Oh!' It's the smallest sound of surprise. She closes her eyes, and thanks to Susannah's poisonous vengeance, now I understand exactly why. I sit watching her, completely helpless to relieve the visible pain she is in, and it makes me want to hurt someone.

'Timothy hasn't come back because of anything you did, or think you made happen,' I plough on. 'He's just… come back. I know how difficult this is going to be for you, Isobel, how much you love Timothy and how important he is to you – has been for such a long time now after what he did for you that day, but angel, he didn't—'

'Stop, Mum! Please!' she interrupts fiercely. 'Just stop. You're wrong. You don't understand.'

But I do – I know what it is to love someone and not be able to be with them, *of course I understand, my darling. I promise you.* I reach out and tenderly stroke her hair again. 'Mothers know everything.'

I mean it to be a comfort, but she ducks away from my touch, clouding over and becoming so darkly furious that I falter. 'No, you don't.'

It is a shock to suddenly realise that she hasn't kept her secret from me because she was worried I'd be angry or think less of her – she simply didn't want me to know. I feel really quite desolate as the penny drops. This is too much change for one day.

'I don't want my door locked tonight.' She glares at me.

I pointedly look down at my bruised wrists. 'I'll very happily give it a go if you think that you'll be OK?'

'I'm asleep,' she says quickly. 'I don't mean to hurt you. I don't know I'm doing it. I never remember doing it.'

'I'm not having a go at you, Izzie.' I stand up. 'I just want you to stay safe, that's all, but of course we don't need to lock it if you don't want to. Are you going to go to bed now?'

She nods.

'OK. I'll go and get your water then.' I hesitate. 'You wouldn't be asking me not to lock your door because actually you want to go back to Fox Cottage and look for this candle, would you?'

She flushes guiltily. You see I *do* know, Izzie.

'You said you'd burnt it down?'

'I did.' I wait, but she stays sullenly quiet. 'Isobel?'

'OK, OK! There are some other things there that I need to get!' she confesses. 'I have to. Well, I think I do. It'd probably be safer.'

I want to collapse into an exhausted heap on the soft, new carpet. I would happily sleep there. 'Isobel, you're not going back tonight. They'd think it was very odd indeed if you did.'

'Well, you go then, and I won't have to!'

'What can you have possibly left behind that could be *so* important, that I need to go back *again*?' I gesture wildly. 'And I'm warning you, Isobel, if you say it's anything to do with magic – blood or otherwise – witchcraft or any kind of spell at all, I'm going to get *very* cross indeed.'

*

I march back downstairs to find Adam waiting in the kitchen for me. 'I actually thought that seemed to go pretty well?' he says as I yank out a chair from under the table to sit down, before adding soberly. 'All things considered.'

I rest my elbows on the table and pinch the bridge of my nose, eyes closed – like I'm praying – but I am in fact trying to calm myself down. 'Well, apart from the fact I've got to go back to Fox Cottage to retrieve something inexplicable that she's shoved up the chimney there, yes – it went fine,' I retort, more acidly than I intend.

He looks thrown. 'What do you mean, she's shoved something up the chimney?'

My voice is suddenly thick with tears. 'She made two *poppets*… dolls,' I try to explain as Adam still looks blank. 'I don't want to say voodoo dolls, but apparently their purpose is to symbolise a particular person that you might want to… manipulate.'

Adam stares at me, stunned.

'I know, I know! That IS a voodoo doll, isn't it?' I try to exhale deeply to calm down, but even my breath is jagged with stress. 'She made one of them out of an old T-shirt of his she had from when they were together and if that wasn't mad enough, she's *consecrated* it – I don't even really know what that means – and performed a ritual that, among other measures, is apparently why he's now come back to Fox Cottage. But now it's worked, she wants the doll back in case it falls into the wrong hands and *bad things happen.*'

Adam sits back in his chair.

I look up at the ceiling. 'This is too much. I don't have the strength for this any more. I think it might have been OK if she and Timothy hadn't actually got together that summer before he went to university. That was when everything stopped just being inside her head and he made her believe he felt exactly the same way about her.'

'Yeah, well I can't really blame him for that,' Adam says quietly. 'She's beautiful and she worshipped him. He's a decent bloke, but he'd been shut up in an all-boys' school. It was a done deal. To hear she's genuinely been waiting for seventeen years for him to come back though?' He closes his eyes briefly. 'That's so very sad.'

I reach up my sleeve for a tissue. 'I'm sorry,' I say quickly, dabbing at my eyes. 'This must be so painful for you too. It's all just…' I trail off. 'She really believes she's brought him back here!' I begin to sob, and Adam frowns, worried, and leans forward again, placing a comforting hand on my arm.

'You're exhausted, Eve. Today has been so stressful. I'm not surprised you're this upset.'

'I'm sorry! Susannah Vaughan came to the house earlier and had a go at me, too. She said…' I hesitate, but I feel so dejected and so desperate for someone to tell me I'm *not* a bad mother and that Susannah Vaughan is the bitch here, not me – I blurt it out anyway. 'She said she helped Izzie get rid of Timothy's baby. She even made her have a DNA test to prove it was his! Can you believe that?'

Adam freezes. 'Izzie was pregnant?'

I regret telling him instantly. He has turned ashen.

'I shouldn't have told you.' I am suddenly wracked with guilt as he removes his hand. 'Izzie didn't want to tell either of us. This was very, very wrong of me. Timothy doesn't even know.'

'There was a baby?' I can see the disbelief all over his face.

'It was that same summer. He ended it with Izzie just before he went to university, didn't he?'

'Yes,' Adam says automatically. 'After a séance we did together at Fox Cottage… it was nothing – just a kids' game,' he adds quickly at the sight of my face. 'Timothy has a very overactive imagination. Always has. He got spooked and dumped her. A baby… oh Izzie…' He shakes his head again and covers his mouth, stunned.

'You know what, Adam?' I say suddenly, standing up, appalled at myself and desperate to do something, anything, to atone for such a hideous indiscretion. 'I *am* going to go and get those bloody dolls for the poor girl. Will you wait here for me? She's gone to bed anyway; I won't be more than five minutes. And when I get back, I'm going to work out what the hell I'm going to do about all of this. I can't let her carry on with this witchcraft nonsense any more. It's past being a harmless hobby. It's becoming dangerous.'

'I honestly don't think she'd hurt anyone.' He looks bewildered. 'She—'

'I mean dangerous for Isobel, as in, it's unhealthy. I don't believe in it – not for one second.'

'I'm sorry, I misunderstood. You should get the dolls if it makes you feel better and perhaps it's advisable that the Vaughans don't find them in any case. Is she locked in?' He nods at my wrists.

'No, so just be aware she might come downstairs.'

'Of course. You go.' His eyes are still wide with shock. 'I'll look after her.'


The cold makes me more alert as I march down the street and start to wake up a bit. The faster I walk and the angrier with myself I become – I should not have told Adam about the baby – the more defensive I also begin to feel. I've moved a whole house on my own today, with no help from anyone else bar Adam taking Izzie out and the men I've paid. I've unpacked at the other end. I've been confronted and verbally assaulted by my former lover's wife. I've recovered my daughter from our old house and discovered her 'witchcraft' is most definitely escalating out of control and now, *now* I'm going to go and remove voodoo dolls from a chimney. You couldn't make this up.

I laugh out loud in desperation, but all I can hear are my footsteps and my breath becoming shorter. I round the corner and pass the back gate to Fox Cottage, before marching right up to the front door and knocking. I wait, but there is no answer. Their car is still here, so they are blatantly in. I tut angrily. I know exactly what they are doing right now: peeping from behind a curtained window – there are some new ones hanging in the small sitting room and the upstairs left bedroom which I suspect is now theirs – and deciding to ignore me.

The thought of this makes me furious. Trapped in this house for the best part of thirty years, and now I actually *need* to get in, I can't. I step back and look at it. Nothing. *I know you're there!*

Well, I'm not having this. I'm not coming back *again* for these bloody dolls. I set off determinedly, this time to the metal back gate. I push in through it and crunch over the gravel of the path, past the back door. I shall appear at the dark dining room French windows, knock on the glass and scare the living daylights out of him and his precious Claire. I'll take great pleasure in telling them that I knocked on the front door; didn't they hear me? I smile grimly, but then I glance up and my mouth falls open in shock. They are indeed in my old bedroom that overlooks the back garden, the fields beyond and even our new house eventually – but they haven't bothered putting curtains on the back window yet, having decided no one can really see them from so far away. Except *I* can see Claire and Timothy standing there, clearly visible and laughing. She is naked from the waist up and he is hurrying to do up his shirt as she leans forward and kisses him, causing him to lose his balance slightly at which point he reaches out, grabs her and urgently puts his mouth all over her breasts. I exclaim as she lets her head fall back in ecstasy, closes her eyes then reaches her hands up to thread her fingers into her hair as his head moves lower, out of view. She puts her hands on her breasts and I turn away, disgusted.

How she must have laughed at my earnest warning – written me off as a frumpy, crazy old woman with an equally mad daughter... and where is their *own* child while they are shamelessly revealing themselves to the world like this, might one ask? Who is looking after Rosie while her parents rub my poor Isobel's face in their happiness?

Furious, I turn and march back round through the garden, twigs snapping under my feet, shoving a low hanging branch of the apple tree out of my way, towards the gate. I cannot believe I was so taken in by Claire. I was right the first time: she's not sexy, pretty or attractive but men like Timothy are drawn to her because she looks like she will. And obviously does. How cheap.

I arrive at the front door and, angry enough to be unafraid, push my thumb down on the latch. It is unlocked. I let myself into the small sitting room, which is empty and oddly quiet given they are at it like rabbits upstairs – I was expecting a cacophony of distressing sounds. I march over to the chimney hole, reach up into it, and feel around the space. My fingers grasp at nothing and I'm starting to think this is a wild goose chase, until I brush what feels like the edge of a piece of material. I clasp it – pull… and something tumbles down into my hand in a flurry of dust and bits of grit. I remove two small, crudely made dolls, one red, one white – tied together with a ribbon, facing each other, as if kissing. *Oh, Isobel!*

'Mrs Parkes?'

I whirl round to see Timothy stood at the bottom of the stairs, shirt undone apart from one button at the neck, jeans on, barefoot and staring at me.

'Tim? *Is* someone there?' I hear Claire shout down, and I quickly raise my fingers to my lips and hold the dolls aloft to show him.

His eyes widen and he calls back: 'Um, no. I'm not sure. Hang on – I'll be right back.' He looks at the dolls, swallows nervously and whispers: 'What the hell are they?'

*Timothy has a very overactive imagination.*

I should, of course, be apologising: I am standing in his living room, uninvited – but if you're going to jump in the water you might as well swim. I draw myself tall and raise a disapproving eyebrow. I am the very epitome of authoritative teachers he has spent the most formative years of his life obeying.

'You must learn to lock your front door, Timothy,' I say sternly. 'It's foolish in the extreme to leave it open just because you live in the country now. These were still in the house.' I push the dolls towards him and note that he shrinks back instantly.

'Do those belong to Isobel?'

'Certainly not!' I retort as if he's just offended me. Embarrassed, he looks at the floor. 'I remembered about them at home, a moment ago. They're supposed to absorb negative energy – become a focal point rather than the people living in the house. A priest who performed a service in here for me recommended we try it as a solution, but I didn't want *your* daughter finding them and coming to any harm. They have to be properly disposed of, apparently. The priest was most insistent. It's probably all rubbish, but you get to a stage when you'll try anything, you know?'

'A solution to what?' he says slowly. 'What's been happening in the house?'

'Nothing really to me,' I shrug. 'Izzie is the one who has borne the brunt of it, the poor child.'

'Tim?' shouts a voice from upstairs. 'Are you coming back up?'

'The brunt of what?' He is fixated on me, staring at the dolls in my hands.

I wave a hand, vaguely. 'No, you'll think us ridiculous. It probably *is* ridiculous. Look at me! I'm clutching two dolls that were up the chimney for God's sake!'

'When you say a priest performed a service – do you mean an exorcism?' Pleasingly, he looks as if he's about to throw up.

'I don't want to drag it all up again.' I deliberately don't give him a direct answer. 'But these dolls really are the last of everything. You can put it from your mind now.'

'Well thank you for coming to get them and thinking of Rosie, that's kind of you,' he says sincerely, and for a moment I almost feel a twinge of conscience.

'I'm sorry to have disturbed you; in every sense,' I reply and turn to leave. 'Do take care.'

At least I've got the dolls back, that's all that matters.

As I walk grimly back up the road, however, I pause in the still, night air and turn them over in my hands. They really are horrible, creepy little things. One is obviously the girl; she's got actual human hair – very obviously Izzie's – stitched to her head, God help us. The red one is bald, thankfully. I imagine Izzie leaning over a sleeping Timothy holding a vast pair of scissors, and shudder – thank God she didn't lose the plot *that* much. I'm suddenly reminded of a dreadful book my parents read to me as a child: *Shockheaded Peter* – a collection of ten tales mostly about wilful children and the occasionally fatal consequences of such behaviour. A little boy is warned by his mother not to suck his thumb, but he disobeys while she is out, whereupon a tailor with giant scissors appears in his bedroom and cuts his thumbs clean off. I swallow and stare at the small dolls in my hands. Glancing over my shoulder to check no one is around, I carefully place the girl on the ground, before pulling at one of the stiches on the boy's head, working them loose and looking inside to see what it's stuffed with. It seems to be a mixture of herbs. I pull some of it out and lift it to my fingers to sniff, but whatever aroma they once possessed has long gone. I powder the leaves between my fingers and let the dust sprinkle onto the cold pavement, watching some of it catch on the wind and blow away, before shoving the dolls in my coat pocket.

If only it *was* that easy to affect the will of others. Mind you… I chew my lip thoughtfully at the memory of Timothy's terrified expression… maybe it's not *that* hard.

\*

When I walk back into the new kitchen, Adam is sitting at the table on his phone. 'She wants you to go up,' he says flatly, looking up as I appear next to him, before getting to his feet himself. 'I might make a move now, if that's OK?'

'Of course. Thank you so much for all of your help today.'

'It's no problem.' He hesitates. 'She was insistent that her bedroom door stay unlocked. I said to her, "No one is trying to keep you here against your will, we only ever do it when you *ask* us to".'

I sigh. 'I can't deny I sleep a lot better when I know she's safely contained in her room, though.'

Adam looks at me sympathetically, 'I know. It's so hard, Eve, but what can we do? She's thirty-four years old. Maybe she'll surprise us and have a really good night.'

I try to smile. God bless him for his continued optimism and patience. As he goes to pass me, I take his arm. 'Hang on in there, Adam. He's no threat to you.'

He swallows. I see the apple bob in his thin throat. 'I just want him gone again. All he had to do was stay in the past, where he belongs. It's not much to ask, really, is it?'


I think about that as I climb the stairs to Izzie's new room. He's right – it isn't. As I walk in, Izzie's sat bolt upright in bed, waiting for me.

'Did you get them?'

I shake my head apologetically. 'I only found one of them, darling. This girl doll. Are you sure there were two there? I looked and looked?'

I pass the single doll over and lay it down on the duvet in front of her.

She picks it up, clutches it to her and strokes the hair, worriedly. 'But they were together, *tied* together.'

I don't say anything for a moment. 'Well, at least you've got one back. Won't that do?'

'No. You have to bathe them in salt to remove the disassociations with any living person, then dismantle or burn or bury it,' she says, distracted. 'I don't understand how one was there without the other. It doesn't make any sense. Maybe someone else found it?'

'I don't see how, Izzie? Only you knew they were there.'

She looks at me, frightened. 'You didn't destroy it, did you? Promise me, Mum?'

'I promise,' I say truthfully. 'You need to get some sleep, my darling. It's been a long day. You're safe and Timothy is safe – I've just seen him and he's *fine*.'

She smiles suddenly at that – the sweetest, happiest smile. 'I can't believe he's just down the road!' She shakes her head in excitement and snuggles down under the duvet. 'Can you turn my light off, please, when you go? Good night, Mummy.'

'Good night, Isobel. Sleep well.'

Once I'm safely back downstairs, I open the draw to the sideboard to reveal the red doll. I need a better place than this to keep it. Somewhere Izzie won't find him.

This situation is already everything I worried it was going to be – after one day. What happens next? Now that Timothy's back, will that be enough for her? Will she be satisfied with worshipping him from afar? I hardly think so. It is only going to become worse and worse – and more painful for her. I cannot allow this disturbance to continue. It *must* stop here. I pick up the doll. I genuinely do not believe desecrating this scrap of sewn material will have an effect on anything at all – except my mood. And yet the force of my grip sends another puff of cranial dust into the air.

Well now. He's really not very robust at all…

# CHAPTER TWELVE

## Claire

Tim looks at his watch and chucks the books he's holding back in the packing box rather than on the shelves. 'Can we go now? We've done another hour. Or shall we stay and pick up where we left off before we were interrupted?' He grabs my arm as I pass him, but I pull it back.

'The moment's passed, don't you think? I don't fancy any more neighbours popping round and letting themselves in, halfway through.' I shudder. 'Which ones were they by the way? Just so when I meet them I can die of embarrassment that they've probably heard us having sex?'

'I don't remember his name, sorry. I'm sure he didn't hear anything at all and I've locked the door now, but fine,' he sighs, 'let's just go then, I'm properly cold anyway.'

'But it's still pretty early,' I look around us at the mess of our belongings strewn everywhere around the bedroom, 'and we've got so much to do.'

'You said let's wait until we've painted in here though.' He nods at the walls.

'Well, yes, but we could at least move some of the boxes out so there's a bit more space to get started tomorrow.'

'Fine, I'll put them in Rosie's room.' He picks one up and I follow him out onto the landing. 'I just want to go back, I'm tired.'

'Hang on a minute.' I change my mind. 'I *might* want to freshen up Rosie's room too. Can't the stuff just go on the other side for now?' I nod at the door, beyond which lies the empty three-storey part of the house. I walk up to it, throw back the bolt and yank it open. The vast hallway beyond echoes as I step up and onto the wooden floor, reaching for the switch and blinking as a vicious strip light on the ceiling flickers into life.

'Bloody hell.' I wince. 'I don't remember seeing "interrogation area" on the particulars. We just need to get ourselves a wooden chair, duct tape and a rope, and we'll be all set.'

I look back at Tim who has put the box back down and is glancing around the space nervously – peering at the doorways to the two dark bedrooms on our left and right, and the narrow stairway between them leading to the third floor above. 'I hate this bit of the house,' he says suddenly. 'I stayed over once when I was seeing Izzie – I'd had a row with Mum and Dad – and Mrs Parkes put me in that bedroom there.' He nods at the door to my right. 'This is going to sound crazy, but I felt the room didn't want me there. It didn't mean me any harm, as such, but was just hostile – like I was intruding.'

'The room itself made you feel like that?' I repeat.

He nods. 'It took me ages to get to sleep, but when I woke up in the middle of the night, I couldn't move – it was like I was pinned down to the bed with something really heavy on top of me. I could see there was nothing there, but I couldn't do anything. I was terrified.'

I put my head on one side sympathetically. 'Poor thing. That's called sleep paralysis. It's when your mind "wakes up" before your body does and you try to move, but can't, for a second or two, until it all catches up with itself.'

'It lasted a lot longer than that. It was more like a good minute or two,' he says. 'I couldn't breathe properly; something was definitely pressing down on my chest. I knew I was awake because I saw a figure walking down the road outside, behind the curtains, but there was nothing I could do. I couldn't scream, nothing.' He swallows. 'In this country it's called an *incubus* – a sleeping demon that lies on your chest. Lots of other cultures think it's a night hag – a witch that sits on you and sends you nightmares.'

I snort. 'Eve Parkes was unkind to me earlier tonight, but I think it's a bit harsh to call her a night hag.'

He doesn't laugh. 'You didn't hear what I said, did you?'

He takes a deep breath and steps into the bedroom, switching the light on. It's a manic bright pink, not in the least restful, but otherwise a very average room. The window is right in front of us; but it's hard to notice anything but the colour of the walls.

'We used to call this the bubblegum room,' Tim says, unnecessarily, as I look at it in disbelief, then up at the thick polystyrene ceiling tiles. The whole look is completed by the white Formica built-in wardrobe… this one has faux gold handles – luxury – and a peach-fringed lampshade that I'm not surprised Eve has left behind.

'See? I saw someone walk past behind the curtains that night,' Tim repeats. 'I *definitely* saw them… and we're a floor up, aren't we?' he adds triumphantly.

*He's actually serious.* 'I honestly think sleep paralysis is quite a common phenomenon,' I say gently, 'but you know what? It doesn't matter that this side of the house creeps you out – you don't have to sleep over here. We already said we're going to keep that door locked, so Rosie can't go wandering around.' I walk over and rub his arm. 'Try to relax a bit. As soon as I can get a locksmith, I'll get him to put an extra bolt on it, OK?'

I expect him to rebuke me for taking the piss or being patronising, but in fact, he nods and shivers. 'I don't even want to put the boxes out here, if that's OK.'

'Sure. If it makes you feel better.'

He looks at me. 'Can't you feel anything?'

I raise an eyebrow. 'Like what? A funny atmosphere or something?'

'I'm not sure what I mean really; a negative energy – a sense of hopelessness?'

I laugh at that, I can't help it – and he looks wounded. 'Yes! I bloody do!' I say. 'This place is a shithole and I've got to spend the next year here making it look pretty because you gave all of my money away – of course I feel a sense of hopelessness!'

He looks down at his feet. I've broken my earlier promise already.

'Sorry,' I say instantly. 'Come on.' Grabbing his sleeve, I flick the harsh light off and pull him back through the door into the middle bit as we plunge into darkness. I throw the bolt across while he shivers awkwardly and rubs his arms again.

'It's really rattled your cage, all of this, hasn't it?' I say, looking at him more carefully. 'It was unsettling to find Izzie just standing in the living room like that, but like you said – you probably left the front door open.'

'Oh, I'm not worried about *her* at all,' he says quickly, 'but yes, we do need to get into the habit of locking up. We can't just leave it because we live in the country now.'

'Very true,' I agree. 'Come on – just leave the boxes. Let's get you home.'

'We *are* home,' he says bleakly.

There's an uncomfortable silence and I clear my throat. 'Can we please not descend into a pit of gloom, Tim? I'm doing my best to stay upbeat. Help me out here, OK?'

It's his turn to apologise. 'Sorry. You're right. I'll shut up now.'

'That'd be good, thanks. Let's get back to your mum and dad's,' I say pointedly. 'We've all had enough excitement for one day. Where did I put my bag?' I look around me. 'I have no idea where it is.' I start to wander around looking on top of boxes, and Tim follows me.

'You didn't leave it in the kitchen?'

'No, because I took a phone call from your mum upstairs in the front spare bedroom…' I pause. 'Ah! Look – there it is!' I spy it through the door to Rosie's room, lying on the floor. As I bend over to pick it up, Tim follows me, walks into the en suite and with the vocabulary of a man who has an eight-year-old and now automatically moderates his language even when she's not there, announces: 'I'll just have a wee before we go.' He still leaves the door wide open as he unzips his fly, though. Not all habits die.

I roll my eyes and look away, wandering around the bedroom as I wait for him, glancing at the birds on the walls before something on the floor catches my eye. It's a small stubby piece of candle with what look like thorns shoved into it. I bend again to pick it up. It's only when it's in my hands and I twist it directly under the light that I can see it has been intricately carved.

'What's that?' says Tim over my shoulder, having finished, and looking at it warily.

'A candle.'

'I mean what's it got all over it?'

'I know. Odd, isn't it?'

'Where did you find it?' he says quickly.

'Just on the floor. Why?'

'No reason.' He reaches out and takes it from me. 'I'll chuck it. I don't want Rosie finding that – she might hurt herself.'

'OK.' I watch him shove it in his back pocket.

'Any other weird things like that you find – will you give them to me?' He looks around him and his gaze settles on the tree and birds. 'I want to paint over all of that too.' He points at it. 'They creep me out.'

'You're kidding me.' I'm amazed. 'Rosie will be *gutted* if you do that. At least let her see them for herself and make the call. I've already told her about them.' I watch him exhale heavily. 'Honestly,

Tim – they're just birds. I'm not having this for the next *year* that we're here. Calm it down and take a breath, yeah?'

'Do you think we should get a priest in to bless this place?'

I blink, I'm so astonished at what he says. 'A priest to do *what*?'

'Bless it,' he says awkwardly. 'Get rid of any negativity – and make it safe.'

'What on *earth* are you talking about?' I exclaim.

He clears his throat, widens his eyes like he's just appreciated how that sounded out loud, and exhales slowly. 'You're right – this is just stupid. I'll feel better in the morning. It's been a very long day.'

I take his hand. 'I know this place holds memories, but like you said to me – it's just a building. That's all.'

He hesitates – then nods. 'You're right. You're absolutely right. I need a massive dose of grow the hell up. I was a kid the last time I was in here and I'm not that person now. You know, Adam, Izzie and I did a séance right here in this very room.' He laughs when he speaks, but it's an anxious sound.

I roll my eyes. 'What were you thinking?'

'Isn't it just the sort of thing you do when you're seventeen and a bit bored?'

I shake my head. 'Nope. I've never done one.'

'Maybe it's a living in the country thing.' He shrugs. 'We did the lot; waited until it was dark, lit candles… Adam and Izzie put their hands on the planchette and it began to spell "Michael" – which was Izzie's Dad's name. Izzie started crying and saying: "Is that you, Daddy?" I was *terrified* and I almost wet myself when it spelt out "Yes". I couldn't say a thing. Adam was really calm though, he took her other hand and told her not to be afraid.'

\*

'"It's comforting. This is OK," he said, and looked at her. "We can stop this any time you want, all right?" He took charge pretty much straight away.

'She nodded, before asking out loud: "What do you want to say to me, Daddy?"

'The planchette spelt k-i-s-s-e-s and then h-e-a-r-t-s. Then it spelt h-e-a-r-t-s again and again, getting faster and faster. Their hands were going mad over the board when Adam gasped and suddenly sat back, letting go and just staring at Izzie. "You're glowing!" he said, in amazement. "Oh My God – I can actually see your aura! That's incredible! It's violet… and blue!" He reached his hand out towards her then rubbed his fingers together very gently, like something tangible was slipping between them. His eyes widened and he slowly pointed at her head. "And you've got a halo! An actual *halo*! That's crazy!" he started to laugh.

'I didn't think it was funny. I made myself look at Izzie, but the only abnormal thing I could see, was how still she was sitting. When she suddenly jumped like something had touched the back of her neck, I leapt out of my skin too. She whipped round and looked over her shoulder – which *really* freaked me out – only for her hand to start moving again, apparently against her will, because she gasped. The planchette was flying around the letters a-n-g-e-l, a-n-g-e-l, a-n-g-e-l. I thought her dad was trying to tell her she was his angel, or that she wasn't to worry, he was in heaven; something like that – but then it slid suddenly and it started spelling h-a-h-a-h-a-h-a.

'There was nothing comforting about that.

'Izzie started to panic straight away. I could hear the fear in her voice when she said "Daddy?" She looked up at us, worriedly. I didn't do anything, but Adam put his hand back over hers only for it to move to P-A-U-L. The second it landed it on the L Izzie screamed and snatched her hand back. I jumped up as well. I couldn't believe it was Paul Jones. It was like he'd been *waiting* for us.

'Only Adam still had his hand on the planchette. "We have to say goodbye!" he said desperately, "that's right, isn't it, Izzie? Otherwise the gate stays open?"

'She nodded – she had turned completely white – and we watched Adam fight to move the planchette to "goodbye". It was like he was pushing a mountain. He shouted: "Thank you for speaking to us, but we need to go now!" and managed to somehow force the planchette across the board, before collapsing onto the floor, and looking up at the ceiling, panting.

'I honestly don't think I took a breath the whole time.

'"We need to blow the candles out now." Adam sat back up quickly. "Do we wrap the board in a cloth next? I can't remember?" He looked at Izzie, his hand pushing up through his hair. "My mind has gone blank. I saw *him* – or someone – stood next to you." He pointed in Isobel's and my direction, and I jumped to my feet instantly, looking around me, terrified.

'"Wow, that was scary." He let his head drop. "We shouldn't have done this in the house. What were we thinking?"

'"Can we burn the board, so nothing can get back through?" I suggested, flattening up against the wall. I wanted to vomit – but Adam looked at me like I was mad. "You never, ever burn a board, Tim. You'll be haunted forever if you do that. You have to bury it – and in a different location to the planchette."

'"Some people say it doesn't matter, once you've made the connection with the spirit world, it can never be undone," Izzie whispered. "Your fate will be bound to the other side forever."

'I wanted to cry. Why the hell was she telling me that now? Fat lot of good that was! "You said it was safe!" I stammered, but she ignored me.

'"Do you think it was all Paul Jones?" she asked Adam. "Do you think my daddy was there at all?"

'"Yes, I do," Adam said earnestly. "I really believe that, Iz. He got pushed out, but he was there. There's no doubt in my mind."'

*

Tim looks at me and swallows nervously.

'I don't know if I agree that it was her father, but Adam seemed certain *someone* was there.' He looks around the room and exhales slowly.

'Right,' I say eventually. 'Well firstly, I can't believe that, even as a kid, you thought that any of that might have been real.' I turn around and start to head off downstairs, Tim following close after me. 'There have been about a hundred studies showing that Ouija boards are down to something called the ideomotor effect, which is basically when you make movements unconsciously – almost involuntarily – when you're asked a question to which you already know the answer.'

'Sorry?' says Tim, looking doubtful.

'Like when you're doing a quiz and someone asks something random like "By what name is *La Gioconda* better known?"'

'Er... I want to say *Mona Lisa*?' He sounds unsure.

'Exactly!' I say delightedly. 'You didn't know you knew it but it's locked away in your subconscious. Same principle with Ouija boards.' I reach the bottom of the stairs and turn to face him. 'Adam and Izzie already knew who they'd be thinking about and subconsciously moved the planchette to spell it out. Although it was probably even simpler than that. I expect Adam just did it to try and be "comforting" to Izzie because he fancied her.'

'Hmm.' Tim stops short for a moment. 'That has *literally* never occurred to me until now. Maybe that was why he spelt out "Paul", because he knew it would freak *me* out?'

I shrug modestly, feeling secretly rather pleased with myself. 'Probably. Plus, loads of other studies have shown when you blindfold Ouija users and flip the board around so they don't know where the letters are, the planchette spells out gibberish, because the users haven't got sight to guide them to the right letters. If it were "spirits" you'd get clear answers anyway, right? It's complete rubbish.'

'You really should think again about your psychology degree. It's not fair that you never got to do it. We should look into how we could make it happen,' Tim says after a pause.

I shake my head. 'It'd be too expensive now – and it's not practical; definitely not this year, that's for sure. I think I would have enjoyed university – but my sister needed me more, and I've done all right without it, so…' I shrug. 'Shit happens.'

He reaches out and takes my hand, giving it a supportive squeeze. 'You honestly weren't ever tempted to use a Ouija board yourself?'

I shake my head. 'No – never. I read quite a lot about spiritual stuff – mediums and that kind of thing – after Mum and Dad died. I think some people really want to believe stuff like that, to the point where they genuinely believe they've heard or seen something supernatural. I find *that* interesting, but only because it shows how powerful the brain can be – but it's also why I think when your brain stops – everything stops – that's it. Game over.' I shrug. 'No one more than me would like to believe in there being something beyond this world, but there just isn't.' My smile becomes a little sadder and Tim hugs me, kissing the top of my head.

'I'm sorry, now I've upset you, talking about this.' He hesitates. 'I *have* sometimes wondered if it had anything to do with the acid we did.'

I wrinkle my nose. 'How can I have been with you for ten years and not known you did acid? You'd have been about twelve, surely, when it was all about raves and smiley faces. I know you smoked dope at school; I didn't know you'd done more than that?'

He looks embarrassed. 'It really only was once or twice in the sixth form – and that time with Adam and Iz.'

It's all starting to make a lot more sense now. 'So what you actually mean is when you were all seventeen and eighteen and tripping your tits off you did a Ouija board. No wonder you were scared stupid.' I snort. 'Come on, let's go. I'd have been more worried I'd unlocked a part of my brain I wasn't going to be able to shut back off if I'd been you. I read an article recently about working professionals using LSD to treat depression and mental breakdowns.' I skirt over the fact that I was scanning to see if there were any helpful pointers for how to handle what Tim might be going through. 'It suggested that it can help shrink down your sense of self,' I'm also very careful not to use the word *selfish* or *ego*, 'and make you feel more connected with the world around you. Apparently LSD can have a really profound effect on some people and they can experience "memories" or echoes of a trip for some considerable time afterwards.' I cross the room to turn the lights off and wait until Tim walks past me.

'I honestly only did it a handful of times, I promise,' he says.

I shut the front door behind us and diplomatically don't comment. Bloody boarding schools. It was probably rife for most of the time he was there, not just in the last year. Thirty grand a year to mess your kids up forever. What's *wrong* with people?

Scrabbling through my bag in the dark car, however, I realise I've not got *all* of the answers.

'Don't go yet, my phone is missing,' I exclaim in frustration. 'What's wrong with me today?' I look up at the house and nudge him. 'Hey – look at that! It's in the front spare room – I can see it lighting up! Someone must be calling me.' I watch as the glow in the room dulls and returns back to black. 'You stay here, I'll go and get it.'

'You don't want me to?' Tim eyes the window nervously.

'You're all right,' I say kindly. 'Thanks, but I really don't mind.'

I unclip the seat belt, open the door and using the overhead light, search on the unfamiliar keyring, before selecting the front door key as Tim shivers in the cold.

'I'll be right back.'

I climb out and walk back up to the door, unlocking it and pushing it open, as it judders, catching on the tiles and swings wide. I throw the hall light on and flick the small sitting room switch. As I walk into the room, I catch my reflection in the dining room window, visible through the door on the far side of the room, and do a double take, before tutting at my own foolishness and bounding upstairs. The landing creaks as I walk into the front bedroom and put the light on, glancing down to see Tim waiting in the car below, engine still running – and there indeed is my phone, on top of a box. I pick it up and press the home key to see who rang, but I have no missed calls. I also don't have a single new notification. I frown, pick it up and slide it into my back pocket, turn and flick the light off.

It's as I reach the top of the stairs that I suddenly feel it. An alertness. I'm not alone.

It makes no sense whatsoever, but the house is noticeably different; quietly wary, whispering, watching. It didn't feel like this at *all* when Tim was in here with me a second ago. I catch my breath and swing round, staring over my shoulder, my heart starting to thump as I focus on the locked door leading to the other side of the house. In my mind, I see the door bang open. Isobel is framed in the doorway – she hurtles towards me, eyes wide, hair streaming and arms reaching out, fingers splayed, ready to push on my chest and shove me backwards down the stairs. I gasp aloud and blink.

There is no one there. The door is still closed.

'Isobel?' I whisper and feel the hairs on the back of my neck stand up. 'Are you there?' I *knew* I heard him talking to a female voice earlier. Has she let herself in again after all? My breathing is so shallow I can hear everything as I wait… but the house is completely silent.

I don't know I'm going to do it, but I turn and run down the stairs, clattering down so quickly I am panting by the time I get to the bottom. In two strides I'm across the sitting room, flick the light off, bang the door shut behind me, turn the hall light off and escape back onto the forecourt, to find Tim talking to Adam, who has pulled up alongside our car in the van again.

'Of course, mate, it's really no problem at all.' Tim is doing his jolly, confident chap voice. You'd think he hadn't a care in the world. 'We'd be happy to help, honestly. I'm just sorry you had to go to the trouble of moving it all out only to put it all back again!'

'I don't mind that at all. Thank you, Tim. This is really kind of you.' He looks up to see me approaching the car, smiles politely, says 'good night', climbs back into his van and drives off.

I'm still shaking as I pull the seat belt around my body.

'Freezing, isn't it?' Tim says, noticing. 'Got your phone? Hang on, let me check I've got mine, now I think of it.'

As he fumbles around in his pockets, I glance up at the house again. *Did* someone – more accurately, Isobel – touch my phone? Is that what made it light up? Or is that a completely absurd thing to think? We pull away, and I look at the screen again. I do a second search: there's not a single new message, or email. Nothing that should have made the screen light up – but have I missed something? Does a WhatsApp or Facebook notification make it light up, too? I've never thought to check before; I've never needed to.

'What did Adam want?' I chew my lip as the connection drops out and the screen freezes.

'He was asking if he might use the barn to finish a painting and some prep he's got to get done for an exhibition he's self-funded. He used to rent it as a studio from Mrs Parkes, apparently.'

I look up. 'I know, *I* told you that earlier, remember? You said no, though, right?'

Tim glances at me. 'Well, I explained the builders were starting a week today, and he said that was fine, that's all he needs. The space he was going to isn't available yet and he's not got any room at home, apparently.'

'Tim!' I exclaim. 'You should have asked me first. I don't want some bloke we don't know coming and going!'

'He's not a bloke we don't know, he's an old friend who asked for a favour. It's not like we're using it. It's just a week?'

'Have you given him a key?'

'He said the French doors in the barn don't lock properly anyway, so he can just let himself in and out.'

'Great,' I say incredulously. 'Well I'll add that to the locksmith's list.' I begin an online search immediately.

'He didn't have to tell us that, he was being nice. Not everyone I know is a dick, Claire.' He sighs sadly.

'Fine.' I put a hand up. 'He can work there until the builders start. But that's it.'

I fire an email off to the only locksmith locally who boasts an 8 a.m. to 8 p.m. response window, entitled 'emergency help required'. I'm getting that house secured first thing.

'Are you listening? What did you say that phenomenon was called?'

'Sorry?' I look up from the screen to see Tim is waiting for an answer to something else. 'The phenomenon? Oh – you mean the ideomotor effect?' I respond automatically. *Funnily enough, Tim, if you'd been inside a second ago, you would have seen it in motion – no pun intended – after my legs absolutely took off on their own.*

'Have you still got a connection? Could you do a quick Google search on sleep paralysis if you're looking at stuff? I want to know more about what you were just saying upstairs. You really think it can be simply explained?' he asks a moment later.

'Of course I do. "REM sleep can sometimes occur when you're awake",' I read aloud. '"REM is the deep stage of sleep when the brain is very active and dreams often occur. The body is unable to move, apart from the eyes and muscles used in breathing, possibly to stop you from acting out your dreams and hurting yourself. In many cases, sleep paralysis is a one-off event that occurs in someone who is otherwise healthy, but can be triggered by sleep deprivation, stress or trauma. It can also be accompanied by hallucinations, a feeling of pressure on the chest or the sensation of a shadowy figure entering one's room or lurking outside one's window. These hallucinations are driven by fear and REM-induced sexual arousal." There, see?' I glance at him. 'You were just a frightened, slightly horny teenager who woke up too soon. Nothing to do with demons whatsoever – sleeping or otherwise.'

He snorts. 'Thanks. Succinctly put.'

'"It can also be accompanied by hallucinations, a feeling of pressure on the chest or the sensation of a shadowy figure entering one's room or lurking outside one's window",' I repeat. 'And that's your person behind the curtain walking down the road a storey up, too.'

'I *have* only experienced it that once,' he concedes.

'Coincidentally around the same time as you were doing acid,' I remark, checking my mail again. Still nothing.

He shifts awkwardly. 'Yeah… it was a pretty messed-up period for me. I honestly didn't do it loads though, I didn't have a problem or anything. It was just a stupid school thing. Everyone was doing it. You all right?' he glances at me. 'You seem a bit preoccupied.'

'Just waiting for a locksmith to email me back, that's all.' Regardless of anything else, she *was* in the sitting room earlier and I do not intend to find Isobel standing in my house unannounced, ever again.

'Have you honestly never had any unusual experiences?' Tim challenges me. 'Never thought you'd seen something as a child?'

'No! I haven't. Tim, *please!*' I look up from my screen, irritated. 'Like I said, I'd love to know for sure there's something more out there, call that whatever you want, spirits, ghosts, an afterlife. But it's crap. There just isn't, and that's that.'

# CHAPTER THIRTEEN

## Eve

I wake up with a jolt, confused by where I am, in the unfamiliar shape of my new bedroom. Turning my head on the pillow, I reach out to the alarm clock lying on the carpet and blearily squint at the time. 1.36 a.m. I drop the clock and automatically pick up the monitor instead. It's completely silent, no flickering lights. I turn onto my left side, then roll over and out onto the carpet, before pushing myself first to all fours then stiffly up onto my feet, having to place my hands down on my thighs before I can straighten up. I need to make time to build my bed tomorrow. I can't sleep on a mattress on the floor at my age – suppose I was to get stuck down here, unable to get to my feet – just lolling around like a Weeble until someone finds me? The shame.

I stagger to the doorway and take the two steps across the small hall into the bathroom. Blinking in the bright light I promised to leave on all night for Izzie, should she need to come and find me, I sit down heavily on the loo for a wee, yawn and glance around the strange, warm and inoffensively bland, cream room. I feel as if I'm in a hotel and must be going home tomorrow. This is going to take some time to sink in.

As I'm washing my hands and drying them, I wonder why I've woken up. I don't normally, unless I'm disturbed. I emerge back onto the landing and look up the small flight of stairs in front of me to Izzie's master suite. The door is closed at the top. If I go up and open it, I risk waking her if she's actually asleep. I hesitate, shuffle back to my bedroom, sink onto the mattress and slide my legs under the duvet. I pick up the monitor again and hold it right to my ear. I can't hear a thing. Not even her breathing. I place it down on the carpet, turn onto my back and stare up at the ceiling, one hand on my brow. It's no good, I'm going to have to check on her.

As I start to creep up her stairs, I realise how blissfully creak-free with newness they are; unlike my knees, which sound like beanbags stuffed full of silly putty and ball bearings... squishing and rubbing with every stair I climb. It would be impossible for me to sneak up on anyone these days.

On the small landing, I reach out and turn the handle. The door pushes luxuriantly over the thick, new carpet and, peering into the gloom, I can see the outline of her bed, the doll's house, her chest of drawers... but one drawer is hanging open as if someone has been having a good old rummage around. I deliberate for a moment – but walk into the room, padding across to the edge of her bed. It's empty.

My heart sinks with resignation but my adrenaline surges. It's a horrible combination of sensations. Fuck, fuck, fuck. I must have disturbed because I heard her leaving the house. Oh *Isobel*! I hate it so much when she does this. I can't stop her from coming and going as she pleases – she's a grown woman – but she has no idea what it does to me when she disappears off in the middle of the bloody night. I won't sleep now until she's home and I am so, so tired. I want to weep with the unfairness of it all. Just one night? Couldn't I have had *one* night? I reach out and rest my hand lightly on the sheet, in the dent where her body has lain. It's cold.

I should have tried harder to persuade her to let me lock her in. I thought the bruises on my wrists were impressive enough to have shocked her into contrition, but obviously not. I should have used a little more eyeshadow; I was too conservative with my efforts. It's only when I am beyond exhausted and need to know that she is safe so that I can properly rest, that I fake them, or like tonight, embellish what is already there – because what if she gets confused and goes back to Fox Cottage by mistake rather than remembering she lives here now? I moan aloud at the thought and then almost pass out with shock as someone gives a little shriek of their own, right behind me. I swing round to see Isobel flattened back against the wall in her nightie, next to the now-open en-suite door, visibly shaking.

'Mum?' she gasps. 'What are you doing? You scared me half to death.'

'Oh darling, I'm so sorry!' I'm appalled to have frightened her so badly. 'I was just checking on you – and you weren't there!'

'Because I was in my bathroom!' she says perfectly reasonably. 'That's all. Urrgghhh. I feel sick.' She puts her hand on her stomach and half bends over. For a minute I think she might be about to pass out or actually throw up on the brand-new carpet we've had for less than twenty-four hours.

'Of course you were, I'm so, so sorry. Here, come and get back into bed.' I hold a hand out to her and she takes it. She's breathing fast and feels warm to the touch – even a little clammy.

'Are you all right, sweet?' I ask. 'You don't think you're coming down with something?'

She shakes her head. 'I'm OK.'

*Unless – have you just run home from somewhere and that's why you're hot and your bed is cold?*

I don't ask her of course. Just think it privately as I help her climb back in and tuck the duvet round her as her head sinks back into the pillow.

'That's better. You go back to sleep now, angel. I can't apologise enough for scaring you like that.'

'I don't understand,' she says bewildered. 'I only woke up because I heard *you* moving around downstairs.'

'Well I'm so pleased you were getting some good rest.' I beam. 'That's wonderful! Maybe things will be a lot easier for you in this house than they were before?'

She nods and yawns. 'I think so. Good night, Mummy.'

'Good night, Isobel.' I say softly. 'Sweet dreams.'

She has already closed her eyes as I creep back down to my own room and get back onto my mattress, picturing her picking her way across the dark, freezing fields behind the house in boots and her thin nightdress, wild hair flowing. Please God she didn't go to *their* house to peer in at the windows.

Or at the very least, let no one have seen her. And thank the Lord, she's back in bed now – safe. I find I'm unable to debate the issue any more and as good as pass out myself.

I wake in the morning to the sound of Isobel *singing* and the clatter of a cereal bowl and spoon as she makes herself some breakfast. I appear in the kitchen to discover she has in fact laid the table for both of us – she won't have washed any of the stuff before getting it out of the packing boxes, but never mind. She turns round and flashes me a smile of heart-stopping beauty. 'Hello, Mama!'

*Mama?* 'Hello, darling.' I regard her warily. 'You seem very happy this morning. Did you sleep well?'

'I really did!' She beams. 'And I *am* happy!'

I don't ask why. I don't want to know the answer, or rather, I don't want to hear the answer. Instead, I sit down and watch silently, sipping the tea she's set down in my place, as she moves about the room with purpose. She has a high colour to her cheeks and her eyes are glittering. If I didn't know better, I'd say she was feverish, but she sits down opposite me and hungrily wolfs a bowl of cereal as if she hasn't eaten for a week.

'I need to go,' she remarks glancing at her phone. 'I'm working today.'

'Are you sure?' I don't want to sound sceptical but I think I would have remembered if she was. 'I thought you weren't in until tomorrow?'

'No, it's certainly today.'

I don't argue the point any more and can't help but brighten at this unexpected gift of a morning to myself. I might have a nice bath before I start the rest of my unpacking.

'Text me if you want anything from town while I'm in there – for tea I mean – and I'll bring it back with me later.' She stands up and carries her bowl to the dishwasher before turning and coming to give me a kiss. 'Have a good day. I love you.'

'I love you, too.' I watch her walk from the room and listen to her start singing again as she puts on her coat and shoes. *Pick up something for tea?* She has never, ever said such a thing. I hear the front door open.

'Byeeee!' she calls cheerfully, but before I can answer, it bangs shut again.

I put my tea down carefully.

Well now, this is all wrong. Yes, last night she saw Timothy, but *with* Claire. I told her they have Rosie – that Tim hasn't returned for her. She should be devastated, not euphoric.

My mind returns to the bed I caught her out of last night and I push my chair back slowly, walking into the hall and sliding open the sideboard drawer to retrieve the horrid little boy doll. Whatever is now gathering pace – she's planning something for sure and it seems to all be coming together from the way she's behaving – I'd really rather not have a voodoo doll constructed from Timothy's T-shirt, DNA loaded to the hilt, lying around the house. That's not paranoia, just common sense.

Only, what to do with the ghastly thing? I turn it over in my hand.

*Bathe it in salt to remove all associations to the living person.*

I hesitate, but then tut crossly at myself. As if I don't have enough to do without bulk buying table condiments and then finding something deep enough to submerge it in. This is absurd – I will just throw it away. She'll never know. I pick him up to shove him in the kitchen bin, but pause and find myself deviating off to the downstairs loo. I roughly remove a much larger pinch of the head stuffing than last night; as good as leaving it empty and floppy. Perhaps I will flush away the contents first, then decide what to do with the skin? I release the herbal powder into the bowl, casually watching it land and then float on the surface of the water. I'm reminded suddenly of scattering my father's ashes on top of a cliff, only for the wind to suddenly gust and blow it all back in our faces. Michael laughed and said that was just like my father; I was less amused. I shudder at the memory of struggling to shake him from my hair – much as I did when he was alive, in fact – then jump guiltily as someone knocks on the front door behind me.

Dusting off my hand on my dressing gown, I shove the boy doll at the back of the drawer in the sideboard as I pass – but the whole thing jams in trying to close it; the shoebox I keep the bills in always catches on the frame. I need a better storage box. Cursing under my breath, I'm forced to leave it ajar and open the front door to find Adam on the step in his large parka. Too big, really. It swamps his thin frame and is hardly appropriate. If he was seventeen, perhaps – but not at his age.

'Hello,' I say, surprised. 'You've just missed Izzie, she said she was walking?'

'But she's not working today, I didn't think?' he looks confused. 'I've just come to tell her I can't see her this morning as planned. She's not picking up so I thought I'd pop in.'

From within the kitchen my phone starts to ring with her ringtone. 'That's her now, hang on.' I hurry through to pick it up.

'Hello, darling, is everything OK?' I return to the hall where Adam is waiting patiently, hands in his deep pockets, having closed the front door to stop the heat escaping.

'You've forgotten your purse and your book?' I repeat aloud and Adam rolls his eyes at me good-naturedly. 'The book is on your bed but you don't know where the purse is. OK – no, don't worry, I've got some pennies you can have to buy lunch. Adam is here; I think you were supposed to be seeing him today?' I tut and mouth 'sorry' to Adam. 'Can I ask him to bring the things to work? I don't know – hang on.' I look enquiringly at Adam and he nods. 'He says yes. All right, sweetest. Have a good day.'

I sigh and hang up. 'I'm *so* sorry, Adam.'

'It's fine,' he says and smiles, but he looks terrible: even thinner than usual, with pallid skin, dark shadows, greasy hair, and jeans just visible under the coat that have gone soft and creased from repeated wearing without washing. I think wistfully of my peaceful bath, disappearing off down the plughole before I've even climbed in.

'Tell you what. I'll go get the book from upstairs while you get me your laundry from the van. Let me stick it on while you take Her Majesty what she needs, then come back and have some breakfast. Have you got time? We need to talk about your current living arrangements. You can't sleep in the van at this time of year, Adam.' I speak gently but firmly. 'It's too cold and that's that.' I pat his arm sympathetically and turn on my heels to go upstairs.

Most people by now would have said to me: *Mum, my boyfriend has nowhere to live – could he stay with us for a bit?* I don't think Izzie's noticed, or even still thinks of him as her boyfriend for that matter, despite him referring to the Valentine's Day lunch they had yesterday – the one he very evidentially couldn't afford at all. Poor chap.

I collect the book from her bedside table; she's rereading *Anne of Green Gables* again. Adam is waiting in the hall when I return, holding a large, battered Ikea holdall stuffed full of dark clothes.

'Thank you,' he says, unable to meet my eye for fear of dashing away the last of his pride completely. 'This is really kind of you. I guess I can start a little later this morning.'

'Oh that's great!' I say brightly. 'You've found somewhere to paint then?'

He nods as I pass him the book and a £10 note from the drawer for her lunch. It's too much and she'll lose the change but it's all I've got to hand.

I watch him walk back to the van. I've barely closed the front door when my phone starts to shrill with Izzie's ringtone again. I sigh and pick up with a second bright: 'Hi, darling!'

She's remembered she's working this afternoon, not this morning after all – so in fact, she's just going to come home again.

'I don't know what I was thinking!' she laughs. I can hear her footsteps on the pavement, then the sound of a horn. 'Oooh! Here's Adam – he can just bring me back. It's all worked out perfectly! See you in a minute, Mum!'

I close my eyes briefly as I hang up. She has no idea. None at all. It hasn't worked out perfectly in the slightest. Adam's got work to do, I've got a house to unpack. She really doesn't get it.

The phone rings *again*.

'What, Isobel?' I pick up, trying not to snap.

'All right…' she sounds injured at the tone I've obviously not hidden well enough. 'Adam said you're making breakfast. Can you put some on for me, that's all I was going to say. You're doing a cooked one, I mean?'

I am now, it appears. 'Fine. What do you want?'

'I'll have a bacon sandwich please, with an egg in it. Thanks, Mum. Oooh! We're here now! Hey open the door and see!'

I'm so used to doing *everything* asked of me – I automatically obey before I remember the blasted drawer is still open and the doll's legs are visible. She's standing on the doorstep, phone pressed against her ear delightedly.

'It's me!' she exclaims, 'talking *and* here!' She hangs up as Adam appears behind her.

'So you are!' I shove the drawer desperately with my hip – mercifully, the contents loosen and the box drops low enough for the drawer to bang shut this time. I herd them straight through into the kitchen. 'Come and tell me how many bits of bacon you both want!'

I'm pathetically pleased with my diversion as they obediently follow me. In another life I probably could have been an excellent spy. I could have done a *lot* of things.

Once we've all eaten and Adam is finishing a cup of tea with Izzie in the sitting room, I sneak off – supposedly to wash up but actually to retrieve the doll… only I'm too late.

It's gone.

I swear under my breath and slam the drawer shut again. That's the thing about Izzie. She appears away with the fairies, and often she is, but then she will have these maddening moments of lucidity and competence when you least want her to. It's utterly infuriating.

'Mum!' she calls. 'I've knocked over my cup. Have you got a tea towel?'

'Don't touch it,' I shout back. 'If you scrub it you'll wreck the carpet. I'll sort it out.' I swear again, less quietly this time, and march back into the kitchen to snatch up a cloth. Not even twenty-four hours. She's unbelievable.

When Michael died, Izzie understandably wanted to sleep in my bed. I was grateful for the comfort, at first, but God help me, it wore off very bloody quickly. She's an appalling bedfellow – always has been – and I started to resent the poor girl when she'd appear next to me in the wee small hours: a motionless little figure whispering 'Mummy' – because I didn't even get respite from her at night. It got worse after the shooting. Understandably she didn't want to leave my side, especially at bedtime, and when she was ill, it was maddening; she'd chase me round the bed, coughing in my face, dragging me into a feverish neck hold, jerking, thrashing around, often turning direction wildly on the pillow on the cusp of sleep and smashing her skull onto the bridge of my nose as she did so. I would just about manage to hold it together, digging my nails hard into the palm of my hand to stop myself from losing my temper completely and shouting at her to lie still because I was so desperate to sleep and escape my day. Hot tears of frustration and guilt would run down my cheeks into my ears as I lay there wishing someone, anyone, was there to share the shift with me.

I love her so much but, my God, it was tough. And here I am – fifty-six-years old now – and not only am I *still* on the go with her all the time, I *still* I haven't learnt how to do the right thing either; I should have thrown that doll away while I had the chance, instead of playing with something that doesn't belong to me.

*

I'm putting the tea towel in the brand-new washing machine and frowning at the mass of programme options in the tiny utility room when Adam appears behind me, in his enormous coat.

'I'm off. Listen, Eve, I feel like I should mention, I asked Timothy if I could use the barn at Fox Cottage for one more week until their builders start.'

My jaw must drop, because he says miserably: 'yeah, I know. Selling my soul. Hypocritical beyond belief – all of the above. But I'm desperate. My mate's space hasn't come off and an extra week buys me the chance to look for something else and get finished in time to ship the paintings to that exhibition I told you about.'

'I understand,' I tell him. I don't actually, but it's not my place to tell him what to do when I can't offer him an alternative. 'What a shame you had to clear it all out only to put it back again.'

'It's fine. I'm only putting the easel up. I just want the light really, just to keep the conditions consistent. I should have been finished before now anyway, to be honest.'

'It's done when it's done,' I say kindly.

He smiles. 'Thanks for understanding. It's only for a week anyway. Hopefully they won't even notice I'm there.'

# CHAPTER FOURTEEN

## Claire

'What you two got stashed under the sofa so that you need me the day after moving in, then?' The locksmith grins, folds his arms and looks around the small sitting room. 'The crown jewels?'

'I wish. Although my husband also wants every single lock in the house replaced, so I can see why you might think that.'

The locksmith's smile fades. 'Not really?'

I point up the stairs and mouth 'he can hear us' before putting my finger to my lips and motioning for the locksmith to follow me through into the dining room.

'I know, it sounds a bit mad,' I whisper conspiratorially, 'and I also know the French windows are rotten in the barn and so are some of the downstairs windows in the three-storey bit – I've been round them all properly this morning. I can see that if someone really wants to get in to *either* end, they'll still be able to. All *I* want you to do, is make sure this middle portion of the house is secure. This is the bit we're actually going to live in.'

He shrugs. 'I can do that. You've already got that massive bolt across the door upstairs that joins the house to the three-storey bit, so no one's getting in there. I'll change the front and back door locks, so that only leaves this one here.' He points at the glass-panelled door at the back of the room we're standing in, connecting to the grain store where Adam had his stuff stored – and the barn beyond, where he'll no doubt be painting his messed-up pictures again later. Just as I think that, the light is suddenly dimmed by a van pulling up on the forecourt. I walk to the window and see Adam climb out, open the back of it and start rummaging around inside.

'I can fit a new lock on this frame,' the locksmith has started talking again and I force myself to turn back to him and concentrate, 'but basically, if a burglar really wants to get in here, all he's got to do is smash one of these panes, reach through and undo it from the inside. It's the door that's the problem in this case, not the lock.'

I picture Isobel standing the other side of the glass, rattling the handle. 'I definitely want it done. What about if you change the lock and I'll keep the key someplace else instead then?'

He shakes his head gravely. 'That's a major hazard, Ms Waters. In a house fire, the smoke will overcome you long before you remember where you've hidden the key.'

'OK.' I rub my eyes tiredly. 'I hear what you're saying and I can see it's a waste of money, but can you change the lock anyway? Just as a short-term measure?'

'It's your party.' He shrugs again, adding kindly: 'It ain't like down south here, though. We don't have a massive crime rate. Where have you moved from?'

'Surrey.'

'Near my old stamping ground! I'm a Surbiton boy!'

'No!' I exclaim. 'That's where I'm from! What a small world!' I'm overcome by such a wave of homesickness, I have to sit down on the sofa. 'Do you go back much?'

He shrugs. 'Not as often as I'd like. The journey's a bit meaty for a weekend and I've got two boys a bit older than your girl – you said she was eight, didn't you? Well they get too tired, don't they? All that driving in two days. Anyway, they're Shropshire kids now. I'd go back properly if it were just about me – the South East will always be home – but it's better for them here really. I expect it was what brought you up here too, eh? All this space. Perfect for kids.'

I nod with difficulty. 'Something like that. I'll go and get the kettle on.'

'Now you're talking!' He grins. 'And we'll make sure we really do get you safe as houses, don't you worry. I've got a few bits to get out of the van and we'll get going!'

As he disappears, I go upstairs to see if Tim and his dad want a cup of something.

'Tea break, gentlemen?' I stick my head round Rosie's bedroom door. 'It's officially eleven thirty.'

'I thought as much.' Tony smiles at me, holding a paintbrush. 'I was starting to feel a little bit Winnie the Pooh-ish. My tummy was telling me it needed something in it.'

'Well, I'll see if I can find a biscuit as well as the tea or coffee then. You're making good progress. Promise you won't paint over the mural wall, though?' I look at Tim as I say that, who ignores me.

'No, no – of course not.' Tony wipes his brow. 'I wouldn't want you to think the whole thing is any more than a lick and promise wash, though, Claire.' He puts his brush down. 'But it *will* liven it up for the time being and that's the important thing.' He looks at Tim, who doesn't say a word, just carries on painting. 'Isn't that right, Timothy?'

'If you say so,' Tim replies tersely, and my heart sinks. They've been up here for less than an hour. They can't have fallen out already?

'Timothy is having a sulk because I've told him not to pull out that wardrobe,' Tony explains, gesturing at it in the far right-hand corner of the room.

'It's a bloody horrible old thing!' Tim explodes and glares at his dad, who bursts out laughing. 'Me or the wardrobe?'

Tim looks pained. 'It's an unsightly piece of furniture and we've already got a wardrobe that can go in here.' He speaks with exaggerated patience.

It's Tony's turn to look annoyed. 'Old chap, I already told you – it's fixed to the wall and the plaster is so shot that if you try and pull it off, you'll probably pull great chunks of wall with it. Leave it until the builders get to this bit and they can rip it all out when it doesn't matter about dust and debris. Same story with those built-in shelves over there.' He points at a large bookcase. 'I wouldn't disturb them either. It's asking for trouble.'

'I really don't want plaster dust everywhere,' I agree hurriedly. 'Rosie has her hanging rail and chest of drawers in any case,' I remind Tim. 'Let's not pull lumps out of the wall if we can avoid it?'

I watch him clench his jaw, then smile widely. 'Of course. No problem. To be honest the poxy furniture is the least of my worries. I've got other, far more important things on my mind.'

I wait for him to elaborate, but he doesn't and I can't be bothered to go through the routine of winkling it out of him like I usually would. I've got too much to do.

'So, tea or coffee, then?' I remind them quickly. 'I'll make them and head back to The Rectory if that's OK? We've got a playdate this afternoon with a little girl at Rosie's new school that your mum has arranged – one of her friend's granddaughters.'

Tim noticeably softens. 'I'm really pleased to hear *that*! I hope Ro has fun!'

'I'm sure she will,' I say hopefully. 'Adam's arrived by the way.'

Tim nods and doesn't say anything, but Tony looks up enquiringly.

'Tim's said he can use the barn to paint in until the builders start next Wednesday,' I explain.

Tony doesn't say anything but I can tell from his raised eyebrow he shares my feelings on the matter. Tim carries on painting crossly.

'Anyway, you'll be here for a while, then? The locksmith won't be done for a bit yet. I'll tell him to come up if he needs anything, shall I?'

'Yes, do, and well done for getting him in so quickly. Thank you.' Tim starts to paint again then stops and rubs his eyes. 'This paint is giving me a cracking headache,' he complains. 'Are you sure it's fast drying, Dad?'

'Yes, I am – you've also had it for free, so maybe don't knock it,' says Tony, before turning to me. 'Tim's right – it was very sensible to get the locks replaced so speedily. The mind boggles at how many people don't take that measure once they move into a new house. Think about how many people could potentially have a key to this place?'

'I know. Imagine someone letting herself in off the street when she felt like it?'

Tim pauses and glances at me carefully. We both know exactly whom I'm talking about. I can see Isobel now, stood motionless, staring at Tim.

I can't seem to stop thinking about her, in fact. I don't know what's wrong with me.

*

'Well I think the point is you make a conscious decision *not* to let her bother you,' says Susannah, cutting straight down the centre of the conversational cloth with no hesitation, as we sit at her kitchen table having a post lunch coffee. 'It's a terribly sad situation really. I mean, Isobel's always had that sense of other-worldliness about her – even when she was Rosie's age she'd whisper to herself and when you asked her who she was talking to you'd have to try several times to get an answer because she just wouldn't hear you, she'd be miles away.'

'You've known her that long?'

'Well, yes. Directly after the *incident*.' Susannah is deliberately oblique in front of Rosie who is sitting at the kitchen table with us doing some colouring. 'Tony felt it would be helpful for the children to play together a few times over the remainder of the Christmas holidays to cement the feeling that everyone was OK, it was all happy, happy again, etc, etc. So she and her mother came over once or twice.'

I lower my eyes discreetly, thinking about what Tim told me yesterday. Surely Tony and Eve didn't begin their affair as early as that? How horrible for Susannah. 'Isobel was probably still deeply traumatised though,' I say. 'In fairness.'

Susannah shrugs. 'But with careful management those personality quirks wouldn't have become any more significant, that's my point. Timothy and Adam are completely normal; they were there as well.' She takes a sip of coffee. 'I daresay she'd have always been a bit ditsy and floaty, but nothing like the girl she's become. That voice, for example.' She rolls her eyes. 'Total affectation.'

'She's always had that too?' I'm astonished.

Susannah nods. 'A private doctor friend of mine saw Izzie once when she was seventeen – long story – it's called Puberphonia. The voice stays permanently artificially high. Physiological causes are very rare, apparently; it's mostly due to emotional stress.' She glances at Rosie and whispers: 'It's the mother, squashing her down all the time and refusing to let her grow up.' She shakes her head in disbelief and takes another sip of coffee before returning to *her* own normal level of voice again. 'It's almost as if the poor girl is desperately trying to remain the child her mother wants her to be.'

Rosie doesn't look up from her picture. 'Who are you talking about?'

'No one sweetheart, just a grown-up you don't know,' I say quickly. 'Do you want to go and get your unicorn, if you're taking it to show Grandma's friends? We're leaving in five minutes.'

'OK!' Rosie says eagerly, the chair screeching nosily as she pushes it back and runs off to her room.

I wait until she's out of earshot and turn back to Susannah. 'Isobel is obviously not all there, but she's not *dangerous*, is she?'

I expect Susannah to laugh and tell me of course not, it would be like fearing a kitten's bite, but in fact, she hesitates and I sit up a little straighter in anticipation.

'I once had a bit of a set to with Isobel,' she confesses, 'after she and Timothy split up. Oh, about this, that and nothing really.' She waves a dismissive hand at my enquiring gaze. 'Some of the letters she wrote him at university came back unopened and she wanted me to give them to him personally. I said I would, but I didn't. When he still didn't respond, she challenged me about it and when I confessed, she got terribly cross and it was a little intimidating, I must say.'

*Susannah* found someone intimidating? I'm astonished… and immediately worried.

'She's very sweet until she's *not*, if you know what I mean. Really though, her problems are *entirely* due to the mother wrapping her in cotton wool and packing her away like the angel on top of the Christmas tree. I have a very nice friend in Harrogate and *her* daughter has struggled with various ailments of the psyche over the years. They finally accepted she wasn't going to get any better and she lives in a really super…' she pauses, 'I don't want to say unit, that's not the right word, because it's so much more homely than that.' She wrinkles her nose.

'Hospital?' I volunteer.

'No, because of course medically there's nothing wrong with her either. *Centre!*' Susannah beams. 'A really lovely centre. It has structure, discipline… and I *do* think that would be the best thing for Isobel too. The mother isn't getting any younger, after all; what will happen when she dies, one wonders? Anyway,' Susannah gets up and walks her mug over to the sink, 'in the short-term, it's *very* unfortunate that Mrs Parkes wasn't able to keep Isobel away from Fox Cottage yesterday and I see it would have been unnerving. She's a very beautiful girl, but I can assure you, Claire – Timothy has no interest in her whatsoever. It was barely more than a teenage crush as far as he was concerned.' She rinses out her mug and puts it in the dishwasher. 'Although Timothy has always had an unnerving knack for doing everything you rather hoped he wouldn't.'

I laugh and swallow the last of my drink.

'Dear chap. He was what you might call a challenging child.' Susannah leans on the side and crosses her arms, smiling. 'I didn't know any better, of course, I'd had no other experience of children at all, but *my* mother told me Timothy was harder work than all four of my brothers put together. He was totally fearless – erring on stupidity. My God, the things that child would stuff in his mouth! Insects, pennies, buttons, sand – you name it.' She sighs. 'And the tantrums. He would hit, scratch and kick if he didn't get his own way when he was small. I've told you before – it's no coincidence we didn't have any more; I was exhausted because, of course, he also didn't sleep properly until he was five. If I'd have had a darling like Rosie first, I might have felt brave enough for another, but I couldn't risk a second Timothy. One is enough!' She laughs and looks at the kitchen clock. 'Shall we go?'

I finish circling my finger round the outside edge of my mug as I listen carefully to all of that. 'Did he really not sleep until he was five?' I say lightly. 'You poor things.'

'It was *hell*, Claire. Nothing worked. Pleading, scolding, closing his door, smacking him. He would lie there for *hours* shouting for us sometimes.'

Smacking? I think about how Rosie can only sleep when she has the bathroom light on and her door open, and how when I was scared as a little girl, *I'd* go and climb into bed with Jen – often forcing her to get up and accompany me to the loo in the night, making her stand sleepy sentry outside the door while I called 'are you there?' to check she hadn't deserted me mid-wee. My heart actually aches for Tim, lying there in the dark alone, frightened and no one coming to him. How terrifying that would be for a small boy.

'Don't judge, Claire,' Susannah says sharply, and I blush. 'Until you've had a very challenging child, you can't possibly understand. It was also a different era; of course you wouldn't smack a child now, but then we didn't know any better,' Susannah sighs again, 'And actually I'm not altogether sure some problems *wouldn't* be solved these days if parents gave their little dears a swift tap on the back of the leg to remind them who is actually in charge.' She picks up a cloth and gives the table in front of me a quick wipe before throwing it back in the sink and drying her hands. 'You know, now I think of it, I'm not convinced Timothy learnt to sleep properly until he started boarding. I knew it would sort itself out when he shared a dorm with the other boys. It's the camaraderie, you see. Tony wasn't convinced, but,' she taps her nose and looks conspiratorially at me, 'mother knows best.'

I think about how even now as a grown man, Tim sleeps in the foetal position, his hands shoved protectively through his ankles, unable to make himself vulnerable. The first time I saw him asleep like that, I almost cried. 'Didn't Tony want him to board then?' I ask casually. 'I always thought it was his decision to send Tim back after the shooting?'

'What?' Susannah pulls a face. 'Of course not!'

'I mean, to send him somewhere safer.'

Susannah hoots. 'Darling girl, Oswestry is hardly the ghetto! Tim was always going to board. He'd already done a term and come home for the holidays when the shooting happened. Tony didn't send him off *because* it happened. In fact, Tony wondered if maybe we shouldn't keep him at the local school after the event – Isobel and Adam were there – but I felt that would be both pointless and cruel. Timothy had already done the hard bit of settling in the first term and made friends, it would have been a waste of so much effort, and money. I was determined the sports hall incident wasn't going to be allowed to dominate our lives – and it hasn't.'

She speaks proudly but I can also hear a slightly defensive tone creeping into her voice. I don't want to sound like I'm criticising. What would be the point? It's all done now, but I don't think I will ever get my head around why some parents think it will make their children happy to be sent to live with a bunch of strangers at age eight – even under the best of circumstances, let alone after what happened to Tim:

*Nice Christmas, Vaughan?*

*Yes, Sir, I got shot, Sir – it was awfully exciting!*

*Jolly good! Now, textbooks open to page ten, boys!*

'It was just what everyone in our set did, Claire. Not sending Tim to boarding school would have been unthinkable.' Susannah is still watching me carefully. 'Yes I missed him, I missed him dreadfully – but that was the way things were, and the discipline did him good. It's too funny though, that after all of that effort he's going to be a *builder*. Tony *is* right though – much as it pains me to admit it – Timothy needs a trade, or a profession. He really doesn't want Tim to have to spend the next year realising he's never going to make it as an actor. Better to let Timothy wonder what if, than have yet another failure shoved down his throat, don't you think?' She lowers her voice. 'You and I both know he wouldn't have lasted five seconds as an actor. He'd never have coped with the rejection. Now, Claire, darling – I don't mean to rush, but we *really* have to go, if we're going.'

She straightens up and runs her fingers through her well-cut, blown-out blonde hair – she's had the same style about as long as Camilla Parker Bowles – and smooths a crease from the front of her trousers. 'Don't let Isobel or her mother give you a moment's more worry. Timothy told me what Eve Parkes said to you yesterday. She really is the most unpleasant woman.'

Susannah pauses and for a horrible moment I think she's about to unburden herself about the affair to me. I really, really don't want her to confide anything that I'd feel duty-bound to discuss with Tim, and might upset him more than he already is right now. If he's forced to delve any further into his shitty past he might just implode completely. I'm not sure I can take much more either.

Thankfully, she seems to change her mind. 'The important point is, in answer to your question, on balance I don't think

Isobel is dangerous, no. Now – time to go!' She strides across the room, elegant wide leg, navy trousers swishing as she gives me a dazzling smile. 'Chop, chop! You've got five minutes.' I must look as confused as I feel because she raises an eyebrow and says sternly: 'You're not getting changed?'

I look down at my jeans and Converse. No, I'm not, because I don't live in Surrey any more. That's at least one good thing about having moved to the countryside, surely? 'I'll do, won't I?'

'You look lovely,' Susannah says sweetly. 'I'll get our coats and call Rosie, shall I? Let's go and make you some new friends!'

# CHAPTER FIFTEEN

## Claire

'So Rosie, this is Anna, and she's going to be in your class at your new school!'

The two girls stare shyly at each other. Rosie is leaning on my leg and twirling lightly on the spot, her unicorn tucked under her arm.

'Anna *really* likes unicorns too, Rosie. Look – she's got one on her top!' Jo, Anna's mum, points it out, placing her hand gently on her daughter's head as she passes on her way to collect my cup of tea from the vast, very smart kitchen we're sat in – all sharp angles, clinical surfaces and bi-folds… not unlike the expensive Scandi top and wide-leg cropped trousers combo she's wearing. I'd look like a triangle in an outfit like that – she looks edgy, unflappable and glamorous. I absolutely should have changed.

'Hey, why don't you take Rosie upstairs to see your room? She might like to meet Twilight? That's Anna's new *talking* My Little Pony.' Jo raises her eyebrows enticingly, and Rosie looks up at me.

'That sounds amazing! Go and look – I'll be right here.' I smile back at her, and Rosie lets go of me, following Anna out of the room. We hear them begin to chatter as they walk up the stairs.

'Children's ability to make friends in an instant is remarkable,' says Susannah, sipping her tea. 'Like water off a duck's back.'

'It really is. Anna's so been looking forward to meeting Rosie,' Jo says warmly, sitting down opposite me on the grey corner sofa and smiling – the perfect Sunday supplement 'at home with' shot. I pull the sleeves of my jumper over my hands, becoming acutely embarrassed by how scruffy and frumpy I look. I'd have made the effort to dress nicely back at home – I should have done it here too, and not made assumptions about the local mums before even meeting them.

'Is Rosie excited about starting at Midbourne House on Monday?'

'I think so, yes.' I try to relax, feeling like I need to make up for looking like a potato by being confident and amusing instead. 'She hasn't actually seen it yet, so I think it's hard for her to visualise, but when we came to look at the school in January, we were very impressed. That's my partner and I… when I say partner,' I add quickly, 'I of course mean Rosie's Dad… we're just not married, that's all. After ten years and a child, *boyfriend* doesn't really cut it any more.' I laugh. 'And lover sounds unpleasantly 1970s satin sheets, so partner it is…' I trail off as they both look at me in surprise.

'Would you like a biscuit?' Jo politely passes me the plate as I take one and wonder what on earth is wrong with me. Susannah shoots me a look which says that's exactly what she's thinking too, before helicoptering in to rescue me from the small-talk rock I've just smashed into. She winches me out of the water with a smooth: 'It's all been so terribly quick, Jo! Poor Claire is utterly *exhausted!*'

She pauses long enough to let the 'she's not mad, just tired' defence register, then continues: 'Timothy has been longing to start a renovation project and they wanted some proper outdoor space for Rosie. Claire is very fortunate in that she can work from home and is able to be flexible. So the stars suddenly aligned and here they are! We're delighted, of course!' She smiles at me, willing me to get a grip and act like a normal person.

'I can confirm this,' Jo nods. 'My mother says Susie's been counting down the days until your arrival. So what is it you do, Claire?'

'I've had about a million jobs,' I try to bolster the beige-ness of what's to come, 'but right now I work in data analysis. I help clients formulate their media activity.'

'Does that mean you sell data?' Jo says shrewdly, sipping her tea.

'Sort of,' I admit. 'But all licenced and above board, I promise.'

Jo laughs as Susannah reaches into her bag, pulls out her phone and stares at the screen before standing. 'Ladies will you excuse me a moment? I have a brief work call to make.'

We murmur agreement and she leaves the room, closing the door discretely behind her as I realise with embarrassment that she's deliberately left us alone to 'get to know' one another. Unfortunately I immediately become tongue-tied as a result, and in the awkward moment of silence where I ought to ask Jo what *she* does, but don't – Jo is forced to step in with: 'So Susie mentioned you've moved from Surrey? This must be a bit of a change of pace for you?'

'Well, it was Greater London really.' I think of our old street longingly, the line of terraces, anonymous cars parked outside, bumper-to-bumper, someone else always around while never in your face, 'but yes, it's a bit different. Obviously we've been coming to visit Susannah and Tony for a long time though, so we kind of knew what we were letting ourselves in for. Rosie is really excited.' The harder I try, the more I am becoming the conversational equivalent of a damp flannel.

'Ah – that's great.' Jo smiles blandly. 'I'm so glad we got the chance to do this today so that Rosie has a friendly face on Monday, but Midbourne House is such a lovely school, I'm sure she'll be very happy there.'

'I hope so.' I clear my throat. 'I've taken next week off as well as this one to be around and help her settle in. Her last school was a little bigger, so I'm sure she'll enjoy it being more homely, and she's very excited about wearing a hat. There's a lot of uniform to get though, isn't there?'

'There really is,' Jo agrees. 'The amount of PE kit is ridiculous. You don't need half of it though, don't worry. Just the tracksuit will be fine. They're doing hockey this term, so you might want to buy her a stick, but it's not compulsory. The school have got plenty.'

'Hockey? Is that safe at their age?' I blurt, and Jo smiles kindly. 'Their teacher is an ex international, she's got it covered, don't worry, but you do need to get Rosie a mouthguard and shin pads.'

'Thanks for the heads-up.' Hats and jolly hockey sticks indeed. Wow. I take too big a gulp of tea, have a huge coughing fit as a result and am forced to take a moment before I can speak again, having gone bright red in the face.

'Are you all right?' Jo says in concern, putting a glass of water down next to me as I whoop and nod, still trying to catch my breath. 'Midbourne House sounds really great,' I splutter, coughing deeply again and grabbing my water, slopping it slightly as I take a desperate mouthful. 'It's a big change for all of us and she needs to be happy. I'm sure she will be.'

Jo looks actually worried that I might expire on her kitchen floor. 'Absolutely. You're sure you're OK?'

'Yes,' I insist, although my eyes are now watering. I look up at the ceiling and try to steady my breathing before giving another involuntary bark of a cough.

'Well, it sounds like you've made some very wise decisions.' Jo valiantly attempts to talk over my splutters. 'And how exciting to be just upping sticks and starting a new adventure! I really admire you for just going for it. Do shout if you want some help renovating Fox Cottage, won't you? I don't know if Susannah mentioned it, but I'm an interior designer. Sometimes *really* big projects can feel a bit overwhelming when you're starting out.' She smiles. 'I'll happily come round and take a look if you'd like me to?'

*

'She seems very nice,' I agree as we walk down the main street, not wanting to say I think she liked the prospect of doing up Fox Cottage more than she liked me. That would sound ungrateful and it was kind of Susannah to arrange a date for us. 'Not too far ahead, Ro!' I call as Rosie skips off down the road looking in windows. 'My feet are hardly touching the ground,' I say unhappily. 'New house, new school, new friends… new backstory.'

Susannah eyes me keenly. 'New backstory? How so?'

'Um,' I wish I'd kept quiet and so choose my words carefully, 'Jo obviously thinks we're moving from some big house in Surrey and that we have plenty of money for private schools and house renovations. None of that's true, is it?'

Susannah waves a hand airily. 'We're happy to do fees for Rosie. We've wanted to for some time, but you wouldn't let us! If it's only for a year it makes so much more sense to just get on with it and go private, rather than mess around waiting to hear on a possible place here or there, in this or that oversubscribed school. It's nobody's business who pays what – and who cares if Jo thinks you came from a mansion rather than a two-up two-down? Isn't that what today's world of social media is all about? Presenting an image rather than the real picture? It's what people think they see that matters.'

I fall quiet.

'Just leave out the bit about my little bastard of a son stealing all of your money and you'll be fine.'

My mouth falls open, shocked. Susannah can still pull the rug from under my feet after all this time and, knowing it, she laughs. 'Oh come on, Claire. You're not the first woman who's faking it to make it, and you shan't be the last. We women must stick together: '"There's a special place in hell for women who don't help other women".'

'Sheryl Sandberg,' I remark, recognising the quote.

She laughs. 'No dear: Madeleine Albright, former Secretary of State.'

'Mummy!' Rosie breathlessly arrives back alongside us. 'Come and see this!' She drags me by the hand to a butcher's window and the huge, halved dead pig hanging by a pierced back leg on a large metal hook. Behind it are several strung-up pheasants, fully feathered, their leathery black eyelids shut. I'm reminded immediately of Eve Parkes's comment at Fox Cottage about needing a river to sluice away blood in the olden days.

'Wow,' I say faintly. 'That's quite something, isn't it? Come on darling.' I tug on Rosie's hand gently, but fascinated, she stares at the pig.

'Where have its insides gone?' She points at the empty stomach and intestinal cavity.

'The butcher does something called "gutting it",' says Susannah, matter-of-factly, arriving alongside us. 'After they kill the pig, they let all of the blood run away and then they take the bits out that we don't like to eat.'

'But it's still got its head?' Rosie points to the whiskery snout, and I start to feel sick. 'We don't eat that? Do we?'

'No, we don't,' I say quickly. 'Come on, let's go.'

'How do they get the blood out?' Rosie is not to be deterred.

'With a knife,' Susannah says. 'They cut the veins and —'

'Ooh! We've done about veins in school!' Rosie is excited. 'They carry blood away from the heart.'

'No, darling, other way round. Veins take blood to the heart.'

'Do they do that after the injection?' Rosie asks, and Susannah frowns.

'The injection that makes the pig fall asleep,' I say quickly.

Susannah hesitates then says clearly: 'They don't give the pigs injections, Rosie. They give them an electric shock so the pig doesn't know what's happening and can't feel anything, then they kill the pig with a knife, or shoot it. After that, they let the blood out and take out the bits we don't eat.'

I stare at her, slightly stunned myself.

'Oh.' Rosie frowns. 'Poor pig. That's not very nice.'

I open my mouth, but Susannah gets there first again. 'It's just how it happens. Otherwise we wouldn't have any bacon. Or sausages.'

Rosie nods. 'Like in *The Lion King* where they have to eat the zebra to stay alive?'

'Exactly!' beams Susannah, and Rosie skips off happily to look in a bookshop window a few doors down.

'I know you're cross,' Susannah doesn't skip a beat, 'but honestly, Claire – you can't tell the child they put the animals to sleep first!'

'Why not? It's true – in some cases,' I say defensively.

'Not unless it's a domestic pet being put down by a vet,' Susannah retorts. 'There are plenty of landowners' children in her school with working farms. They'll tell her if you don't – and she was fine. She took it all in her stride. Children ought to understand exactly where their food comes from and how it arrives on their plate. I didn't go into detail about how they exsanguinate the pigs – or that, actually, it's often done while the pig is alive.'

Luckily, before I am forced to say anything to *that*, Rosie calls: 'Mummy! Can we go in the pet shop over there? I want to buy a treat for Badger!' She points over the road at PetTime!.

'Oh darling, that's so sweet of you,' says Susannah as we arrive next to her, 'but Badger has lots of lovely foodie treats at home. Grandpa bulk buys them all on the Internet. Along with those enormous sacks of food that arrive four at a time on a blasted pallet.' She looks at me, deadpan and rolls her eyes.

'Well can I get him a toy then? We need a new ball?' Rosie wheedles, and Susannah softens. 'Why not? Come on then, Rosie-Posy. Let's see what we can find!'

We cross the road, and Rosie runs off ahead into the shop. I'm about to call after her to stay where I can see her, like I do at home, but Susannah puts a hand out.

'She's safe. Let her start finding her feet. This is exactly what I mean – let her grow up a little.'

Chastened, I close my mouth. Perhaps she's right, everything *is* different now and I need to realise that.

Susannah wrinkles her nose as we walk in. 'I do so hate the slightly *sweet* meaty smell of pet shops. It's different to a butcher somehow – it's the mixture of all of those lovely doggy choc drops, straw and cow hooves, I think. Yuck.'

'I can't smell a thing,' I remind her. 'For which, right now, I'm very thankful. Where's Rosie gone?' I look down the main aisle in front of me, but can't see her anywhere. 'Ro?' I call, peering down the other one to my left. Still nothing. Squashing down an extra heartbeat of panic, I push past Susannah to the right side of the shop and look past the shelves full of bags of food, bedding, collars, treats and chews – to see Rosie stood at the far end, facing and *holding the hand* of a kneeling Isobel Parkes. Isobel is staring up into Rosie's shy face with a bewildered but rapt delight as she whispers something to my daughter, her long red hair flowing over her shoulders and down her back.

'Get away from her!' I yell immediately and fly down towards them.

Rosie starts to cry at the completely unfamiliar tone of my voice, and as Isobel straightens up I see that she is wearing a green apron and a name badge, but it doesn't register in time to stop me from shoving Isobel on the shoulder so hard with the heel of my hand that she gives a little cry of shock and stumbles backwards.

I watch, confused and frightened, as Isobel almost falls over some large sacks behind her, but just about stays on her feet, as a much older woman puffs over to us, also in an apron and badge.

'Hey, hey! What's all this about, then?'

No one speaks for a moment as Susannah arrives alongside me and the facts shuffle into place. Isobel didn't follow us, she isn't attempting to lure Rosie and abduct her – but she was still touching my daughter, talking to her… except I then shoved her. Shit. I shouldn't have done that.

'She was calling, "Mummy"!' Isobel is rigid and breathless with fear.

I can't help it, I know I'm at fault here, but I cannot stand the sound of the little girl voice coming from the mouth of entirely the wrong person, this adult woman. It's as if Rosie herself is somehow speaking through the lips of this life-sized, wide-eyed, human doll. I step back away from her, dragging Rosie with me.

'She was sad,' Isobel continues, 'and I said, "don't worry, Mummy's here!"'

My eyes widen in horror as Susannah steps forward and places a calming hand on my arm. 'You saw Claire come into the shop, didn't you, Isobel?' she says smoothly. 'That's what you were telling Rosie; her mummy was in the shop and she didn't need to worry – not that you were telling Rosie *you* are her mummy. Take a breath, Claire.'

'Mummy?' It's Rosie squeezing my hand that brings me back. I look down to see she's biting her lip and her eyes are still full of tears. 'I'm sorry. I remembered I couldn't see you and you *always* say stay where I can see you.'

I snap out of it immediately, furious with myself for making her feel as if this is in any way her fault. 'It's OK, darling. I can see you and I'm not angry with *you*.'

I pull her into a fierce hug and glare over her head at Isobel. I ought to be apologising for pushing her, but instead I'm accusative. 'Did you say anything else at all to her?'

Isobel shakes her head violently. 'No. Just not to be frightened.'

'Why would she *need* to be frightened of you?' I demand aggressively.

'Claire,' Susannah's calm, steady voice interjects again. 'That's not what Isobel meant either and you know it.'

'Can I go now, please?' Isobel whispers to the older lady.

'Of course you can, lovely. You go and answer that phone for me. I can hear it ringing out the back!' The older woman frowns at me and crosses her arms.

Rosie pulls her hand free from mine. 'Good bye, Belle,' she says as Isobel turns to leave, and gives her a small wave.

*Belle?*

Isobel's face breaks into a smile of incredible sweetness and warmth. It's almost angelic, for fucks' sake.

'Bye bye, Rosie,' she says softly, looking down at my daughter.

She knows Ro's name too? Once she has gone, I gently turn Rosie by her shoulders to face me, and stroke my little girl's soft cheek. 'You're sure nothing else happened, sweetheart? You're OK? That lady didn't say or do anything you didn't like?'

'Claire,' Susannah says, 'they were alone for a matter of seconds. Let's not make a mountain out of a molehill.'

'Isobel is a lovely girl, she wouldn't hurt a fly,' the older woman says warningly, still staring at me, 'She wasn't even supposed to be working today. She made a mistake and came in on her day off. I don't want her any more embarrassed than she already is, thank you.'

'We understand completely,' Susannah says soothingly. 'Come on, Claire, time to go home.' And without another word, she leads *me* out of the shop as if *I'm* the one they all need to be worried about.

*

As we drive back to The Rectory, I stare at the road in front of me, unable to get the picture of Isobel whispering to Rosie out of my head, but I also know I crossed a line there. Would I have shouted at anyone else like that? Of course not. And I shoved her – these days that probably counts as assault.

Rosie is calmly drawing in the back, and Susannah appears to be tapping away on her phone, but out of nowhere she casually remarks: 'I'm obviously aware of little ears, so I'll be circumspect, but I was clueless that particular individual worked there, for the record. It must be a new thing. Had I been aware I wouldn't have suggested a visit.'

'Of course. It's OK,' I say quickly. 'It wasn't your fault.'

'Oh darling I know *that*.' She looks up, surprised. 'I'm just explaining. It wasn't *anyone's* fault. In fact,' she peers at me over the top of her glasses, 'nothing *actually* happened. *I* didn't see you push Isobel at all.' She takes her glasses off, puts them back in their case with a snap and slides them into her bag. 'Can I give you a word of advice, however? It won't go down well – particularly with some of the older locals – if you were seen to be less than sympathetic to the limitations of the particular individual's capabilities. An out-of-towner is unwise to come in and appear to be laying down the law. She may be the village oddity, but she's *their* village oddity. Do you understand what I'm saying?'

I nod silently, glance at Rosie in the rear-view mirror and decide not to mention that the strength of the anger I felt at the sight of Isobel holding my daughter's hand is at best unnerving, and at worse, frightening. Never mind pushing – I pretty much wanted to kill her.

*

Safely back at The Rectory, I put CBeebies on for Rosie, then return to the hall where I can hear voices coming from the kitchen. To my surprise, Tim is sitting at the table nursing a steaming mug of bright yellow liquid.

'Hey,' he says as I appear in the doorway and come to sit down opposite him. 'I had to stop painting at the house, I'm sorry. I needed some meds.' He raises the mug and sips gingerly.

*Meds?* What's he talking about? 'That's just a Lemsip, isn't it?' I say slowly. 'You were all right a couple of hours ago. What's happened?'

He clears his throat. 'Nothing's "happened"; I just don't feel very well, sorry.' He shrugs tiredly. 'Did you have a nice time this afternoon?'

'It was great, thanks,' I lie, as Susannah is in the room too. 'We had a nice cup of tea and then popped to the pet shop for a treat for Badger. So what are your symptoms?'

He gives a resigned 'so you think I'm making it up' sigh and puts his mug back down. 'I feel slightly shivery, light-headed and I ache all over. I haven't taken my temperature yet, but I will in a minute if you like? I don't know if it's paint fumes or I'm coming down with something, but I had to drive Dad's car back. I'm not doing this to annoy you, Claire. I promise.'

Susannah doesn't say anything, just carries on rummaging around in a cupboard, her back to us. I narrow my eyes at Tim and nod my head in his mother's direction, silently making the point that I don't intend to have a row with him in front of her.

He rolls *his* eyes like I'm being ridiculous and silently puts his hands up – I don't know if he's sarkily saying he surrenders or is asking me to back off, either way, none of this is improving my mood. We've got an entire house to unpack. I don't have time for man flu now.

'Do you think you might be able to go and get Dad?' he adds, as the final cherry on my cake-of-crap day. 'Again. I'm sorry, I know this is really irritating for you, but he can't get home otherwise.'

'The only thing is,' I say tersely, 'I've got Rosie's tea to cook, then I need to bath her and put her to bed before I go back over to the house to unpack her bedroom there. I think I'd like to try and move in tomorrow, if possible.'

Tim looks puzzled, but before he can speak, Susannah cuts in with: 'I can do Rosie's tea,' as she emerges from the cupboard. 'I'll be back to work again next week – play the granny card while you can. You might like to get out of the house and have five minutes to yourself, Claire – or I can get Tony. Whichever you prefer.'

'Thanks, Ma.' Tim massages his temples with his eyes closed. 'God – this head! I can hardly see straight. That would be great, if you don't mind.' He opens his eyes, blinks and winces before looking at me again. 'Dad had practically finished Rosie's room by the time I left but if you want to move in tomorrow now, the other rooms might have to wait. I'll do the best I can.' He sighs as if the whole burden of organisation is on him. 'I'm just a little overwhelmed today by everything, that's all.'

That's the comment that tips me over the edge. I jump up quickly. *He's* overwhelmed? All of my promises from last night have completely vanished. Right now I hate him – all of them, actually. Except Rosie, obviously. 'Fine. I'll go and get Tony now then. Tell Rosie where I've gone, please.'

I march out of the room without another word.


Rather than head straight to Fox Cottage, I drive too fast out further into the countryside, over the border and up into the hills. Pulling into a layby, I stop the car suddenly with a gasp. I feel jittery. My skin is prickling with a fear and fury I have no idea what to do with. I am not myself. Tim's the one who loses control and builds up repressed anger. This is not me.

I turn off the engine and feel the stuffy artificial warmth of the heating start to bleed away as I look down at the motionless bare trees and dotted cows plodding through cold, distant fields. There's just enough light to catch the pale reflection of the river as it snakes through the bottom of the darkening valley. I try to draw on this steady, open space to calm me – but as the weak sun slips rapidly out of sight, turning the hills a darker purple, the emptiness becomes oddly claustrophobic.

Desperate suddenly to speak to Jen, I grab my phone… but it's one o'clock in the morning in Sydney. I'd phone Mel but she doesn't know anything is wrong, and I don't want to break my promise to Tim or worry her by blurting everything out in a mad rush. Instead of calling, I type a WhatsApp message to my sister.

*Freaking out a bit! Am being absorbed into a life that belongs to someone else, not me. Wrong place, wrong house/friends/school mums/shops/roads. V homesick. Tim being a wet weekend, moaning about the place. I shouted at his ex-girlfriend in a pet shop today. Also went to posh house of school mum dressed like a tramp. She thinks I've got cash to splash on doing up Fox Cottage. Can't be honest and tell the truth so feel like building new friendships based on lies… barriers already up, so couldn't think of a thing to say and said nothing but boring twatty stuff the whole time I was there. Also got hole house (not typo – intentional) to unpack. Am v tired. Want to cry. Love you.*

Seeing it down in black and white, I *do* start to cry. It's times like these that I would give anything to ring my mum. I can just hear her voice saying delightedly *Hello, my sweetheart!* Dad would be pottering around in the background, making a cup of tea.

Perhaps if I were in one of Rosie's Disney movies they would appear right now, maybe ethereal blue, certainly smiling and alongside each other, to tell me what to do. They might sing a song that would be about not giving up, recognising my inner strength and being a brave girl. We could fly through starry skies or be on top of a cliff so I could see the world spread beneath me that has so much to offer. They'd finish it by telling me they're so proud of the woman I have become and that there is nowhere I can go that they are not with me. It would feel so real that I would be sure they were actually here with me. I lean my head back. Unlikely to happen in a Volvo on a hilltop in Wales to a forty-one-year old woman though, however much I want it to.

I breathe out and wipe the tears away, before looking down at the WhatsApp message in my lap. I can't send this to my poor little sister. I delete it all, apart from the bit about shouting at Isobel in the pet shop, because it's so ridiculous and so not me, it will at least amuse Jen, although I don't think it's funny.

I can't believe I pushed her. I'm far too old to allow myself to feel this way about some poor girl Tim once had something with, however beautiful she is. I look out over the fields again, it's now almost completely dark. The next 365 days will pass just like this one… steadily I will do this. One year. That's all. Then we can go home.

I sit up, resigned once again to getting a grip and turn the car around to head back to Fox Cottage.

# CHAPTER SIXTEEN

## Claire

Tony is still upstairs finishing off the last of the painting, when I shout 'Hello?' from the small sitting room.

'Ah! The cavalry!' He appears, brandishing a brush. 'Just a tiny last section to do, if that's all right, then I'll wash my brushes and we'll be done up like a kipper! I've made rather a good job of Rosie's room as it happens. Want to come and see?'

Not really, no – but I can't refuse, and trudge upstairs after him as he disappears off. He's waiting delightedly in the room having painted the three walls either side of the cherry tree a primrose yellow.

'Marvellous what a lick of paint can do, eh?' He looks around the room, pleased. 'One wall still needs a second coat – but I'll do that in the morning. I'm going to come back tonight after supper to put the first one on your room. No, I insist. It won't be done in time otherwise. Ah – something else,' he reaches into his pocket and pulls out a bunch of keys, 'your chap left these with me. All of the new locks are fitted. There are two of each key for the front and back door and the inner door to the small sitting room. He's also put a second lock on the one out here.'

We walk into the hall and he points to the large new bolt on the door leading to the three-storey section. Our own, personal, Fort Knox.

'You're all set.' He holds out the keys and drops them into my hand. 'That was a job well done, Claire. You're getting there!'

'Thank you.' I force a smile. 'And thank you for your help too. Do you think I could ask you to do one last thing and take this lock *off* when you get five seconds?' I point at the old-fashioned, black, turn-key mechanism on Rosie's door. 'I know I can just take the key away so Rosie can't lock herself in – or out – but I'd rather the whole thing just came off completely.' I want to add how bizarre I think it is to have it there in the first place, but then I suppose Isobel is a grown woman – in body at least – and entitled to privacy. Anyway, I have no desire to discuss Eve Parkes with Tony, after what Tim told me yesterday.

'Of course,' he says easily. 'I'll bring the tools with me tomorrow.'

'Lovely. I'll wait for you downstairs.'


I wash up the mugs in the kitchen staring unseeingly out of the window into the small, dark courtyard, because I'm actually focusing on my own reflection in the glass – hair scraped back, make-up worn off, up to my elbows in suds. Isobel briefly appears in the glass instead, smiling beatifically as she did at Rosie earlier, before I firmly push the picture away, pull my hands from the water and dry them off on a damp tea towel which I hang over the Aga – no, *Rayburn*, I correct myself – which seems to be finally working and is hot.

Thank goodness for Tony. I lean back on it for a moment and close my eyes, feeling the welcome warmth spread through the tired, aching muscles of my lower back. I groan suddenly, realising that's probably in part why I've been so out of sorts. I'm due on any day. That explains a lot – and is also all I need. The older I get the worse they become. Men just have no idea, the bastards.

I look around the kitchen and feel completely exhausted at the thought of having to unpack so many boxes. Perhaps I'll just burn them all instead – that would be considerably easier. I wander back through to the sitting room to see if Tony is ready.

I can hear him still pottering around upstairs, so flop down onto one of our sofas for a minute and stare up at the beams, watching a small spider creep along and disappear into a hole. I'd like to disappear like that. So now I'm jealous of a spider... but as I peer more closely, I realise that among the grooves, missing chunks, knots and frankly worrying worm holes – the survey would have picked that up surely? – someone has scratched elaborate stars into the beam. That must have taken quite some effort. Several of them are five-pointed, some six – and there's one... I squint... eye? How odd.

Before I can think about them any further, there is a sudden hammering at the front door, so insistent, I exclaim aloud 'All right!' in amazement, and get to my feet.

Before opening my shiny new Yale lock, I flick on the outside light – to reveal a furious Eve Parkes staring back at me, eye pressed right up to the glass panel as she stands on the doorstep with Isobel a little way behind her. My heart sinks as I open the front door. It swings easily – someone has already fixed the hanging too – and I jump back as Eve literally falls in through the doorway, having put her shoulder to it through habit, expecting it to stick... determined as she is, to come in.

'Are you all right?' I gasp as she sprawls on the floor in front of me, while I reach out to try and pull her to her feet. Isobel just stands there, hands over her mouth, and I realise Adam is present too, dressed in paint-splattered clothes, doors to his van open and a folded-down easel on the ground. He's obviously packing up for the night. He dashes forward to help Eve as Isobel starts to chuckle, watching her mother drag herself to her knees. It turns into the peal of uncontrollable laughter of a child being tickled; the sound that adults worldwide can't help but smile at. I stare at her in disbelief, it's so incongruous; but then I realise she's shocked

– this reaction is just a reflex – and I remember someone telling me that's why you mustn't tickle a child too much, even though the sound is addictive, because they can't control their laughter… it doesn't mean they're enjoying what you're doing to them.

'Don't touch me!' Eve waves my hand of assistance away from her undignified position on all fours.

She is practically crying as Adam begins to help her up, but I'm pretty sure they are angry, frustrated, humiliated tears. I cried like that when I told my then-boss that a man called Harry Asquith had pulled me behind the marquee, pushed me down to my knees like Eve is now – but on the soft, summer grass – then shoved his hand up my skirt… before we both heard Tim tipsily calling me as he staggered back from the loo and Harry vanished. The boss told me it was 'just what happens' when guests at weddings get a bit drunk and letchy with the waiting staff.

Not for the first time, I wish I'd told Tim instead. Then maybe none of us would be standing here right now.

Eve staggers to her feet, leaning on Adam, her face bright red either with rage or the effort of getting up.

'You!' she exclaims, pointing at me wildly. 'How dare you – *how dare you* do what you did today? You and your wretched mother-in-law sought my daughter out at her place of work to insult, intimidate and *assault* her? I don't put anything past Susannah – but you? What kind of woman *are* you?'

'Eve!' I blanche. 'Of course we didn't! It was nothing like that.' I glance at the house over the road. Her accusations are carrying clearly on the still night air and it's a matter of seconds before a curtain begins to twitch. Immediately mindful of Susannah's earlier warning, I hold out a hand. 'Look, come in, please – I don't want to do this on the doorstep.' I open the sitting room door, and Eve blasts into the room, followed reluctantly by Adam and then Isobel, who is looking past me curiously. She's come alive and is visibly excited. It takes a moment for me to realise she's waiting for Tim to appear.

'Isobel has told me everything,' Eve says, turning to face me. 'She was in tears when she came home. Her employer called and confirmed her version of events. I'll say it again – what kind of woman are you?'

'I'm really not sure this is helpful,' Adam says worriedly, watching Isobel. 'Let's not do this.'

'There's been a misunderstanding, I think,' I start to try and explain myself. 'I didn't know where Rosie was and I found Isobel holding her hand and whispering to her. After Isobel appeared in here last night out of nowhere, I thought she had maybe followed us into the shop. I had no idea she worked there. I didn't mean to upset anyone. I accept I might have overreacted.'

Eve stares at me silently, then swings to point at Isobel. 'So tell *her* – not me. She's right there. She can hear you.'

That throws me, which is probably the point, but obediently, I turn to face Isobel. 'I apologise for frightening you, Isobel.'

She looks away uncomfortably, wringing her hands, her delicate wrists twisting awkwardly as she mutters something inaudible.

'What's that, Isobel?' says Eve, irritably, in a teacher's voice. 'You're going to need to speak up if anyone is to hear you.'

'I said, it's OK – you were only being a good mother.' The words tumble from her mouth in a silvery twist. She darts a glance and a flash of a nervous smile at me, before looking worriedly back at Eve. 'Can we go home please, Mummy? I didn't want any of this. It was only because Mrs Hughes phoned and told you. I wouldn't have said anything. I didn't want to make trouble.'

The poor girl is utterly caught between us, and in spite of everything, I feel sorry for her. I instinctively liked Eve so much, but *this* woman who accused me of deception yesterday and verbal assault tonight is vile. I think about what Susannah told me: the way Eve treats her daughter... and the lock on what was Isobel's bedroom door... then I notice the bruises on Eve's wrists. Was Isobel forced to restrain her mother? What was Eve trying to do to her? I breathe in sharply and step away. I shouldn't have invited them in. This isn't a situation I want to be involved in. I want them all to go, immediately.

'Eve, we need to take Izzie home now,' Adam says firmly, and I can see he's right, Isobel is becoming visibly agitated.

'You stay away from my daughter,' Eve delivers her parting shot, stepping closer to me and pointing a warning finger in my face. 'The Vaughan men really must have done something evil in a former life to deserve the pair of *you*! "What a tangled web we weave, when first we practise to deceive."'

It's the sheer hypocrisy of that last dig, on top of the day as a whole, that finally causes me to snap.

'I am no liar!' For a moment all I can hear is the sound of my own breathing as my courage gathers. 'I apologise sincerely for what happened this afternoon, but you're in no position to lecture me in my own house about deception. I get that all of this is pulling the skin of old wounds apart for a lot of people, but it's opened my eyes too. What kind of woman are *you*?'

Eve's mouth falls open.

That's right, Eve – I know all about you. An affair with your friend's husband… a special place in hell.

'I have no idea what you're talking about!' she splutters a moment later.

'Stop, both of you,' Isobel says suddenly. 'She's a good mother too.' She gestures towards Eve and then shakes her head. 'This is all wrong. Something has gone very wrong. I can feel it.' She looks around her wildly for a second before laughing again, except this time there is nothing endearing about the sound at all. 'I don't like this,' she whispers. 'Something isn't right.' She places her hands on the side of her head and closes her eyes tightly. 'Adam?' she pleads. 'I need to leave!'

He springs towards her and puts his arms round her waist. 'I'm here! I've got you – you're safe. We need to get her out, Eve, now!'

He's trying to drag Isobel backwards when her eyes suddenly snap open and her face goes first blank with shock, then contorts into a violent scream of absolute fury. I have never seen anything like it. She breaks away from Adam's hold and standing freely on her own two feet appears to grow taller and taller in front of my very eyes; white-hot with rage. I cover my ears in horror as the dreadful high pitch of her shrieking continues. I half expect the windows to implode, sending darts of glass flying into our faces and hands – but then the sound simply cuts off with no warning.

'Get out of here,' she says, after a moment's pause, but her voice is completely different: low and adult.

It's like a scene from a horror movie when a possessed child opens their mouth and the demon's voice coming from within their body is heard for the first time, except this is real.

I stumble back as she points in my direction. 'Get out!' she shouts again. She's talking to me.

Adam has backed off too, hands up – as if afraid of being burnt.

She stands there for a moment, towering and furious before suddenly sinking to the ground, crumpling into a small heap on my sitting room floor and sobbing like she's melting away. Is she even conscious? Eve gives a strange little cry and rushes over to her daughter.

'We should call the crisis team.' She looks up at Adam in panic, no hint of the angry, forceful woman from a moment ago, just a terrified mother who doesn't know what to do.

'No,' he says flatly. 'Not after last time. I *told* you, we shouldn't have come.' He rolls up his jumper sleeves to reveal wiry arms covered with intricate tattoos – he has no bare skin at all – right down to the wrists. I watch in disbelief as, despite his slight frame, he lifts Isobel's lifeless body from the floor with almost no effort, gathering her in his arms and carrying her from the room in some bizarre reverse version of a husband carrying his wife over the threshold.

The room falls silent as the three of them vanish. I am stunned and can only stare at the spot where they were all stood moments ago.

'And thus the circus left town, packing up the big top and leaving under the cover of darkness,' says a voice drily behind me. I whip round to see Tony standing on the stairs, looking down into the room, holding a paint tray containing a clean brush. He pulls a sympathetic face. 'Are you all right?'

'Did you see and hear all of that?' I gasp.

'I did,' he agrees, shaking his head. 'Dear, dear.'

'Her voice when she shouted at me! It sounded like it belonged to a completely different person.' I swallow and wobble back over to the sofa to sit down. My legs aren't able to hold me up.

'Ah, come now!' Tony chides gently. 'It was all just theatrical smoke and mirrors! Creative types like nothing better than a dramatic scene. They call it passion, the rest of us call it a complete breakdown of decorum. Don't let it fool you. I can see what she was trying to achieve but I confess myself a little disappointed. The "strange local girl possessed by something evil" trick is somewhat of a cliché, don't you think?'

I glance at him. 'You think she did that to scare me?'

'Well I certainly don't think anything "unworldly" took her over, that's for sure.' He hesitates and scratches his head. 'I had a chap in the dock once who adopted no less than seven different voices – complete with accents – because his entire defence rested on him having multiple personality disorder, and he maintained his main personality was not guilty of the offence one of the others had committed. It was a masterful performance, but ultimately, a performance was all it was. So yes, I suppose either one could conclude Isobel Parkes has serious mental health issues or there was an ulterior motive behind that display. Certainly ignore what you heard her mother say about calling the crisis team. Isobel will be *fine*,' he says firmly. 'She's always fine.'

I'm aware of getting into very uncomfortable territory. 'I know that Isobel historically has always had very strong feelings for Tim...' I try and steer us away from Eve, 'and obviously this was her house. It must be difficult for her to see me living here with him now. I can also see she's not very well – but could I ask you something I asked Susannah? Do *you* think she's dangerous?'

He sighs, comes downstairs and sits next to me. 'Over the years I've seen the effects of trauma on a huge range of people from all walks of life: witnesses, victims, professionals... and I've realised it's impossible for some people not to manipulate the effects of said trauma to their own end. Subconsciously or consciously. I think Isobel Parkes has effectively played the part expected of her, *when* it has suited her, but I think it's wise to be at least wary of her.' He pauses while I digest that. 'If I may offer you another piece of advice that applies here? "It's a good rule in life never to apologise. The right sort of people do not want apologies, and the wrong sort take a mean advantage of them."'

'I'd guess who said that, but I've already got one quote wrong today,' I manage eventually. 'I take your point though.'

'It's P. G. Wodehouse.' He rubs his jaw. 'Another of his is: "Boyhood, like measles, is one of those complaints which a man should catch young and have done with, for when it comes in middle life it is apt to be serious".'

I snort sadly. 'Yes, perhaps, could we not tell Tim about Isobel's *Carrie* act? I'll never get him back in this house otherwise. He already thinks it's haunted. I'd rather just tell him the truth; they came over to have a go at me for shouting at her in a shop and I apologised. End of story.'

'Of course. That's exactly what happened, after all.'

'Thank you,' I say gratefully. 'He really wants to make this work, and so do I.'

'I know you do and I really think this could be the making of him. You're very sensible not to let unnecessary distractions derail you.' He nods at the door through which Isobel has just vanished. 'Come on,' he stands up, 'they'll be wondering where we are.'

# CHAPTER SEVENTEEN

## Claire

It seems Tim is feeling a little better once we get back to The Rectory. I decide to wait and tell him about my latest Eve Parkes showdown once Rosie is in bed. I don't want him discussing it in front of her in case she gets upset again and thinks it was her fault when it wasn't.

Managing so many different agendas is exhausting and I'm glad to have Tim's help with bathing Rosie and reading stories before snuggling her into bed. He does all of the different voices of the BFG, to her rapt delight, as I sit quietly at the end of the bed watching them. I used to love *The BFG* as a child; now as a parent I don't particularly like it: a fast-running giant planting dreams or nightmares in your mind with a silver trumpet. I shiver involuntarily, but keep quiet, because Rosie is fascinated, snuggled in Tim's arms. Part of the thrill is her daddy bringing it to life rather than the story itself and she's right – he's very good at it. Once he's finished, I take over and sing her songs, before promising I'll come and check on her in two minutes.

When I appear in the kitchen, Susannah is wearing her apron and standing over the Aga, conjuring up one of her amazing meals out of nowhere. She's an excellent cook and although I can't smell whatever is in the pan, the sound of it sizzling and the sight of the laid table makes me immediately hungry.

'Glass of wine?' Tony offers, getting up from the table where he's reading the paper as I walk into the room. 'There's a rather nice Malbec open, or I can get some white from the big fridge if you'd prefer?'

'Malbec sounds great, thank you.' I look over at Tim who is leaning on the side, arms crossed, looking pensive. I get the feeling I've interrupted a conversation between the three of them. 'How is your head?'

'A bit better thanks,' he says tiredly, closing his eyes for a second and rubbing his brow with his hand. 'Dad was just telling me about the visitors you had at the house earlier. I'm so sorry, Claire. I don't know what to say.'

Ah, that explains the atmosphere. I shrug helplessly. 'It was partly my own fault. I *did* shove Isobel away from Rosie in the shop earlier. It may well have hurt and upset her.' I clear my throat awkwardly. 'I suppose if I'm being objective I can see why her mother was angry.'

'You pushed her?' Tim looks surprised. 'Mum just said in the shop all you did was tell Izzie to let go of Rosie, which is fair enough.'

'It was barely an outstretched hand, never mind a push.' Susannah doesn't turn round but carries on energetically stirring. 'The whole thing has been taken massively out of proportion.' She puts the spoon down and licks her finger before reaching for the pepper. 'One always likes the idea of doing risotto, but you forget what a faff it is.' She adds another fierce twist of seasoning then steps back and wipes her brow as Tony reappears carrying my wine. 'Ant, I'll have some of that white, please, actually, while you're out there.'

Tony hands me my glass then salutes her. 'Right away, *memsaab*.'

'You probably can't say that any more, dearest,' she says archly.

'I'll say whatever the bloody hell I like in my own house,' he replies amiably and disappears off to the fridge as I return to Tim.

'In any case, I apologised to Isobel, in front of her mother,' I confess. 'I probably shouldn't have let them in but I just didn't want them standing outside making a scene.'

'That was very sensible of you, Claire,' Susannah says over her shoulder, having returned to stirring.

'It was hard to know what to do for the best really,' I continue. 'One minute I was sat on the sofa looking at the stars and eyes on the ceiling beam, the next all Hell was breaking loose and I—'

'Hang on. What stars and eyes on the beam?' Tim interrupts.

'There are loads of symbols on the beam in the sitting room.' I take a sip of my wine. 'They're rather beautiful actually. A bit hippy, but—'

Tim has straightened up completely. 'What sort of stars? Five- or six-pointed?'

I stare at him. 'Just stars. That's all. I can't really remember to be honest. Events took over after that.' I cross the room and sit down at the table.

'I think I'd like to get the house blessed before we move in tomorrow,' Tim blurts suddenly as Tony reappears in the doorway holding Susannah's wine.

'"Blessed"?' Tony repeats in astonishment. 'I thought we weren't saying anything about all of that?' He looks at me, confused.

'*I* didn't,' I reply pointedly, as Tim simultaneously says: 'about what?'

Tony scowls, cross with himself at having made such a basic mistake and waves a dismissive hand as he sits back down and snatches up his paper. 'Isobel Parkes had an ethereal moment, shall we say, at the house. Nothing but utter tosh.'

'She became agitated, then quickly went ballistic,' I'm forced to explain to Tim. 'Her voice was all low and growly and she shouted at me to "get out" of the house, then she collapsed on the floor crying. Adam had to carry her out.'

Tim's eyes widen with fear. 'That's horrible. It's lucky Adam was there to help, but whatever it was threatened you? I *definitely* want the house blessed now.'

'*Whatever it was?* Christ, Susannah!' Tony glowers over the top of the article he is clearly not reading at all. 'This is what happens when you will insist on a Catholic school. Several years at the monk factory and the boy wants Father Whatsit-fiddly to flick some water about the place before he can so much as sleep there.'

'Yes, *thank* you, Tony!' Susannah snaps, lifting the pan off the hot plate. 'We all know my beliefs are not important to you, but they *are* important to me.'

'When it suits you,' replies Tony shaking the pages out. 'Cherry-picking the pomp and leaving out the nasty bits – in other words liking cathedrals and reflexively crossing yourself when you pass a hearse – does not a Catholic make.'

'On the other hand, I've put up with ridiculous comments like that for years because I happen to believe in the sacrament of marriage. So, swings and roundabouts.' She slams the pan down on the mat, wipes her hands on her apron and turns to Tim. 'I don't see any reason why you shouldn't perform a blessing at Fox Cottage. I think it's a very nice idea, actually.'

Tony simply snorts in disgust and turns the page.

'I'll call Father Mathew in the morning,' Susannah says smoothly. 'I'm sure he won't have any objections to popping round. I know he's having lunch with the Dicksons tomorrow, so I don't see why he couldn't come on to Fox Cottage after that.'

'Thank you, Ma,' says Tim looking relieved.

'Sorry, can we hang on a sec.' I put a hand up. 'This is all getting a bit OTT, isn't it?'

'Thank goodness,' murmurs Tony, turning the page. 'A voice of reason at last.'

'I don't really want Rosie seeing a priest wandering around the place praying, on the day she moves in.' I set my wine down carefully. 'It would properly freak her out.'

'Well, she doesn't *have* to move in tomorrow?' Tim reasons. 'We could stay another night here, as originally planned?'

'No, Tim, we couldn't,' I say firmly. 'We need to get Rosie settled. She starts at her new school on Monday. She needs to know where she's at. Also, we've got a huge amount of unpacking to do tomorrow; I'd rather we just got on with it. I mean – a blessing would be a nice extra to make it a happy place and all that – but it's not exactly essential, is it?'

'I'm genuinely not sure I want any of us to sleep there yet,' Tim says quietly. 'We need to make that house safe.'

*Safe?* He really thinks that?

In the moment of stunned silence that follows his extraordinary statement, we all hear it; the faint, eerie sound of a little sing-song voice calling 'Mummmmy? Mummmmy?' echoing down the draughty rectory corridors. Poor Tim looks as if he's about to be sick. There's even a sheen of light sweat on his forehead.

'It's Rosie. I promised I'd go and check on her and I haven't.' I get up quickly enough to make the chair scrape noisily on the flagstones, and Tim flinches at that too. He is a bag of nerves. Maybe he really has come down with something, but either way, he needs to take a moment.

'Hold those thoughts,' I say. 'I'll just check on Rosie and come right back.'

I pad off down the corridor in my slippers, emerging back out into the draughty hall and jog up the wide staircase. How on earth Tim can have slept *here* as a child – and even now – with no problems, but wants to exorcise Fox Cottage, is completely beyond me. It's just a house. One he had an upsetting séance in as a teenager with Adam and *her*, granted, but the building itself is no more than bricks and mortar. He must see that, surely? I make my way down to Rosie's room, but when I stick my head round the door, her bed is empty.

'Rosie?' I go right into the room expecting to find her in front of the bookcase selecting something else to read, but she's not there either. I frown and then jump so badly I almost hit the ceiling as a small hand is placed on my back. Spinning round I find Rosie standing there in her pyjamas.

'Sorry, Mummy!' she looks anxious. 'I just went for a wee.'

'Back into bed, you little monkey,' I scold in relief, and she grins and jumps in under the covers.

'Two minutes,' she says, 'but will you really come back this time?'

'I will, I promise.' I cross my heart and blow her a kiss before heading back down to the kitchen. Perhaps I'm being unfair to Tim. This has even got to me a little bit. We all need to calm down.

Susannah has dished up and they are all waiting for me in silence. I slip back into my place, and Susannah picks up her fork. 'She's all right?'

'Absolutely fine,' I confirm.

We start to eat. Wishing I didn't have to, but knowing I must, I return to the scene of the crime. 'So, this exorcism you want to do…'

Tim sets his fork down and looks at me.

'Will you feel happier if we do it?'

Tim clears his throat. 'It's not about me being *happier*. I wasn't going to tell you this, but seeing as we're getting everything out in the open, earlier on, when we arrived at Fox Cottage and went up to Rosie's bedroom, there was an old newspaper cutting, right in the middle of the room, lying on the carpet. Now, I know it wasn't there last night, because we moved everything out, didn't we, to have a clear run for painting? Yes?'

'Yes, OK.' I take a sip of wine, slightly taken aback by his tone.

'That newspaper clipping was of me as a child, taken after the shooting, so it's what – nearly thirty years old? And you're telling me that's nothing to worry about, that it just turned up in the middle of the floor out of nowhere?'

I chew more slowly. 'Are you saying some*thing* put it there? I thought you wanted every lock in the house changed because you were worried some*one* was going to let themselves in – again.' I take another forkful of rice. 'She must have been very disappointed to find you weren't there.'

'"She"?' It's Tim's turn to look bewildered. 'I'm not talking about Isobel. I actually want all of the locks replaced and working so we can get *out* in an emergency, not to stop someone getting in.'

An extremely uncomfortable silence follows. 'Right,' I say eventually, 'so you don't think this cutting on the carpet is Isobel playing silly games? Or to put it another way, illegally trespassing?'

'The thing is, you *have* had the locks changed now,' Susannah says soothingly. 'She can't get in any more – if we assume Claire is right. I'm certainly not sure you want to call the police *just* yet and mention trespassing, do you?'

'Sorry.' Tim holds up a hand suddenly. 'I think I can hear Rosie again.'

I sigh. 'Hang on. I'll be right back.'

I retrace my steps on autopilot to her bedroom. Susannah's right, everyone local will find out and hate me for persecuting poor, disturbed, beautiful Isobel if I call the police. Maybe it *is* better to wait and see what happens tonight, now that she will discover it's impossible for her to get in and leave Tim any little gifts. Plus, I suppose it could have just as easily been Adam? He knew we weren't there last night. He saw us leave – and he told *us* the French windows in the barn were rotten. Although I can't see why he'd do something odd like put that cutting on the floor? What would be the point?

Back in Rosie's room I discover she's fast sleep. So poor Tim is now even hearing things. Perhaps it would just be easier to let some priest perform a blessing, or whatever it is they do. I tuck the duvet round Rosie and creep back down. I can hear raised voices coming from the kitchen as I reach the bottom of the stairs and my heart sinks.

'I'm not making anything up!' Tim is insisting as I approach the doorway. I stop in the hall and listen carefully.

'All I'm saying is that I didn't actually see this piece of old newspaper,' says Tony calmly. 'How can I back you up to Claire when I didn't see anything? I am concerned, however. You promised all of us that you were committed to this plan. Claire and Rosie have given everything up to move here, and I've paid out a not inconsiderable sum of money to make it all happen and put a roof over your heads. You've *got* to move into Fox Cottage, Timothy. If you really, absolutely must, get the place blessed, exorcised or whatever the hell it is – but then—'

'I know you don't believe me, Dad, but—'

'For God's sake!' Tony bangs the table in frustration, making the knives and forks leap up and clatter back down. 'It's not about anyone's beliefs, Catholic, agnostic or otherwise! It's about a state-ment of fact! Nothing has happened at that house that doesn't have a rational explanation. You're in danger of starting to appear a little touched yourself, if you don't mind my saying so. Time to get on with the job, hey?'

I cough to show that I'm approaching and walk back into the room. 'She's asleep. Sorry to interrupt the meal with all this getting up and down. So,' I take a deep breath, 'we're going to see how it goes tonight now the locks are changed, get Father Mathew in tomorrow too, get unpacked, take stock and hopefully sleep there, but if it's OK by you, Susannah, we'll play that by ear a little? There, everyone's happy.'

'That sounds like a plan.' Susannah takes a sip of wine.

'Thank you,' Tim says, reaching out to take my hand and squeezing it tightly. 'I do just have one other thing to say though? If that's OK?'

'Sure!' I smile patiently and lean back in my chair. I've more or less completely given up on my food now anyway.

'I just want you all to know – in case you were worried that I'm not committed to making this situation work – that I had a call from my agent earlier and I got that part I went for.'

My mouth falls open and I sit up straight. 'Oh my God! Why didn't you say anything earlier?'

'Because I've turned it down,' Tim says looking straight at Tony. 'I wanted to prove that I understand what I did with the money has consequences. The most important thing to me is my family. I've made a commitment to you and I won't walk away from it.'

'But if you'd talked to me about it, we could have made something work, I'm sure,' I look at him bewildered.

He shakes his head. 'It would have meant filming on location for two months. I couldn't have left you here, having dragged you away from home in the first place. It wouldn't have been fair. It's just the way it is. You're more important.'

'Well I think that's very honourable of you, don't you, Tony?' says Susannah.

'Very,' says Tony. 'Good man.'

Tim nods and exhales heavily. He looks exhausted.

'Strange hours your agent keeps, though,' Tony remarks, wiping his mouth on his napkin. 'Did they call you with this news once you were back here this evening then?'

Tim frowns. 'Yes. Why?'

'I didn't see you take a call today, that's all.'

'You're saying I made this up, too?' Tim's voice is light but Susannah closes her eyes briefly before starting to clear the plates.

Tony laughs. 'Darling! Of course not. It's more a remark on the state of the signal at Fox Cottage if anything. Why ever would I accuse you of making that up?'

'I don't know.' Tim gets to his feet. 'To undercut the significance of what I've just said about sticking it out here? To make me look a twat? To suggest I'm lying again, like I'm lying about why I don't want to move into the house, and finding that newspaper cutting on the floor… the same way I admit I lied about the money at first. You tell me.' He pushes his chair in. 'Thanks for tea, Mum. I'm just going to pop out for ten minutes.' He bends and kisses my cheek. 'I need some air; my head is going to explode and we've run out of paracetamol.'

'We've got plenty of that here,' says Tony. 'Don't be an arse, Tim. You don't have to stomp off in a mood.'

'We could actually use some more Calpol for Rosie, if you're going to the chemist or a petrol station,' I say. It's not true – I've got two big bottles of it, but I can see he really does need an excuse to get away from here for ten minutes, just as I did earlier.

He nods gratefully. 'Will do. See you in a bit.' He shoots his father one last look of sadness and disbelief, which breaks my heart a little, before walking from the room. Once he's gone, Susannah turns and looks at Tony pointedly too. She doesn't say anything at all, but it's enough to trigger her husband.

'So I suppose all of that is my fault then?' Tony says crossly as we all hear the front door close. 'I *did not* say he'd made it up about being offered the part. That, along with everything else he's said tonight, is entirely a figment of his imagination.' He stands up and grabs his wine. 'I shall be in my study.' He then stomps off, in a mood.

Susannah stares into the middle distance for a moment before turning back to me, and smiling. 'Would you like some more risotto, Claire?'

I shake my head. 'No, thank you, but it was delicious.'

We lapse into silence but thankfully my phone bleeps with a text from Mel.

*Just to say I'm thinking of you and missing you. X*

'It's Mel, my best friend, asking me to call her,' I lie as I stare at the screen and get up. 'Do you mind?'

Susannah shakes her head absently, barely noticing as I leave the room. I ought to offer to help her clean up, but I just want to escape.

I want to go home.

# CHAPTER EIGHTEEN

## Eve

Isobel has more or less stopped crying and is just lying on the sofa, eyes glazed as she watches the TV unseeingly, when there is a knock at the front door. Adam and I glance at each other. I go to get up but he holds out a hand. 'I'll go.'

I'm so exhausted that I'm more than happy to let him.

I try to stay relaxed and ignore the exchange of low male voices I can hear carrying up the hall. 'Do you want a cup of tea, Izzie?' I ask her calmly, but she's sat up a little and is very still.

'Isobel?' shouts a voice and she gasps. One word – that's all it takes. We both know exactly who is there, now. So, not content with his family harassing her, now *he* has to come to the house too?

She makes it out to the hall before I do, moving so quickly I couldn't have stopped her if I'd tried. Sure enough, Timothy is on the doorstep, his breath forming around him like dry ice against the night sky, hands in the back of his jeans pocket. I can't help sourly wondering if he is seeing stage directions in his mind: *Curtain up. It is a misty, cold night. Enter the hero.*

Adam is blocking the way, however, hand protectively across the opening as he holds the doorframe. 'Mate, please,' he says to Timothy. 'She's had such a rough evening already. Another time, eh? Forgive me being the protective boyfriend, but she's really not up to it.'

Timothy ignores him completely and looks round him, calling out: 'Iz! Please! I really need to speak to you. I need your help – it's important. I want to keep my little girl safe, that's all. Please!'

Isobel walks determinedly down the hall and puts her hands on Adam's arm to move it out of the way.

'I don't want you to be my boyfriend any more,' she says quietly, and I wince for poor Adam. 'I know you want the best for me but I also want you to leave now, so that I can speak to Tim.'

How can he do anything but let go? He steps back, humiliated, hands in the air and shaking his head, disappears off into the kitchen. I should probably follow him and make sure he's OK, but there's no way I'm letting Izzie stay out here on her own. Whatever is about to happen, I think I ought to witness it first-hand. Anything may be given in evidence at a later date, and all that. I stare at Timothy, not making any attempt to hide my hostility. He might not know what Izzie went through after that summer because of him, but I do.

Izzie, however, steps forward and hugs him, wrapping her arms around his neck and laying her head briefly on his chest. 'I'm so glad you've come,' she says. 'Of course I'll help you.'

I watch his arms jerk automatically, unsure for a moment, but then he hugs her back tightly and closes his eyes. I can hear relief pouring out of him when he replies: 'Thank you. I knew you'd understand.'

They draw back away from each other and Timothy glances nervously in my direction.

'Hello, Mrs Parkes, I knew this one was your house because of Adam's van being outside, but I'm still sorry to have to disturb you. I wouldn't unless it was important.' I don't answer, just stare at him stonily – and, embarrassed, he turns back to Izzie. 'Your mum told me when she was collecting the dolls you've not had an easy time of it in Fox Cottage.'

My heart thumps, and Isobel glances back at me briefly.

'Anyway, I'm going to have the house blessed tomorrow,' he continues, unaware of having just dropped me in it. She will have noticed doll*s*, plural, for sure. 'Hopefully that will help. But what I really want to know is – I'm not imagining it, am I? What happened to you?'

'"What happened" to me?' Izzie repeats briefly and her eyes cloud with tears. 'Wow.' She wipes them away quickly. 'Well. You're right to be worried. That house is dangerous—'

I frown and straighten up. *What?*

'And I'm actually so much happier now we're not in it!' She gives a little gasp of laughter, and my mouth falls open. *She is? Since when?*

'It was my home for so long, but it wasn't safe. You're not safe there,' Isobel continues, 'and I'm so sorry that I didn't know you had a little girl. You shouldn't have come back, I can see that now.'

I realise she's apologising for 'manipulating' him back to Fox Cottage. I'm about to intervene, to stop her appearing completely mad, when she blurts: 'I've really not been trying to make trouble though…'

He holds up a hand 'No one is saying that you have.'

She shakes her head, exasperated. 'Claire thinks I am, and I'm not. I don't want to punish anyone. I don't want to create hysteria or cause an irrevocable family split. I just want to make sure it never happens again to anyone else.' A tear trickles down her cheek. 'It might have already started. I really, really hope I'm wrong, but you *must not leave Rosie alone*. Not ever, in that house, at night. It can't be allowed. I feel like something big is going to happen.'

OK, now *I'm* worried. What the hell is she talking about? I know I made up all of that evil presence nonsense to scare Timothy, but she's talking like there really is something to be frightened of and it's working. Timothy nods frantically.

'I feel like I'm being watched,' he whispers, terrified. 'I know I'm not imagining it. I'm so stressed out by it I can't sleep and I'm having these terrible dreams and headaches.'

Isobel shakes her head slowly. 'You're not imagining it. And don't let anyone tell you otherwise.'

I hear a movement behind me as Adam appears in the kitchen doorway, leaning on the frame, arms crossed, watching them quietly.

'OK – well, thank you,' Timothy says. 'Thank you so much for not laughing at me and acting like I'm mad and this is all in my head.'

'You are not mad and it's not in your head,' whispers Isobel. 'Trust your instincts… and the evidence.'

'I'm so very sorry I walked away without helping you, all those years ago.' Timothy says suddenly. 'I didn't understand.'

Isobel doesn't say anything to that. Just nods, her eyes shining and holds out her arms to him again.

I watch them hug briefly, her eyes flutter closed as if she is fixing the moment in her mind forever. She moves her head briefly and kisses his cheek so lightly I'm reminded of the butterfly kisses I used to give her as a child. I also distinctly hear her whisper 'I love you.'

I wish I had left them alone now. Not only is this deeply private, hearing those three little words makes me ache with sadness. I can feel she means them with every part of her being and I want so very badly to wave a magic wand; make him love her back, let her have the one thing she has always wanted. But I can't.

Adam exhales heavily and, glancing round, I see him disappear back into the kitchen. Isobel doesn't even notice he's gone.

'So you won't leave Rosie alone now? You promise?' Isobel draws back from their embrace, and Timothy nods.

'Here,' she says, 'let me give you my mobile number.' She turns and scrabbles in the drawer of the sideboard for a pen and scrap of paper, before scribbling on it. 'In case you need it in an emergency, or something.'

I look down. I literally can't endure this. It's too painful, watching her give her all like this.

'Thanks, Iz,' he says, and she flushes with pleasure. 'Good night, Mrs Parkes,' he says politely, still looking wretched, but perhaps a little more resolute as he shoves his hands back in his pockets. 'Sorry again for disturbing you.'

Once Isobel has closed the door behind him, she turns and smiles at me radiantly. 'I think I'll go to bed now, Mama.' She gives an elaborate yawn. 'It's been a long day and I'm tired. I slept so well last night though. I hope that'll happen again tonight. I'm sure it will.'

I wait for her to angrily ask me why I lied about the boy doll's whereabouts, but incredibly, she says nothing. It must be because she's got it back now anyway, seeing as she took it from the drawer. I don't think she cares about anything else except Timothy, Timothy, Timothy...

'I'm so relieved!' she says suddenly and wipes her sparkling eyes briefly. 'I can't even tell you.' She blows me a kiss and drifts off up to bed.

I watch her go in astonishment and then go to find Adam. He is sat slumped at the table, twisting a tissue with one hand, the other in his trouser pocket.

I sit down opposite him. 'Tell me what you're thinking?'

He looks up and balls the tissue in his hand before shoving it in his other pocket. 'Honestly? Entitled, ruthless, smug fucker.'

I sigh in sympathy. Our apple carts have all so badly tumbled over. I told Antony, I *begged* him not to interfere and buy Fox Cottage. Why does a certain type of man always think they know best? It is utterly maddening. And of course he would have been there this afternoon to hear me shouting like a fishwife, and witness Isobel becoming hysterical. I saw the expression on his face when she fell to the floor; his impatience was palpable.

His lack of compassion for her condition is one of the biggest disappointments of my life. You can't be with a person who does not understand your child can't just 'snap out' of it and ought to 'pull themselves together', but I used to wonder if he would have changed over time – had Timothy not existed and I'd been able to stay with him after all, of course. After this afternoon, I can see he wouldn't have. I made the right decision: for Isobel's sake, at least.

'You can get away with anything as long as you're charming enough, can't you? I wish I'd realised this a lot earlier in life,' Adam says, dragging me back to the room.

'Yes, sadly I think that's probably true,' I agree. 'I don't even understand what all of that was about, out there.'

'Neither do they,' he says flatly. 'They were talking at totally cross purposes. You got that he thinks there's something in the house though?' he looks at me again. 'Something that needs "exorcising"?'

I nod.

'Well, that's not what she thinks he means. I know what *she's* talking about and what really happened in the house. She's close to finally confronting it, but it has to be on her terms. I can't intervene.'

I blanch and sit up straighter. 'You can't say all that and then *not* tell me! That's not fair!'

He sits up too and covers his face with his hands before sliding them up and behind his head, arms wide, in a faux-relaxed position, which is anything but. 'Eve... I've wanted her to talk about it for a very long time. I wish I could tell you, but I really can't say any more. I'm sorry.'

There's a long, uncomfortable pause. 'Then it seems I must accept that,' I say tightly. 'I wish I *had* burnt the place down now though.'

Adam frowns at me.

'On the day we completed,' I elaborate. 'I lit Izzie's wacky candle and I was this close,' I lift my thumb and forefinger, 'to dropping it and letting the whole place go up. If there's no house, they can't live there, can they? Except knowing my luck, that wretched Claire would have arrived, and because she can't smell anything, would have been overcome by the smoke, died and then I'd have been done for murdering her. So there we are.'

Adam stares hard at the table, shakes his head and then gets up. 'I'm sorry, I have to leave. I can't handle this right now. I'm all Vaughan-ed out and as I'm apparently not even "the boyfriend" any more, there doesn't seem much point in my sticking around. I've always only been the consolation prize. My gestures were never grand enough.'

'You *are* the boyfriend,' I reassure him, gently. 'You have been for a very long time now.'

'Um, no – I really haven't. Never, in fact.' He looks at me pointedly.

I'm aghast. While no one wants to think of their child having a sexual relationship, Isobel is also a grown woman. She may have mental health issues, but she is not stuck in permanent childhood, whatever Susannah Vaughan and anyone else might think. I admit I talked to her about sex later in life than I otherwise might have done with another teenager. Too late, it would now appear, but I was factual, realistic, positive… I made it stress free. I had assumed she and Adam… that they must have. I mean… all this time? *Nothing?*

'Actually, I don't want to discuss this with you, if that's OK?' He wraps his arms around himself, protectively. 'Sorry. It'd be weird – and unfair. It's complicated.'

'Of course,' I say quickly. 'I don't want to pry, I just—'

'I love her,' he says simply. 'That's all. I've loved her since we were seven – when you first moved here and she was sat on my table at school. People think children that young can't fall in love – but they can. It nearly killed me when Timothy rescued her from Paul Jones and I just stood there, crying like a baby.' He pushes his chair in. 'And now he's back to save her again. Timothy the Hero, forever.' He pats his pocket for his keys. 'I just want to keep her from being hurt.'

'I'm so sorry. What she's said tonight has hurt *you* – deeply – I can see that, but please don't leave. She'll have changed her mind again by the morning and you'll be the boyfriend again. It's also freezing out there. Stay here tonight, like we agreed? I've made the spare room up?'

'I know, and I'm sorry – but I can't,' he says miserably, scratching his head. 'I won't sleep in the van though, I promise. I've got somewhere I can go.'

I nod. I don't like it and I wish he wouldn't, but I understand why he can't stay. It's too painful to be that close to someone you love – only a wall apart – and not be able to hold them. So near and yet so far. Agony.

'Can I just get my washing please?' he says.

I stand up. 'Of course, it's in the upstairs airing cupboard, actually. I'll get it.'

'It's OK,' he says quickly. 'I'll go.'

I let him, appreciating that even though his heart is breaking, he still, nonetheless, hopes to get one last look at her, exchange a good night on the landing. Any little scraps.

He disappears, and I sit there thoughtfully for a moment. *So, more secrets, Isobel?* Have I misjudged this? Is it Timothy's *daughter* she's becoming fixated with, rather than Timothy himself? Christ, I hope not. I close my eyes for a moment and take a deep breath. Timothy really is terrified about moving in, though. Antony must be spitting feathers about an exorcism. I can't help but give a brief smile of satisfaction at that. "Misery and guilt hiding behind bells and smells" was his damning summation of the Catholic church, I seem to remember.

I open my eyes again and my gaze alights on Adam's rucksack in the corner of the room. He's left the zip slightly open having clearly shoved his phone back in, only it's lying on something: the red doll. My eyes widen with shock. *He* took it from the drawer? I hurry over and open the zip a little more widely… to discover a woman's scarf – not mine or Izzie's – and a pink, glittery hairclip, complete with a unicorn's smiley face.

I lift it out, turning the small item over in my hand. It very obviously belongs to a little girl. Rosie.

'Eve?'

I turn around to see him standing there, holding his bag of now-clean washing. I hold the clip aloft.

'Why have you got this? You couldn't possibly want to hurt that little girl? And that scarf under the poppet?' I point to them. 'I understand Timothy, and at a push, Claire too – but *Rosie*? She's just a child!'

'You think *I'm* going to use them to make more dolls?' he says slowly. 'I was going to get rid of them. I'm trying to protect Izzie. I'm always trying to protect her. I saw them in her bag when I picked her up this morning, so I took them out. Please don't challenge her about them, she'll only get upset.'

I must hesitate just a fraction too long as I consider that explanation because he walks past me, grabs the scarf and the doll from the bag and tosses them onto the table.

'You take them then if you don't believe me. Destroy them yourself if it'll make you happier.'

I place the hairclip down on the scarf carefully. 'I'm sorry. I didn't mean to sound accusative.' I think of Izzie's cold bed last night when I wondered where she'd been. 'I've obviously made a mistake.'

'Yes, you have,' he says angrily, picking his bag up. 'You honestly think I could hurt a little girl?' He slings it over his shoulder. 'You don't know me at all then. Even after all this time.' He quietly walks out of the room. The front door closes behind him with barely a click.

# CHAPTER NINETEEN

## Claire

My alarm goes off at 1 a.m. I wake instantly to stop it before it disturbs Tim, only when I turn over, I discover he's not there and his pillow is missing.

I sit up in the dark room, blinking fully awake, all thoughts of sneaking off downstairs to call Jen, gone. Where is he?

I get up and shiver into my dressing gown. Creaking out onto the hall landing, I glance at the bathroom, but the door is open, the light on, and the room empty. I pad across the landing – only for Tony and Susannah's door to drift slowly open. I freeze, thinking I've woken one of them – except when I look down, two liquid brown eyes stare up at me and a tail thwacks against the doorframe.

'Shhh, Badger!' I whisper. 'Bed! Go on! Shooo!'

He looks at me balefully and vanishes back into the gloom as I hear Susannah or Tony snore loudly, wake themselves slightly with the noise and turn over to go back to sleep.

Tiptoeing towards Rosie's room, I push the door open enough to see her sleeping peacefully, but I also spy a familiar leg sticking out from behind her bed, lying on the floor.

I walk round to discover Tim flat out on a duvet, his pillow under his head, and another duvet with no cover on it pulled over him. He's fast asleep.

I stare down at him. Is Ro ill? Did she come in and I didn't realise – so he got up with her? I'm about to reach my hand out and put it to her skin to check for a temperature when Tim suddenly wakes up, wide eyes staring at me – and scrambles backwards so fast he hits his head on the chest of drawers. It makes such a thud, wobbling the china ornaments on the top of it and the lamp, as he sits upright – I'm sure Rosie will disturb, but she doesn't. Just sleeps on through.

Tim stares back at me, breathing fast, and swallows, before wiping his mouth with the back of his hand. 'What are you doing just standing over me like that?' he breathes hoarsely. 'I almost had a heart attack!'

'Sorry,' I whisper back. 'What are you doing in here? Is she all right?'

'Um,' he blinks again, confused. He was obviously deeply asleep. 'Just give me a second.'

Rosie twitches and turns over, starting to restlessly sense our presence in her sleep.

I put my finger to my lips. 'Come to the bathroom,' I mouth and creep back out.

I wait in there for a moment or two, looking at my reflection in the mirror and am just beginning to wonder if he's gone back to sleep, when he shuffles in, hair all over the place, eyes squinting in the light.

'What's going on?' I ask, concerned.

'Nightmares,' he says and scratches his chest before pushing the door to, reaching for some loo roll and blowing his nose deliberately quietly.

'Poor little thing,' I sigh. 'That'll be my fault for shouting in the shop. I must have stressed her out.'

He frowns, then shakes his head. 'No. I had nightmares. About her.'

'Oh Tim!' I reach out and put a hand on his arm.

'I couldn't get to sleep. I closed my eyes for literally ten minutes and had the most horrific one I've ever had, about Rosie.' He crosses his arms making my hand fall away from him. 'I needed to go and make sure she was OK.'

'Of course. Are you coming back to bed though? It can't be comfy on the floor in there?'

He shakes his head. 'I think I'll stay with her.'

I look at him carefully. 'Are you sure you're all right?'

He hesitates and I'm astonished to see tears forming in his eyes, which he wipes away quickly.

'Why don't you tell me about the nightmare?' I encourage. 'Sometimes it can help to say it out loud? It doesn't feel as scary then.'

He gives a small, desperate laugh. 'No, thanks. I don't want to think about it ever again, let alone discuss it. It was terrifying.'

'But just a dream,' I remind him. 'Come on, tell me.'

He looks at me and takes a deep breath. 'It involved Paul Jones being in Fox Cottage. I could hear him laughing but I didn't know where he was or where Rosie was either. I kept rushing from empty room to empty room and the laughter was coming from a different place each time. Then I heard Rosie screaming. It got worse after that.'

'OK, just stop,' I say quickly. 'It's all right.' I put my hand back on his arm. 'You don't have to continue.'

'Everything is feeling very real to me at the moment. I'm sorry. I know I'm stressing you out and I don't mean to. What with these bits of candles, séances, carvings all over the ceilings, newspaper clippings from nearly thirty years ago and exorcisms, my head's a mess.'

I cross my own arms, shivering in the cold, my teeth giving an involuntarily chatter as I try and think of something to say – but I'm not fast enough for Tim.

'Look, just go back to bed,' he says brusquely. 'We'll talk more about it in the morning. I know you don't believe in this kind of thing, but I do, and I'm freaking out. I feel like we're playing parts in some improvisation horror movie I don't even know I've been cast in.'

'Sweetheart, you've always had a wild imagination. It's what makes you a good actor.'

'Don't, please!' He lets his head hang back in despair. 'This is not bullshit. I promise you.'

'I know it isn't! You *are* a good actor. The fact that you got the part proves it. That's what we need to talk about in the morning – how we make that work.'

'I told you, I already refused it – and we won't talk about it in the morning anyway.' He rubs his eyes and mutters. 'I think she's right. Something big is going to happen, I can feel it.'

'Of course she's right. You have an *amazing* agent. She's spot on, this is just the start. You got one part – you'll definitely get others. We just need to find a way of getting you to auditions.'

He shakes his head. 'No, that's not what I'm talking about. And I can't get to auditions from here anyway, that's just crazy!'

'Why not? I'm going to have to get to work from here!' I can't help but make the point.

He yawns, involuntarily. 'OK, I really don't want to fight with you now, it's what – 3 a.m.?'

'One,' I correct him.

'Whatever. It's late. Honestly, go back to bed.'

'No, come on – you're right, we need to discuss this. If you won't go to auditions, why don't you finally ask Sam for some help? You've proven you're still good enough to get parts. Get him to fast-track you. If he can't open some doors, no one can.'

He exhales heavily. 'You really don't get it. It's not your fault, but you don't. Stuff just isn't black and white like that. For one, if this ever happens, I don't want to use any connections – it means everything to me to get it on my own merit. For two, Sam would never push anyone he sees as a threat. I couldn't say this to anyone but you, but I'm a better actor than him.' He shrugs. 'I know it, he knows it. I got all the parts at school he didn't. I was like Neil in *Dead Poets Society* and he *hated* it. He could have got me seen for a hundred things by now if he wanted to. And he hasn't.'

I can't help but think that's absolute rubbish. Sam is an A-list star. Why would he feel threatened by Tim? This is all starting to sound increasingly paranoid. Worryingly so.

'I know you won't agree with me,' he whispers urgently, 'but Harry would have done it in Sam's position. No question.'

I can't help it. I snort with disgust.

He looks up at the ceiling. 'Harry really didn't set out to screw us.'

'That's exactly what he would have done, given a chance,' I retort before I think. It's the middle of the night – my brain is not working properly.

Tim looks confused. 'I don't understand what you mean by that?'

I hesitate, on the verge of finally telling him, after ten years, what his beloved friend, his 'family', did to me that first night I met him. I want to explain that back then, I didn't think he would believe me over Harry, but the longer we've been together the more it's become about not wanting to torpedo his most important male relationship because I love him. But yes, I was frightened and no, it wasn't OK. I know Harry doesn't like me – he's been downright rude to me at times – and although he's not laid a finger on me since that night, it's pretty sad that I consider him managing such a basic principle of acceptable behaviour a positive. I won't care if we never see him again, but as that doesn't seem a likely prospect anyway, and I know Tim is already very hurt – do I need to stick the knife in a little bit harder, twist it a little more? Probably not. Although something occurs to me randomly: 'Did Harry know it was *my* money from the start?'

Tim looks at me in disbelief. 'You want to do *this* now too? I don't know! We didn't discuss it. He asked if it was Dad's money and I said no. By default I suppose he knew it was yours?'

I nod. Maybe Harry did do this deliberately to spite me and drive a wedge between us, knowing it would cause huge problems. I wouldn't put it past him, but even if he did it's badly backfired and he's deeply damaged the person he claims to love most in the world. Tim is on the verge of spiralling out of control.

'I'm sorry that I'm handling everything so badly.' He echoes my thoughts, sitting down on the edge of the bath and looking up at me. 'This whole thing – the move, all of it – has really done my head in. It's not just raked over the past, it's dug it right up; all of my anger about being sent away after what happened – I still can't believe they did that to me, to be honest, now that I'm a parent myself. I was already struggling and now we're actually here, it's even worse. I got the part but I can't take it and that bloody house,' he shudders. 'I really, really don't want to move in tomorrow. Something terrible is going to happen.'

'You feel like you've had a premonition? Is that what you mean?' I'm starting to take this seriously. I don't think he's well at all.

'Kind of. This fear is in my head the whole time.' He taps his skull. 'But not just for me – more for you and Rosie. The Parkes tried to get rid of whatever is in that house and it didn't work. What makes us think we can? How do I keep us safe?'

'Whoa – stop now. They tried to get rid of what, and how?'

'Whatever is in the house,' he repeats, looking back at me, frightened. 'They got a priest in too! Mrs Parkes told me!'

I narrow my eyes. 'I think we can discount anything that woman says, don't you? Look, let's see how you feel about it all in the morning, OK? No one is going to make you do anything you don't want to. We should go back to bed now, though. You're going to be so tired in the morning otherwise.' It's exactly what I might say to Rosie if she woke up in the middle of the night, and he knows it.

'You go,' he's resolute. 'I'm going to sleep in with Ro again. I don't want to leave her on her own.'

I don't push it. I just kiss him good night and return back to our room. I slide under the cold covers and type 'Paranoia' into my phone before landing on the page of a mental health charity.

Paranoia is feeling or believing that you are under threat when there is no evidence that you are. There are different types of threat, from thinking people are trying to take over your mind, through to believing you, or your loved ones are at risk of being harmed or killed. You might be convinced that you are being watched or that people are talking about you. Sometimes these suspicious thoughts might be justified. They can help to keep you safe, if there is evidence to support the thoughts. For example, if you saw lots of people being sick after eating from a tray of food, you would be right to be suspicious. However, it would almost certainly be paranoid to believe all of your food is being poisoned by an organisation hired to kill you. Sometimes this paranoia can take the form of a delusional disorder called PSYCHOSIS, where you see the world in a different way to everyone else around you. You might experience delusions (thinking you are all-powerful/ something is trying to harm you) or hallucinations (seeing things others don't, like faces, or religious figures. Hearing voices that can seem hostile). People might tell you they are worried you are losing touch with reality. It can be upsetting when people close to you don't seem to believe you. This can make you feel more scared and frightened, sometimes angry and frustrated. It's important to remember psychosis is an illness just like any other and can be treated in a way that enables you to function day-to-day and feel supported.

I lie back on the pillow and stare up at the ceiling. Is that what this is about? Has moving back here triggered some sort of post-traumatic thing that's led us to this point; full-blown paranoia or psychosis? I've been so busy focusing on Isobel's 'psychological issues' – except she knows *exactly* what she's doing – that I've totally missed Timothy's genuine ones. Has he been steadily losing the plot right under my nose?

I don't know what to think any more. Everything is falling down around me.

\*

'It's just here.' Adam points to the newly puttied window frame. 'When I shut the door, literally a whole lump of the wall crumbled out. I didn't want you to think I'd damaged it, then just left it.'

'Thank you. It's kind of you to have taken the trouble to fix it back in.'

'I've not done a professional job or anything... obviously,' he smiles briefly, 'and I know you've got the builders starting on Wednesday, so they'll rip it out again in any case, but... anyway, I've told you now.'

'It'll stop any rain getting in for a few days though, which is great.' I shiver. 'It's so cold in here.' I eye his fingerless gloves and glance across at his tray of brushes. 'I've probably got a heater in a box somewhere. I'll see if I can find it.'

He hesitates. 'I've got one, I just didn't want to be cheeky and plug it in. It's your electricity. You've been kind enough, letting me use this space.'

'Oh, you must plug it in! We really don't mind,' I say sincerely.

'Thank you,' he says quietly. 'I did want to ask you another favour though: I hope I won't need to, but if I run out of time today, would it be all right to come in tomorrow too? Even though it's a Saturday?' He scratches his stubble. 'I'm just desperate to get this last work finished, that's all.' He motions towards a canvas sitting on the easel: a dark swirling mass of purples and blues. I think it's supposed to be a sea. It looks finished to me, that's for sure.

'Of course. That's no problem.' Then I get to the point of why I've come in. 'How's Isobel this morning?'

He looks uncomfortable. 'I don't know. I haven't seen her. I'm really sorry about what happened yesterday. All of the shouting and crying. It was very upsetting. Isobel is so fragile at the moment. She doesn't sleep well and things seem even worse when you're overtired, don't they?'

I nod.

'She's a sensitive person at the best of times – by that I mean she's very attuned to how other people are feeling. She has a very highly developed sense of empathy. When other people are upset – like her mother was last night – she finds it hard.'

'Her mother doesn't seem to be *quite* as delicate as Isobel is,' I can't help the tartness in my voice.

Adam looks down at the floor. 'Eve has a tendency to speak before she thinks sometimes, that's for sure. Have you been out on the back road to Lake Vyrnwy from here?'

I'm slightly startled by what appears to be such a random question. 'Not for a long time. Why?'

'That's the road she and her husband were on when they had the crash that killed him. You wouldn't want to break down there at night on your own, it's very rural. It's also a pretty straight bit of road where they were, yet Eve's husband swerved off it for no apparent reason. Eve had to run for quite a while on her own to get help, and because it was in the middle of nowhere, the emergency services took a long time to get there. She had to sit in a stranger's Land Rover with the farmer she'd woken up, waiting, behind her own crashed car containing her dead husband. So she's not had it easy.' He sighs deeply. 'I'm not trying to excuse her having a go at you yesterday, she can be very hurtful when she wants to be, but she's… got issues.'

I hesitate. 'That's really horrible and I know what happened to you, Tim and Isobel wasn't long after that, either, which must have affected her too. But don't we all have a story to tell? My parents died in a car crash.'

He looks horrified. 'Oh, I'm so sorry, Claire. I didn't mean—'

I hold up a hand. 'Please don't feel bad. That's not why I'm telling you. I'm just not sure having a damaged past excuses bad behaviour later in life. That's my point.'

'It doesn't. I'm not saying that, it's just… oh.' He trails off and gestures suddenly out of the window overlooking the forecourt. 'Looks like you've got visitors.'

I glance behind me to see a small red car has pulled up and a grey-haired priest in glasses is climbing out. 'Oh God,' I sigh.

'No, he probably just thinks he is,' Adam remarks, and I half smile.

'I better get on. Needs must when the devil drives.'

'I'm sorry you're having a tough time of it and I'm really sorry about your parents.'

'Thanks.' I mean it sincerely and as I walk back through to the middle bit of the house, I feel glad Tim said he could work there. He does seem like a nice bloke.

*

Father Mathew turns out to be a nice enough man too, although a pretty condescending one. Tim offers him a tea or coffee as we sit down on the sofa in the big sitting room, to which he replies a coffee would be lovely, and beams straight at me. I let it go, because he is here at short notice on a Friday and, if it helps Tim, I'll make him all the coffee he wants. I disappear off to make it like a good little wife, returning with a steaming mug to hear him saying gravely to Tim that the difference between blessing a house and providing an exorcism is that to perform the latter, you need a possessed person, which we don't have.

'Popular culture usually depicts the possessed as teenage children because people subscribe to the notion that children have a particular energy that demons are attracted to. As a father myself I can't deny that's true about the energy, but—'

He must see the look of surprise on my face because he holds a hand up to show me a wedding ring. 'I crossed over from the dark side myself.' Tim laughs heartily, and Father Mathew smiles. 'That is to say, I'm a former Anglican who converted to Catholicism. You aren't expected to give up your wife and children if you already have them.' He turns back to Tim. 'I'm sorry, where was I? Ah yes – teenage children. So that's where the idea of possession comes from – a demonic entity taking over a living human – but historically it was used in all sorts of situations that, today, we would quite rightly understand is a person suffering from a mental health issue. In that instance they need medical help, of course. Genuine demonic possession is a very rare phenomenon.' He takes a sip of his coffee.

'An interesting one though,' I say politely. 'What are the criteria for being considered genuinely possessed? Is there a check list?'

Tim gives a slightly nervous laugh that I know means 'don't take the piss'.

'I'm serious,' I say innocently. 'I really want to know.'

But Father Mathew isn't concerned. He's seen my type many times before. 'Well, I suppose there is, in a way.' He sits back comfortably and crosses his legs. I suddenly wish my sister was here. She'd love this. 'You'll have seen films like *The Exorcist*,' he says to me cosily, 'so you'll know that one of the associations with possession is the afflicted person having unnatural postures, possibly levitating,' he eyes me keenly and I keep a completely straight face, 'sometimes odd facial expressions or their voice might change and become guttural.'

I stop grinning inside and remember Isobel yesterday, before reminding myself quickly that her voice didn't become guttural, just normal in comparison to her usual stupid dreamy-fairy one. I'm not feeling quite as charitable towards Isobel this morning given that she's pretty much the main reason I'm wasting my time talking to a priest when I've got a house to unpack. Funnily enough, there were no old newspaper cuttings on the carpet when we arrived this morning, now the locks have been changed.

'The film was actually based on a true story, you know. A fourteen-year-old boy was introduced to a Ouija board by his aunt which then began the apparent chain of events: shaking beds, an aversion to religious artefacts, scratching behind the walls – that sort of thing.'

I sincerely wish I hadn't asked now. Tim looks terrified. Father Mathew notices too, as he rather hurriedly says: 'but as I've already mentioned, this was back in the 1940s and now it's believed the poor child was actually suffering from schizophrenia. Not so understood a condition as it is these days. My job now is to provide relief to unquiet souls.' He looks Tim directly in the eye.

Tim gives a small bark of laughter, catching his meaning straight away. 'That sounds about right, don't you think, Claire? Wouldn't you describe me as an "unquiet soul"?'

'I'd say you have genuine anxieties about this house,' I reply carefully. 'And I see no reason why a blessing from Father Mathew wouldn't help relieve them.'

'Do you think it's possible for a house to be evil?' Tim blurts suddenly. He looks really distressed and I wish I hadn't taken us off down this route. It wasn't kind. The poor man is on the verge of tears again.

I reach out and take his hand as Father Mathew says gently: 'I certainly believe it's possible for acts of evil to happen within a house, and I think, as Claire says, it's perfectly reasonable to want to bless a house and celebrate a new beginning, in which that evil – or any evil – will play no further part. Some orthodox churches believe in demonic infestations – I think that's what you mean by a house being evil, perhaps? Or are you talking about human ghosts? Spirits of dead people you might have known, that sort of thing?'

Tim nods.

'Well, *we* believe when a person dies there is an encounter with God. A merciful God who welcomes us into a place of peace and rest.'

It's my turn to shift uncomfortably. Is a theology lesson really necessary? I just want to get on with ticking the box so Tim feels better.

'My God, who I believe to be your God too, doesn't abandon his child to roam the Earth without him,' Father Mathew says confidently.

'There you go, Tim, no such things as ghosts,' I say briskly. 'What does the blessing you're about to do actually involve, Father?'

'I'm glad you've asked, Claire.' He places his mug on a box next to him, temporarily acting as a coffee table. I look up to see Adam walking past the window to get something from the van, and distracted, miss the first part of what Father Mathew says. '… so it will be going from room to room with some holy water, saying prayers that you may well be familiar with. You'd be very welcome to join me, or I can perform it alone?'

'Every single room?' I say in disbelief. He'll be here all day.

Father Mathew looks at Tim carefully. 'Yes, I think so.'

'May I join you, if that's OK?' Tim says.

'Of course,' Father Mathew says kindly. They both look at me.

'I'll get sorted down here if I may and come and find you en route, if that's all right?'

'We'll start on the three-storey side, I think.' Tim gets up bravely, although he's actually shaking, which makes me change my mind.

'You know what, I'll come with you now and then leave you to it, once you've done a couple of rooms.'

I take his hand and he grips mine in return so tightly, I almost wince.

\*

'So if we're starting on the other side – as it were – we'll need to go through here, Father Mathew.' I point to the interconnecting door in the upstairs hall, right in front of the three of us, and start to fumble with the new, heavy bolt. Just as Tim steps forward to do it for me, I finally manage to throw it back and the door slowly swings open onto the bare, freezing landing. It's like unsealing a tomb. I think we all feel the rush of dead air escape past us.

Father Mathew steps forward and puts a reassuring hand on Tim's arm. 'There is nothing to fear.'

We traipse up the steep staircase to the very top floor of the house and the front bedroom. I don't even remember this one from the viewing. Did I see it? Despite the gloom of the low ceilinged and small windowed space, the thin curtains are open and a brave pale sunlight is fighting with sugared-violet walls. It's so bare and bleak with the naked bulb hanging in the light socket, it's not hard to imagine things going bump in the night up here. In fact, Tim immediately says: 'Can you feel how cold it is?' as Father Mathew steps in over the creaky boards.

'It's a little fresh,' he agrees, 'but then I see there's no heating in these top rooms, and it's a chill wind out there today.' Holding aloft the silver ball on a wooden stick that he's brought up with him, he flicks it around the room – I *think* I see some drops of water come out – and begins to quietly pray. Tim, next to me, seems to know the words and starts to join in, head bowed. I can't help but catch my breath – but the lights don't flicker, nothing implodes. It's a bit of an anti-climax really.

I wait respectfully until they've finished. Tim lifts his head and exhales heavily, I think with relief.

'I'll go and get on now, OK?' I smile encouragingly. 'Come and find me when you're finished.'

He nods. He already looks better. It's amazing what blind faith can do. I give his hand another reassuring squeeze and head back off downstairs. I'm certain this is nothing more or less than him finding comfort in the familiar – if not necessarily pleasant – rituals of his childhood being repeated now, but I'm not going to say that. If it means he moves in here tonight and doesn't fall apart, that's fine by me.

I head down a level, back through the door into the middle section of the house and into Rosie's room. I better start here really, because *God* – there's so much to do. I groan aloud as I look at the boxes and check my watch. Susannah and Tony are bringing Ro over at 3 p.m. I need to get cracking. At least the room looks brighter now Tony's painted it. The cherry tree catches my eye, however; it looks different, as if the blossom has bloomed more fulsomely – which is ludicrous. I peer at it more closely, something is written – or more accurately painted – on the leaves in red:

*Get out*

My eyes dart to another leaf.

*Get out*

*Get out, Get out, Get out…* relentlessly, over and over again. I imagine the sound of the threat being whispered repeatedly, mimicking the soft swish of the leaves moving in a malicious breeze.

Only it has been deliberately painted all over the beautiful tree, which is now ruined. *You bitch, Isobel.* I feel my chest tighten with fury. When the hell did she do this? Rosie will notice, of course she will. She doesn't miss a trick – and what do I say to her then? How do I explain this to a child?

My eyes suddenly fill with tears; the resolve that I've been managing to hold together starting to crack at the sheer unkindness of such an action. Rosie is a little girl, she's no threat to anyone. She is bravely moving here, starting a new school on Monday. She does not deserve this.

I hear Tim and Father Mathew come back downstairs on the other side of the house, which instantly creates another problem.

They'll be coming in here soon. Tim already thinks this tree is creepy – he's going to think this is another sign. He'll ask me how I think Isobel got in to do this last night when the locks have all been changed? And I don't know the answer to that.

She must have done it on Wednesday night and I just didn't notice. Although, Tony and Tim were painting in here *yesterday*. Surely *they* would have seen it? I did tell them to ignore this wall though, and it's meticulously and neatly on each leaf rather than daubed in obviously large red, dripping letters like graffiti. Isobel is certainly committed. I thought she liked Rosie – she seemed to, when she was holding her hand and whispering to her in the pet shop. Perhaps that was all an act too.

I grit my teeth at that thought of her touching my daughter, threatening her like this. Right now I need a solution rather than an explanation. Isobel Parkes will learn – just like the rest of us – that you can't always get what you want; but more importantly, I need to get these words off the walls before Ro arrives.

I hurry downstairs into the small sitting room, through the passageway and past the grain store room to the barn. Thank God – Adam is still in there. He turns at the sound of my footsteps.

'Have you got a minute?' I pant. 'I need a favour.'

*

Tim is understandably surprised to discover Adam carefully repainting the tree in Rosie's room.

'Hello!' I say cheerfully. It's no less weird than flicking a pastry brush of water around each and every room asking God to banish the darkness and let in the light, after all. 'Adam is just touching this up for me; putting some personal little touches on for Rosie, which is very kind of him. Could you bless this room last, do you think, Father Mathew?' I don't move from the doorway, blocking both of their entry.

'Of course,' says Father Mathew.

'And cheers, Adam!' Tim calls quickly, over my shoulder. 'That's really decent of you.'

'No problem, Tim, it's a pleasure,' he says, not turning round.

They move on to the bathroom and I sigh with relief. 'Thank you.'

'It's fine.' Adam speaks calmly, concentrating on what he's doing. 'It's much easier to get rid of something like this than to put it on in the first place: just the sweep of a brush and no one will be any the wiser.'

'Well, it's very kind of you.' I feel a little uncomfortable about keeping this from Tim, but it's definitely for the greater good.

Adam hesitates. 'I'm just sorry that it's here at all.'

I want to tell him what I really think – but Isobel is his girlfriend. It's not his fault, but he's still kindly helping me put it right. Instead, I settle on: 'I hope she gets the help she needs,' which is a lot more generous than I actually feel, before I go to find Father Mathew and Tim.

*

'So maybe I'll see you at Mass with your mother on Sunday?' Father Mathew tries, as we reach the front door, once they've finished.

'Absolutely!' Tim replies enthusiastically, while I smile politely and refuse to make false promises. Father Mathew notices and says kindly: 'we're here when and if you're ready.' He hesitates. 'You know, Claire, I do a lovely marriage celebration too.'

I glance at Tim. Wow, he really has unburdened his soul. I open my mouth to say that while I'm grateful for Father Mathew's help, I don't actually believe in God. Not one who takes the lives of good people who are loved and needed, because if He's that powerful, they could have been saved, surely? And if I don't believe in God, it would be hypocritical to get married in a church. Tim, on the other hand, doesn't see how any old person off the street can declare a couple married. Only a priest can do that. So here we are, ten years on, still at the impasse, still unmarried. Good luck with sorting that one out, Father M. There isn't enough holy water in the world.

But I keep my peace, deciding it can be a conversation for another day.

'Can I ask you one last thing?' says Tim. 'Have you ever come across people advocating leaving objects around the house that absorb negative energy – a sort of spiritual lightning rod? What are your thoughts on that?'

Father Mathew hesitates. 'I have a small wooden crucifix next to my bed. Is that what you mean?'

Tim hesitates. 'I was thinking more about dolls?'

'Dolls?' Father Mathew looks confused. 'Er – that represent saints, perhaps? Statues and figurines? That sort of thing? Well, I would see no harm in that. A statue of Our Lady could certainly provide a sense of calm and comfort.'

There's a pause before Tim says heartily: 'That's very helpful. Thank you.'

Father Mathew smiles. 'Well, I'll be off then. God bless you.'

'Should we have paid him?' I ask as we watch him hurry to his little red car, presumably relieved to be heading to the Dicksons' house for lunch.

'No!' says Tim, appalled by what's obviously a 'bad form' suggestion. 'I'll make a donation on Sunday.'

'You've not been to Mass in as long as I can remember. You're really going to go?'

'Maybe. I don't know… but I feel much, *much* better about the house now.' He smiles.

'Good,' I say carefully. 'So what was all that about dolls that absorb energy?'

Tim shrugs. 'Just something I read about online. I got the wrong end of the stick, I think. Anyway, it doesn't matter now.' He checks his watch. 'Don't we need to pull our finger out? Rosie's going to be here soon. Talking of money though, I think we probably should pay *Adam*, shouldn't we, for whatever it was he was doing in Rosie's room?'

It's my turn to be horrified at the thought of Tim handing him a couple of tenners. 'No! Don't do that – he'll be really embarrassed.'

Tim frowns. 'Looking at the state of his van I think he'd be glad of it?'

'Well, I'd feel embarrassed. Please don't,' I beg. 'It'd feel really condescending when I asked him for a favour.'

Tim sighs. 'Fine. I'll nip out and get him a bottle of something instead then. Has he done a good job?'

It's quite hard to explain what Adam's done, actually. Whatever I could say wouldn't do the end result any justice. He has added a deep cherry pink blossom alongside Eve's more delicate pale flowers, cleverly blotting out most of the leaves completely, and sweeping the brush cleanly over the ones that are left. Butterflies and two fluttering doves hold either end of a banner, which says 'Rosie' above the tree.

'What do you think, Ro?' I lift my hands away from her eyes, when she finally arrives to see it later on.

She smiles, and looks around, shyly biting her lip, obviously delighted. 'I like it.'

'Pretty cool, hey?' says Tim. 'Daddy's friend did this for you.'

I know it's petty, but I can't help but feel annoyed that he's making out *he* organised this. Maybe that's not what he means. I'm probably just being touchy.

'Tim, will you stay with Rosie just for a minute? I want to thank Adam before he disappears.'

'Sure. Come on, Ro – let's put some of these books away on the shelves.' He points to a stacked pile, next to the wardrobe in the corner of the room, and picks up the first one. 'You could decide which one I'm going to read you tonight, too.'

I *am* being touchy. Tim is just trying to make everything OK. I need to hold onto that.

I find Adam in the barn, crouched over a pile of brushes that he's packing into a box. He turns to look over his shoulder as I appear in the room. 'I'm sorry to disturb, I just wanted to say thank you. I have a very happy little girl upstairs looking at her very beautiful tree.'

He smiles. 'You're welcome. I'm glad she likes it.'

'I don't even know how you did that so fast!'

He shrugs. 'It's very rough and ready – but also much easier when you have no pressure and you're doing something for fun, rather than knowing someone is going to critically pull apart the components of whatever you've created. I enjoyed it. Isobel never let me paint her anything on that tree, so I should be thanking Rosie, really. I got there eventually. Tell her to look for the lucky ladybirds. There are five of them hidden for her to find. Each one has a letter of her name on its back.'

'That's so lovely of you!' I'm enchanted.

He straightens up. ''Night, Claire. Have a good evening.'

'You too. See you Monday, if not tomorrow? Adam,' I say as he lifts up the box, to leave, and he turns back. 'I also just wanted to say, that snippy comment I made about Eve earlier,' I speak clearly and hold my head up, 'it didn't need to be said, and I apologise.'

'It's honestly OK. If I'm being truthful, I had words with her myself yesterday. Explaining to you why she's the way she is has helped remind *me* that she struggles a lot and no one is perfect, so I kind of owe you one. No one gets it right all the time. And she really has been good to me.' He puts the box back down and crosses his arms. 'I don't really get on with my own folks. My dad's not around and my mum thinks I should get a proper job. This,' he gestures at his painting materials, 'doesn't make a lot of sense to her or my stepdad. Eve let me stay here countless times when things got really bad for me at home. She did the same for Tim too, when his parents chucked him out.' He's assuming I know what he's talking about, and I don't – in fact I'm astonished to hear Susannah told Tim to leave. What could he have possibly done to deserve that?

'That was that summer when you all did the séance, wasn't it?' I hazard, carefully piecing together what Tim told me himself about his night in the 'bubblegum' room here.

'Yeah. When Iz got plastered in their pool.'

'Remind me what happened again?' I try to sound casual, but I don't fool him.

He hesitates and looks sideways at me. 'I don't really want to gossip, Claire.'

'Please tell me.' I must sound desperate because he runs his fingers through his hair and exhales heavily.

'We were just sunbathing and swimming, being teenagers. Tim was a bit over-excited, going on about how it was hardly ever hot enough to use it.' He pauses. 'His dad came down and gave us some beers and opened some wine for Izzie. Then Tim's mum came home and went ballistic.'

*

'"You're all *drunk*!" she shouted. "Have you any idea how bloody dangerous that is? Get out of the water! Now! What on earth do you think you're playing at?"

'I climbed out instantly and so did Tim.

'"You too." She glared at Izzie, who was giggling behind her hand in the water as she swayed slightly, then sank slowly beneath the surface and blew bubbles which popped, before she re-emerged, flicking her long hair back and spraying an arc of water, which Mrs Vaughan had to dodge to avoid.

'"Ooooh, sorry!" giggled Izzie. Tim's mum looked like she wanted to jump in and slap her.

'"What's going on?" Tim's dad appeared on the patio.

'"What does it look like?" Mrs Vaughan swung round on him accusatively. "They're all several sheets to the wind. They could have drowned! You weren't aware of any of this?"

'Mr Vaughan eyed the empty wine bottle on the grass and the beer bottles lolling next to it. "I was in my study, working. For God's sake, Timothy!" He looked furious. "Have a little common sense."

'I don't know if he meant not to leave the evidence lying around, or perhaps he only expected us to have one bottle of beer each, but before Tim could answer, Isobel swam over to the steps and attempted to get out; placing a foot, unsteadily, on the first rung. She managed it and hauled herself out of the water, only to slip forward, banging her head on the metal handrail and falling back into the water with a splash. Mrs Vaughan gasped and we lunged towards her but Mr Vaughan was already there, calmly kneeling down on the wet paving, offering her his hand as she re-emerged, coughing and spluttering. She shrank back from him and started crying.

'"It's all right," he said kindly, "we've all been tipsy and embarrassed at least once in our lives. Take my hand and get out of the pool or I'll have to jump in and haul you out myself, which really will be mortifying. Come on!"

'She gave in and he practically landed her on the side like a lifeless fish; her silver swimsuit glittering in the sun against her white skin. He had to pick her up in his arms, getting soaking wet himself, because she'd gone all floppy and was still sobbing and holding her head. He laid her down on a lounger. "You let her drink that whole thing?" he asked Tim, pointing at the wine bottle. "You silly idiot!"

'"When I asked you to take her out, Timothy, I did not mean get her dangerously intoxicated in our swimming pool. Oh my God!" Mrs Vaughan wrinkled her nose in disgust as Izzie, who had sat up, started to be sick on the grass.

"'You don't have anything you want to add to this, Dad?" Tim said, standing ramrod straight like a private on parade. I thought that was brave of him, challenging his dad to admit that *he* had given us the drink in the first place.

"'Only that I'm very disappointed," his father said. "Not the actions of gentlemen, I'm afraid chaps." He looked at us both regretfully. "Poor show. Very poor show indeed."

'Tim stood up a little straighter, a hot flush of humiliation spreading around his neck and jaw. I looked at my feet.

"'I'll take her home now," his father sighed. "Explain to Eve how she's wound up in this state." He began to walk towards Izzie.

"'No, thank you," Mrs Vaughan said quickly. "I'll do it."

"'It's no problem, Susie. You've just got home." He patted his pockets for his car keys.

"'I said *I'll* take her back – and Timothy, you can jolly well come with me and explain yourself."

"'That's no problem. Mrs Parkes will understand. She knows I'm not like that. She won't mind and she won't become all hysterical either." Tim glared at his mum. "She's cool."

"'Really?" Mrs Vaughan's voice became icy-cold. "Well if she's that marvellous, you won't want to come home here tonight, will you? She can worry about you all, take you off my hands. Go on," she jerked her head in the direction of the house, "pack a bag."

"'You're chucking me out?" Tim was incredulous.

'Mrs Vaughan was so angry she was shaking. "I wouldn't dream of making you suffer me a moment longer, so yes, you should absolutely feel free to leave."'

*

I can practically hear Susannah voicing hurt words really intended for Tony rather than her son. I also understand that because he obviously sees Eve as a surrogate mother figure, Adam is probably far from Tony's number one fan either – I expect he knows exactly what happened and why it all ended, too. Nonetheless, I'd feel disloyal overtly acknowledging their affair with him, so I don't say a thing and an uncomfortable silence follows.

'Anyway,' Adam says eventually, 'all water under the bridge now.' He picks up the box again. 'Good night, Claire.'


'You've done very well indeed,' says Susannah, as we all sit around the kitchen table eating fish and chips. 'Congratulations on your first meal in your new house!' She raises a plastic beaker – I haven't unpacked glasses yet – and we all lift ours too. I even cheer with an enthusiasm I wish I really felt.

'Obviously I'll keep it oblique and not go into detail – but I'm so pleased that Father Mathew helped earlier.' Susannah delicately cuts her fish. 'Isn't he a nice man?'

'He mentioned he was a former Anglican,' Tim says.

'Which means he's joined the Pope franchise because he doesn't want women bishops.' Tony forks up a chip.

'Nobody's perfect, Antony,' Susannah smiles, and Tony sits back and shakes his head in disbelief.

I'm pretty stunned to hear that too. Susannah is a fierce advocate for women's rights. If that's true, how is she OK with that?

'The point is, you are all finally in your new home,' she says firmly. 'What do you think of your new bedroom, Rosie?'

'It says my name on the wall,' Rosie announces proudly. 'I *really* like it, but Mummy,' she turns to me, 'can you stay with me in there tonight? I just feel a bit… funny.'

I reach out to her and she slips from the table and into my arms. 'It's just because it's a new house.' I kiss her head. 'It'll take a bit of getting used to, but of course I'll stay with you. New rooms can make you feel a bit strange, but it's nothing to worry about, I promise. I'll get the airbed out though, because your bed definitely isn't big enough for both of us.' I wink at her, and she smiles with relief.

'You're really tired though,' Tim says quickly. '*I'll* do it so you can get some kip. Rosie won't mind if it's me instead, will you, Ro?'

*Does he just not want to sleep on his own?* I watch him carefully as he smiles at me. Perhaps he's just being nice though. He does seem much more relaxed.

In the event, it's much later than her usual bedtime once she's finally tucked up, sleepy and on the verge of drifting off. I stroke her head and whisper the words I always say.

'Go to sleep, sweetheart. Mummy's here. You're safe and I'm not going to let anything happen to you.'

I wait until her body softens and her breathing slows and deepens, then creep back out onto the landing. Tim is already upstairs in our bedroom, in bed and reading a book.

'You're not going to watch some TV?' I ask, surprised.

He shakes his head. 'Too tired. Thought I'd just come up.' His smile is a little nervous now.

'Me too. I'm absolutely knackered.' I peel off my socks and chuck them in the corner of the room by the door. 'Are you all right?'

'Fine, thanks,' he says brightly, watching me unhook my bra and put it away in the drawer, before reaching for a T-shirt to sleep in. 'Did you manage to catch Adam to thank him?'

'Yes, I did.' To my irritation, I feel myself blush as the T-shirt slips over my head.

I watch him notice, before he returns to his book. 'Do you want to start off with Rosie and come and find me to swap over later, or shall I just go in there now?' He doesn't look up from the pages.

'I'll start off there and, unless I wake up, I won't disturb you.' I walk over and kiss him good night. 'But you know where I am if you need me, OK?'

As I walk out of the room I glance back to see he's turned onto one side and is huddled in the foetal position, gripping the pages of his book tightly, like a little boy in a dorm all over again, too afraid to turn the light off.

# CHAPTER TWENTY

## Eve

'I *need* you to give me the scarf and the clip!' Isobel shouts, her hands clenched into small, tight fists, as she sits up in bed in her nightie, the duvet tucked round her middle.

'Darling, that's enough,' I say in my best calm voice. 'These weren't yours to take in the first place and you know that. They belong to Claire and Rosie, don't they?'

She hesitates, then nods.

'Did you take them from the house last night, while I was getting cross with Claire? After I fell over?'

She folds her arms and refuses to answer me.

'I found them in Adam's bag when we got home and thought *he'd* stolen them. He's now very angry with me and I don't blame him. He explained he actually took them away from you, didn't he?'

Still, she says nothing, just thumps back onto the mattress and pillow crossly, so she's lying down and looking up out of the dark skylight at the thick cloud – there are no stars tonight.

I sigh deeply. 'What is it that you want to do with them? And tell me the truth.' She says nothing and I shrug. 'Fine. You're not having them until I get an answer.'

She glares at me silently. I can see her getting angrier and angrier until eventually she shrieks aloud in frustration, kicks the duvet away, leaps up and snatching a teddy from the shelves, flings it violently across the room in temper. The hard glass nose scratches down the en-suite door, and I inwardly count to ten. She could be a toddler again right now, although when she actually was, I don't ever remember her behaving this appallingly. She could always be distracted or cajoled; Michael was particularly good at both. He understood her far better than I often feel I do. She glowers, waiting for a reaction, and when none is forthcoming, stamps her foot so hard with frustration that the room shakes.

'I said that's enough!' I repeat sharply, aware that we now have neighbours the other side of the paper-thin, new-build walls who can probably hear everything. 'I will simply throw them away if you behave like this.'

'You don't understand!' she wails, by turns a teenager despairing of her aged, out-of-touch parent not allowing make-up to be worn to school. I only wish this situation were that uncomplicated. 'I can't tell you – you won't get it!'

'Try me,' I insist.

She throws her hands up and flings herself face down on the bed this time, so that her voice is muffled. 'You say this, Mum, but you won't. You get frightened and you just overreact.'

'I will keep an open mind, I promise.'

'OK, then yes – I want to make two dolls using them.' She rolls onto her side suddenly and points at the scarf and the clip in my hands, then looks at me, waiting for my reaction. 'You see? I TOLD you! You're immediately thinking this is a bad thing. You're worried already.'

'I'm not, actually,' I lie, 'it's half past ten on Friday night and I'd just quite like to go to bed too.'

'Then GO!' she says through gritted teeth. 'No one is stopping you.'

'I'd like you to get some rest as well,' I say pointedly. 'Rather than making all of this fuss and then sitting up making horrid little dolls.'

Her eyebrows flicker. '*Horrid* little dolls?' She repeats instantly and sits up again. 'Why are they horrid?'

'Oh come on, Izzie!' I'm starting to lose my own patience now. 'Everyone knows what a voodoo doll is!'

'I'm talking about poppets – they make *good* things happen – and sometimes they prevent harm. Did you ever stop to think I might be going to use them to help keep Rosie and Claire safe?'

'How!' I practically shout. 'How is making an effigy of someone from one of their stolen belongings keeping them safe? It's all a load of complete... rubbish!' I'm trying so very hard not to swear, not to lose control. I can feel myself failing. *I'd* like to throw something now. Instead, I sink down, exhausted, into the faded old armchair in the corner of her room; one of the first items of furniture I proudly bought after Michael and I married. I should throw it out really, the springs are finally going and I can see Izzie has been picking at the loose threads on the arm that I asked her to leave alone. She's made an un-mendable hole out of which the horsehair is now escaping, but replace it with what? Furniture these days isn't built to last. 'You are wasting your life on completely made-up twaddle!' I tell Izzie as calmly as I can manage.

'Well then if it's made up, not real and not going to do anything, why can't you just give me the scarf and the clip anyway?' she reasons triumphantly. 'You can't have it both ways, Mum.'

'Tell me what you would do, if you were me,' I say suddenly. 'I've just come upstairs to find you standing in my bedroom, in the dark, watching Tim, Claire and Rosie moving around in our old house. That makes me feel so sad, Isobel. I can't even tell you.'

She was lurking by the curtains when I discovered her; an oversized Victorian child looking longingly out of the nursery window at the big children playing, wearing only her long night-dress but incongruously holding binoculars. I could see the lenses were trained on the lit-up rooms of Fox Cottage, and as I glanced across the hard, icy fields, through the hedges and spindly bare branches of the trees on the boundary of our old garden, I had to concede the house looked almost cosy. It reminded me of the Brambly Hedge illustrations in Isobel's favourite: *Winter Story*. She has always liked the bit where the snow starts to fall and all of the mice must rush back to their tree trunk homes, little lights flickering along the hedgerow.

'It's not a normal thing to do, Isobel – to spy on people like that,' I remind her. 'Where did you even get those binoculars from?'

'A friend,' she says sulkily. 'I just borrowed them, that's all. I'll give them back.'

I decide to let that one go. 'Why were you watching the Vaughans? What were you hoping to see?'

'I wanted to know who was in the house. If they were all there.'

'But why?' My confusion starts to give way to worry. 'Isobel – you're to stay away from Fox Cottage – do you hear me? You are *not* to go there again. Whatever it is you're up to – it's to stop.'

She hesitates, and then she repeats what she said to Timothy on our doorstep last night. 'That house is dangerous. They need protecting. Why don't you trust me, Mummy?'

'Don't,' I say warningly. 'Don't "Mummy" me when it suits you.'

'I'm *not*,' she insists. 'I know I made a mistake bringing Tim back here, but—'

'You do not have any control over anybody, Isobel!' I slap my hand down on the tired old chair arm hard enough for a small puff of dust to cloud into the air, close enough to my face to make me cough and splutter. 'For the last time, you did not bring him back here!'

'OK, so I didn't.' She gestures helplessly. 'If that's what you believe, that's up to you, but all I'm trying to do now, is put it right again. I thought Tim understood, but I can see he doesn't, so now this is something *I* need to do. They have to leave that house. Please, give me the scarf and the clip.' She holds out her small hand. 'I need to make the dolls.'

'No – you need to *stay away from that family!*' I finally lose my temper. 'You know what? Have them then, if you won't listen to me!' I fling the clip and scarf meanly at her. 'In fact—' I jump up, clatter downstairs into my bedroom, yank open my knicker drawer and pull out the red doll, before puffing back up to her room and shoving it in her face. 'Have this too!'

She gasps. 'I knew you had it! What's happened to him?' She puts the scarf and clip down on the duvet next to her and puts her hand over her mouth as she looks at the doll and then up at me incredulously. 'Did you do this?' she points at the hole in the stitching and the doll's collapsed face. 'No wonder Tim doesn't understand me. He must be in such pain!'

'Oh sweet Jesus,' I whisper, looking in total despair at the ceiling, 'it's a bloody doll, Isobel!'

'Mummy, what have you done?' She doesn't hear me. Her expression is one of dismay and deep disappointment. I half expect her to say the words I've used myself in a million classes over the years: *you've let me down... but most of all – you've let yourself down.*

I can't bear it any more. I rush out, and once back in my own bedroom, throw myself down on the bed and thump the pillow in frustration, at an absolute loss as to what I do next. I wish Michael were here.

But it's just me.

I stare up at the ceiling and try to think. I know from experience that an out-of-hours intervention involves calling the crisis team. Unless Isobel poses immediate harm to others or herself – which I can't prove – they won't action anything. What exactly are you supposed to do when your child is talking about unsafe houses, making voodoo dolls and watching every move of her former lover and his family – but is otherwise lucid and calm? Although somehow, that makes it all the more frightening.

I reach into my pocket for my phone and call Adam. I know he was angry yesterday and he's stayed away all today too, but surely by now he will have forgiven my mistake?

I wait as the phone rings and rings. For the first time in as long as I remember, he doesn't answer.

I hang up and realise there is no one to help me. I won't be able to convince her to be locked in tonight – she's already too animated for that. I listen to the agitated, busy footsteps as she paces around above my head. It's already begun. She's gearing up for something, there's no doubt about it – why does she need to know who is in Fox Cottage right now? What is she intending to do? And how do I stop her? I swallow, now dreading the night ahead.

Another sound begins to carry down through the thin floor to me. She's singing. I crane to catch the words, but it's the tune that I identify as she repeats it over and over again.

'Ring-a ring o' Roses

A pocket full of posies.

A-tishoo, A-tishoo – we all fall down.'

# CHAPTER TWENTY-ONE

## Claire

I wake suddenly and reaching for my phone on the floor, squint at the time. One a.m. I try to turn over quietly on the airbed but it groans with every move. I feel like I've been kicked in the stomach and realise I'm going to have to get up and hunt for a tampon. Rolling off the mattress as quietly as possible, I get up and, shivering, make my way across the landing to the family bathroom rather than Rosie's en suite. Thankfully, I find them in a box by the sink, and once I've sorted myself out, head back towards Rosie's room, passing our bedroom on the way.

The light is still on. Confused, I go in to find Tim asleep but with the book still in his hand. I start to remove it but he jumps awake.

'It's just me. I'm sorry!' I say quickly. 'I didn't mean to disturb you.'

We both pause as we hear light footsteps running down the stairs.

'Bugger,' I sigh. 'I've woken her. Hang on, I'll be right back.'

I walk out onto the landing. She *would* bloody get up the second I'm not in there and go looking for me. Never mind the three hours I've put in on an inflatable mattress on the draughty floor. But when I stick my head back round her door, she's already jumped back into bed.

'Rosie?' I whisper, but she doesn't answer – just pretends to be asleep.

'I know you can hear me. I'm just going to finish what I was saying to Daddy, then I'll come back to you, OK?'

She snores for an added sense of conviction. This is a relatively new thing – the pretending to be asleep game. I roll my eyes – and go back to our room to find Tim is up and pulling on some pyjama bottoms.

'She's fine,' I say. 'What are you doing?'

'I'll go in with her now. You stay in here and get some rest.'

I glance longingly at our bed. 'Are you sure?'

He nods. 'Go for it.'

He shuffles out as I quickly click the light off and clamber into the warm dip left by his body. Sighing with relief, I burrow under the duvet. The house is so silent, it's almost a relief when it starts to rain outside, slowly getting heavier and heavier until it's blowing in thwacking gusts against the window, making me feel safe to be inside. Thank goodness Adam filled the gap around the window with that putty. Slowly the rain subsides and settles into a gentle pattering, which quickly lulls me to sleep.

*

I wake up at just gone eight, a whole hour later than normal, and head through to Rosie's room to find her sitting up in her bed watching the iPad, Tim lying on the airbed next to her staring up at the ceiling.

'Morning!' I smile, and Rosie doesn't look up from the screen and, while Tim glances at me, he doesn't speak as he rolls off the mattress, gets up and walks out of the room.

Frowning, I let him go, and turn to Rosie. 'You all right darling? Sleep well?'

She doesn't answer me either.

'ROSIE!' I practically shout; she jumps and looks up. 'Sorry, Mummy! What did you say?'

'Did you sleep well?'

'Yes, thank you!' She flashes me a quick grin and goes back to *Vamperina*, or whatever it is she's watching.

I turn and head off to find Tim, who is stood in the bathroom splashing water on his face. He looks terrible – puffy eyed and baggy skin. One of the first times I've seen him look much older than me.

'I'm so sorry,' I say. 'You haven't slept a wink, have you? I should have stayed on the mattress; I'm lighter than you. It's more comfy for me.'

He reaches for a towel and buries his face in it. 'You're right, I haven't really slept.' His voice is muffled but then he re-emerges. 'Not because of the mattress though. I woke up at 2 a.m. feeling like someone was watching me. Actually standing over me, Claire. I could see the shape of the body, but because I was on the floor, I couldn't put a light on or anything. I reached up for Rosie's lamp, on her bedside table, and nearly knocked everything off. When I switched it on, there was no one there. No one at all – but I know, I *know* someone was in that room with us.'

My early morning optimism drains away from me completely. 'Sweetheart, that's not possible,' I remind him. 'All of the locks have been changed. No one except us has keys. It may have felt like someone was there, but—'

'It didn't feel like it – they *were* there. Don't look at me like I'm mad. I'm absolutely certain of it. The figure was looking down at me. I thought I was going to die, I was so frightened. I was actually too scared to go back to sleep after that.'

'No one can get in – and Father Mathew blessed the house yesterday. You felt so much better, remember? Why didn't you come and find me?'

'I didn't want to leave Rosie on her own, not even for a second. What if the figure had come back? What if it had hurt her, or taken her?'

'"Taken her"?' I repeat incredulously.

'I know how that sounds now, in daylight – but in the middle of the night it all felt very different, believe me.'

'Sure, I can see that.' I put a steadying hand on his arm. 'Why don't you have a shower while I give Rosie breakfast, and we'll work out what we're going to do, OK?'

He swallows and nods.

I give him another encouraging smile, and leave the room – but the truth is, I'm out of ideas now. I don't know what to do about Tim's paranoia. I didn't feel a single thing out of the ordinary last night – and I slept fine. I go back into Rosie's room and walk over to the window to pull the curtains.

'Can you leave them, Mummy?' she looks up briefly. 'I like it darker.' She points at the screen.

'Just for one more minute. It's not good for your eyes to watch it like you're in a cinema. Rosie, can we pause the iPad?' I reach over and touch the screen. 'So did you really sleep OK last night? No nightmares or anything?'

'I was fine,' she says. 'I woke up when Daddy walked around a bit, but then I went back to sleep.'

'Daddy was walking around the room?'

She nods. 'I saw him.'

'It was definitely Daddy?'

She frowns. 'I think so, did you come in?'

'I swapped with Daddy. I was in here when you went to sleep, remember?'

'Oh yeah!' She laughs. 'Can I have the iPad back on now?'

Not exactly a reliable witness. I let her get back to the screen and look around. Nothing is any different than it was last night. I absent-mindedly close the wardrobe door that has drifted open, but it won't shut properly. Something is in the way. I open it to push back whatever hanger is sticking out, from where I hung up Rosie's dresses yesterday, but something lying on the bottom of the wardrobe catches my eye. It looks like a board game – I can't really see in the gloom and bend to fish it out. An arc of letters sits over a line of numbers. A smiling sun and an angry moon reside in the top corners, two five-pointed stars like the ones on the wooden beam downstairs are positioned in the left and right bottom corner. Finally, my eyes scan over the words 'Yes', 'No' and 'Good bye'.

I am looking at a Ouija board. In my daughter's wardrobe.

'Rosie,' I say slowly – then raise my voice, 'Rosie! I'm just going downstairs to make a cup of tea. Will you tell Dad when he comes out? If you want him, he's in the bathroom, OK?'

'OK,' she says, not looking up from the screen.

I march downstairs into the kitchen. Grabbing the matches from the kitchen drawer, from where I placed them carefully yesterday next to some candles in case of a power cut now that we live in the country, I stride out into the wash room – the old pub urinals, I suddenly remember Eve telling me – and slide my bare feet into my cold wellington boots by the back door.

Turning the key, I gallumph angrily out through the courtyard breathing in the damp, very cold air, turn left and squelch across the grass, sodden from the night's heavy rain. Once I reach the far end of the garden by the barn and the apple tree, where there is a compost heap, the pile of cut back branches I remember seeing on it are way too wet to burn – they actually have drips hanging from them. I walk over to the barn and peer in through the French windows to see if there's any newspaper or rubbish I can shove under the board instead, to make it catch, but start when I see Adam is there. He looks as equally surprised to see me as he turns round, flattened up against the glass in my PJs staring in.

To my embarrassment, he wipes his hands on a cloth, comes over to the door and opens it. 'Morning.'

'Hi.' I self-consciously cross my arms over my braless chest. 'Sorry to disturb you,' I say quickly. 'I didn't realise you'd arrived.'

He looks at his watch. 'Am I too early? I figured you'd be up with Rosie anyway so anything after eight was probably OK. Sorry. Would you like me to go again?'

'No, it's fine. I was just going to have a bonfire. Have you got anything that needs burning?' I try and smile brightly, but it's obviously a completely ridiculous thing to say.

'Er, I have got some rubbish, yes, but…' he scratches his head and looks around him, obviously not sure where to start. There are lots of canvases stacked against the wall wrapped in blankets and a couple of large boxes containing yet more throws. 'I'm starting to pack everything for the exhibition in London,' he explains absently, 'I don't like to use bubble wrap, it's expensive and not very eco-friendly.' He looks back at me. 'Sorry, I'm not trying to be rude, but are you really having a bonfire now, in your pyjamas at 8 a.m. on a Saturday?' He laughs. 'It's just it's a bit wet for it – you might struggle to get it going, I think?'

I glance over my shoulder, expecting Tim to appear round the corner at any second, looking for me, but no one is there. 'I need to burn this.' I turn the board over to reveal the symbols.

'Oh!' His eyebrows shoot up in surprise.

'I found it in Rosie's bedroom this morning. In her wardrobe.'

'OK,' Adam says carefully. 'That's not great.'

'Not really, no – and if—'

Before I can continue, I hear Tim calling worriedly: 'Claire? Are you out there? Claire?'

'Shit!' I exclaim, panicking.

'Here – just give it to me. Quick. I'll get rid of it,' says Adam, holding out a hand and beckoning with his fingers.

'Are you sure? Thank you so much!' My relief is huge as I pass it to him.

'It's fine. I understand. You go.'

I've already turned to hurry back to the kitchen when he calls after me: 'Claire?'

I stop and twist back to face him, arms crossed again.

'It was definitely in the wardrobe, in Rosie's room?'

I nod and start to walk back across the lawn, waving cheerfully to Tim as I come round the corner. 'Hi love! Just needed a breath of air to clear my head. Shall we have some breakfast?'

I'm cross to find myself thinking, as I slip my boots back off in the washroom, that Adam has just seen me with no make-up on and unbrushed hair.

I've just attempted to burn a Ouija board at the bottom of the garden. Not looking pretty while doing it – for some bloke I barely know – ought to be the very least of my worries, frankly.


'Let's go for a quick stomp, shall we?' I say brightly, as we're finishing up breakfast.

'Haven't we got quite a lot to do?' Tim ventures, and Rosie looks between us uncertainly.

'Yes, we have, but I think it would be an idea to have a change of scene.' My tone doesn't invite disagreement. 'A walk would do us all good.'

'Can we go and get Badger first so he can come too?' Rosie asks eagerly but slumps as I shake my head.

'We won't be gone long enough for that, darling, and there might be sheep. I thought we'd just go up to the hill fort, get some air and come back. Oooh! Look your binoculars are on the side there, that's handy! Why don't you bring them and see what we can see? We'll park at the cricket club?' I look at Tim. 'Let's go and blow away the cobwebs! Come on!'

\*

It is absolutely bloody freezing at the top and unnervingly gusty. I have to gasp to catch my breath at one point and I hold onto Rosie tightly, almost worried the poor little scrap is going to be snatched from my hand like a dandelion seed and blown away forever into the fields stretching out below us.

'This is a fort from a long, long time ago called the Iron Age,' Tim shouts over the roar of the wind. 'That's what all of the banks and ditches are for: to stop people getting into this stronghold – which was a sort of little village – at the top where we are now. A very beautiful queen was born up here too! She was called Guinevere and she married a king called Arthur. Some people think she was able to do magic!'

Rosie's eyebrows shoot up. '*Real* magic?' she yells.

Tim nods. 'She was a sorceress, which is like a girl wizard. Actually, I think it was someone called Morgan le Fey who was the sorceress, and she didn't like Queen Guinevere.'

'So she was a baddie and the queen was a goodie?' Rosie has to cup her hands so he can hear her.

'Rosie, our house is down there,' I interrupt. 'See if you can find it!' I pass her the binoculars and point them at the town in the distance. She looks politely but then hands them back to me and turns to Tim. 'What did the baddie girl wizard do, Daddy?'

'Well…' Tim widens his eyes dramatically, holding out his hand, 'let's start walking back and I'll tell you.'

Delightedly, Rosie runs to him and they head across to the path, disappearing out of sight as they make their way back to the car.

I linger and raise the lenses myself, looking first across to the town, then out over miles of Shropshire countryside. The clouds are scudding across the sky so quickly, it's almost like watching a sped-up film – the passing of time feels palpable here; there's a restless energy in the earth and on the wind. These ramparts have stood for thousands of years and will be here long after I'm gone… but this sudden and unwelcome confrontation with my own mortality – one day I will have no choice but to leave Rosie – physically jolts me and I have to force the fear away.

Instead, I concentrate on the view, taking one last look beneath me. Queen of my castle and a kingdom I don't want. I don't know I'm going to do it – but I scream suddenly. The sound is completely lost on the buffeting air. No one hears.

There is nothing for it but to turn and begin the walk across the exposed flat settlement and return back to the house.

*

We put on the TV for Rosie and light the fire in the big sitting room as clouds begin to gather on the other side of the window – making it dark enough to need to switch the lights on, even though it's not yet lunchtime. I watch the flames leaping in the grate as we start to unpack in silence alongside each other, and realise that would have been a far more logical solution to my Ouija problem. Except didn't Tim say it's not a good idea to burn them in the house? I exclaim aloud at such a ridiculous thought. It's a piece of bloody card – what am I talking about?

Tim looks up, holding a handful of books. 'What's the matter?'

'Nothing.' I shake my head. 'Sorry. Deep in thought.'

He nods briefly and turns back to the box. He's clearly got his mind on other things too. He's still adamant he saw a figure; someone in the room, watching him and Rosie sleep… I think he'd pass out completely if he knew what I'd found in the wardrobe, too. He'd never set foot in here again.

There's no doubt Isobel Parkes wants to believe she is not as other mortals: stars carved in the beam downstairs, that stupid bit of candle, the shouting and collapsing, the floaty voice. She freaked me out enough to have me running out of the house the day we moved in and I thought she was upstairs; I hold my hand up to that – but I'm wiser to her act now. I get that she doesn't want to live in the real world – maybe it scares her too much, I don't know and I'm not sure I care – but the important thing is, she's not *actually* magic, and there is no physical way she can be getting into the house. I've changed all of the locks. In fact, I have no proof whatsoever that *anyone* else was in the house with us last night.

Even the Ouija board – that Adam will have got rid of by now anyway – is hardly evidence. I can almost hear the police: 'people leave the strangest things behind when they move. It happens all the time. Isobel doesn't mean any harm, Ms Waters. It's just her way. You'll get used to her.' The board has probably been in the house all along and I just haven't noticed it until now. The newspaper cutting on the carpet, the nasty little paintings on the wall – they could all have happened before the locksmith arrived. So why can't I just put Isobel from my mind? Why does everything keep returning to her?

'You think I'm making all of this up as an excuse to move out of this place, don't you?' Tim says suddenly.

I look at him in surprise. 'No. I was thinking about Isobel, actually. Kooky, witchy little Isobel.' I hear the malice in my voice and it surprises me as much as him.

'That's not kind,' he says slowly. 'She's been through a lot.'

I throw down the cushion I've just unpacked. Haven't we all? And why's he defending her anyway? I'm starting to feel very out of sorts indeed and I don't want to say something I regret. 'I think I need a break and a cup of tea. Do you want one?' I glance at Tim, who silently shakes his head and carries on.

'No, thank you, Claire,' I say pointedly, because I'm pissed off – but unfortunately I only make myself sound very petty, and like I'm talking to a five-year-old rather than my partner, which makes me even crosser.

'I'm genuinely frightened – I wish you could see that,' he says quietly.

'So you keep saying.'

I leave him with that thought and march through into the small sitting room. 'Come on!' I say bossily to Rosie who is tucked up on the sofa, happily watching an *Aladdin* DVD. 'Screen break. We're going out in the garden.' I hold a hand out. 'I'm going to have a quick cup of tea and *you* can have a go on the swing.'

'OK,' she says reluctantly. 'Can I have a hot chocolate and a biscuit when we come back in, though? In front of the TV?'

'Yup,' I agree briskly. 'Go and find your coat, it's cold.'

It's actually more than cold as we pick our way through the long tufts of grass in the back garden. I have to return for an old spoon to chip frozen bird shit off the swing seat and the temperature has fallen away because of a wind chill that bites through to my very bones, but even though I huddle miserably over my tea, I still feel better for being out of that bloody house. I stare out over the fields through the gaps in the hedge as my hair whips about my face and I'm forced to peel strands of it from my mouth.

Rosie valiantly attempts another swing, then shivering, turns to me and begs: 'Can I go in now, please, Mummy?'

I nod, feeling bad that I dragged her out in the first place as she legs it in relief back towards the house. I watch her running off and sink down onto the swing myself, looking around the forlorn garden; everything dead and cut back. A birdbox is half hanging off one of the tree trunks. Even the wildlife has had the sense to move out. I try to imagine how nice it will be in the summer, when it gets warmer. We've had glorious picnics at The Rectory before. I know it can happen here. I just have to hold on. I gently push back with my feet, still clutching my tea, about to let go as I come in line alongside the trunk of the tree, only to notice it has barbed wire embedded into it. The twists of metal have somehow sucked into the body of the tree, as over time it's grown up and around the wire – both forced to coexist unhappily alongside the other. It's pretty much the definition of bleak.

I shudder, sip my now-almost cold tea and glance up at the flaking white picket fence and the wooden back gate – to see Isobel stood on the other side of it, completely motionless – just watching me.

I scrabble to my feet, spilling some tea down my jeans. Her loose, red hair is lifting in a cloud around her on the wind. She's wearing a full-length, black trench coat over a longer eccentric green velvet dress, which is just visible beneath the bottom of the gate. She has her hands in her pockets, and doesn't say a thing, just holds my gaze unflinchingly. A robin flits past and lands on the grass by the compost, cocking his head on one side and trilling at us. The same one that sang on the day I looked round this garden with Isobel's mother, when she still lived here and I had a happy life miles away? Isobel's face breaks into a sweet smile at the sound and, to my amazement, she lifts a hand and *blows me a kiss*.

My mouth falls open. How *dare* she taunt me like this? Furiously, I turn on the spot and walk off. I will not be provoked into another confrontation – but two steps more changes my mind. I want to ask her exactly what she thinks she's playing at, hanging around outside? *She does not live here any more!* This is my house now! MY family!

Except, she has vanished. I blink in astonishment. She was definitely, *definitely* there. I rush over to the gate and look up and down the road. There is no sign of her. Chucking what's left of my tea over the lawn, I stride round to the French windows and pull them open, but Adam is not there either. The stacked paintings in their blankets are still leaning against the wall, and the rest of his belongs are lying around too. He's clearly coming back, but has just as obviously popped out. I look through the front window to see that his van isn't on the forecourt either. So he didn't let Isobel in here then. She's just – gone. I walk back out into the garden and look around again. There is no sign of her. The swing is moving gently in the wind, to and fro, but remains empty.

\*

'Can you eat just a little bit more, darling?'

Rosie shakes her head and pushes her beans on toast away from her. 'I don't feel hungry.'

'Well if you're not hungry enough for beans on toast, you won't be hungry enough for this either.' I reach behind me for the plate on the side, which has the most enormous doughnut on it that I bought when I nipped to the shop for the beans.

She shakes her head. 'I don't want it. Can I get down, please?'

My eyes widen in surprise. 'You don't want a *doughnut*? Come here!' I tease, holding out my arm. 'Are you ill?'

She comes round the table to lean on me, and heat radiates from her small body.

'Actually, I think you might be.' I place my hand on her forehead. 'You've got a temperature. Poor bunny. You come and sit down while I get you some Calpol.'

I lead her into the sitting room, then once she's on the sofa, I jog upstairs to find the bottle and a clean plunger.

'That's come on quickly,' I say sympathetically as she swallows the mouthful. 'You were fine this morning. Does anything hurt?'

'Just my tummy,' she says unhappily and leans her flushed face down on one of the sofa cushions. It's clear she doesn't feel well at all. I get her settled in front of *Moana* with some water to sip, little and often, as well as a sick bowl, because I've learnt the hard way that it's always a good idea to have one, just in case.

I'm unpacking warily around her, thinking that today can't really get much worse, when quite simply, it does.

The front door goes. 'Tim?' I call. 'Can you get that?'

I wait, but there's no response, just another knock, so swearing under my breath, because Rosie will undoubtedly be sick the second

I leave the room, I head out into the hall, only to see through the glass panel that *Harry Asquith* is standing on my doorstep.

I open it and don't say anything – even though he's standing in front of a *Porsche* and it's as much as I can do not to snort in derision.

'Hello.' He gives me the ghost of a smile. It's more of a brief twitch of either end of his mouth. 'May I come in?'

I shake my head. 'No, you may not.'

He opens his mouth, but unfortunately, Tim – who obviously did hear the door, but apparently just didn't feel like answering it – appears behind me. 'Harry?' he says in astonishment. 'I thought it was your voice! What on earth?'

Harry takes a deep breath and reaches into his back pocket for a small, folded-up piece of paper, which he passes to Tim.

Tim unfolds it and his mouth falls open. 'This is a cheque for two hundred and fifty grand!'

'It's every penny of your original investment. I said I'd repay you, and now I have.' He scratches his head and blinks in confusion. For a moment I wonder if he's had a drink, but not even Harry would be stupid enough to drive pissed from London to Shropshire. He doesn't look well though; his eyes are piggy slits sitting in uncooked pastry. Perhaps he's hugely hungover.

'I sold my house,' he blurts, looking at me, as if I've just asked aloud where the money came from.

I raise an eyebrow and look at Tim.

'Come in,' Tim steps to one side, 'please.'

Harry holds up a hand. 'No. Claire's right. I shouldn't. I've got to get back to town tonight anyway. I'm supposed to be meeting someone.' He rubs the back of his neck; he seems to be crawling within his own skin. 'Although I'm not going to make that, I don't think.' He checks his watch and looks around him, although quite what for, isn't clear; a magic portal back to London that is big enough to fit his ridiculous car and enormous ego into? That would be some black hole.

'You're driving *back* to London now?' Tim says in disbelief. 'But that's crazy!'

Harry laughs. 'Yes, it is a bit, I suppose. I don't know what I'm doing here to be honest with you. I can't lie, I wasn't going to give you this back.' He motions at the cheque. 'It wasn't why I sold up and I still maintain it wasn't my fault the business went under. I didn't intend to use your money to bail anything out. It really was a straightforward opportunity that I wanted you to get in on. That said, if I hadn't offered it to you, you wouldn't have lost everything.' He throws his hands up, helplessly. 'Nothing is black and white, as they say.'

I peer at him more closely. It's freezing out here but he's actually sweating. I can see small beads of perspiration forming on his top lip and round his hairline. I'm almost certain it's pure alcohol weeping from his pores rather than from any social embarrassment.

Harry swallows. He's gone very pale. 'When you told me you'd got the part and you weren't going to take it because of being here…' He shakes his head. 'I know how long you've wanted this and what it means to you. It's not my fault, but I can't be the reason it doesn't work out for you. Take the money and go home. Tell your dad to get someone else to labour for him. You bloody *have* got a proper job and don't let him or anyone else tell you otherwise.' His voice trembles with emotion, and his eyes fill with tears as he suddenly leans over and hugs Tim tightly, kissing him quickly on the cheek. He stares at the cheque between Tim's fingers and for a minute I think he's going to snatch it back after all and rip it into tiny pieces, but he turns abruptly on the spot, marches back to the Porsche and folds himself back into it without so much as another word.

He doesn't look at either of us as he starts it up, staring blankly ahead as he roars off the forecourt in a spray of loose grit, leaving us staring after him in astonishment.

*

'I'm not having this conversation until the money is actually in your account,' I insist, sitting at the kitchen table with my head in my hands. 'I don't trust him at the best of times and that was just plain *weird*. Who drives all that way to hand over a cheque? He couldn't just get your details and do a transfer like a normal person?'

'Oh come on, Claire. It was about the gesture! Yes he's a drama queen, but like he said, he didn't have to do this. Would you give the money back, in his position?'

'Yes! Of course I would!'

'Really and honestly? You can say that hand on heart?'

'Yes, I can,' I insist. 'And while we're on the subject of ethics, if this money *does* credit back, you're telling me you're prepared to simply walk away from this house that your dad bought us, leaving him completely in the lurch, despite promising to do it up with him?'

'Well, like Harry said, we can pay someone to take over my role,' Tim says eagerly. He's like a different person all of a sudden. This lifeline seems to have completely re-energised him. 'I'm hardly a skilled labourer, am I?' he reasons. 'Maybe I should ring Jan back and see if they've offered the part to someone else yet? I suppose there's a chance they haven't? It *was* late on a Thursday night? She might not have even called them yet to say no.' His eyes dance with excitement. 'Imagine if it happened after all!'

'Rosie is supposed to start at her new school on Monday,' I remind him quietly.

'We can find somewhere to rent back home and ask for her old place back, I'm sure. She'd be fine with that.'

'They probably won't have one any more. I imagine there's a waiting list.' I hold up a hand as he opens his mouth again. 'I'm honestly not prepared to talk about any of this until I see proof that the money is in your account, and I really don't think we should mention this to your parents yet either.'

'It'll clear and we'll be able to go home. We won't have to spend another night in this horrible, spiteful house.' He shudders.

Spiteful? What's he talking about? It's a bloody house, not a person. 'Try not to get too excited. Just in case.' I get to my feet. 'I need to go and check on Rosie. She's all I want to concentrate on right now.'


At bedtime, Rosie's temperature is still high, despite my tagging doses of Calpol and Nurofen. I put her to sleep in our bed so that I can keep an eye on her, and lie alongside her as she dozes fitfully, looking through my phone. The signal is so slow, however, I give up on Facebook and flick through my pictures instead, especially the ones I took of our leaving party. There's a lovely one of me and Mel, although I can see Mel is trying not to cry. I close my eyes and try not to think about Harry rocking up like the cavalry and waving his cheque.

I can't pretend I wouldn't give anything to go home and not have to live here for a year after all – and is it unkind of me to be so sceptical of him suddenly returning the money? Maybe he really doesn't want to stand in the way of Tim's dreams coming true… except this is real life – not an *X Factor* backstory.

And how exactly *are* we supposed to tell Tony and Susannah? It's a *house*. They bought a house for us. It's not like returning a birthday gift I don't much want and swapping it for something else on the sly. I don't see how we can possibly leave them in the lurch – but most of all, MOST of all – what will this do to poor little Rosie? She won't know if she's coming or going. Literally. I look at her again, breathing faster than normal, her eyes fluttering under the lids as she sleeps lightly, her small body fighting whatever infection is trying to take hold. I can't believe I made her go and sit on that freezing swing earlier. What the hell is wrong with me?

I turn back to my phone and scroll through the rest of the pictures, right up to the latest, only to see one of me and Rosie asleep in her bedroom, taken last night at 23.03, apparently. Rosie is curled up sweetly like a hamster, I however am flat out on the airbed, arm draping off the side, mouth hanging attractively open. Thanks, Tim.

I think about him for a minute more, 'terrified' one moment, skipping round the place excitedly the next, and start to feel crosser and crosser – finally slipping downstairs to find him in the sitting room where he's half watching TV and half on his phone. He looks up as soon as I come in. 'How is she?'

'Hot as a dog. I'm going to keep her in with me. Can you sleep in her room tonight, please?'

He blanches. 'On my own?'

'Oh my God, Tim!' It's all the excuse I need to let rip at him. '*Please* don't start this again! The house has been blessed. You are very tired and very stressed out right now. You said it yourself: coming back here has raked up a lot of feelings from the past. But that's *all* this is. You are a grown man.' I pause and he looks down at the floor. 'Your daughter is ill. If you *really* feel you can't sleep in her room, you'll have to sleep in with Rosie instead and come and find me if you need me, OK?'

'Yes, I'd rather do that,' he says quietly. 'Thank you. I'll go up to bed now so that she's not on her own and you can get some rest. I know you're tired too.'

I'd expected a defensive attack, not an apology and wrong-footed; I'm not quite sure where to go next.

'Good night then.' He doesn't look up from his phone.

I realise suddenly I'm not sure when we stopped kissing each other good night. 'OK. Good night. Thanks, by the way, for that lovely picture you took of me and Rosie last night.' I attempt to inject some light-heartedness back into the conversation, and finish the day on a positive note. 'I was practically dribbling.'

He frowns in confusion. 'Sorry, what now?'

'The picture you took.' I walk back over to him, unlock my phone, find the picture and show it to him.

He stares at it, and looks up at me. 'I didn't take this.'

I laugh, thinking he's joking.

'No, seriously, Claire. I didn't take this.' He sits up straighter and takes the phone from my hand, looking at it closely, becoming increasingly wide-eyed.

'Well, *someone's* holding that phone,' I say. 'It's taken from the doorway. It's not me, because I'm in it. Rosie's flat out, so it must have been you.'

'Now do you believe me about the figure I saw?' Tim says, his voice trembling.

I stare at him. 'What? But you're the only other person who knows my phone code!'

'You don't need to unlock someone's phone to take a picture – you just press the home button and swipe up. I promise you, I didn't take it. I was in the other bedroom.'

'Well, this picture didn't take itself, did it?'

Tim shivers visibly and swallows. He looks like he's about to pass out.

'No, Tim! It didn't!' I insist. 'This is completely ridiculous!'

'I want to take Rosie up to Mum and Dad's now,' he says. 'I don't think I'm happy with her being here. We can all just stay there tonight.'

'No, she's ill.' I put my foot down. 'It's not fair to wake her when she's got a temperature and drag her out in the cold in the middle of the night. I know you don't want to live in this house. I *know* you want us to leave. I get it – OK? You don't have to do stuff like this.' I hold the phone aloft.

'It's not me! I am not making this up!' he insists. He looks haunted. It might just be his best performance yet.

'Right – have it your way then. If you're certain that you didn't take this,' I hold the phone up again, 'it means someone else was in the house last night. That is *the only* possible explanation. Tonight, you will sleep in with Rosie and I will sleep in her bedroom, like we just arranged.' I'm now adamant. 'Everything seems to be specifically happening in that room, so if Isobel wants to put in another appearance tonight,' I pause and wait for him to register what I've just said, 'I'm going to be waiting for her.'

# CHAPTER TWENTY-TWO

## Eve

'Darling, do you think I could lock your door tonight?' I look down at Isobel lying in her bed. She's exhausted, with shadows under her eyes so pronounced, the skin looks bruised.

'No!' She twists her head on the pillow in such alarm that I put a hand out to steady her, the other one holding onto the dirty washing under my arm.

'All right, all right!' I reassure her. 'I won't.'

'You promise?' she says. 'I've not had any panics or night terrors since we've moved in.' She's almost pleading.

'That's true actually,' I admit. 'You haven't.'

'I feel safe here,' she says suddenly and sighs.

Concerned, I sit down on her bed. 'You *are* safe here, dearest. Of course you are.' I put the washing down on the floor and turn back to her. 'Isobel, you know I love you, don't you?'

She nods.

'Is there anything you want to tell me? Something that's bothering you?' I hesitate and risk reaching out to stroke her hair. She flinches slightly but then closes her eyes: her signal that I'm allowed to carry on. I wait to see if she's going to say anything, but she doesn't.

'There is nothing that's happened, or that you could have done, which would be so bad you couldn't tell me, or that would stop me loving you,' I tell her truthfully, stroking her gently. 'I love you whatever happens. Nothing is ever, ever going to change that.'

She doesn't open her eyes, but a tear escapes down her cheek.

'Oh darling, what is it?' I say desperately. 'I can't help you unless you tell me what it is?'

She reaches up and takes my hand. At first I think it's to stop me smoothing her hair, but she holds onto me tightly.

I want to tell her I know about the baby, but something prevents me. If she wanted to confide in me, she would. I cannot force her to share intimacies. A child is not duty-bound to tell their parent anything, however painful that might be. Unconditional love between a child and parent must only ever flow in one direction.

She suddenly sobs and turns her face towards me, not letting go of my hand and gripping across my knees with her other hand. She hasn't held me like this in years and, for a hideous second or two, I'm briefly back in the sports hall – like an old-fashioned camera flash popping – with her clinging to my legs in fear.

I don't risk moving; I simply hold her hand and put my other arm around her shoulders, and lean as close to her as I can. 'You're safe, Isobel. I'm here. Mummy's here.'

'It wasn't my fault,' she whispers. 'I promise.'

'What wasn't, darling?' But she squeezes her eyes more tightly shut and tenses her shoulders. I can see she's starting to panic.

'Isobel, listen to me,' I say gently but firmly, 'whatever it is, I promise you, I know it is NOT your fault. I mean it – nothing would ever, ever stop me loving you.' I wait, to see if she can hear me, if my words are soothing her at all. 'It just couldn't, no matter how bad it was. So whatever it is, you can tell me when you're ready, but it WILL NOT change how I feel about you.' My voice trembles slightly as she twists and looks up at me with frightened eyes, then nods, wiping her tears away.

'I want to go to sleep now,' she whispers.

I lean forward and kiss her head briefly. 'Good night then, darling. I hope you sleep well. Try to stay in your bed tonight, won't you? I wondered if perhaps I heard you leave at about quarter to eleven last night? I don't think you came back until just after two o'clock?'

She shakes her head and her expression becomes blank again. 'I was here all last night. In bed.'

I smile. 'OK. My mistake then. I'm sorry.'

'I have one last little thing to do,' she blurts. 'It'll be finished by the morning, I'm sure.' She smiles suddenly, with relief.

I look at her worriedly. 'Please stay safe, Isobel.'

'That's *why* I'm doing this. To keep everyone safe. He won't leave her on her own after this.'

I don't know what that means, and perhaps it's better that I don't. I get up, gather the washing in my arms and nod in the direction of her en suite. 'Can I get your things? I'm going to put this lot on before I go to bed myself.'

'Yes.' She yawns and snuggles down contentedly, pulling the duvet up around her shoulders.

I walk into her bathroom and gather the whites from her washing basket. I pull out the long nightie she was wearing last night. It's been bundled into a tight ball and is damp. Shaking it out, I realise the hem is covered in mud; as if someone had trudged through a field in it and got caught in heavy rain. Again, I decide not to confront her about it – not to march back into her room and demand she explains herself.

What could I do to stop her in any case? She is far more likely to tell me the truth herself if I bide my time. I think she's finally on the verge of telling me everything.

I can wait until the morning.

'Good night, darling. I love you,' I tell her, as I walk back through her room.

'Mummy?'

I turn back.

'I love you too,' she says.

I blow her a kiss, turn off her light, and gently close the door.

# CHAPTER TWENTY-THREE

## Claire

The longer I stay awake, to wait and see if anything is going to happen, the more stupid and cross I feel. It's now 11.47. I could have been asleep at least an hour ago.

I toss and turn in Rosie's single bed, the iron frame creaking loudly under adult weight it's not designed for. I text Jen, to see if she's around – the light from the screen illuminates the cherry tree on the dark bedroom wall and casts odd shadows – but she doesn't reply. It's almost eleven a.m. on Sunday morning with her, she's probably out getting brunch or something. She might even still be in bed herself. I sigh and turn onto my back, looking up at the ceiling, before restlessly turning back on my side and logging on to the *Daily Mail* TV and showbiz page. After ten minutes of scrolling through endless Kardashian stories, my eyes start to close and the phone becomes heavy in my hand. I yawn and place it next to my head on the mattress within easy reach. I'm done. The house is quiet. I can't hear a sound. I don't feel anxious. I don't even feel on alert any more – just completely shattered. I start to slip into sleep and it's a blissful release…

*

…but I'm dragged back, what feels like moments later, by something tapping the bare skin of my arm. I'm so deeply gone, it takes me a second or two to work out a dark figure is stood right next to me, about an inch away from my body. I have a split second of sheer panic before I realise the figure is also whispering.

'Mummy.'

It's Rosie.

'I woke up and you weren't there. I feel hot.'

I slump slightly, feeling sick and a bit dizzy myself. On autopilot, I reach up to her forehead: she's right – she's very warm indeed and needs another dose of paracetamol or ibuprofen.

'Hang on, sweetheart, I need to look on my phone and see which medicine you need.' I squint at the screen to check my note of what time she last took something… ibuprofen it is. 'Come on, let's get you back to bed and comfy again.'

'Can't you stay in with me and Daddy go in the other room?' she whispers as I lie her alongside Tim after dosing her up. He is flat out and snoring, oblivious to us holding a conversation beside him.

'Let's not wake poor Daddy to move him,' I suggest, generously. 'He's fast asleep.'

'Can you wait until *I* fall asleep and then go back into my room?' she pleads. 'Please, Mummy.'

'OK,' I concede, too tired to argue. 'Scoot over a little and I'll get in with you.'

She does as I ask, but it's not comfy for her any more than it is for me. It's an average-sized double bed, and she's getting so tall these days, that actually three of us is a bit of a squash. Especially when one of us has a temperature. I perch on the very edge of the bed, attempting to doze as she thrashes about trying to get comfy. There is no way on God's green earth I can sleep in here all night, on an inch of mattress with my head barely on any pillow at all.

It's 1.18 a.m. before I'm certain it's safe to ease back out of the bed. I go to the loo and shiver across the landing clutching my phone, to get back into the now-cold bed I started off in several hours ago. It's going to be one of those nights where Rosie is up and down like a jack-in-the-box, I can tell. It always happens when I'm most tired; it's one of the many unwritten rules of young children. I've lost count of the times that I've been jolted awake to find that small body – like something out of *The Shining* – motionless alongside me, whispering 'Mummmyyyy'. It's not the most relaxing way to wake up.

I plump the pillow and settle down again, yawning deeply. I'm facing the doorway and I've actually left the door open wider than need be; the light from the bathroom is just that little bit *too* bright, but I can't be bothered to get up and push it to. Rosie will be back in a bit anyway. I close my eyes, sigh and start to drift again…

…only this time when I open my eyes, it feels completely different. There's no Rosie next to me. I don't understand why I am so suddenly awake. The house is completely still and very cold. I shiver under the duvet before rolling over onto my back to lift my head slightly, staring out into the hall and through to the bathroom with its spotlights brightly shining in the ceiling. I half expect to notice that a window is open, it's so draughty, but it's to my left that my gaze moves. The mirrored wardrobe door is slightly open – just a crack – and as I stare at my reflection in the half-lit glass and my brain begins to make sense of the confused repeat images, I realise one pair of the unblinking eyes staring back at me, is not my own.

Someone is crouched in the wardrobe.

My breath catches in horror and, very slowly, I push myself up onto my elbows. The eyes don't move, but the tips of three fingers begin to creep around the edge of the doorframe, as if they are preparing to very, very slowly and noiselessly climb out. I cannot move. My heart is thumping an insistent fast, squishy alarm in my chest, and my breath begins to rasp as my own hand reaches around the mattress for my mobile. My fingers close around it, I drag it forward and fumble with the home button; swipe up, *swipe up*! My hands are shaking so wildly that I simply can't keep it steady. If it was a gun and I was pulling the trigger right now, I'd hit the ceiling – without a doubt. I scramble up to seated, but the fingers shoot back, the eyes disappear and the door slams tightly shut, as if a life-sized human cuckoo clock has just finished chiming.

I stare at the now-closed door, unable to breathe. Are they about to burst out and attack me? I wait for what feels like an eternity – but is probably no more than seconds. The door doesn't open again so much as a hair's breadth. I am still too scared to move. This is every worst childhood nightmare coming true: *there's something under the bed, behind the curtains… in the wardrobe.*

I can feel my breath quickening, becoming shorter. I don't know that I'm going to do it, but I suddenly scramble out of the bed and hurtle from the room to our bedroom where Rosie and Tim are still asleep. I hasten round to Tim's side and shake him.

'Tim,' I whisper urgently, while trying not to disturb Rosie. 'Wake up.'

His eyes flicker open and he stares at me confused for a moment, then sits up, alert. 'What's wrong. Where's Rosie?'

'She's right there.' I put my finger to my lips, but realise I am shaking violently. 'I think there's someone in her bedroom, in the wardrobe! They were watching me sleep. I saw them start to push the door open but I sat up and they disappeared.'

'What, vanished?' He looks terrified.

'No! They went back into it and the wardrobe door closed shut.'

'Where's my phone?' He looks about him desperately. 'I had it because I was watching a movie. I'm going to call the police.'

'Wait – the police?' I hesitate. 'Are you sure?'

'You just said there was someone in the house!'

'I think so, I definitely saw something... I'd just woken up!' I swallow, trying to concentrate. *I did see a person, didn't I?*

'I've found it. Oh my God, it's got no battery.' He pushes a button furiously. 'It's died completely. Where's yours?'

'I must have left it back in the room. I didn't think about it, I just ran.'

'Do you know where the car keys are?' he whispers. 'We could just drive to Mum and Dad's?'

'They're by the front door. Tim, wait. Rosie's ill – I don't want to just...' I try and think straight.

'We need to do *something*!'

I look at him, frightened. 'It felt real, but I was half asleep.' I swallow. 'We can't just call the police and tell them we think there is something in the wardrobe, plus half the town probably already knows we had the place blessed earlier. We're going to seem insane. I'm going to go and look.'

'No!' Tim says instantly and gets up. 'I'll go.' He looks around him. 'Where's that pole to open the skylights with? I want to take something with me.'

'It's already in her room, by the en-suite door, but it's pretty lightweight. Maybe this isn't a good idea after all?' I'm starting to feel frightened again.

'No – you're right. We can't just call the police because you woke up and thought you saw someone looking at you in the wardrobe mirror.' He takes a deep breath, but looking faint with fear. 'Wait here with Rosie.'

I watch him walk uncertainly from the room, and get into bed, next to Ro, my heart thumping as I listen carefully. After a moment more, Tim reappears in the doorway, still clutching the pole.

'It's empty, just some of Rosie's clothes and dressing-up dresses hanging in there.'

'I was sure I saw something.' I rub my eyes. 'I'm so sorry.'

'Don't apologise, I believe you. I think you did see someone. Claire, can we just go, please? Something is really wrong. I don't want us to stay here. We need to get her up.' He points at Rosie. 'Now.'

I hesitate, then nod. I know I saw those eyes, and the fingers edging round the frame.

He props the pole against the chest of drawers, then reaches down and grabs his jumper, lying on the floor next to him.

'Rosie?' He turns to her and touches her skin lightly. 'We need to go to Grandma's. Can you put this on to keep warm?' He sits her up, all floppy and sleepy, and pulls the massive sweater on over her head, rolling the sleeves up until her hands emerge. 'Daddy's going to carry you.' He lifts her up and she reaches her arms round his neck and cuddles her head onto his shoulder; she's barely awake.

We reach the bedroom door, Tim hovers on the threshold briefly but then rushes across the landing and plunges down the stairs, me following closely behind him. In a matter of steps we are across the small sitting room and out in the front hall. Tim moves to one side and I see the keys hanging in the lock, lit by the moon shining in through the glass panel of the door.

We burst out onto the freezing forecourt, the sharp gravel digging into the soles of my bare feet as I hobble over to the car and open the back door so Tim can strap Rosie in. I jump into the passenger seat, shivering wildly as I stare up at the house. I can't see Rosie's bedroom from the front of the house but the other rooms are still in darkness. Tim jumps in and we roar off the forecourt.

Neither of us speak as we hurtle away round dark corners, only beginning to slow down as the roads turn into narrower lanes, the closer we get to The Rectory.

'Now do you believe me?' says Tim eventually, glancing at our sleeping daughter in the rear-view mirror.

I leap out of my skin and, gasping aloud, clutch a hand to my chest as a ghostly shadow drifts out of nowhere and breaks right before gliding off into the night – a hunting owl.

'Yes. I believe you,' I say. 'There was something there. I'm sure of it.'

'I didn't tell you – I should have – but the night we moved in, Eve Parkes came round to remove some sort of doll they'd had up the chimney in the sitting room. A priest had put it there to refocus "negative energy". She told me whatever it was had mostly persecuted Izzie. No wonder the house took so long to sell.'

I think instantly of the words painted on each leaf of the cherry tree in Isobel's bedroom.

*Get out Get out Get out*

So maybe they weren't threats after all, but a desperate wish made over again and again.

Or worst of all, a warning… that I ignored.

\*

'It's very confusing!' Rosie chatters away happily over her cereal as we adults sip coffee silently. 'I went to bed at home but I woke up here!' She laughs. 'Daddy had to put me in his jumper, Grandma! It was hanging over my hands!'

'How very funny!' Susannah agrees, rolling her eyes conspiratorially. 'What an adventure! Would you like anything else to eat, darling? I'm so glad you're feeling a little bit better this morning!'

'No, thank you.' Rosie shakes her head. 'My tummy doesn't want any more now. It's still a bit hurty. Can I get down, please?'

'Of course you can. Grandpa will come and put the TV on for you in the sitting room, won't you, Grandpa?'

Tony gets up, wiping his mouth with his napkin. 'Come on, Rosy-Posy. Let's get you sorted out, shall we?'

Susannah waits until they have left the room. 'You're here for Sunday lunch, of course?' she says, pouring herself some more coffee, as if it's not out of the ordinary at all for us to have arrived in the middle of the night, half dressed and gibbering with fear. 'So, what are your thoughts this morning?'

'I don't think we know, do we?' Tim looks at me, and I shake my head.

Susannah hesitates. 'Please don't take this the wrong way, but I do think you were sensible not to call the police during the night. Wouldn't it be better to go back to the house first, in the cold light of day, as it were, and just make absolutely sure you want to go down that route, before you escalate things? I'm not saying *don't* call them, just maybe walk around outside and check to see if there are any signs of someone having broken in, at the very least? I'm just thinking how it would sound to them otherwise; "we woke up in the night and saw someone in a wardrobe, so we ran up to my parents' house and we haven't been back since". Their resources are so strapped, and I worry you're going to get a bit of a name for yourselves at this rate; Father Mathew in on Friday doing a blessing, the police poking around in wardrobes on Sunday.'

I sigh. 'I wondered that myself and hearing you say it out loud, it *does* sound ridiculous.'

'That's because it *is* ridiculous.' Tony comes back into the room.

'It wasn't just me, Dad – Claire saw something too,' Tim says instantly.

Tony sits down heavily and looks at me.

'I'm almost certain I did,' I agree.

He looks at me steadily. 'So if I asked you to bet your life on it now, would you?'

I shake my head.

'Exactly,' he adds, disappointed. 'I must say, I've always thought you made of sterner stuff, Claire. These two…' he gestures at Tim and Susannah and shakes his head, 'but we're the sensible ones.' He looks sad and rather wistful.

'Tony!' Susannah says sharply. 'That's enough.'

'I'm not sure it is, actually.' He scratches his chin thoughtfully. 'I worry when we find ourselves dragging an ill child out of bed in the night because we "think" we saw something. This is becoming a fait accompli. It's just a house. The builders start in three days' time, for goodness' sake – they're going to rip most of it down.'

No one says anything.

'Very well.' He sighs. 'If you really can't bear it, live here until they've done the worst of it. In fact, perhaps we ought to reconsider our plans and attack the whole lot in one go. It would certainly speed things up if you weren't living on site.'

'Tony, shouldn't we?…' begins Susannah.

'Shouldn't we what?' he looks at her and shrugs helplessly. 'Got an alternative? No? I thought not. So, Rosie can stay here with us today while you move whatever you need in the short-term, up here. The bigger items, we'll discuss tomorrow. But I want to hear no more of this exorcism rot, or figures *watching* you. It is not real. It does not exist.'

'Thank you, Dad,' says Tim, standing up with almost military obedience. 'That's very kind of you. We'll go and get packed up now.'

I think about the eyes I am sure I saw looking back at me, and say nothing.

And just like that, I'm moving back in with my in-laws.


As we pull up outside Fox Cottage, nothing seems out of the ordinary at all. We let ourselves in and walk around cautiously, but it's all exactly as we left it in the middle of the night. Tim takes a deep breath and starts off slowly up the stairs, with me following behind him. The rooms are light and bright and I begin to wonder if I had the most odd of turns last night. Did *I* have a night terror of some sort? Was I in a mental state halfway between dreaming and reality?

We both walk into Rosie's room, and I pull the curtains, looking at the crumpled covers thrown back by me with such urgency. My phone is lying in the middle of the mattress, and I pick it up. Just a message from Jen saying yes, she is up and some Facebook notifications. No calls made or received. No new photos, except the ones of the dark ceiling I took last night.

Tim walks over to the wardrobe and opens it again. Just as he said, an assortment of puffy princess dresses and Rosie's actual clothes. He exhales. 'Well, let's start getting packed up anyway.'

'You're sure?' I say. 'You really want to move in with your parents for what could be months?'

'Well, I don't think it will be. I'm certain Harry's cheque is going to clear. Don't you think it's actually *better* this way? Dad suggested it himself; we didn't even have to ask him.'

'I suppose so.' I sink down onto Rosie's bed and put my hands on my head. 'We're still going to have to send her to the new school tomorrow though?'

'If she's well enough to go,' he points out. 'The way things are going at the moment, I think we should just take one day at a time, don't you?'

We spend the morning boxing up belongings that we unpacked the day before. We break for lunch and head back to The Rectory, me in a daze, Tim starting to chat excitedly on the way about the possibility of discovering that maybe his agent won't have refused that part *and* getting the money back, all in one day.

'Tomorrow could be *amazing*.'

I eat roast chicken with my in-laws on autopilot, then head back down to the house again.

At 5 p.m. – exhausted – we are almost ready to start the car runs up to The Rectory of items we need immediately.

'If you start taking Rosie's stuff down to the car, I'm just going to shove all of the dresses and her hanging clothes in a plastic bag, it'll be easier.' I look around us, in her room.

'Can't we just leave them?' Tim says. 'Cinderella costumes aren't exactly a priority right now, are they?'

'Well we're not coming back, it seems, are we?' I shrug, and he sighs.

'Fair enough.'

He bends and grabs one of the boxes and leaves the room, while I open the wardrobe door again. Reaching in, I put my arms around the gathers of brightly coloured satins and full net skirts, attempting to lift them out in one go. It sort of works – only her Ariel costume gets stuck and I pull gently to try and free it. It slips off the hanger and I think I've done it, only it's still snagged. Swearing, I'm forced to pull most of the dresses free and dump them on the bed, as I go back for Ariel. The mermaid tail seems to have caught on something right at the back and, as I reach in to free it, instead, my fingers find a small metal latch hook. Confused, I stick my head in and start to fumble with it, pushing it up and out of the metal loop it's secured to… at which point the whole of the back of the wardrobe simply swings away from me – opening out like a door… stopping as it bashes onto something behind it.

My mouth falls open and I climb in – pushing a second back panel with my hand, only to realise it is, in fact, another wardrobe door, that in turn swings open and allows me to climb *out* of the wardrobe into the bubblegum bedroom, on the *other side of the house.* I turn and stare back through what is essentially a secret passage into Rosie's room, in shock.

'TIM!' I yell, at the top of my voice.

*

'I just can't believe this,' he says incredulously, as he stands alongside me in the bubblegum room and we stare back through the wardrobes into our daughter's room. 'Someone really has been getting into the house. You saw them in there last night and I saw them standing over me the night before that.' He turns completely white. 'Do you think they were expecting to find Rosie, not one of us?'

I feel sick. Utterly, completely sick. 'Yes, probably.'

His shock bleaches away into fury and I watch his fists clench. 'I will kill them,' he whispers softly.

'We need to phone the police.' I put a steadying hand on his arm.

'Yes, you're right. We do.' He walks over to the window and stares out onto the street below. 'You've thought all along that Isobel has been getting into the house,' he says, his back to me. 'You were frightened when you saw her talking to Rosie in the shop; obviously she turned up here the night we moved in and she was with her mother when Mrs Parkes came round to have a go at you.' He turns to look at me. 'Do you still think it's her?'

'Now that I've seen this?' I point at the passageway. 'One hundred per cent. No question. She was hanging around the back gate yesterday, too. I'd been pushing Rosie on the swing, I looked up and she was just standing there, watching. I didn't tell you, because I didn't want to freak you out, but I found a Ouija board in Rosie's room and someone painted nasty little messages over the leaves on the cherry tree on the wall; that's what Adam was sorting out. I thought it was *you* she was obsessed with,' I say truthfully. 'I was obviously wrong.'

'I trusted her.' Tim stares into space.

'Those dolls you said Mrs Parkes came to collect,' I remember suddenly. 'The ones she told you were shoved up the chimney to absorb negative energy. Don't you think now it's more likely they were something to do with us, and Rosie?' It's my turn to stare through the passageway in horror. I can just see the foot of my little girl's bed. 'What was Isobel planning to do?' I stammer. 'Take her from us?'

Tim stands up abruptly. 'Let's get the car loaded up first. Rosie needs her things. Then we'll call the police.'

*

We're putting boxes in the boot when Adam pulls up onto the forecourt in his van. 'Hello! Busy Sunday all round,' he smiles, climbing out. 'I've just come to get everything out of the barn. I hope that's OK?'

'It's fine,' Tim says briefly and waves in the direction of it. 'Help yourself.' He walks back into the house without another word, leaving Adam staring after him in surprise.

'I'm sorry about that,' I say quickly. 'We've had a rough day. It's not you.' I hear the tremor in my voice and cough to cover it.

'Are you all right?' He looks at me carefully.

I nod, trying not to cry. The reality of my discovery is just starting to sink in. 'It's a bit complicated. Lots happening. I better get on; Rosie's ill up with Tim's parents and I want to get back to her as soon as possible.'

I want to hug her to me and never let her go, ever again.

'Of course,' he says. 'Let me know if I can do anything to speed things up – bring another load, or something. I'd like to help if I can.'

'That's kind of you, thanks.' I make myself smile at him before I disappear back into the house to get a bag of Rosie's toys.

When I return, he's crouched over on the forecourt chucking what look like rags in a cardboard box and swearing under his breath.

I put the bag in the car and walk over to him. 'Everything OK?'

'I've just spilt a load of linseed oil.' He looks up, anxiously. 'I'm so sorry. I've cleaned it up with these though, don't worry. You don't need any more on your plate today.'

I hesitate for a moment, then hold out a hand. 'Here – give me the cloths. I'll wash them for you.'

'No, no – please don't worry.' He pushes the flap over on the box. 'I'll sort them out later.'

'It's not a problem – I'll just whack them on a twenty-minute cycle.'

'It's such a kind offer,' he insists, 'but I don't want to make more work for you.'

'You're not. I promise.' I make it impossible for him to refuse.

He picks up the box. 'Let me carry them in for you, at least, so you don't get covered in the oil.'

Once we're in the washroom he insists on shoving the saturated cloths in the machine, and as he crouches down I notice a spliff tucked behind his ear.

'I didn't know you smoked,' I say, to acknowledge that I've seen it.

He blushes, glances over his shoulder and straightens up. 'I don't, except the odd one here and there. I won't do it in the barn, I promise.' He reaches up and removes it, holding it in his hands. 'It's pathetic really… and nothing to do with being "creative", it's just for when I'm particularly stressed. I suffer from anxiety attacks now and then.'

'I'm sorry to hear that,' I say immediately, thinking back to Susannah dismissively referring to Timothy and Adam as being 'completely normal'. The thought of someone pointing a gun at Rosie and firing makes my skin turn cold. She can't really believe those poor children genuinely grew up unaffected, can she? 'Doesn't smoking weed make it worse, though?'

He looks amused, and I colour.

'Is that not right? I don't know what you call it – dope? Gear?'

'In answer to your question, no,' he says gently, 'it doesn't make it worse for me. I tried antidepressants, but they made me feel like a zombie. It was like wading through treacle all the time. I couldn't paint, I couldn't do anything really. This is better in comparison.' He holds up the spliff.

'Maybe you just need to try a different antidepressant?' I hazard.

'Maybe,' he agrees, rolling the joint between his finger and thumb. 'This isn't a good look, that's for sure – the older I get the

more crusty hippy it makes me appear. Like I live on a campsite.'
He smiles sadly. 'You're probably right, I should try something
more conventional. *Or* go a little bit further in the other direction.
I read a big newspaper piece recently that says treatment with LSD
could be the way forward.'

'I read that too!'

'Yeah? Interesting, wasn't it?' he says. 'I also read that a mental
health charity is crowdfunding half a million dollars to continue
research into the use of LSD to treat post-traumatic stress disorder;
they think it might be able to help change your way of thinking.
Which would be nice.' He sighs. 'Maybe Tim was onto something
all those years ago. I should have listened to him and not wussed out.
He must have told you. That séance we did?' he continues as I look
confused. 'Tim did a tab. He was very cool back then, very worldly-
wise… I was just the village boy.' He laughs. 'Anyway, I didn't have the
balls to do it, so I pretended I'd "dropped" one instead. Although poor
Tim had a really rubbish trip. He totally freaked out. I never much
fancied it after that to be honest. Do you mind if I wash my hands?'

'No, of course not.' I step to one side so he can get to the sink.
'It's dreadful that you didn't get any help after what happened to
you all.'

'The shooting, you mean?' he says conversationally.

I nod.

He dries his hands on the towel hanging from the hook. I
catch sight of the tattoos finishing at his wrist, covering as much
bare skin as possible. 'It is what it is.' He shrugs. 'We all survived.
My mum made me go to those classes because she fancied Paul
Jones. They'd been on a few dates but he lost interest. She used
taking me as an excuse to get to see him. He scared me, though.
I only suffered it because I got to hang out with Izzie.' He smiles,
straightens the towel and turns to me. 'While we're on the subject
of anxiety – are you sure you're OK? Tell me to mind my own
business, but you seem a little on edge.'

'Me? I'm fine,' I insist.

'Honestly?' He waits. He has such kind, sad eyes. I barely know this man and yet I suddenly want to tell him *everything*. It's probably nothing more than I want to tell someone, anyone, but…

'You can trust me,' he says. 'I'm a good listener.'

I hesitate, but then I remember he's *her* boyfriend, and I shake my head, my eyes filling with tears.

'Hey!' he says worriedly, putting a gentle hand on my arm. 'Please don't cry! I didn't mean to upset you. I should probably go – I'm sorry.' He steps away. 'I'll let you get on. Thanks again for this…' He points at the washing machine, then quietly lets himself out of the back door.

I exhale heavily and – as I wipe my eyes, my hands shaking – I hit a wall. I actually feel it happen. I simply can't cope with any more of this. It's not dissimilar to when they told me Mum and Dad had died: a total mental detachment from reality. It was too much; *this* is all too much. I just want to leave and never come back. Tim was right – this house was a terrible mistake. I want to get away from all of them. Rosie is not safe from that woman here. *I* don't feel safe any more. I don't want my daughter ever setting foot in this house again.

I reach out slowly, put the cloths on the thirty degree, twenty-minute wash – and head off to find Tim.


He's sitting on Rosie's bed, still staring at the open passageway.

'The only problem with calling the police *now* is that I don't think for a minute they'll actually catch who did this,' he says. 'They'll bring down a squad car or two which they'll park outside, the whole town will start talking about it and whoever's responsible will just stop and get away with it.' He stands up. 'I want to think about everything a little bit longer, if that's OK? Are you nearly ready to leave?'

I nod. 'I want us gone by half seven at the latest. I'm tired now. I've had enough.'

He looks up at me. 'I bet you have. I'm so sorry. I don't even know what to say to you any more.'

I turn without answering and leave the room. I'm not being rude, but there's nothing more *to* say. I'm done here.

*

At 7 p.m. I return to the washroom to retrieve Adam's cloths from the tumble dryer. As I bend and open the door to remove them, a faint haze of smoke appears in front of my eyes. I can't smell anything, though, so I don't let myself worry about it. No doubt I'm *so* tired, I'm simply seeing things. Blinking and swallowing a sudden cough, I quickly and carefully fold up the hot cloths, placing them back in the cardboard box, deliberately leaving the lid open.

Nearly there.

*

'Wow! Thank you.' Adam peers into the box and gratifyingly inspects my handiwork before I place them in the corner of the room. 'That's some service!'

'You're very welcome. I'll tell you a secret,' I say. 'I worked as a chambermaid in a B&B when I was younger. I can actually make a swan out of a towel; it's a dying art.'

I don't mention that not only did I have to strip the beds and remake them, I also had to take the dirties to the local laundrette and service wash them. I spent a *lot* of time watching machines going round while learning the do's and don'ts of the laundrette trade from the very knowledgeable attendant, Lillian. 'Now,' I look at my watch, 'I don't mean to be rude, but we're leaving in about ten minutes. I think it would be good if you could finish up and leave when we do tonight, if that's OK?'

'Of course. Claire – have I offended you in asking if you were all right? I didn't mean to overstep the mark, or pry.'

'You didn't,' I assure him. 'Everything is fine.'

I turn and head back to the main house. 'Tim!' I yell upstairs. 'I've messaged your dad to come and get the last bits. Are you ready?'

'Yes, I am.' He appears at the top. 'Just wait until I tell him about the door in the back of the wardrobe. If he says he saw this coming, he's a bloody liar. He owes me an apology. *Ridiculous*, is the word I believe he used?'

'Can you just come on, please?' I say. 'I want to get back to Rosie *now*. Grab your stuff quickly so I can lock up. I'll be in the car. Go!'

'OK, OK!' He disappears and I head to the front door.

As I emerge onto the forecourt, the driver's door to Adam's van is open. He's obviously sitting in it, because I can see his leg and the fingers of one hand drumming restlessly on his knee.

I walk up to the door. 'You all done, too?' I say purposefully. 'We're off now as well. Could you?—'

But I don't get any further. I've surprised him and although he quickly tries to hide the picture on his phone that I've caught him looking at – it's too late. I've seen it.

'That's Tim and Isobel!' I reach across and grab his wrist, forcing him to turn the screen back up, as he swears under his breath and closes his eyes briefly.

It *is* them – embracing. Her kissing his cheek.

'When was this taken?' I say slowly, my heart thumping, letting go of him.

'Thursday night,' he says quietly. 'Tim came over to see her at Eve's. I'm really sorry. Just because I've been torturing myself looking at it over and over again, you shouldn't have to. I didn't mean you to see it, I'm—'

'Ready?' Tim appears next to me, clutching a key, and glances at the mobile, too, before doing a double take. 'Er, what's that?

And why are you showing it to Claire?' He stares at Adam, bewildered.

'I wasn't!' Adam climbs out of the van quickly and we both step back. 'I promise you. I was just looking at the picture and Claire saw. I'm so sorry, I've been in pieces.' He shrugs miserably. 'This last few days has been like stepping back twenty years and having you come home from sixth form all over again. I know it's shit, I can hear myself saying it – but I can't help it. It's how I feel.'

'But it's nothing like that time,' Tim says and gestures towards me. 'I've got—'

'I know, I *know* you have,' Adam interrupts. 'But it's what you being here does to Izzie. She – wait. ' He pauses, sniffing the air suddenly. 'Can you smell something?'

Tim frowns but obediently breathes deeply, then looks surprised. 'Yes, I can actually. Where's that coming from?'

Adam steps backwards onto the forecourt and looks up at the house. 'There!' he says urgently.

We turn to face Fox Cottage and see what he's pointing at. A silent plume of smoke is rising above the roof, virtually invisible against the night sky.

'Shit!' Adam exclaims. 'It's coming from the barn.'

He breaks left and runs around the front of the house to the white wooden gate, which Isobel was stood behind only yesterday. He yanks it open and pelts into the back garden, with Tim and me closely behind him.

The back of the house tells a very different story to the façade of the front. Flames are leaping around the dining room windows in the middle section of the house. The barn is fully ablaze and I have to step back because the heat is already intense. As I do, I think I see the light turning on and off in Rosie's dark room.

'Wait – is someone there?' I say sharply.

'What? Where?' Tim spins round.

I shake my head. 'Ignore me. I thought I saw the light flickering like some sort of bloody Morse code in Rosie's room,' I point at it, 'but it's just the flames reflecting on the glass… or the fire reaching the room itself.' I try to exhale and calm down.

'Morse code? Like someone's stuck? Oh Jesus!' He puts his hands on his head in panic. 'I have to go back!' He is about to run back towards the house when Adam grabs him.

'Are you insane? Leave it! It's just stuff!' I see him look desperately at the barn, full of his paintings.

Tim turns and stares at the house again, abject horror on his face as we hear someone else shouting.

'Tim? Claire?'

Antony comes running into the garden. 'Oh thank God!' he says. 'I got out of the car and I could see flames licking over the edge of the ridgepole – and the smoke! Thank God you're safe!'

He pulls Tim into a hug as more people start to arrive, neighbours I've yet to meet. Adam starts talking to one of them and pointing to the barn as he speaks, but my attention returns to Tim who has grabbed Tony's arm.

'I have to go back in, Dad!' he says. 'I think Isobel is in there!'

'What?' Tony freezes and looks at the house. 'Quickly! Tell me Tim. Which room?'

'Rosie's,' Tim says frantically. 'The one we were painting. Dad, no! Wait – you can't!'

Tony is already running towards the burning building, to shouts from Adam and the neighbours to stop, as they realise what he's doing.

'No, Dad! The door to the room is locked!' Tim shouts but it's too late. His father has already disappeared around the corner, heading for the back door.

Tim turns to me, distraught. 'I phoned Isobel. I told her to come to the house and find me in Rosie's room. I told her I knew about the passageway – and I waited. I was so angry. I thought I heard something, so I locked the wardrobe door in the bubblegum bedroom, then I ran round and locked Rosie's bedroom.'

He unfolds his palm to reveal the key to the big lock I asked Tony to remove and then clean forgot about.

'I deliberately trapped her,' Tim says frantically, as my mouth falls open in horror. 'There are no windows in that room, apart from the skylights, and the pole is in our room. She's got no way out. Dad won't be able to do anything, even if he gets to her.' He looks at the key in his hands and shouts out loud, as if psyching himself up, before he turns and runs after his father, to rescue Isobel Parkes for the second time.

My shriek of 'NO!' echoes redundantly around the empty garden.

He does not stop.

# CHAPTER TWENTY-FOUR

## Claire

A&E wards at night unnerve me: disorientated patients trying to doze under artificial lights, as the poor staff deal with numerous dramas around them. The bloke in the curtained bay next to us throws up so violently – several times – I'm convinced he's on the verge of death… only for us to hear him slurrily insist, moments later, that he's only had 'one drink tonight, doc, honest'. On the other side is a confused old lady who seems to have fallen over at home and wants very much to go back there, becoming increasingly distressed and starting to swear like a trooper when she's not allowed to. Tim has suffered some smoke inhalation and, mercifully, they come and move us to a more private room to treat him with oxygen. He never made it past the kitchen before being forced back. We still have no news about Antony. Adam has kindly insisted on waiting with us, because I came in the ambulance with Tim and he's worried we will need driving to The Rectory at some point.

The only difficulty is, I know Tim desperately wants Adam to leave, and of course I understand why. Neither of us has said a word about Isobel, but any second now, surely the police are going to tell us that they've found a body in Rosie's bedroom? I can almost *hear* Tim wondering – is it murder if you lock someone in a building that then burns down through no fault of your own…

or perhaps manslaughter? I don't think I should be able to consider that dilemma as rationally as I am. Probably the paramedics are right – I'm in shock. Tim is also becoming increasingly agitated by the lack of news about his dad.

'They should have found him by now,' he keeps repeating, pulling the mask away from his mouth before clamping it back on again.

At half past ten we all jump as Adam's mobile rings. He looks at the screen in surprise. 'It's Isobel's mum. I'm sorry – do you mind if I get this. Hello?' he says, as Tim and I look at each other nervously.

'Why were you at the hospital?' he says, frowning. 'That's where I am now. What? Oh My God! She can't be.'

I close my eyes. They've found her and they've told Eve first as her next of kin. Of course they have. Oh, Christ.

Tim pulls the mask away from his mouth and retches. I grab the bowl the nurse gave him and thrust it under his chin. They told us he might expect to feel nauseous but I know that this is a reaction to the news Adam is getting. I put my hand on Tim's back as Adam hangs up and blurts in shock: 'Isobel's died.'

Tim retches again as there's a knock on the door and two uniformed policemen, accompanied by a nurse, walk in – followed by a porter with a wheelchair waiting in the doorway.

'I didn't know this was going to happen!' Tim blurts and starts coughing violently.

'It's OK,' I say quickly, leaping in to cover his tracks. 'It's a normal reaction to smoke inhalation. It's nothing to be frightened of. Try not to talk, darling.'

*Don't say anything. Not a word.*

The two officers look at Tim sympathetically and one of them clears his throat. 'Mr Vaughan, I'm very sorry to have to tell you that a body has been recovered from your house, in what appears to be a child's bedroom at the front of the building.'

'Oh no!' I don't say that for effect – it's genuine fear. Tim shut her in the room, the house burnt down and now she's dead.

Everyone looks at me and for a horrible moment, I have no idea if I've just said that out loud.

'We believe it's your father,' the officer continues. 'Would you be willing to identify the body?'

'My what? But... there has to be a mistake,' Tim blurts. 'It can't be Dad!' His voice wavers, and I reach for his hand, to steady both of us.

*Antony?* Oh dear God.

Tim clasps me so tightly, as he starts to fall through space, that it hurts. 'He was there, in the garden with us. Not my dad.' His voice breaks completely and he gulps, putting his other hand up to his mouth.

Adam looks away; the police officer looks at the floor. We are all respectfully silent as Tim struggles to make sense of what he's just been told.

'The door was locked. I had the only key – Dad couldn't have got in there.'

'It appears he used the other entry point,' the police officer explains. 'Via the other bedroom. The false door through the wardrobes was open when we found him collapsed on the floor.'

'But that was closed too. I know it was, and how would Dad know to?...' Tim looks at me in shock before trailing off.

I shake my head, imploring him to stop talking. 'Tim, just do as the officers ask,' I tell him. 'Everything else can wait. I'll be here.'

Tim looks stunned as his eyes fill with tears. 'OK. I'd be willing to do the ID, yes.'

The nurse takes the mask that Tim is holding. 'You'll be fine to stop that now in any case. Ron's going to help you over there, though, all right?' she says, as the porter steps forward. 'Just so you don't take a turn on the way.'

They wheel him off, leaving Adam and me alongside each other. 'Do you mind if I call Eve back?' he says quietly. 'I pretty much hung up on her.'

'Of course, please do.' I sit back on my plastic chair as he starts to talk to Isobel's mother, and it begins to sink in that Tony *knew* that the secret door was in the wardrobe. He *knew* there was an access point to Rosie's bedroom there and that he could get into the room, despite the main door being locked. My breath has become very shallow.

'I cannot believe this is happening,' Adam says suddenly and I realise he's off the phone again. 'Isobel died in her sleep last night. Eve went to wake her up this morning and she couldn't. How can that happen to someone who is thirty-four? That's just not possible! People don't just die like that when they're not old? This doesn't make any sense!'

I try to focus and take *his* hand. I have so many questions I want to ask him – he's *sure* she was at home, being one – but I can't say a thing. He's understandably devastated. 'I'm very sorry for your loss,' I tell him. 'I don't know what to say, Adam. I really am so sorry.'

'I'd say the same to you, but I'm glad Antony Vaughan is dead.'

I let go and shrink back from him.

'You know what the police just said – about the wardrobe with the false back?' He's angry. 'Do you understand what they're talking about? Had you found it?'

'I discovered it today. I didn't know Tim's father knew about it.'

'*Knew* about it?' Adam laughs and looks up at the ceiling. 'He fucking made it! All those times he was over there "helping" Eve to fix things, here and there. He was quite the handyman. Isobel told me what he'd done to her, but I didn't know until recently that she fell pregnant. She told Susannah it was Tim's baby. Susannah even made her have a DNA test before she helped her get rid of it. Imagine that, Claire? Imagine what Isobel went through? She made me promise not to tell anyone what he did to her, and I haven't. All this time... I know he's Tim's dad but I hope he rots in Hell. I'm not sorry. I'm not sorry at all.'

I can't take this in. 'But Tony was having an affair with Isobel's mother.'

'Yes, he was, but he used Eve as an excuse to get access to the house. He visited her at night. He told Izzie he loved her – because that's how you treat someone you love, of course. When she told me, and this was ten years ago now, I tried to convince her to go to the police, but she wouldn't. I don't think she didn't wanted the truth to come out and annihilate Eve. *I* paid him a visit, and she told me it stopped, but… then you all moved here. She was terrified when she saw Rosie. She was so frightened he was going to use the door in the wardrobe again and that it was why he bought Fox Cottage in the first place. She wanted you out of there. She wanted to keep Rosie safe.'

My head is swimming. Adam's words don't feel real, yet I know I believe him. 'How old was Isobel when this began?'

'She said sixteen. I always believed that, because I couldn't see Antony Vaughan doing anything obviously illegal that he would never be able to argue his way out of, if he was caught. But because of her reaction to Rosie, I can't be sure now…'

'Are you going to tell Eve all of this?'

'I don't know.' He blinks in confusion. 'I don't know what to think. She didn't tell Eve herself, so do I respect her decision? And how can I tell Eve something like that when Isobel isn't here for her to discuss it with? What does she do with that information then? On the other hand, why should Antony Vaughan get away with it by dying? His wife shouldn't waste her time mourning him. And how can Izzie be *dead*?' His voice wavers.

'I would never recover from discovering something like that about my child who has just died – knowing I could never talk to them about it. I think I would rather not be told, on balance.' To say that's an understatement doesn't even come close. 'If that helps?'

There's another knock at the door and a doctor peers in 'Mrs Bradbury?' He looks at me hopefully.

'No. I'm not. Excuse me though,' I ask quickly, as he's retreating. 'Paternity tests. If two alleged fathers are biologically related – as in, father and son – can it give you a false positive result?'

The doctor looks completely thrown, as well he might. 'Er, yes. Fifty per cent of the son's DNA comes from his father, so unless both men are tested, there's a high possibility of a false positive result.'

'Thank you,' I say, and he glances at both of us as if we're mad.

'Happy to help?' he ventures and disappears quickly in case I ask him anything else.

'I'm telling you the truth, I swear,' says Adam.

I turn to face him. 'I believe you. Tim told me from the start that he's never had a sexual relationship with Isobel. I believe him too.' I pause. 'May I tell him what you've told me? I would feel uncomfortable knowing this about his father, and not saying anything, as he starts to work it out for himself and wonders if he's right. As for telling Eve and Susannah, you've made a good point, just because Antony has died doesn't mean people shouldn't know what kind of person he really was. But there are other lives this will devastate if we do something now that we might regret later. Eve doesn't know how Antony was found. Neither does Susannah.'

Adam doesn't say anything.

'Most of all though – Isobel.' I swallow. 'I can't believe how strong she was.'

'I'm sorry for all of the things she did, that frightened you – but that was her intention,' Adam says. 'Rightly or wrongly, she didn't want you leaving Rosie on her own for one second. She wanted you out of that house; she wanted you to go home. She really believed that she was able to protect you.' He pauses, miserably. 'Claire, the fire…'

'Don't,' I say quickly. 'Don't ask me anything; don't tell me anything.' I take his hand again, and briefly squeeze it. 'Some secrets are better left untold.'

# TWO WEEKS LATER

# CHAPTER TWENTY-FIVE

## Eve

'I know this is a lot to take in, Eve,' says the GP sympathetically. He's a young man – not a dissimilar age to Isobel, I imagine. I glance up at the wall to see a picture of him with his arms round a smiling wife and two small children. 'But there was nothing that you could have done to stop this from happening. The post-mortem found that Isobel's death in her sleep was caused by sudden adult death syndrome, or SADS. They couldn't find anything wrong with the structure of her heart, but she might have had a disease which affected its electrical functioning – that's unfortunately something you can't determine at post-mortem, only when someone is alive. The very difficult thing about SADS is that these apparently healthy young people are walking around completely unaware that something is wrong, because there are no symptoms. Some people occasionally have blackouts, but…' he trails off.

'Isobel did faint from time to time. I put it down to her stress and anxiety issues. My daughter did not have an easy life. Things were often difficult for her.'

He nods and I wonder if he has a clue what I'm talking about, if he's read her copious notes.

'Isobel experienced a traumatic event when she was a young girl that triggered a lot of issues,' I explain, in case he hasn't. 'She was puberphonic—'

'But presumably tested to make sure the high voice wasn't down to anything being physiologically wrong with her?' he interrupts.

I take it back. This one knows his stuff. 'Yes. She was seen repeatedly by numerous medics over the years. She also suffered from night terrors and was quite socially challenged. I'm worried I missed something I should have seen because I was too busy concentrating on the wrong details, as it turns out.'

'Oh, no – absolutely not,' he says emphatically. 'You didn't overlook anything. You couldn't have foreseen this, neither could any of the doctors she saw. The conditions don't even always show up on an ECG when someone is specifically tested to see if they are a carrier.'

'It's genetic then?'

'If Isobel had any siblings or children, we would now be testing them to see if they had inherited the same condition, yes. That's the recommendation when there is a sudden death of someone young in the family. Often carriers die in their sleep, like Isobel, but sometimes it happens after more strenuous exercise, or they just collapse.'

'My husband died when he was young,' I say suddenly. 'We had a car crash. I was there. He had significant head injuries but I've never been able to determine why he suddenly veered off the road. We were driving at night. I wondered if he'd seen something that I missed because I wasn't looking out of the windscreen – something that he tried to avoid. That said, we'd also had an argument and for a while I considered that he might have swerved deliberately to get my attention, but he wasn't really like that – it never made sense. It's tormented me for years, to be honest,' I laugh and I can hear the desperation in it. 'Could he have had a heart attack, like Isobel, only while he was behind the wheel, do you think? Does that sound ridiculous?'

'Not at all. There is research to suggest SADS carriers are often mistakenly believed to have died from injuries sustained in car accidents, when actually they died suddenly while they were driving and the car subsequently crashed. The opportunity to find a genetic link that other family members could be tested for would then be missed because it would be mistakenly assumed, as possibly in your husband's case, that he died from his head injuries.'

'Well, well, well…' I say slowly, my voice shaking. 'That would make a lot of sense to me. Can I ask you something else?'

'Of course,' he says kindly.

I take a deep breath and, with great difficulty, make a huge effort to hold it together just a little longer. It's so hard trying to talk factually like this. 'Isobel didn't feel *cold* when I found her in her bed. She wasn't breathing and felt cool to the touch, but I did CPR. I'm not sure I did it right, although I did the best I could until the ambulance arrived and they took over. I've been terrified for the last two weeks that I did something wrong, that she died because I wasn't skilled enough to save her, and no one is telling me.' Silent tears begin to course down my cheeks.

'No, no. No. It wouldn't have made any difference at all,' he assures me. 'She felt cool because she had already died in her sleep; it would have been very peaceful. Her heart would have just stopped.' He waits as I wipe my eyes and nod. 'I'm so sorry for the loss of your daughter, Eve. And for your husband.'

'Thank you,' I swallow. 'It's not the order of things, is it? To have to bury your child.'

'No, no it isn't,' he agrees. 'It's not the order of things at all.'


'But she didn't suffer, that's the main thing.' I blow my nose as Adam sits opposite me at the kitchen table. 'The last thing she said was that she loved me. She loved you too, Adam.'

He looks up at the ceiling, his eyes full of tears, but doesn't respond.

'She really did.' I genuinely believe that to be true. Although it wasn't the kind of love he wanted... on her part perhaps more that of a friend, or a brother.

'I don't feel like I ever managed to properly save her,' he says quietly, wiping his face with the heel of his hand. 'I wanted to, but I didn't succeed. I should have called him out.'

'You were a child. Paul Jones was a nasty bully.'

Adam glances at me then looks away.

'I mean it – what goes around comes around. He got what he deserved.' I try to calm myself down. 'Isobel was on the verge of telling me something, I think, the night before she died. She said it was nearly finished. I can't help thinking it has something to do with Timothy. Particularly as the last message she had on her phone was from him on the night of the fire, asking her to meet him at Fox Cottage, that he knew about the passageway to the other side?' I shake my head in despair at their willingness to believe such supernatural rubbish. 'She was already dead by that point, of course. That was when I was at the hospital with her and the police still weren't letting me tell anyone she'd died while they ruled out foul play.' I exhale slowly. 'The night Timothy came here and was very frightened, *you* were angry. You told me Isobel knew what had "really happened in the house". What did you mean?'

'I meant that Isobel knew what was scaring Tim,' he replies without missing a beat, 'because it was her. She broke into the house several times after they moved in. She left him newspaper cuttings on the floor, about the shooting. She painted threatening messages over the leaves on Rosie's cherry tree. She visited them in the night, she took photos of them sleeping, she left a Ouija board in Rosie's room.'

'What?' I am appalled. 'But why? She told me she was trying to protect them! She made two more dolls. I found them in her bedroom after she died. You know how much store she set by that kind of thing.' I get up and walk out to the hall, open the drawer and retrieve the little family. The red boy doll, the girl doll – made from Claire's scarf – and the little baby doll, complete with the glittery hairclip holding back its yellow wool hair. They are all tied together with a red ribbon round their middle. I set them down on the kitchen table and a brief flash of pain passes across Adam's face. He picks them up and turns them over and over in his hands, before closing his eyes and holding the dolls tightly.

'I asked her to stop,' he whispers. 'I tried to step in. You saw me, and you heard her tell me it was none of my business – that I wasn't her boyfriend.'

'You don't think she had anything to do with the fire, do you, if she was persecuting them like that – trying to make them leave?' I push the thought of Antony cowering in a smoke-filled room from my mind. Everyone locally is talking about how tragic it is that Antony should lose his life running back into the burning house to rescue the box of things belonging to Claire; the last mementos of her late parents. 'I know Isobel had already died by the time the fire caught,' I continue, 'and the investigation said it was an accident – it was the cardboard box of linseed rags combusting in the barn that started it,' I pause, watching him, 'but Isobel would have known all of your flammable oils were in there. She wouldn't have been able to pinpoint the moment when it would combust, but she could well have set it all up and simply not lived to see the outcome.' I look searchingly at Adam and he looks away, refusing to hold my gaze. There is a long pause. All I can hear is the ticking of the kitchen clock that I've finally got round to hanging, and the whir of the cogs as it gears up to chime. I let it strike three and once the sound has died away, I clear my throat.

'Even *I* know you never pile linseed-soaked rags in cardboard boxes,' I remark. 'You've told me before that they can self-combust. In fact, you stopped using linseed oil for that very reason. *You* wouldn't have done something like that, much as I know you hated a certain Mr Vaughan, would you?'

He sits forward and rubs his face with his hand. 'I did hate him, yes. I can't deny that.'

'Now I think about it – it's very fortunate that Rosie was at her grandparents' and Tim and Claire weren't upstairs either, but downstairs, arguing with you. Almost as if great care had been taken to ensure no one would be hurt. Did you start it deliberately, Adam?' I whisper. 'You couldn't have known Tim's father would run back in. It was an idiotic thing to do. He should never have risked it. That wasn't your fault.'

Adam snorts. 'Why would I start a fire that would burn a year's worth of my work that I was just about to exhibit?'

'Why do we do any number of things in the name of revenge, jealousy and love? I gather that now Timothy has no house to live in, the local grapevine has them going back to where they came from. Mary Morgan tells me they're buying a house in Surrey with Susannah, and once the funeral is over, The Rectory will be going on the market. The Vaughan family will be gone. A job well done, I'd say. Had Isobel lived, your lives would have returned to normal.' I hold my breath and wait.

He looks straight at me. 'Claire cleaned and dried the rags I was using. The fire investigator said *that* was what caused them to combust. The oil doesn't come out of the material unless you wash it at high temperatures. I don't see how she could have been expected to know that. There was enough oil still on them to heat up when she put them in the dryer and it began the chemical process of combustion. She put them in the cardboard box, gave them back to me, then they caught properly in the barn.'

He reaches into the pocket of his parka, hanging on the back of the chair he's sitting on and pulls out a small tin. I watch him open it to reveal a pre-rolled joint. He picks it out, gets to his feet and makes towards the back door, putting the joint to his lips and sparking a lighter he's retrieved from his pocket.

'It was an accident,' he says as it catches and a puff of sweet smoke fills the room. He lets himself out into the garden and closes the door behind him.

*

After he's gone, I put the dolls back in the drawer. I've bathed them in salt thoroughly, like Izzie told me to. She would have wanted that. They have no connections to anyone any more. They are inanimate objects, yet somehow I cannot bear to throw the little family away.

I return back to the table, in my too-quiet house – just the ticking clock. I allow my eyes to close briefly. I see Fox Cottage burning, as I have in my nightmares of the last two weeks. I swallow and try to think of Antony as I would rather remember him: in my bed, laughing with me, telling me he loved me.

I cannot believe Fox Cottage simply isn't there any more. I can see every single detail in Isobel's room. The skylight, the tree, the birds, but I picture *her* in her new bedroom upstairs, sitting on her bed, telling me how happy she was that Timothy had come home... and now, I'm so glad. I am sorry if the intensity of her love made her act in ways that she shouldn't, if it tipped over into obsession. But if this was all the time she had left, I'm grateful that she at least had the chance to feel the warmth of such love again, to hold Timothy – albeit briefly – and tell him how she felt, one more time.

''Tis better to have loved and lost than never loved at all.'

My darling little girl, like the beautiful birds I painted for you with all of my love, may you now finally fly free.

# NINE MONTHS LATER

December 2018

# CHAPTER TWENTY-SIX

## Claire

I make my way up a rainy Old Brompton Road after a morning sales pitch wondering if I've got time to stop for a quick coffee. I'm on a half-day today – and meeting Susannah at the train station so that we can go back together to watch Rosie perform in the school Christmas concert. Tim has a matinee, so will have to miss it, but I've promised to film it for him. Jen is coming too, which is a treat for Rosie. She has been so amazing in coping with everything. Never mind *another* new house and a third new school of the year; Tony's was her first experience of a family death – followed by careful questions that Tim and I had no choice but to ask our daughter, and also necessitated having to tell Susannah everything. I was profoundly shocked by her immediate response: 'But Adam Owen alleges Isobel was sixteen? So nothing *illegal* then, at least.'

Faced, however, with the irrefutable proof of the DNA test she herself had orchestrated, she crumbled once Tim explained he had never had *that* kind of relationship with Isobel. Tim also wanted answers of his own. Why didn't his mother tell him at the time his recent girlfriend had come to her for help with a pregnancy? How could she have done what she thought she did?

They are very slowly rebuilding their relationship, alongside a shared grief that's devastating enough, without having anywhere to put the anger they won't ever be able to talk to Tony about. I don't really know if the three of us buying a house together will work. A granny annex doesn't quite do justice to the section of the house Susannah will be living in, but we'll see. Time will tell. Eventually it always does.

I decide I probably have got ten minutes to get a cappuccino, when I realise with a jolt of shock that I'm outside Adam's exhibition. I saw coverage of it in *the Metro* and was curious then, but stayed away. I hesitate. He won't be there, after all. I could just look quickly.

I open the door and tentatively walk into the white space of the gallery with its light wooden floor, only to gasp and cover my mouth with my hand. The walls are full of Isobel. Canvas after canvas of her. Isobel smiling, laughing – happy.

'Hello,' says a voice behind me and I turn to see a young woman smiling at me. 'Beautiful, aren't they?'

'Very,' I manage. I had expected the sheep skulls and storms. Not this. I'm lost for words.

'These are by a new artist called Adam Owen, who we're really excited about. He painted this entire exhibition in nine months, which is just…' she pauses and shakes her head in disbelief, 'well, it's a phenomenal achievement, let's say that. It's almost feverish really, in its intensity, and it has been a huge success. He's attracting a lot of international interest.' She lowers her voice to a whisper. 'My advice would be to snap one up before he becomes *outrageously* expensive.' She winks at me.

'Well we've just bought a new house,' I find myself telling her, 'there's a great deal of wall space to fill.' The thought of some of Harry's returned £250k being spent on supporting an artist from the very place his actions banished us to is quite a pleasing one.

Her eyes light up. 'Perfect! I'll leave you to look around. There's an umbrella stand right there and do come and find me if you have any questions.'

'Thank you.'

I walk slowly through the space – through Adam's love letter to his Isobel – and overwhelmed, my eyes fill with tears. She was so loved, her whole life, by him. What it would be to inspire someone like this? I look at the walls in wonder – painting after painting of her… and then right at the centre of the back wall, at the heart of the exhibition, is the portrait I saw in the barn the day Eve showed me round Fox Cottage: a restless Isobel on the verge of sleep.

'That was the only painting to survive a huge fire in the artist's studio,' the woman calls out from behind her desk as she sees me looking at it, but the phone rings before she can tell me any more about the house I burnt down.

'Excuse me,' she smiles and answers it, leaving me to inspect the paintings so carefully she must believe I really might be about to buy one, when actually I'm trying to steady myself, having rushed right back to the fire. Those rags were smoking when I put them in the box, a fact I chose very deliberately to ignore. Although I still can't quite believe they would have caught *that* quickly. Not without a helping hand. Adam really has risen from the ashes of Fox Cottage.

I cross to a larger image of Isobel in the garden as I never saw it – a summer riot of colour and glory: lupins, blowsy hydrangeas, fat roses shedding petals on the grass as they weave around a pergola laced with honeysuckle… almost a wedding bower… and Izzie walking beneath it, having escaped the house behind her. She is dressed in one of her eccentric, long gowns and I'm reminded of Tim telling Rosie all about Morgan le Fay, that windy day at the top of the hill fort. No wonder Izzie chose to live in her fantasy world of magic. It was better than real life, and I imagine it at least gave her some sense of control. I look more closely at Adam's faithful depiction of Fox Cottage in the background, and notice suddenly that he's painted a watchful face at the skylight of her bedroom. It could be mistaken for no more than abstract brushstrokes, but I see it.

'You've spotted the ghost at the window?' The woman calls across to me, having finished on the phone. 'Really creepy isn't it? I hate that sort of thing.' She shudders. 'My husband teases me about how I can't so much as watch a spooky advert on TV. I think you're either built that way or you're not. I am – while my husband is just like, "no – there's *nothing* under the bed."' She laughs and I smile politely, but don't comment. She's wrong. As Tony himself said, everything that happened in that house had a rational explanation. It's *people* we should worry about. Had that man not shot Tim, Adam and Isobel, Tony wouldn't have suggested the children play together to 'reassure' them afterwards. Eve and Tony may never have begun their affair. So much might have been different had those ten seconds never happened. One person's actions can devastate so many others in the blink of an eye. Isn't that far more frightening?

But while it resulted in Isobel having the sort of life so tragic it might be considered too uncomfortable to contemplate, I'm glad Adam has forced everyone to look at her now and see how amazing she was, because I think she's a hero. What extraordinary quiet courage and strength she had.

I walk to the small portrait I was so struck by, the first time I saw it. I should like to buy it, but of course I can't, and I won't. It occurs to me as I study her face, that Isobel probably wasn't chasing sleep at all, but trying to fight it. She must have been so afraid of the night coming – and yet she bravely shone a light in the dark for my daughter.

I take one last look at the girl who loved Tim with her whole heart and did everything in her power to protect Rosie and I blow *her* a kiss.

'Thank you, Isobel,' I whisper as I stare at her searching eyes. 'May you be at peace now. You were loved.'

Back by the door, I turn to say goodbye but the woman at the desk is on the phone again. I hope she's right and this *is* the start of huge success for Adam. I wish him well. I slip back out onto the rainy street, brightly coloured Christmas lights above my head reflecting in the wet pavements beneath my heels, put up my umbrella and make my way home.

# A LETTER FROM LUCY

Thank you so much for reading *The Memory*.

I'm not a plotter – I make the story up as I go along – and the direction this book ended up taking was a surprise to me. There are some difficult themes in *The Memory*, but it does allow me the opportunity to direct anyone who might like to find out more about cardiac risk in the young, to visit c-r-y.org.uk or sads.org.uk.

I'd also be particularly glad for your feedback on this one, so if you have time I'd be really grateful for any reviews you might want to leave.

If you'd like to keep up-to-date with all of my latest releases, you can sign up at the following link. Your email address will never be shared, and you can unsubscribe at any time.

*www.bookouture.com/lucy-dawson*

If you'd like to download a free short story by me you can join my readers' club via the following link:

*www.lucydawsonbooks.com/join-my-book-club*

Alternatively, if you'd like to contact me personally, you can reach me via my Website, Facebook page, Twitter or Instagram. I love hearing from readers, and always reply, despite the best efforts of my two small children.

Many thanks again for reading *The Memory* and I look forward to having another book ready for you soon!

With all best wishes,
Lucy x

 www.lucydawsonbooks.com

 lucydawsonbooks

@lucydawsonbooks

# THANK YOU

Dr Camilla Dawson, Ceri Flavell, Wanda Whitely, Vanessa Jones, Jenny Blackhurst, Clare Mackintosh and Sally Dawson. All errors are my own.

Sarah Ballard, Eli Keren, Jane Willis, Georgina Le Grice, Yasmin McDonald, Zoe Ross, Hannah Beer, Alex Stephens and all at United Agents.

Kathryn Taussig, Jenny Geras, Maisie Lawrence, Kim Nash and all at Bookouture.

But most of all, thank *you* for buying this book. I'm very grateful indeed.